A DIME NOVEL HERO

Kit shook her head, unable to resist the glimmer in Jake's dark eyes. Despite the gunbelt slung low on his hips, she glimpsed a piece of the teasing young man she'd known before he'd left to track down his father's killer.

She took one of Jake's strong hands in hers, pretending to inspect it. The long slender fingers curved around her palm for a moment, and the light sprinkling of hair across the back of his hand tickled her. Her breath seemed to rasp more loudly in her ears as her heart kicked her ribs. Startled by her body's response, she glanced at Jake. His rugged face had gone still except for his untelling eyes which studied her closely.

She swallowed, releasing him like a hot branding iron. "You pass inspection."

Other **AVON ROMANCES**

Captain Jack's Woman *by Stephanie Laurens*
Highland Brides: The Lady and the Knight
by Lois Greiman
Mountain Bride *by Susan Sawyer*
A Prince Among Men *by Kate Moore*
A Rose in Scotland *by Joan Overfield*
A Tough Man's Woman *by Deborah Camp*
The Wild One *by Danelle Harmon*

Coming Soon

The Heart Breaker *by Nicole Jordan*
The Men of Pride County: The Outcast
by Rosalyn West

And Don't Miss These
ROMANTIC TREASURES
from Avon Books

After The Thunder *by Genell Dellin*
Brighter Than the Sun *by Julia Quinn*
Waltz in Time *by Eugenia Riley*

A Dime Novel Hero

Maureen McKade

AVON BOOKS ◆ NEW YORK

AVON BOOKS
A division of
The Hearst Corporation
1350 Avenue of the Americas
New York, New York 10019

Copyright © 1998 by Maureen Webster
Inside cover author photo by Bezy Photography
Published by arrangement with the author
Visit our website at **http://www.AvonBooks.com**
Library of Congress Catalog Card Number: 97-93796
ISBN: 0-380-79504-3

First Avon Books Printing: January 1998

AVON TRADEMARK REG. U.S. PAT. OFF. AND IN OTHER COUNTRIES, MARCA REGISTRADA, HECHO EN U.S.A.

Printed in the U.S.A.

WCD 10 9 8 7 6 5 4 3 2 1

Thanks to the Friday night gang—Cheryl, Bernadette, Barb, Lea, and Janie—who keep each other going with love, encouragement, and chocolate;

Edie—I will always be grateful that our last names started with the same letter;

Mom, who instilled in me the love of reading at an early age and who continues to share that love of the written word;

and my real-life hero, Alan, who believes in me even when I falter.

Prologue

Wyoming, 1880

"Fatty Fatty Four-Eyes, blind as a bat; take off her glasses, she don't know where she's at."

The boys' cruel words stung like salt rubbed in a wound, and Kit Thornton's eyes filled with tears. Blinded by the moisture, she tripped on a loose slat in the boardwalk and fell. Her wire-rimmed glasses skidded off her face, and her books flew out of her arms. Cutting laughter erupted around the ten-year-old girl as she groped for her spectacles. She wished the earth would open up and swallow her, taking her far away from her taunting schoolmates.

"What's going on here?" Seventeen-year-old Jake Cordell's glare sent her tormentors scurrying away.

The lanky young man hunkered down beside Kit, but she kept her watery gaze on his boots, humiliation washing through her.

He settled gentle hands on her shoulders. "Are you all right?"

"Fine," she managed to say past the lump of embarrassment in her throat.

1

Jake snagged her glasses and handed them to her. "Here you go."

With trembling fingers, Kit hooked the curved ends over her ears and settled the spectacles on her nose. His scuffed boots came into focus.

"C'mon, let's get up." Jake took hold of her arms and helped her stand.

Dull, throbbing pain in Kit's knee brought an involuntary groan.

"What is it?" Jake asked.

She shook her head. "Nothing. I'm fine."

"Did they hurt you?"

The anger in his voice startled Kit. She gazed up at his handsome face, the cleft chin and square jaw, and nearly forgot her name. She glanced away, heat rising to her cheeks. "It's my knee."

She leaned over and lifted her hem a couple of inches. Her stockings were torn, and blood welled from a cut.

"Looks like you scraped it pretty bad." He removed his red bandanna and handed it to her. "Tie this around it."

Kit accepted the neckerchief with a mumbled thanks. The material was warm and slightly moist from resting against Jake's neck, and she concentrated on tying the makeshift bandage around her wound.

"You'd best get home and have your ma clean it up for you," Jake said.

"I don't have a mother," she said softly.

Jake appeared surprised. "What's your name?"

"Kit Thornton."

"Your pa owns the newspaper?"

She nodded.

"Then I'll take you over to his office so he can take care of you," Jake said.

Blue eyes widened behind the glass lenses, and she

took a step back. "No. He doesn't like me pestering him. I can take care of myself."

She leaned over to gather her scattered books, and Jake picked up a couple. "You like to read, huh?"

Kit's round cheeks reddened. "Yes."

He handed the books to her, then pushed back the brim of his hat and grinned. His roguish smile nearly stopped her heart. "Not many girls I know like to read."

"I do." She lifted her chin, daring him to challenge her.

Jake's grin grew. He liked the young girl's spirit. "You won't get any arguments from me." He leaned close to her. "Don't tell anyone, but I like a good book myself."

She stared at him. "But you're the marshal's son."

His smile faded. "So?"

Her blush deepened. "Everybody *likes* you." He stared down at her a moment, and Kit's embarrassment grew. "I have to go."

She turned to leave, but Jake grabbed hold of her arm. "I'll walk you home."

"You don't have to."

He shrugged. "I want to make sure you take care of that cut." He held out his hand. "Come on."

Trembling with nervousness, Kit reached out and wrapped her fingers around his palm. Wonder filled her as she walked beside Jake, who'd reduced his stride to match hers.

The handsomest boy in Chaney was walking her home! Too excited to speak, Kit gripped Jake's hand and allowed him to lead her around to the back door of the newspaper office.

Once there, he released her. "Are you going to be all right by yourself?" he asked.

She nodded. "I won't be alone. I have my animals."

He frowned. "Animals?"

"Would you like to see them?" she asked, her blue eyes suddenly sparkling.

"Theodora Katherine, where are you?" a man's voice sounded from within.

Her expression dulled. "I have to go."

"Would it be okay if I came over some day to see your animals?" Jake asked.

She nodded, too tongue-tied to speak.

He laid a hand on her shoulder. "If you ever need any help, just holler and I'll take care of those boys for you." He bowed at the waist gallantly. "Your wish is my command, madam."

Tears filled Kit's eyes again. "Thank you."

He chucked her chin lightly. "Don't mention it. You take care of that knee, Kit Thornton."

He waved and turned away, his long legs eating up the distance.

As Jake disappeared from view, Kit sighed wistfully. She knew the marshal's son was a troublemaker; her own father had often complained about Jake's no-good behavior. But Kit had seen the gentle side he hid from everybody else—and no matter what anyone said, he would always be her hero.

Chapter 1

1894

Jake Cordell's search had finally come to an end.

He leveled the brim of his worn brown hat against the bitter north wind. After having been gone for so many years, he had forgotten how cold an April day in Wyoming could be.

His palomino sneezed and shook its head.

Brushing a gloved hand through the horse's cream-colored mane, Jake said, "Look, it's not my fault. It's supposed to be springtime."

Standing in his stirrups, he stretched his stiff legs. He studied the drab landscape, the withered grass and skeletal trees still hibernating in winter's embrace. "Besides, I want to see if Maggie's still around." Jake smiled, remembering the good times they'd shared in her room above the saloon.

Zeus snorted.

"You're probably right. Odds are she's married with a couple of screaming kids, not to mention a husband, making her life miserable." Jake sighed. "But then, I've got nothing better to do."

He rode on in silence, his thoughts centering on the

changes coming about in his life. For six years he'd searched for Frank Ross, the man who'd murdered his father, Judge Jonathan Cordell. Now that Ross was behind bars, it was time to settle down. The problem was, Jake didn't know what he wanted to do with the rest of his life. He'd considered putting his law degree to use, something his father would have approved of. However, the prospect of twisting words into unintelligible sentences brought a frown to his lips. More to Jake's liking was the idea of raising horses, preferably on the old family ranch.

The woods on either side of the road opened up to reveal a bustling town and Jake drank in the sight, surprised by how much he'd missed it. He urged Zeus down the middle of the busy street, noting how much his hometown had grown and changed. The mercantile where he used to make mischief was gone, replaced by a stonefront bank. And the little saloon where he'd had his first drink had been rebuilt into a fancy dance hall, complete with hurdy-gurdy girls all the way from Chicago, according to the sign. Rose's House of Hospitality, where he'd lain with his first woman, no longer existed. A church stood in its place, and Jake grinned at the irony.

He stopped at the first livery and tossed the stable boy an extra nickel to brush Zeus's coat and give him fresh hay. The towheaded kid pocketed the coin and promised to take good care of him.

With his rifle in one hand, Jake threw his saddlebags over his shoulder and walked across the street. His gaze scoured the false fronts, and he wondered where to start looking for Maggie Summerfield. While he had searched for his father's murderer, he'd made the sheriff's office his first destination in every new town. Most of the lawmen had known everyone in their jurisdiction, and Chaney was bound to be no different.

The old sheriff's office now sported a recently painted sign that read Police Station, proclaiming Chaney's transformation from frontier town to civilized city.

Stepping up onto the boardwalk, Jake entered the jailhouse. There were some noted changes since the days when he'd been an overnight guest, sleeping off a rowdy evening. The cells were now hidden from view by a brick partition with a solid wood door. Two desks instead of one adorned the office, with a brown-uniformed policeman behind each.

The younger officer, his feet propped on his desk, looked up and down at Jake's dusty clothes, then scowled. "Are you looking for something, mister?"

"Someone. Maggie Summerfield."

The man shook his head and yawned. "Never heard of her."

Jake took a step forward, not liking his insolence. "Have you ever thought about using your brain for something other than filling up that canyon between your ears?"

The police officer's face flushed a deep red and he sprang to his feet. "You son-of-a—"

"Hold on, lads." The older man insinuated himself between them and turned to his colleague. "Now, Jameson, don't you be gettin' in over your head. If I'm not mistaken, the gentleman you're tanglin' with is Jake Cordell." He spoke with a deep Irish brogue.

Surprised, Jake looked at the husky red-haired man. "How'd you know?"

The officer smiled, revealing even white teeth beneath a bushy moustache the same rusty color as his hair. "Sergeant Patrick O'Hara. It's a pleasure to be makin' your acquaintance, Mr. Cordell."

Jake shook his beefy hand.

O'Hara pointed to the other policeman. "And the barkin' pup there is Officer Will Jameson."

Recognition dawned on Jake, and he studied the younger man. "I remember when you were a snot-nosed brat throwing rocks at old lady Harrigan's place."

Jameson dragged his palms across his trousers, his face ruddy with anger, embarrassment, or both. "Look who's talking. Seems to me you done more than your share of raising hell yourself." Guarded respect glinted in his eyes. "I read in one of them books where you're faster'n a rattler on a hot rock."

"Take my advice, kid, and don't believe everything you read." Jake looked back at O'Hara. "Is that how you recognized me?"

O'Hara shrugged sheepishly, then retrieved a dog-eared book from a desk drawer and held it up. "Aye. I've read them all, but this is my favorite."

Jake reached for the copy of *Ambush at Andrews Crossing* and thumbed through the worn pages. He swore in disgust. "I remember when this happened. I was only eighteen—my father took me with him to track down a gang of bank robbers. That's when he was still a marshal." He clapped the book shut with irritation and glanced at the author's name. "What the hell did I ever do to T. K. Thorne?"

The Irishman appeared startled by his outburst. "I'd be thinkin' you'd be flattered to have so many books written about you."

Jake shook his head in frustration. "All it's given me is a reputation. Every young buck trying to make a name for himself wants to gun down the famous Jake Cordell. If I ever find this T. K. Thorne, he's going to wish he never heard of me."

"Well, he seems to be knowin' a lot about you."

Reluctant curiosity prodded Jake. He'd never read one before, scorning the exaggerated lies, but now that he'd put that life behind him, he felt the urge to do so. "You mind if I borrow this?"

"Be my guest, lad. You were inquirin' about the whereabouts of Maggie Summerfield?"

Jake stuffed the book in his jacket pocket. "That's right. Do you know her?"

A grim expression sobered O'Hara's round face. "I'm sorry to be havin' to tell you this, but she died a few years back."

Jake's breath caught in his throat. "How?"

O'Hara shook his head. "I don't know, lad. Considerin' what she did to make a livin', it could've been most anything."

"Because she worked in a saloon?" Shock made his words bitter.

O'Hara cleared his throat self-consciously. "It's a tough life for a lass."

Sadness overwhelmed Jake. He'd known he might find her gone or married but hadn't even considered her death. He hoped she'd found some happiness before she died. Maggie had deserved a better hand than life had dealt her.

"She didn't have a helluva lot of choice," he said. "Her mother had to sell herself to keep them off the streets, and people figured Maggie was the same way. Folks in this town didn't give her a chance."

O'Hara stepped up to Jake and gripped his shoulder. "Sounds to me like you gave her a chance. Let's go across the street, Cordell, and I'll buy you a pint."

Jake nodded and followed O'Hara into a small saloon. Sitting at a corner table, the officer caught the attention of the barmaid. "Two ales please, lass."

A few moments later a young woman set two filled mugs on the stained table. Jake stared after her, thinking how Maggie had been in her place not so long ago.

"Drink up, laddie," O'Hara urged, his voice surprisingly gentle, considering his massive size.

"To Maggie." Jake clinked his mug against

O'Hara's, then drained the cool beer in a few swallows.

Now, when he was finally ready to quit bounty hunting and come home to stay, Maggie was gone. She'd been a friend and a lively bed companion. He didn't know if he'd loved her, but he sure would miss her.

Jake ordered a bottle of whiskey.

"Had you known her a long time?" O'Hara asked.

"Ever since I was about sixteen," Jake said, his voice as hollow as his insides.

The waitress set a bottle and a shot glass in front of Jake. He poured some of the amber liquid into the glass, then swallowed it in one gulp and refilled it. If he closed his eyes, he could almost hear Maggie's husky voice and smell the perfume he'd bought her when he'd come home for his father's funeral.

"Did you come back just to see Miss Summerfield?" O'Hara asked.

"I came back to start over. Thought I could do it right this time."

O'Hara leaned back in his chair and threaded his fingers across his belly. "Do you think it'll be that easy? Being a legend, and all?"

Disgust twisted Jake's lips into a grimace. "I never asked to be some kind of dime novel hero."

He tossed down another shot of whiskey.

"Easy does it, lad. I didn't think you were a drinkin' man."

"Why? Because those books say I'm not?" Jake grinned without humor. "I'll tell you a secret, Sergeant: T.K. Thorne doesn't know me half as well as he thinks he does."

The officer rubbed his whisker-stubbled jaw. "What'll you do now?"

Jake shrugged listlessly. "Drink this bottle of whiskey, and if I'm lucky, get drunk."

O'Hara shook his head and stood. "Take it easy, Cordell. I wouldn't want to be throwin' you in our new jail.''

Jake only poured himself another shot and lifted it in a mocking salute. ''It wouldn't be the first time Jake Cordell slept it off behind bars.''

Kit Thornton dismounted in front of the Chaney *Courier* building and retrieved her round spectacles from her jacket pocket. Slipping them on, she stepped up onto the boardwalk and walked into the newspaper office.

''Good morning, Kit.'' David Preston gave her a welcoming smile.

''Hello, David.'' She glanced at the smudged apron he wore to protect his immaculate shirt and trousers. His sleeves were rolled to his elbows, revealing ink-dotted forearms. She could recall her father looking much the same when he'd owned the *Courier*.

''What're you doing in town?'' David asked.

''Business,'' she replied vaguely, not wanting to burden him with her problems. She'd just come from the bank, asking for another extension on her loan repayment—a request Mr. Mundy, the bank manager, had denied.

''Have you eaten breakfast?''

''Before sunrise,'' she replied.

He shook his head as his fingers placed type in the press with experienced ease. ''You wouldn't have to get up at such an ungodly hour if you lived in town.''

Kit was tired of the same old argument. ''The ranch is my home.''

Crossing the room to the press, she studied the letters David had strung together: FRANK ROSS SENTENCED TO LIFE IMPRISONMENT.

Her knees unexpectedly trembled, threatening to collapse beneath her. ''Wasn't that the man who killed Judge Cordell?''

David nodded. "That's right. His son finally captured him. You haven't heard, have you?"

"What?"

The newspaperman's hands paused in his task, and he gazed at Kit. "Jake Cordell is back in Chaney."

Panic widened Kit's eyes. "Jake's back in town?"

Disgust flitted across David's classically handsome features. "Cordell got drunk last night and Jameson threw him in jail. Some legend." He brushed back a lank of sandy hair from his forehead with ink-stained fingers. "How long will you be in town?"

"I'm not sure," she replied distractedly.

Jake had returned to Chaney! The last time she'd seen him had been at Judge Cordell's funeral six years ago. Jake hadn't even recognized her, and she'd been too busy with her own ailing father to offer her condolences.

"Is he still in jail?"

"I suppose," he said. "I was planning on interviewing him later, after he's sobered up."

Kit moved toward the door. "I've got to go."

"You just got here."

She shook her head. "I have to go see Jake Cordell."

He sighed. "I know you've read all those dreadful novels about him, but the real Cordell is much different from the fabricated hero."

Kit glared at David. "How would you know? Maybe he had a good reason for getting drunk."

"Or maybe that's his usual state."

"Or maybe you're jealous," she retorted.

"Don't be ridiculous. I knew those books would be a bad influence on you, Kit, but I didn't say anything. Perhaps I shouldn't have been so lenient."

"Lenient?" Incredulous, Kit stared at him. "You bought my father's newspaper, *not* his daughter."

Hurt replaced David's haughty expression. "It's only that you need a man to take care of you. I knew your father, and he'd have wanted me to look after you."

Livid heat crawled up Kit's neck. "I'm perfectly capable of looking after myself. I have to go."

"All right, but when Cordell doesn't measure up to his reputation, remember what I said."

Kit wanted to deny his words. Jake Cordell *was* a hero; he was *her* hero—but the words stuck in her throat. "Good-bye, David."

Ignoring the bustling people on the boardwalk, she hurried to the police station. There was no reason to think Jake would recognize her now; she bore little resemblance to the shy, chubby girl with spectacles he'd protected as a child.

Suddenly uncertain she wanted to see Jake after a night of drunkenness, she slowed as she approached the stone building. Would he resemble the boy she'd known at all?

It didn't matter. She owed him.

Kit opened the door and entered.

"Top o' the mornin', lass," O'Hara said with a wide grin.

Met with such a friendly greeting, Kit smiled back. "Good morning, Patrick."

"What can I be doin' for you on such a beautiful mornin'?" O'Hara frowned and leaned forward. "Nothin's happened to Johnny, has it?"

She laid a reassuring hand on his forearm. "No, he's fine. Pete is watching him."

"Old Two Ponies still around?" Fondness fringed Patrick's tone.

Kit nodded. "And still as ornery as ever."

"I know it's not my ugly mug that's brought you here so early, so what is it, lass?"

She glanced at the door blocking her view of the cells. "I heard Jake Cordell is in there."

"Word gets around fast."

"With someone as well known as him, are you surprised?"

"Nope, can't say that I am. Don't be tellin' me you just want to get a look at the hero?"

Kit shifted her weight from one foot to the other. "No. I knew him when we were younger. He was good to me, Patrick. The least I can do is get him out of here. I'm hoping Freda will let him stay in her extra room."

"It's true Cordell doesn't belong in a cell, but I'm not certain I should let you help him. He's not a pretty sight."

Kit frowned, wondering how Jake could have changed that much.

Jake Cordell was accustomed to the attention he garnered in the many towns he passed through—especially that of the fairer sex. His solidly built body was typically clothed in tan jeans that hugged his muscular thighs, and a navy blue shirt spanned his broad chest and shoulders. Dark brown hair highlighted with fiery tints was kept trimmed above his collar, and clear, alert eyes the color of maple syrup surveyed the world with an intensity matched by few other men.

It was his face, however, that caught the admiring gazes of all ages of women. Carved in granite like the ancient mountains, his features were a landscape of angles and planes. His profile was that of a hawk's, sharp and proud. Lines etched around his mouth testified to an easy smile or an unforgiving frown, depending on whether the object of the expression was friend or foe.

The ladies, however, never saw the violent side of Jake Cordell, for in their presence, he was always a gentleman; a cavalier, as in days past.

Retching sounded from behind the wood door.

Patrick flushed, his face matching his hair. "It's no place for a lady."

Despite her embarrassment, Kit propped her hands on

her hips. "There's not many folks who think I'm a lady. Now, are you going to let me take him out of here or not?"

He studied her a moment, then nodded slowly. "All right, but I warned you."

He plucked a ring of keys from the wall behind his desk. Her heart in her throat, Kit followed him to the back room. The sour smell of vomit assailed her nostrils and she nearly gagged. When they reached the cell, she stared at the curled-up figure on the floor. Was that pitiful piece of humanity Jake Cordell, hero and defender of justice? She glanced at Patrick, who shrugged helplessly.

"He's not exactly what you expected, is he?" he asked gently.

Kit shook her head. She cleared her throat of bitter disappointment and squared her shoulders. "He's not how I remember him, but I owe him."

"Would you two shut up and let me die in peace?" Jake Cordell growled.

Tears welled, threatening to roll down Kit's cheeks. He wasn't anything like the dashing hero of her dreams. Did the polite gentleman of the dime novels even exist? Pain stabbed deep in her chest. Maybe David was right; maybe Jake Cordell was nothing but a common drunk.

"She said I was the only man she ever cared for," Cordell slurred.

Kit studied his bleak expression. "Who?"

"Maggie. She deserved better." Self-disgust bled into his tone.

Kit stared into Jake's bloodshot eyes. Grief glimmered in their dark depths. Keeping her gaze locked with his, she said, "Let him out, Patrick. I'll take him over to Freda's."

"Are you sure, Kit? With the liquor in him, he's got a surly tongue," Patrick said, concern in his voice.

Turning away from Jake, she nodded and smiled in reassurance. "I'll be fine. Besides, I don't know him well enough for him to hurt me."

Liar, a little voice shouted in her head. She knew Jake Cordell too well.

With a resigned sigh, Patrick unlocked the cell door.

Kit stiffened her spine and tried to hold her breath as she entered the enclosure. She wrapped her fingers around his arm. "Come on, Jake. Let's get you out of here."

"Who are you?" he asked, as he tried ineffectually to escape her grip.

"It doesn't matter. C'mon, stand up."

Surrendering to her grasp, he pointed to the hat that lay on the cot. Kit grabbed it and slapped it on his head.

"Take it easy, would ya?" Cordell grumbled.

Patrick handed her Jake's gunbelt, and she slung it over her shoulder.

"If you have any trouble, lass, give me a holler," Patrick offered.

"Thanks, but if I have any trouble, I'll just shoot him."

Jake stiffened as he turned startled eyes toward her.

"Don't worry," Kit reassured. "I'll aim for your head. Won't hurt a thing."

Jake only managed an indignant grunt.

She supported much of his weight across her shoulders as she tried to keep her nose turned away from his grime-encrusted clothes and stale liquor breath.

"Where are we going?" he asked.

"Freda Finster's. If we're lucky, she'll let you rent her room."

He stumbled along beside her. "Why're you helping me?"

"Because I used to know a Jake Cordell a long time ago."

He turned to study the blond woman's profile. Her thinned lips were set grimly in a mask of distaste, and a pair of wire-rimmed spectacles balanced on her nose. Despite his hangover, he noticed she wore trousers that emphasized her long legs, but the soft body pressed against his side told him a woman's body lay beneath the masculine clothes. With a firm hold, she steered him toward a neat whitewashed house with a porch that ran across the front.

"Freda," she called out.

Her voice ripped through his brain like a dull plow and he covered his ears with his palms. "I've known Apache war cries that weren't so damned loud."

She ignored him, and despite her apparent disgust, which he admittedly deserved, she continued to steady him. Jake wondered why she cared if he fell flat on his face or not.

A tiny woman wearing a food-stained apron opened the door. Wisps of flour streaked her flushed cheeks, and her eyes twinkled with fondness. The aroma of fresh-baked bread and cinnamon trailed after her, triggering a recurrence of nausea. Jake swallowed back the bile and concentrated on the conversation.

"Kit. Good to see you," Freda Finster welcomed her visitor, with a German accent as thick as molasses. "I do not see you enough. You must not spend so much time at that house with only Johnny to keep you company."

The woman named Kit smiled warmly. "Johnny is more than enough company, but you're right. Another woman's voice would be nice once in a while."

Freda glanced at Jake, her lips curving downward with disapproval. "Who is this?"

"His name's Jake Cordell, and he needs a place to stay."

Freda's eyes narrowed and Jake could tell she was

wondering what gutter he'd crawled out of.

"I know he looks pretty bad now, but . . ." Kit's voice trailed off. "Please, Freda, as a favor to me?"

After a moment, the middle-aged woman nodded reluctantly. "If you put it that way, how can I say no? After all you have done for me, it is the least I can do."

"Thank you."

"After he is cleaned up and the liquor is gone, better he will look." She wrinkled her nose. "Smell better, too."

Jake sniffed his shirtfront, his dignity bruised. "I don't smell so bad."

The two women exchanged glances, rolling their eyes.

"I'd best get back to check on Johnny. I left him with Pete, so I'm never sure who watches who." Worry etched Kit's smooth brow. "Do you think you can handle him on your own?"

"I can handle myself," Jake retorted. He drew back his shoulders and nearly toppled over. Kit grabbed hold of him and propped him upright.

Freda nodded. "Go home and take care of your son. This one I will take care of."

Kit eased her support away from Jake. He swayed a moment, then reclaimed his balance.

"Thank you," Kit said. She set down his gunbelt and hurried away.

"Wait!" Jake called after her.

She didn't stop.

"Who is she?" Jake asked Freda.

The German woman frowned. "She helps you, and her name you do not know?"

"I never set eyes on her before today." He tried to concentrate on the woman's features, but all he could recall was cornflower blue eyes behind her glasses. "At least, I don't *think* so."

"Kit. All her life she has lived here, but few folks know her."

Jake frowned. The name sounded familiar, but his head was pounding too much to recall where he'd heard it. "Hell, I grew up here and I don't remember her."

Freda's eyes slitted. "While you're under my roof, cursing will not be tolerated. Understand, do you, Mr. Cordell?"

"Sure, whatever you say." Suddenly tired, he asked, "Which room's mine?"

She shook her head. "After a bath, you will get your room."

"Look, I never had use for a mother when I was growing up, and I got even less use for one now."

Freda's small chin jutted out pugnaciously. "No bath, no bed."

Jake studied his opponent, wishing she wore a gunbelt. At least then he'd know how to handle her. Sighing in resignation, he nodded. "All right, I'll take a damn bath."

Her mouth thinned to a narrow slash. "What about cursing, I said?"

He hooked a thumb over his shoulder. "I think I'll go see if I can get a room at the hotel."

"You do that, then why you did not stay here, you must explain to Kit."

Jake's conscience reminded him that she had done something no one else in town had: she'd helped him. He cursed silently. "Where's the tub?"

"Show you, I will."

An hour later, a damp Jake followed Freda down the hallway to his room. The carpet, though worn, was clean, and gold-bannered wallpaper brightened the dim interior. She swung open a scarred door. "Your room."

He glanced inside. "Thanks."

"You have manners. I was beginning to wonder what

kind of stray Kit had found this time. If there is anything you need, I will be in the kitchen baking." She waggled an admonishing finger. "No boots on the bed."

"Yes, ma'am."

Jake entered the bedroom and closed the door behind him, shutting out his landlady's disapproving clucks. He surveyed his new home, noting the bed and a straight-backed chair, as well as a scratched dresser. A long, narrow cloth embroidered with orange, red, and gold leaves twining its length ran across the dresser top with a chipped porcelain pitcher and bowl sitting in the center of it. A braided rug covered most of the floor, which had been waxed to a bright shine.

Tossing his hat on the chair, Jake collapsed on the bed, crossing his arms behind his head.

A knock sounded and he quickly sat up, planting his feet back on the floor. "What?"

"Your boots, Mr. Cordell," Freda scolded from the other side of the door.

"Yeah, yeah." He tugged them off, muttering, "I wonder if Spinster Finster knows that witches are still burned at the stake."

Lying back down, he stared at the whitewashed ceiling. It was 1894 and the era of the bounty hunter was drawing to a close. Jake could feel it as easily as he could feel the coming of a new century. He had hoped to return home and pick up where he'd left off with Maggie, although asking her to be his wife wasn't something he'd figured on. He'd seen enough of his own parents' unhappiness to know marriage was a losing proposition.

He tried to picture Maggie's face, but her features were indistinct. Instead, spectacled eyes filled with compassion crept into his thoughts and lulled him into a deep, dreamless slumber.

Chapter 2

As her appaloosa mare galloped down the road, Kit leaned low over the animal's neck. The wind whipped her shoulder-length hair behind her, and the pleasant mix of horse and leather filled her nostrils.

Kit eased back on the reins and Cassiopeia responded immediately, slowing to a trot, then gradually to a walk. Cassie blew noisily, snorting a couple of times, and Kit held firmly to the reins with her gloved hands.

Despite her attempts to dismiss Jake Cordell from her thoughts, he intruded like a pesky fly. The years always had a way of changing people, but the transformation of Jake Cordell from a friendly, warm-hearted kid to a cold, mocking man had shocked her. His cynical brown eyes reflected the wealth of experience that had molded him into a stranger.

But it was the haunting loneliness she'd glimpsed that had tugged at her heart. She knew what it was like to be alone, without someone to turn to for comfort or companionship. She'd spent her solitary childhood nursing hurt animals and creating imaginary friends. Always on the outside looking in, Kit had never belonged.

She dragged herself out of her musings. At least she had Johnny to love; Jake had no one.

Ten minutes later she arrived at her home, the home where Jake Cordell had been raised. The first time she'd set foot in the yard over six years ago, she'd felt a sense of homecoming. When she'd gone into the house, she'd experienced a disconcerting déjà vu, of having lived there in another time, another life.

She reined up beside the smallest of the network of corrals and dismounted, giving Cassie a quick pat on the neck. She looped the leather straps about a fence pole and turned around only to be met by a five-year-old whirlwind on two legs. Following on her son's heels, Johnny's dog, Toby, yipped excitedly.

Kit wrapped her arms around Johnny and swung him around until his shrieks of joy mingled with her own laughter, even as a fear clenched at her heart. What would she do if she lost Johnny? She couldn't even imagine her world without her son.

Kit set Johnny's feet back down and he toppled to the ground in a dizzy heap. She joined him as they both regained their breath.

"Did you miss me?" she asked.

Johnny's dark eyes danced. "Yep. Pete teached me how to sneak up behind bad men and scalp 'em clean-like."

Kit groaned. "He was just having fun with you, Johnny. People don't take scalps anymore."

"But Pete said when he was my age, he practiced all the time. He said that if I want to count coup, I have to practice. Pete says that back in his time, I coulda been a great warrior."

Kit made a mental note to talk to the old Indian about his "lessons." "That was a long time ago, sweetheart. Now we're civilized."

Johnny screwed up his young face. "What does civilized mean?"

"It means we can't have any more fun," answered a growling voice.

Kit smiled wryly at the ancient Indian. Coarse gray hair flowed down his back, but Pete Two Ponies' eyes were those of a young man.

"No, it means now we can all have fun without worrying about outlaws," Kit said.

"It ain't the outlaws you have to worry about, it's the railroad and the banks and them politicians." Two Ponies spat a stream of tobacco to the brown soil.

"Maybe, but it also means Johnny doesn't have to grow up wearing a gun for protection. By the way, thanks for watching him while I went into town."

Pete waved a gnarled hand. "Nothing else for an old Injun to do but watch the young'uns growin' up to take their place."

Kit ignored his standard gloom and doom. "Has Charlie been working with the yearlings this morning?"

Pete nodded. "Looks like you'll be havin' some more of them gray men comin' here and lookin' you over."

"Those 'gray men' are businessmen, and they're looking over my *horses*."

"In my day, you woulda been married and borne a whole lot of papooses by now."

"In your day, I'd have lost my scalp to an overzealous warrior," Kit shot back with a grin.

"It wouldn't have been your scalp you'da lost." Pete Two Ponies winked and turned to walk away with an arthritic gait.

Watching his departure, Kit shook her head fondly. Pete had shown up two days after she'd bought the ranch, and he came and went as he pleased. She respected his privacy, and through the years a friendship had grown between them.

Kit brought her attention back to her son. "Have you fed the animals yet?"

Johnny shook his head. "Me and Pete were just getting to it."

"Pete and I," Kit corrected automatically. "How about you and I go take care of them?"

"Okay."

With Toby dancing at his heels, Johnny skipped ahead to the smaller of the two barns. Kit followed, her disappointment with Jake Cordell evaporating beneath the tranquillity of her home. Toby lay on the ground outside the shed, waiting patiently for Johnny to come back out. Inside the building, Kit spotted Johnny on his knees in front of the first cage.

"Looks like Jasper's getting better. He's standing up," Johnny said, his voice low so he wouldn't disturb the injured raccoon.

Kit joined him and leaned over to peer inside. She smiled, laying her hand on the boy's shoulder. "He does look better. You've done a good job caring for him."

Johnny turned, grinning up at her. "Remember how he was at first? He wouldn't let me get near him."

"And you got him to trust you."

"Can I keep him even after he's all healed?"

Kit knelt beside him and shook her head. "It wouldn't be right, sweetheart. Jasper's a wild animal. He'd be sad locked away in a small cage. You wouldn't want that, would you?"

Johnny was silent for a moment. "What about Satan? He was wild."

Kit stared at Jasper's bandaged leg a moment, trying to come up with an explanation of why the stallion was different. "That's true, but horses are meant to be tamed and used by people, just like cattle. But Jasper and all his friends weren't. They belong in the wild."

"I guess so," Johnny said reluctantly. He got to his feet and fed and watered the creatures in the five cages. Besides Jasper, there were two rabbits, a squirrel, two kittens who'd been orphaned, and a possum who'd been cut by a tin can.

While Johnny carried out his tasks, Kit went to the house to retrieve two baby bottles filled with milk. She passed one to Johnny and kept the other.

Opening the wire door of the kittens' pen, she lifted one of the young animals off the cloth-covered floor and gave it to her son. Taking the other one in her palm, she sat beside Johnny on a wooden bench.

Kit glanced at him, noting how he gently cradled the kitten in his lap. She'd known ever since he was an infant that he had an affinity with animals. Johnny had been less than a year old when she'd found Toby, a starving young puppy in Chaney. She'd brought him home to care for, and from the moment they'd set eyes on one another, her son and the gawky hound dog had been inseparable.

The peace and quiet in the barn usually soothed Kit, but her meeting with Mr. Mundy had left her troubled. If she hadn't taken a second mortgage out on the ranch to purchase some mares, the loan would've been paid in full. But she'd taken the risk, and now she might lose everything she'd worked for.

"Can we keep them, Ma?" Johnny asked, startling Kit out of her somber thoughts. "Salty and Pepper aren't wild." He turned his wide, pleading brown eyes to her. "Can I, Ma? Please?"

She lifted Pepper, the black kitten, to her cheek, its soft fur tickling her skin. "I don't see why not."

Johnny's wide grin sent a shaft of brilliant sunlight to her heart. "Thanks."

She swallowed the fragile emotion. If only the ranch were that easy to keep.

After putting the drowsy kittens back in their cage, Kit and Johnny went outside. Toby met them at the door.

"Race you to the house," Johnny challenged Kit.

For a moment, she wondered what the townsfolk would think if they saw her running across the yard for the sole purpose of having fun. It would definitely be an interesting addition to the rest of the rumors circulating about the eccentric Kit Thornton.

"You're on," Kit replied, and broke into a long-legged stride.

Johnny streaked past her and Kit took off after him. She laughed at the sheer folly of it and caught up with her son. Side by side, with Toby barking excitedly beside them, Kit and Johnny raced across the bare yard, their breath coming out in white wisps. Falling back a few feet, Kit allowed him to beat her to the porch. She bent over at the waist to breathe in deep draughts of air.

"Looks like you beat me this time," she gasped.

Johnny nodded jubilantly. "Maybe next time, Ma."

Kit glanced at her son. In that instant she saw his father's face, and dread gripped her heart. If Jake found out about Johnny, he might try to take him away from her. She blinked back moisture in her eyes. He had no right to Johnny. He hadn't nursed Johnny through the chicken pox, or patched him up when he hurt himself. Johnny was *her* son, and nobody, not even his father, would ever take him away from her.

The following morning, after having slept fourteen hours straight, Jake gazed at his image in the mirror. Bloodshot eyes peered back accusingly. His pallid complexion was colored only by slightly ruddy cheeks covered with dark bristles. Scooping up cool water in his cupped palms, he washed his face, then shaved with an unsteady hand.

He glanced around and was surprised to find his saddlebags and rifle sitting on the chair. He didn't remember retrieving them. Tugging on a clean set of clothes, he left the room.

"Good morning, Mr. Cordell."

Freda Finster was placing two settings of silverware on the dining room table.

"Morning, Mrs. Finster."

"Feeling better, you are?"

"Hell—heckuva lot better, thanks," Jake replied. "Who brought my saddlebags and rifle in?"

"Sergeant O'Hara." She turned toward the kitchen. "Breakfast will be ready in a few minutes."

Jake followed her into the oven-warmed room and sniffed appreciatively at fresh coffee and baking bread.

"If some coffee you would like, there is a fresh pot," Freda said.

Jake flashed her one of his most charming smiles. "That sounds real good, Mrs. Finster."

She poured him a cup and handed it to him.

"Thank you," he said.

"You are welcome. Now sit down by the table and drink it."

"Yes, ma'am." He did as she ordered, lowering himself to a sturdy wooden chair. The hot brew was strong, just the way he liked it.

He glanced at Freda and caught her studying him. "What is it? Did I forget to wash my face? Or maybe you want to check behind my ears?"

She almost smiled. "No. I was only thinking that you might not be as bad as I had thought."

Feeling like he was back in short pants and his teacher Miss Evans had scolded him, Jake squirmed in his chair. "I guess I owe you an apology for the way I acted yesterday."

Freda laughed, startling him, and bringing a reluctant grin to his lips. "That was not so hard, was it?"

"I never was too good at saying I was sorry," Jake said with a sheepish grin.

"Why Kit helped you, now I understand," she commented, as she stirred cooking oats.

Puzzled as to why a woman he didn't even know would go out of her way to help him, he asked, "Why's that?"

"She knew there was good in you. Sees things, she does, that other people do not even notice."

He shifted uncomfortably. He didn't like anybody reading him too well, because then they expected something from him. And he'd long ago given up trying to live up to others' expectations. "Who is this Kit, anyhow?"

Freda paused. "When I came here four years ago, I had just lost my Hans. He left me with only a few dollars. Here I was, new to this America and all alone. Kit, she introduces herself and knowing nothing about me, helps me buy this house and start a bakery. Without her, I do not know what I would have done."

Jake digested the information. "Did you say she's lived in Chaney all her life?"

A frown furrowed her brow. "That's right. Yet some people in this town approve of her not."

"What do you mean?"

"Kit is not like other people. She . . ." Freda puckered her lips as if searching for the right words. "Those who need, she helps. Color of their skin or what language they speak, she cares not. And it is not just people but animals she takes in and cares for. Most in this town do not understand her, so they make up horrible things about her. Kit pretends she does not care, but it hurts her."

He searched his memory, trying to remember a girl named Kit. Hadn't she said she'd known a Jake Cordell a long time ago? Usually he had no trouble remembering a pretty woman, and Kit definitely was someone he should've had no trouble recalling. He shrugged aside his musings.

"Would you happen to know of any offices in town that I might be able to rent?" Jake asked.

"A room above the doctor's office, there is. Dr. Lewis is looking for someone to rent it."

"So old Doc Haney isn't here anymore, huh?"

"No. Such a terrible thing. Late one night he fell in a horse trough and drowned."

Jake shook his head in a mixture of amusement and pity. "Probably drunk again. I'll talk to Dr. Lewis later."

"Are you planning on staying in Chaney?"

"For now."

"What about your family?"

"My father's dead. My mother lives back East." Jake quelled the familiar hurt with a forced nonchalance. "She didn't like living in the middle of nowhere."

Freda's hazel eyes clouded with sympathy, but she didn't comment. "Breakfast is ready." She motioned to a plate piled with biscuits and a bowl filled with gravy. "Could you bring those?"

Jake picked them up and followed Freda into the dining room.

She sat at the head of the table while Jake took the seat to her right. Filling his plate, he hoped the food tasted as good as it smelled. The first mouthful told him it tasted better.

Finishing breakfast, he wiped his mouth with a napkin and pushed back his plate. "That hit the spot, especially those biscuits. Thanks, Mrs. Finster."

"You're welcome, Mr. Cordell. Is good to cook for someone who appreciates it. And call me Freda. I think you are talking to Hans's mother when you call me Mrs. Finster." Fondness glimmered in her eyes. "Kit's son also likes my biscuits."

"She has a son?"

Freda nodded. "Yes, but no husband."

The information about Kit intrigued him. "What happened to the boy's father?"

Freda stood and began to gather the dishes, keeping her gaze averted from Jake. "About him Kit does not talk." She left the dining room.

Puzzled by his landlady's evasiveness, he frowned. Freda obviously liked Kit but didn't seem to approve of her son's father. He wondered if Kit had been married.

Jake pushed back his chair, and carried the remaining dishes into the kitchen. "Do Kit and her son live in town?"

Freda shook her head. "On a ranch, southwest of town."

"Just her and the boy?"

"Curious you are about a woman you do not even know," Freda said suspiciously.

Jake shrugged. "I just want to figure out how she knows me. I think I'll go for a little ride."

"Where is it you will go?"

"Unfinished business."

Though puzzled, Freda didn't pry. "Dress warm, Mr. Cordell. Cold it is this morning."

Jake nodded in acknowledgment and grabbed his tan jacket off the coat rack in the foyer. He donned it, then slapped on his hat, pulling the brim down on his forehead. The morning was crisp, but he welcomed the fresh air.

As he strode toward the livery barn, he was hailed by a steady stream of old acquaintances. An hour later, he finally made it into the stable.

"Zeus!" Jake called out.

An answering neigh led him to a middle stall, where his horse munched contentedly on oats.

"It looks like you've really had a rough time of it,"

Jake remarked, running a hand fondly along Zeus's muscled neck.

Zeus continued to crunch his grain, as if ignoring Jake.

"Okay, I'm sorry I didn't come see you yesterday," Jake apologized. "What do you say we go for a little ride?"

Zeus didn't look enthused at venturing out into the dismal morning.

A few minutes later, Jake led the reluctant horse out of the stable and mounted up. Indecision made him pause a moment, then he tapped the palomino's withers with his boot heels and Zeus jumped into a trot.

The cemetery was set on a hill overlooking the town. In the late spring and summer it was lush with green grass, but now it looked as dead as its inhabitants. Jake halted Zeus in front of the two-foot-high weathered fence surrounding the small graveyard. He dismounted and stepped over the slight barrier.

His gaze went first to his father's tombstone, which had a light blanket of snow on it. He brushed the flakes off and placed his hand on the cold stone. He had been at this grave only one other time: nearly six years before, when he had said good-bye to his father.

Jonathan Cordell had started out as a lawman, then become a judge. He'd been away from home often, leaving young Jake with various families. Later Jake had stayed alone, becoming independent at an early age, as well as rebellious. Yet a part of Jake had never given up trying to please his father, and though he'd failed at that, he hoped bringing in Jonathan Cordell's killer had counted for something.

He gripped the tombstone tightly as his gaze swept across the inscribed stones and crude wooden crosses. He walked around until he discovered what he sought in the far corner.

MAGGIE SUMMERFIELD
BORN 1865, DIED 1889
WE WILL MISS HER

Jake concentrated on a bluejay's raucous call and the answering chatter of a squirrel. The silence following their argument forced Jake to acknowledge the grief within him.

Jake stared down at the sod that covered her grave and curled his fingers into tight fists. "I hope you didn't die alone, Maggie. If I'd have known, I'd have come back."

He reread the words on the headstone. "I'm sorry things couldn't have been different between us, but you were a good friend, Maggie. I hope you're in a better place."

Taking a deep breath, he walked back to Zeus and mounted. About to turn the palomino toward town, he noticed the trail running through the trees above the cemetery. The path led to his former home—the ranch that should've been his, that he was still determined to possess. And now was as good a time as any to find out who he was up against.

He urged Zeus up the narrow trail and into the woods. The path continued for nearly a mile before the ranch came into view. He whistled low in admiration of the horses that pranced about in the corrals.

As he approached the house, a nondescript mutt raced out to greet him. Zeus shied nervously at the yapping dog and Jake kept a firm hold on the reins. He dismounted by the porch, tying Zeus to a pole. The dog sniffed Jake's boots, then licked his hand.

Jake grinned and scratched behind the animal's ears. "You like that, don't you, fella?"

The dog raced back to the barn, and Jake shook his head at the animal's antics.

He knocked on the door and it was opened almost immediately, as if by itself. Then Jake glanced down and saw the young boy who stared up at him inquisitively.

"You're not Charlie," the boy accused.

Jake squelched a smile. "Last time I looked, I wasn't. My name's Jake." The kid's guileless stare didn't waver, and Jake cleared his throat. "Jake Cordell."

The boy's dark eyes widened. "You're the one the books are about!"

Jake groaned. "Don't tell me you've read them, too."

"No, my ma reads them to me now, but someday I'll be able to read them all by myself. Ma's teaching me how. And how to spell and do ciphers. Ask me what two and three is."

Unaccustomed to children, Jake hesitated a moment. "All right, what's two and three?" he asked.

"Five!"

The youngster's enthusiastic answer coaxed a suppressed grin from Jake's lips.

"Who's at the door, Johnny?" a woman's voice called from within.

"It's that man the books are about," Johnny hollered back.

Muffled footsteps heralded the entrance of the woman, and Jake blinked in recognition. He glanced down at Kit's trouser-clad legs and thighs. His liquor-fogged memory hadn't imagined her inviting curves. Raising his gaze to her heart-shaped face, he smiled and tipped his hat. "Fancy meeting you here."

She pressed her round spectacles up on her pert nose. "Mr. Cordell. You're looking much better than the last time I saw you." Placing her hands on Johnny's shoulders, she pulled him out of the doorway and protectively stepped in front of him. "What are you doing here?"

"My father used to own this place." He arched an

eyebrow at her apparent unease. "What are *you* doing here?"

"Now *I* own this place," she shot back.

Johnny tugged on her arm. "Ma, that's Jake Cordell, the man in the books."

She glanced down at him, and her expression softened. "I know, sweetheart."

"Please let him come in, Ma," he pleaded.

The boy was on his side easy enough. "I just stopped by to see who was living here now. I should probably be getting back to town before I freeze." He added a melodramatic shiver. "I can't hardly feel my fingers and toes already."

After a moment, reluctant resignation stole across Kit's rose-flushed face. "Come in and warm up, Mr. Cordell. I've got some coffee on the stove."

Jake's victory seemed hollow. He knew he'd used her kindheartedness against her. With a twinge of conscience he entered the house, and memories assailed him. He forced the visions of his autocratic father from his mind, but the restlessness remained.

She closed the door behind him, and suddenly he was unsure what to say. He fiddled with his hat brim. "Do you own this place all by yourself?"

"Yes, I do." She took the Stetson from his hands. "Give me your coat and I'll hang it up for you."

She accepted his jacket without comment and then turned to her son. "Johnny, could you take him to the front room? I'll get the coffee."

"Okay. C'mon, Mr. Cordell."

A slight swagger accompanied the boy's walk down the hall, and Jake hid a smile behind his hand. Inside the room, Jake glanced around at the walls, which had been covered with tan wallpaper and adorned with woven rugs and a few pictures, mostly of horses. When he and his father had lived there, little time had been taken to decorate the interior. She, however, had given the house a woman's touch, and warmth emanated from the home. Jake settled into a chair close to the crackling fire.

"Are you really a hero?" Johnny asked, his long-lashed eyes full of wonder.

Jake shook his head. "Nope. I just did a job that needed doing."

Johnny settled cross-legged on a thick rug at his feet. "But you fought all kinds of bad guys and you always beat them. You must be really strong and brave to get the bad men without anyone's help but Zeus's."

"I was just smarter than they were. Let me tell you a secret, kid: most bad guys aren't very bright. If they were, they wouldn't become outlaws, would they?"

"That's what my ma says, but I'm not so sure. Before you caught Blackjack Banner, he played poker and won lots and lots of money. If he was dumb, he couldn't have done that, could he?"

"That may be true, but I did catch him, didn't I?"

"Yeah, you did," Johnny exclaimed. "I guess maybe he wasn't so smart."

Kit entered the room and set a tray on the oak table. "Cream or sugar, Mr. Cordell?"

"Neither," Jake replied, noting that she had removed her spectacles. Without the glasses to detract from her features, she appeared softer and more feminine. "Are all those your horses out there?"

She handed Jake a cup and nodded. "They're the culmination of five years' hard work."

"I've never known a woman to run a horse ranch by herself."

"Does your horse really talk to you, like it says in the books?" Johnny piped up.

Jake turned to the inquisitive boy. "Not exactly. But you could say Zeus and I understand each other."

Johnny stood and ran to the window. "Zeus looks cold."

"It is getting colder out there," Kit remarked. "Johnny can take him to the barn, if you'd like."

"He's a pretty big horse. I doubt your son could handle him," Jake warned.

A faint smile brushed her generous lips. "Johnny can handle horses better than most grown men."

Jake thought for a moment, debating whether to allow the youngster near Zeus. The boy's expectant face balanced the scales in his favor. "All right, Johnny. I suspect you and him will get along just fine."

"Thanks, Mr. Cordell." Johnny ran for the door.

"Don't forget your gloves," Kit called after him.

"I won't." Johnny pulled on his outer clothing, then disappeared out the door.

Jake stood and crossed the floor to the window. The hound ran over to greet the boy, startling Zeus. Johnny spoke to the mutt and the animal moved away to lie on the ground, but his soulful brown eyes followed the boy's movements. Slowly approaching Zeus with an outstretched hand, Johnny talked to the horse. The youngster reached out and touched the palomino's nose, then he untied the reins from the post and led him to the barn.

Jake turned back to Kit. "He does have the touch, doesn't he?"

Pride shimmered in her eyes. "Yes, he does."

Jake returned to his chair and Kit refilled his coffee cup.

"Would you be interested in selling?" Jake asked, without preamble.

She blinked. "The ranch?"

"Well, I don't have much need for a kid." Jake smiled to temper his words. "I'd like to buy back my father's ranch and do what he planned to do."

The color seemed to leach from her face as she shook her head. "This is our home now. I could never sell it."

He'd suspected that would be her answer. "I'll give you twice what you paid for it."

Kit set her coffee cup on the end table and clasped her hands together, but not before Jake noticed their trembling. "It's not for sale at any price."

Jake leaned forward in his chair, intending to intimidate her by his actions as well as his tone. "It can't be easy for you, raising a son all by yourself. Think how nice it would be to live in town and have Johnny walk to school. You'd have neighbors to help you out. And you'd make enough from selling the place that you wouldn't have to find a job."

Fire sparked in her eyes, and she sat up straighter. "I've built this ranch up from nothing. I bought the bloodlines to breed the best saddle horses possible, and I've done it without any man telling me what to do. I think I've done a damn fine job of it, too."

Startled by her outburst, Jake leaned back. He had underestimated her. "I apologize if I insulted you. It's just that I've never before met a woman who preferred ranching to an easier life in town."

"You've met one now." Quiet steel ran through her words.

Admiration for her independence rose unexpectedly in Jake, but he tamped down the emotion. If he couldn't buy the place, he'd have to find some other way to get it. Legally. It appeared his law degree would come in handy, after all. Changing his tactics, he relaxed and smiled. "Can I ask how you ended up out here?"

Kit glanced down and her shoulders untensed. "My father left me the newspaper office when he died. I sold it and used the money for a down payment on this place."

Jake stared at Kit, thinking back and remembering. "Your father owned the *Courier*?"

She nodded.

Amazed disbelief rocked Jake. "You're little Kit Thornton?"

"That's right, although I don't think I was ever little." Defensiveness crept into her voice.

Jake studied her, trying to reconcile the memory of the chubby girl with the crooked spectacles that kept slipping down her nose and the slender composed woman sitting in front of him. "You've changed."

Kit laughed, the sound like wind chimes in a gentle breeze. "Thank you."

Jake felt his face redden, a reaction he hadn't experienced in years. "You're grown up and you've gotten—" he searched for the right word, "—taller."

"You'd best be careful, or you'll swallow your boot."

Her eyes glinted humorously, catching Jake off-guard. He studied her as if seeing her for the first time: the high cheekbones and upswept brow, the delicate jaw and slightly upturned nose. The only feature that hadn't changed were her startling blue eyes.

"It's been a lot of years since anyone's called me Fatty Four-Eyes." Despite her nonchalant tone, years-old hurt flashed in her face. "Did you ride out all this way just to see if I'd sell?" she asked.

He fingered the coffee cup's handle. "I stopped by the cemetery first."

"To visit your father and Maggie?" Sympathy shone in her expression.

"How'd you know about Maggie?"

Guilt flickered across her face. "She was a friend."

Jake sensed she held something back from him. "She worked in a saloon."

Kit's clear gaze met his. "What's your point, Mr. Cordell?"

Jake lifted a hand in question. "How did you meet her? Did you work with her?"

Her cheeks flamed. "I never worked with her, and she didn't always work in a saloon."

Jake waited, expecting her to elaborate, but Kit remained silent. "Do you know how she died?"

Kit turned to look out a window, giving Jake an unhindered view of her delicately molded profile. "She just got sick."

"Did a doctor see her?"

"No. She didn't want one."

Frustration gnawed at Jake's gut. "Someone should've gotten him anyhow."

Kit brought her attention back to him. Raw grief glittered in her eyes like unshed tears. "I tried, but you knew Maggie. Do you think she'd have let a doctor examine her if I had gone against her wishes?"

Jake's throat tightened at Kit's anguish. It'd been a long time since he'd felt anyone's pain so deeply. He gazed out a lace-curtained window, gathering his thoughts. "Maggie was stubborn once she set her mind to something," he admitted. He balled his hand into a fist, realized what he'd done, and forced himself to relax. "I wish I could've helped her."

Kit stared at the fire crackling in the hearth. "She cared for you more than any other man she'd known."

"Did she die alone?" he asked quietly.

"No. I was with her at the end."

Jake leveled his troubled gaze at Kit. "Do you think I was wrong to leave her working in the saloon?"

Her expression unreadable, she replied, "It doesn't matter what I think."

He shifted uncomfortably. For some reason, it *did* matter what she thought.

Jake blinked back memories. He didn't want to dwell

in the past any longer. "Why did you get me out of jail yesterday?"

"Maggie would've wanted me to."

"Is that the only reason?"

Her fingers curled into fists in her lap, and she shook her head. "I owed you for being my friend when I needed one."

Her poignancy tugged at Jake's heart. "You don't owe me anything."

She gazed at him for a moment, then asked, "Will you be staying in Chaney, Mr. Cordell?"

He flashed her a quick smile. "Call me Jake, like you used to. I thought I'd stay for a little while and try my hand at being a lawyer."

Surprise lit Kit's features. "So you *did* get your law degree."

Jake nodded. "I've never actually been in a courtroom, but with a little brushing up, I should be able to write some wills and contracts."

"From bounty hunter hero to lawyer? That'll be quite a change for you." She reached for the coffeepot. "Would you like some more coffee?"

"Yes, thank you." Jake held out his cup to be refilled. "Maybe now T. K. Thorne will leave me alone and stop writing those damn books."

Kit jerked, spilling hot coffee over Jake's hand.

Chapter 3

"O w!" Jake exclaimed, coming to his feet.

Her face flaming, Kit jumped up and grabbed a napkin from the tray. She thrust the cloth at him. "Here."

As he dabbed at the reddened skin, he managed a crooked grin. "Is this my payback for those rotten things I said to you yesterday morning?"

In spite of her embarrassment, Kit smiled slightly. "If it was, I'd have dumped the whole pot over your head."

Jake chuckled, a full, deep sound that unexpectedly warmed Kit's heart. It'd been a long time since she'd heard his laughter.

She lowered the pot to the tray. "I'm sorry, Jake." Reaching for his scalded hand, she raised it to examine more closely. The angry red skin made her grimace with self-reproach. "I'll get some butter to put on it."

"Don't worry about it. I'll survive," Jake reassured. "At least it's not my gunhand."

Kit released him, her stomach clenching anxiously. Had the books placed his life in jeopardy? She knew a bounty hunter's lot wasn't a safe one, but she hadn't even considered that the dime novels could further en-

41

danger Jake. "I thought you'd like the books, since they showed all the good you did."

He snorted. "Hardly. Besides, nobody but a saint could live up to that Jake Cordell." He lowered himself back into his chair and rested an ankle on his knee. "Don't worry about it. It's not your problem."

Johnny burst in, slamming the door behind him.

Grateful for the interruption, Kit reminded her son with practiced patience, "Don't forget to hang up your jacket."

Johnny did as she said and ran into the room to lay an arm across Jake's shoulders. "Zeus and Cassie got along real good, just like best friends. Cassie was whispering something in Zeus's ear when I left."

"Who's Cassie?" Jake asked.

"Ma's horse. She's smaller than Zeus, but she's just as smart," Johnny said.

Jake gazed at Kit, a twinkle in his eyes. "I'm sure she is."

"You wanna go upstairs and see my horse collection? I got lots and lots of horses—all different colors and sizes."

"Sure, if it's all right with your mother," Jake replied.

"Please, Ma?" Johnny begged.

Kit looked from one expectant face to the other and found she couldn't deny either one. "All right."

Johnny clasped Jake's hand and led him up the steps.

For a long moment, Kit remained rooted in place. Seeing the two of them together had brought a myriad of emotions scurrying for attention, anxiety the most prevalent.

Did Jake recognize his own son—the mirroring brown eyes and crooked grin? Allowing them to spend time together could end in disaster, but Kit didn't have the fortitude to forbid it. She hadn't agreed with Maggie's edict to keep Johnny's birth from his father, yet Kit knew she could lose her son if Jake learned the truth—and it was for that reason that she remained silent.

Sighing heavily, Kit stood and carried the coffee tray into the kitchen.

Footsteps on the stairs fifteen minutes later prompted Kit to meet Johnny and Jake at the bottom of the staircase. She slipped on her spectacles, feeling a familiar security behind the lenses. "Did you show Mr. Cordell your horses?"

"Yep, and he liked them—didn't you, Mr. Cordell?" Johnny asked.

"I sure did, especially the stud horse called Satan." Jake's dark eyes danced with merriment.

Jake Cordell had an uncanny ability to communicate with his famed palomino, Zeus. The prized animal had been given to Jake by a rich Spaniard in appreciation for a job Jake had done for the man. Named after the Greek god, Zeus had lived up to his name with his courage and cunning, as well as his proclivity toward the mares.

Embarrassed warmth spread across Kit's cheeks. "Well, I see you got a thorough description of each one."

"If the real Satan is anything like Johnny's Satan, he must be quite a horse."

"My hired man, Charlie, taught me how to recognize good bloodlines. Satan's the reason my colts and fillies get top dollar," she replied.

"I wouldn't mind a tour of the place sometime when the weather cooperates."

"Like the tour I gave you years ago?"

Jake laughed. "I'd forgotten about that." He looked down at Johnny. "Did your ma ever tell you about the time her pet chipmunk attacked me?"

Johnny's eyes saucered. "Uh-uh."

"I came over one day to bring her a baby bird that had fallen out of its nest," Jake began. "Since I was there, I asked her if I could see the other animals she was taking care of. While I was leaning over one of the cages, this chipmunk jumps onto my back and starts making the most godawful noises I'd ever heard."

"That wasn't the chipmunk making those horrible noises; that was you," Kit corrected with a grin. "I never did figure out who was more scared, you or Chippy."

Johnny howled with laughter. "You were scared of a little chipmunk?"

A sheepish grin slid across Jake's face. "It didn't seem so little at the time."

Kit recalled that day with sparkling clarity. A week after Jake had rescued her from Will Jameson and his fellow tormentors, he had brought the baby robin to her. The bird had seemed very tiny and fragile in Jake's cupped palms. She'd given the young creature extra care, and a month later she and Jake had set it free.

She glanced down at Jake's hands, which hung loosely at his sides. Remembering how they had tenderly cradled the baby bird, Kit wondered if he still possessed such a gentle touch—or if his years as a bounty hunter had changed that, too.

Dragging her gaze up to his face, she asked, "Would you like to stay for lunch?"

"I think I've intruded enough for one day," Jake said.

"C'mon, Mr. Cordell, please stay. Ma makes the best peach cobbler in the world," Johnny added.

"Well, thank you, young man," Kit said fondly, smoothing down his cowlick. She glanced at Jake, noticing a tuft of unruly hair in the same place as Johnny's. Quickly she looked away. Taking a deep breath, she forced the corners of her lips to turn upward. "Really, it's no problem, Jake. I have more than enough."

"As long as I'm not intruding."

"You aren't," Kit reassured. "Johnny, show Jake where the sink is. And don't forget to wash your own hands."

Johnny led him through the kitchen, which had changed little since Jake had lived there. For a split second he could envision his mother next to the stove, her cheeks rosy, ebony tendrils curling about her face. Jake nearly stumbled in his haste to escape the apparition, and he followed Johnny to the enclosed porch.

Standing by the pump, Johnny snorted. "Why does Ma always make me wash up? A little dirt ain't going to hurt."

"Because that's what women do. Besides, don't you think we'd get awfully dirty if they weren't around to remind us?" Jake winked at the boy.

"I don't care. I like being dirty."

Jake tried to remember how his father had handled his stubborn petulance. "Well, let's humor her and clean up, because we may not get any of that cobbler if we don't."

After a moment's thought, Johnny agreed.

When they were done, Johnny wrapped his small fingers around Jake's hand. Surprised by the trusting gesture, Jake instinctively squeezed the boy's hand.

Jake wished his own father had given him some sign of affection. He couldn't remember his father ever holding his hand or telling him he loved him. For a fleeting moment he wondered what it would be like to have a child. He sure as hell would spend more time with him than Jonathan Cordell had spared his son.

Kit placed the last of the bowls on the table and turned to see Jake and Johnny enter the dining room hand in hand. Her heart plowed into her ribs, missing a few beats. She'd often dreamed of seeing father and son together in this house. Yet the reality of it troubled her, and she wondered if someone might see the resemblance between the man and the boy: the deep brown eyes and strong, square-cut jaw. Thankfully, Johnny had inherited his mother's lighter colored hair, as well as her generous mouth. With a little luck, nobody would see the similarities as clearly as Kit did.

"I hope you both washed good," she said.

Jake winked at Johnny, who giggled, and the two of them raised their hands.

"Yes, ma'am," Jake replied dutifully.

Kit shook her head, unable to resist the playful glimmer in Jake's dark eyes. Despite the gunbelt slung low on his hips, she glimpsed a side of the teasing young man she'd known before he'd left Chaney.

Laughing, she took one of Jake's strong hands in hers, pretending to inspect it. The long, slender fingers curved around her palm for a moment, and the light sprinkling of hair across the back of his hand tickled her. Her breath seemed to rasp more loudly in her ears. Startled by her body's response, she glanced at Jake. His rugged face had gone still except for his untelling eyes, which studied her closely.

She swallowed, releasing him like a hot branding iron. Struggling to keep her voice even, she said, "You pass inspection."

Turning to her son, she examined his hands. Would they grow as strong as his father's? Already she could see that the same blunt nails capped Johnny's fingertips. Trembling, she released her son, not noticing if he'd cleaned well or not. "Okay, you can go sit down, too."

Trying to regain her aplomb, Kit brought the food from the kitchen and deposited it on the table, then joined Jake and Johnny.

During the lively meal, Johnny stole the majority of Jake's attention.

"Ma said you used to live here when you were my size," Johnny said.

"That's right," Jake said. "But I didn't spend a lot of time here."

Johnny's face scrunched up. "Why not?"

"Whenever my father had to leave town on business, he'd put me with someone to stay with until he got home."

"What about your ma?"

"It was just my pa and me," Jake replied.

Kit detected the bitter hurt in his voice, and wanted to touch him, to lend him her understanding. Instead, she laid her clenched hands in her lap.

"Do you like living here?" Jake asked Johnny.

The boy's eyes sparkled. "Yep. I play with Toby and Jasper and the other animals. And Ma promised she'd teach me how to ride pretty soon. And I like to explore."

"Don't you ever get lonely?"

Johnny shook his head. "I got Ma and Charlie and Ethan and Pete and Toby."

Jake smiled. "I've met Toby, but who're Charlie, Ethan, and Pete?"

"Charlie and Ethan work here, and Pete is an old Indian who came with the ranch," Kit answered. "I'm surprised he wasn't around when you lived here."

"He teaches me all kind of things," Johnny interjected. "Like how to count coup, and how to scalp folks."

Jake's mouth twitched with amusement, and he winked at Kit. "Looks like you're going to have a little warrior in the family."

"See, Ma? Even Mr. Cordell thinks so," Johnny said in an I-told-you-so tone.

Kit chuckled. "Pete considers himself Johnny's grandfather, and in his tribe, the elders taught the children." She shrugged. "Pete's heart is in the right place."

"Will you teach me how to ride, Mr. Cordell?"

Johnny asked. "Ma said she would, but she's always too busy."

"Johnny, it's not polite to ask such a thing. As soon as I have some time, I'll teach you," Kit said.

Jake finished his dessert and pushed back his empty plate. "I suspect I won't be real busy with my law practice to start with, so I wouldn't mind giving Johnny some riding lessons."

Johnny whooped with joy. "Is it okay, Ma? Please?"

Kit folded her napkin and placed it on the table. One of the reasons she hadn't found the time was because she was fearful for his safety. Despite Johnny's affinity for animals, a horse was still unpredictable, and Johnny could be hurt. Gazing at her son's expectant face, she couldn't come up with a single reason to forbid it. "All right, as long as it doesn't take too much of Jake's time."

The grandfather clock in the front room struck two.

"Time to do your chores, Johnny," Kit said.

The boy slid off his chair and moved to Jake's side. "When can we start?"

"Next time I come visit," Jake replied.

"When'll that be?"

"A day or two. Deal?" He stuck out his hand.

"Deal," Johnny replied, and his small hand was swallowed up by Jake's larger one.

A few moments later, Kit heard the door open and close.

Jake smiled fondly. "He's quite a boy."

Kit planted an elbow on the table and propped her chin in her palm. "He can talk your ear off when he gets going, but on the whole, he's a good boy."

"I remember being pretty contrary when I was his age. My father used to polish my backside good. It must've helped, because I didn't lose my temper half as often."

A smile twitched Kit's lips. "At least not in front of him." She sobered. "I'm sorry about your father. I was at the funeral, but I didn't have time to talk to you. Judge Cordell always used to say hello to me and tip his hat like I was a real lady."

Bitterness clouded Jake's eyes. "My father wasn't around much while I was growing up." He laughed caustically. "Do you want to hear something funny? As much as I resented my father, I've become him."

"I don't understand."

Jake waved a negligent hand. "Forget it." He smiled, though the gesture appeared forced. "I do have something the great Jonathan Cordell doesn't. Thanks to T. K. Thorne, I have a reputation."

Kit shivered at his cynical tone.

"I'd best be getting back to town. I've got to talk to the doctor about that room above his office," Jake said.

He stood and Kit led the way to the foyer. Plucking his hat and jacket off a peg, she handed them to him.

"Thank you for everything, Kit. I enjoyed the company, and the meal," Jake said sincerely. "And if you have second thoughts about selling the ranch, let me know."

She shook her head firmly. "That won't happen, Jake."

He grasped her hand gently, holding her captive. "Think about it, Kit. Think how much better off Johnny would be in town, close to school."

His warm, callused palm pressed against hers, and awareness curled in Kit's stomach. Her mind clouded and she worked to focus on his words. "I've worked too hard to give it up."

"Doesn't hurt to try." Releasing her, he stepped back. "Good-bye."

"Good-bye, Jake."

After closing the door behind him, Kit peeked around

the curtain and watched Jake stride into the barn.

A few minutes later he emerged, leading his horse. He mounted with natural grace and lifted a hand to Johnny, who'd followed him out of the barn. Tapping Zeus's withers with his heels, Jake sent the horse into an easy gallop. Her son waved in farewell until Jake disappeared from view.

Kit leaned against the wall, crossing her arms. Warring emotions roiled within her. She'd enjoyed seeing Jake again. However, she could already see a dangerous bond growing between Johnny and Jake. Maggie had always said Jake was a tumbleweed, and Kit didn't want to see Johnny hurt when Jake left again.

She shouldn't have raised her son's hopes by permitting Jake to teach him how to ride. If Jake didn't return, she would have to explain to Johnny what kind of man Jake was, and destroy her son's illusion—the illusion she'd created with the Cordell stories.

After he returned from Kit's, Jake went to the doctor's office. The bell above the door announced his arrival, and Dr. Lewis stuck his head out of the back room. He scrutinized Jake closely, then frowned.

"What are you waiting for—an engraved invitation? Get in here and take your clothes off so I can examine you." The cantankerous doctor's gray eyes snapped impatiently.

"I'm not sick," Jake replied.

"Then what the hell are you bothering me for? I'm a busy man."

"My name's Jake Cordell."

"So what? My name's Henry Lewis. Now go and bother someone else." The doctor turned away.

"Wait," Jake called. "I understand you have an office upstairs you're looking to rent. Is it still empty?"

Dr. Lewis stopped to gaze at him. "Last time I

looked." He narrowed his eyes. "You aren't another doctor, are you?"

"No," Jake said, feeling insulted. "I told you. I'm Jake Cordell, the bounty hunter." He cleared his throat. "The dime novel hero."

The doctor harrumphed. "Those ten-cent books are all a bunch of flapdoodle and tommyrot."

Seeing past the doctor's crusty facade, Jake grinned crookedly. "So, how did you like them?"

Dr. Lewis blinked, startled, then aimed a finger at Jake. "You're a lawyer, aren't you?"

Laughing, Jake nodded. "And you're a fake, Dr. Lewis."

Humor glittered faintly in the doctor's eyes. "The office is all yours, Mr. Cordell."

"How much do I owe you?"

"Twenty dollars a month. Pay me later. Now go on and let me tend to business."

Dr. Lewis disappeared into the back room once more, and Jake, shaking his head and smiling, left.

He paused on the boardwalk and looked up at his new office. With any luck, he'd only be there a month. That would give him plenty of time to get his father's ranch back. Then he'd show everyone he could do what Jonathan Cordell hadn't been able to—he'd raise the best damn horses west of the Mississippi.

His step faltered. Kit cared about the ranch, too. He had seen it in her eyes when she'd talked about the horses, and the thought of taking the place from her twinged his conscience. He could still picture little Kit sprawled on the boardwalk, her eyes glittering with tears as the boys teased her. From that moment he'd made himself her protector—and now he was plotting to take her ranch.

Sergeant O'Hara crossed the street and joined him,

his expression downcast. "So you're really goin' to be hangin' up your gun?"

Jake slapped his back. "Sure am, and can't say that I'm real upset about it."

O'Hara slipped his thumbs between his tan suspenders and brown wool shirt. "Now, I know you aren't too fond of your reputation, but a lot of folks, meself included, will be missin' your adventures."

Jake pressed his hat back off his forehead. "Can't be helped, Patrick. There comes a time in every man's life when he hits a crossroads and has to decide what path he's going to take. I've decided I'm tired of being shot at, spit on, bit, kicked, and cussed at." He shrugged. "Of course, being a lawyer isn't a whole lot different."

"Aye, there's probably more than a spot of truth there. Would you be wantin' to join me for a pint or two?"

Tempted, Jake considered, then shook his head. "If there's so much as a hint of liquor on my breath, Freda would most likely lock me out."

"She's a brassy lass, isn't she?" Patrick commented with a grin.

Jake raised his eyebrows. "I can think of a lot of words to describe Freda, and brassy isn't even close."

The Irishman chuckled. "If Kit hadn't taken you over, Freda wouldn't have taken you in. I hope you weren't too rough on the lass."

"Kit?" Patrick nodded, and Jake snorted. "She can take care of herself. I stopped by her place earlier today."

Surprise skidded across Patrick's rough-hewn features, replaced by a wary defensiveness. "And what did you think?"

"I think she's done a good job, considering."

"Considerin' what?"

"Well, that she has a son and she's all by herself."

"She's got some hired men. Did you see them?"

Jake shook his head. "No, but Johnny mentioned them."

"So you haven't met them?"

Confused exasperation tested Jake's patience. "That's what I just said. Would you quit beating around the bush and tell me what the hell you're getting at?"

After studying Jake a moment, Patrick sighed. "Kit takes in strays."

"That's nothing new—she's been doing that since she was ten years old."

"Then you'll be knowin' what I'm meanin', and you probably won't be surprised when you meet her hired men." He tipped his hat to Jake. "I'll be seein' you."

Bewildered by Patrick's enigmatic reply, Jake remained standing in place. Although he'd known Kit for over thirteen years, he'd felt like he was meeting her for the first time that day. A part of that little girl remained in her, but the rest of her had changed dramatically. Most obvious was her transformation into an attractive woman with a damn fine figure, made especially tempting in those tight-fitting trousers. Another change was her independence: a trait Jake admired, even as he knew that self-reliance would be his greatest hindrance in regaining his father's ranch.

He uprooted himself and strode down the boardwalk. Zeus would need some exercise tomorrow, and if they ended up at Kit's place, he might be able to meet Kit's hired men and see what Patrick had meant.

Besides, the prospect of seeing Kit and her son again wasn't at all unpleasant.

Jake Cordell leveled his six-gun menacingly. "Throw it down, Ross, or I'm liable to get an itchy finger."

With flat fish eyes, Frank Ross squinted at the tow-

ering bounty hunter. "I ain't gonna be taken in alive, Cordell."

Kit Thornton, aka T. K. Thorne, reread the lines and scowled, then jerked the sheet from the typewriter. She crushed the paper in her fist and tossed it at the wooden box beside the fireplace. The balled sheet bounced on the floor, coming to rest beside the other orphaned scraps of paper.

Her reluctant gaze sidled to the newspaper that lay on the corner of her writing desk. The headline glared at her, daring her to dispute its claim: FRANK ROSS SENTENCED TO LIFE IMPRISONMENT. Although she'd memorized the article, she scanned it again. After she finished, she removed her wire-rimmed spectacles and laid them on top of the paper.

When Jake had become a bounty hunter in the wild and untamed West, Kit had taken the factual newspaper accounts and given them a dollop of creative license to concoct the dime novels. Little did she realize how different the man was from the fictional character she'd created.

Trying to write Jake Cordell's last adventure now, Kit floundered with the words that usually came so easily. How was she to have known Jake would despise the reputation her books had brought him? She'd written them as a tribute to the young man she'd been infatuated with so many years ago. She shuddered to imagine what he would do if he learned she was the nefarious T. K. Thorne.

She stood and pressed her palms against her lower back, trying to massage the tightness out of the knotted muscles.

Trudging out of the office and up the stairs, she paused outside Johnny's bedroom and peeked in. A single candle cast a pale yellow glow across his beloved features as he slept peacefully in the same room his father had slept in as a child. With little imagination, Kit could envision Jake in the bed, and the picture brought a heated warmth to her cheeks. She scolded herself sharply. The Jake Cordell she wrote about was the man she'd been infatuated with, not the drunk she'd helped over to Freda's. Although he'd behaved better while visiting, Kit couldn't allow her hopes to rise. Admiring the mythical hero was much safer.

Melancholy filled Kit as she slipped inside to extinguish the candle. Tiptoeing back into the hallway, she leaned against the wall and slid her hands into her trouser pockets.

Jake threatened the two most important things in her life: her son and her home. She would have to be blind not to see he was determined to own his father's former ranch. And if she didn't pay the note that was due in less than four weeks, he had a good chance of regaining his legacy—and Johnny's birthright.

Shaking aside the dismal thoughts, she returned to her desk in the library. The smooth wooden chair creaked beneath her, and she slipped her glasses back on. She stared at the bulky typewriter, willing it to write Jake Cordell's final adventure without her help. It remained stubbornly silent.

She sighed restlessly and opened a desk drawer, withdrawing a wooden box. Lifting the lid, she gazed at Jonathan Cordell's revolver. He'd given it to her a few months before he was murdered, as if he'd had a premonition of his own death. She had never figured out why he'd gifted her with the gun, but Kit cherished it as a remembrance of her friendship with the elder Cordell. Kit stroked the cool metal, then placed the velvet-lined box back in its place.

Settling her fingers on the round typewriter keys with an intimacy born of familiarity, she forced a couple words onto the paper. The clacking kept time with the grandfather clock's swinging pendulum. But the solace she usually found in her writing eluded her.

Propping her elbows on the desktop, Kit buried her face in her hands. She wished Jake had never returned to Chaney to stir long-forgotten memories. Some memories were best left alone.

"Can we go watch Charlie and Ethan, Ma? I got my chores done," Johnny pleaded.

The afternoon sun glinted across his hair, highlighting the same auburn tints that shone in his father's darker hair.

Kit chastised herself. She had to stop comparing Johnny to Jake. If she continued, she was liable to slip up and comment aloud. She glanced at her son, who waited expectantly. "All right, but you'll have to be quiet."

"I know."

Johnny's indignation rang clearly in his tone. Sometimes she forgot he wasn't a baby anymore.

The training pens were situated a quarter of a mile from the main building, curtained from sight by a grove of hardwood trees. As Kit and Johnny walked, dead leaves crackled beneath their feet. Spring had finally decided to make an appearance, and buds showed on the bushes and trees.

The training pens came into view and Kit slowed their approach. Once they were by the corral, she leaned against the upper rail and Johnny against the lower. Ethan, a nineteen-year-old who shared his heritage equally between the Pawnee and whites, waved at them. Kit returned the gesture, smiling at the young man.

"They're working with Snowflake," Johnny said in a low voice.

It didn't surprise her that her son had named the horse,

and the white mark on the chestnut mare's forehead told her why he'd chosen that name.

They watched Ethan and Charlie, a muscular black man, work with the skittish horse for a few minutes.

"Someone's coming," Johnny announced.

Kit glanced up to see a horseman nearing the corral. The cream-colored horse gave away the rider's identity immediately: Jake Cordell. Why had he returned so soon?

Kit gripped the pole so tightly that her knuckles whitened. Had he guessed Johnny's identity? Or had he already found out *she* was the hated T. K. Thorne?

Chapter 4

~~~~~

Jake eased back on Zeus's reins as he neared the activity around the corral. His palomino snorted impatiently, shaking its mane.

"Yes, I know she's a cute little filly, but you behave yourself," Jake warned in a low voice. Zeus flicked his ears back but settled down to a sedate walk.

Jake's gaze roamed across Kit Thornton, noting she again wore the snug trousers that drew his attention to her small waist and nicely rounded hips that his palms ached to possess. He recalled the soft plumpness of her breasts pressed against his side as she'd helped him to Freda's, and he had little trouble imagining what lay beneath the mannish clothing.

Shifting in the saddle uncomfortably, Jake drew his appreciative gaze away from Kit. "All right, maybe I should be taking my own advice," he said to Zeus.

A few moments later he halted by the corral and touched the brim of his hat with his thumb and forefinger. "Afternoon, Kit, Johnny."

"Hi, Mr. Cordell," the boy said enthusiastically.

"Hello, Jake." Kit's greeting was less exuberant than her son's.

Jake dismounted, the saddle creaking beneath him.

Loosely tying the leather reins around a fence post, he stood on the other side of Johnny. Resting his booted foot on the lower rail, Jake studied the two men in the corral and understood what Patrick had meant.

"What brings you back so soon?" Kit asked, drawing his attention.

"I was cleaning up my office this morning and cabin fever hit. I'm not used to being surrounded by four walls."

"You'll have to get used to it if you're serious about working as a lawyer."

Jake shrugged, hiding the fact that he didn't plan on being in the office long enough to grow accustomed to it. "Time will tell if I'm cut out for the law business."

"Would you like to come up to the house for some coffee?"

"If you don't mind, I'd rather watch for a little while." He gestured to the horse in the corral. "Looks like your wranglers know what they're doing."

Kit turned back to her hired men, her expression brightening. "Charlie's been working here ever since I bought the place, and Ethan, the boy, showed up about a year ago."

"Some bad men hurt him real bad and Ma took care of him," Johnny added.

Knowing Kit, Jake wasn't surprised.

"Part Cheyenne?"

Kit shook her head hesitantly. "His mother was Pawnee."

"Not many folks would take in a half-breed."

Fire flashed in her sapphire eyes. "Don't you ever use that word around here."

Jake would have been disappointed if she hadn't responded with such vehemence, and he tossed her a grin. "Personally, I judge men by what they do, not what they are."

Kit's startled gaze met his. "Be careful who you say that to."

"I suppose a woman raising a child alone, with a Negro and a breed working for her, isn't too popular among Chaney's upstanding citizens," Jake said.

She blinked, then kicked at the dirt. "It hasn't changed much since we were children, has it?"

"Why do you stay here if you hate it so much?"

She lifted her stormy eyes to him. "I don't hate the town, Jake. I hate the narrow-mindedness of some of the people. There's a lot of good folks around Chaney, too."

"I like Freda and Patrick," Johnny said. "Freda lets me help her make cookies, and Patrick always buys me a licorice stick."

Kit ruffled her son's hair, and smiled at Jake. "See what I mean?"

"And then there's Will Jameson," Jake remarked.

"You were the one who taught me how to handle bullies like him," she said.

Jake turned back to the corral, embarrassed by the gratitude in her voice. He had always had a weakness for the underdog.

Charlie slipped a blanket on the horse's back and pulled it off, then repeated the motion over and over. Jake straightened, recognizing the training method.

"I've only known one other person who broke horses that way," Jake commented.

"Your father," Kit said.

"How'd you know?"

"We used to visit quite a bit." She paused. "That was after you'd gone away to college. He told me about his plans to raise horses and how he'd train them."

Bitter betrayal blindsided Jake. "I didn't think he'd told anyone but me what he wanted to do with the ranch." Resentment sharpened his tone. "Hell, I didn't even know you and him were such good friends."

Kit's lips thinned. "He never spoke down to me, and he listened to what I had to say, unlike my own father."

Jake studied her stony profile, and his anger dissipated. "I guess maybe I didn't know my father as well as I thought I did."

Her features softened as understanding filled her eyes. "That's funny. He said the same thing about you."

Jake laced his fingers, resting his forearms on the corral pole. He cursed Frank Ross anew for murdering his father before he had made his peace with the elder Cordell.

Looking around, he imagined owning the ranch and the horses that pranced about in the nearby enclosures. The image brought a peace of mind he hadn't experienced in years, although Kit's presence disturbed him. Whether she knew it or not, and whether he liked it or not, she stood in his way.

"Would you like to see Satan?" Kit asked.

Seeing the excitement brimming in her eyes, Jake wanted to forget she was his adversary. But he'd dreamed his dream for too long. He'd do what he had to do to possess what was rightfully his. "Sure."

Johnny ran ahead of them.

"Does he always have that much energy?" Jake asked.

She smiled, and he could almost touch the love in her expression. "Usually he has more."

Curiously bereft, Jake frowned. "I haven't been around kids much. Sometimes I wonder what I'd be doing now if I hadn't turned to bounty hunting to get my father's killer."

"You sound bitter."

"Maybe I am. I don't know. I see you with your son and this ranch, and it makes me wonder."

"You've done a lot of good, Jake. Think of all the lives you've saved by bringing in those outlaws."

"But what price did I pay?"

Kit adjusted her spectacles, then slid her hands into her jacket pockets. "That's something only you can answer," she said with a husky voice.

She had a point, even though he wasn't certain he was ready to confront his conscience.

"Satan's in here," Johnny stated when they reached the larger of the two barns. "You have to be quiet or he gets upset."

Jake leaned close to Kit. "That sounds like Ma talking."

Her cheeks reddened, and she gave a rueful nod.

Johnny opened the door and led him to a stall at the far end. When Jake had been a child he'd spent many hours playing in the barn, although the building had been empty back then. The rich aroma of horses and fresh hay surrounded him, a strong but not unpleasant mixture. As his eyes adjusted to the dim light, he distinguished the figure of a tall black stallion. Satan threw back his regal head, his ebony mane dancing across his neck.

"He's beautiful," Jake whispered in awe. "Where did you get him?"

Kit stretched out her arm toward the horse, and he nuzzled her hand. Patting his forehead, Kit turned to Jake. "An auction in Denver. He was more dead than alive at the time." Fury colored her words. "The former owners tried to tame him using a whip. The only thing it did was scar him. I took one look into his eyes, and knew he wasn't the devil they thought he was."

Leave it to Kit to buy a horse no one else could handle. Or wanted. "So you bought him."

"I worked with him every day for six months to get him to trust me."

Jake studied the woman and the horse who nuzzled her ear. His throat tightened. The taunts and cruel jokes she'd endured as a child had made her stronger, more prepared to face adversity.

"Something wrong, Jake?" Kit asked.

He forced a smile. "Nothing worth talking about."

"Nobody but Ma can ride him," Johnny said. "But I think when I'm big enough, he'll let me ride him, too. He's a stud horse. What does that mean, Mr. Cordell? Ma won't tell me."

Jake's face warmed as he wondered how to explain horse breeding to a young boy. He glanced at Kit, whose eyes twinkled with amusement. No help to be found there. "Well, ah, I guess it means he's a good daddy."

Johnny nodded. "Ma says my pa was a good man. She says I'm a lot like him. Sometimes I wish he was here now." He glanced at Jake. "I wish my ma would marry you, instead of Mr. Preston."

"I have no plans to marry Mr. Preston," Kit stated, then added hastily, "—or Jake."

"Who's Mr. Preston?" Jake asked.

"He owns the paper."

"He's got Toby breath," Johnny said with a scowl. Jake snorted with laughter. "He was courtin' Ma."

The thought of another man exploring her enticing curves brought a flash of jealousy that surprised him. He cleared his throat. "He's the one you sold the *Courier* to?"

A wistful expression shadowed her face. "That's right. My heart was never in the newspaper business, much to my father's disappointment."

"I thought you and your father got along fine," Jake said.

"As long as I did everything he said. He never really listened to me, Jake. When I tried to tell him about the other kids teasing me, he patted me on the head and said I was too emotional, just like my mother had been.

"And when I used to help him set type, he'd say I

was too slow or I didn't spell the words right. He'd find fault with everything I did. He didn't approve of me taking in strays, either, so I kept them hidden. That was the only time I defied Father.''

Jake could empathize. He hadn't been able to measure up to his father's expectations, either. He glanced down at Johnny, standing beside him; at least the boy wouldn't have to impress a father.

"You should've told me, Kit," Jake said.

She shook her head, a sad smile playing across her lips. "There was nothing you could've done. The only thing that would've made it better was if I'd been born a boy.''

"I'm glad you weren't," Jake said, his gaze straying across her full breasts and down to her hips. Kit blushed.

Jake turned to Johnny. "Ready for your first riding lesson?"

Johnny jumped up and down, startling Satan. "Yep."

Kit ran her hand down Satan's neck to calm him. "Are you sure you don't mind, Jake?"

"I've been looking forward to it," he said honestly.

She scratched the stallion's forehead, a frown marring her face. After a few moments, she looked at Jake. "Treasure's our gentlest horse."

Jake read the concern in her eyes, and leaned close to her, speaking in a voice low enough that Johnny couldn't hear. "Don't worry. I'll make sure he doesn't get hurt."

She nodded, but Jake could tell he hadn't allayed her apprehension.

Fifteen minutes later, in the bright afternoon sunlight, Kit leaned against the corral as Jake and Johnny stood next to the gentle dun. Despite Jake's reassurances, she couldn't stop the fear that climbed up her throat. She locked her fingers together to hide their trembling and hooked her arms over the top rail. Despite the cool day, perspiration pearled her forehead.

"All right, Johnny," Jake began. "First thing you have to do is let your horse get to know you. Let her smell your hand, talk to her, rub her neck; that way she won't be so surprised when you get on her back."

Treasure nuzzled Johnny's hand and the boy giggled, bringing a reluctant smile to Kit.

"See her ears?" Jake asked.

Johnny nodded. "They're kinda standing straight up."

"That means Treasure knows what's going on, that she trusts you. If a horse should ever throw back its ears, you'd best be getting out of its way."

Jake's low easy drawl calmed Kit. For a moment she heard the long-ago echo of Jake's soothing voice as he'd eased her loneliness with a few words and an understanding smile.

Then Jake lifted the boy into the saddle, and Kit's fingernails dug into her palms. "All right, now, keep your heels down in the stirrups," Jake instructed.

Johnny gripped the reins in both hands, and his tongue darted across his lips. Jake remained close to Treasure, keeping one hand on the bridle and the other on Johnny's leg.

"That's right, keep those toes pointed to the sky," Jake said. "You're doing great, Johnny."

The boy smiled, his face glowing.

"What do you say we walk around the corral a couple times so you can get a feel for the reins?" Jake suggested.

Johnny nodded.

As Jake led Treasure around the enclosure, Kit could see him talking to Johnny, and her shoulders untensed. Jake was a natural teacher, and she wondered if he even realized his talent.

Would he act any differently if he knew Johnny was his son? Kit squelched the thought even as her conscience proclaimed her a coward for keeping silent.

After a few circles, Jake stopped Treasure and laid a hand on Johnny's arm. "Do you want to try it by yourself?"

He nodded eagerly.

Kit held her breath as Johnny kneed Treasure into a slow gait.

Jake walked close beside them. "You're doing just fine." He spoke in a low voice that wouldn't startle the horse. "Ease up on the reins—Treasure will feel the leather on the side of her neck and turn that way."

Excitement animated Johnny's face, and something close to pride glowed in Jake's expression.

"All right, Johnny, I think that's enough for today," Jake said. He led the docile horse to the fence near Kit, and Jake smiled. "Looks like your son takes to riding like a grizzly takes to an itch."

Relief poured through her, and she smiled at the carefree expression on his features. "I didn't realize you had a gift for teaching."

He shook his head. "Johnny's just an excellent student." Jake lifted him down from Treasure's back and laid a hand across the boy's shoulders. "You did real good, kid."

"I rode all by myself," Johnny exclaimed with a wide grin.

"You sure did," Kit said with a fond smile. Now that Johnny stood on solid ground, she wondered why she'd been so terrified. "I bet you'll be trotting next time."

"And then he'll be wanting his own pony," Jake said, winking at her.

Kit's lightheartedness fled. She wasn't sure she'd be able to keep the ranch, much less afford to give Johnny his own horse.

"Johnny why don't you take Treasure into the barn? I'll be in there in a minute to help you unsaddle her," Jake suggested.

Eagerly, the boy did as Jake had said.

Once Johnny was out of earshot, Jake asked, "Is something wrong, Kit?"

Dismayed, she wondered if her feelings were as transparent now as when she'd been a young girl. She forced a smile. "What could be wrong? Thanks for giving Johnny the riding lesson. You don't have to feel obligated to give him another."

He shook his head. "To be perfectly honest, I enjoyed it. Johnny reminds me of me when I was a boy."

Kit's breath caught in her throat. "What do you mean?"

"I bothered Pa to no end when I was Johnny's age, wanting him to teach me how to ride." His eyes clouded. "He never had the time. So I know how Johnny feels."

Kit felt the sting of Jake's censure, and guilt gave her voice a sharp edge. "It's hard finding the time in between all the work on the ranch and the recordkeeping, not to mention the cooking and cleaning."

Jake cupped her cheek, and said quietly, "I'm not comparing you to my father, Kit. I know it must be hard for a woman alone to raise a child."

She fought the urge to lean into his gentle hand. "Sometimes I wonder if I'm doing the right thing."

"Maybe Johnny would be better off if you sold me the ranch and took him to live in town," he said.

Betrayed, Kit jerked away. "Stop it, Jake!"

"What?"

"Don't use Johnny to get the ranch," she said hotly. "He's the reason I bought the place. I wanted something to pass on to him."

"But he'd be better off around children his own age."

"Like I was 'better off' with other children?" she demanded bitterly. "You and I both know how cruel kids can be. And we both know how quickly he'll be labeled a bastard. Out here, I can protect him." Her anger abated. "Like you protected me."

Jake studied her with a steady, tight-lipped expression. "You're not going to change your mind, are you?"

She met his gaze without hesitation. "No."

His jaw muscle clenched. "I'd better go give Johnny a hand with Treasure."

With stiff shoulders and long-legged strides, Jake left her standing alone by the corral.

Kit closed her eyes, breathing deeply to calm her thundering heart. She hadn't meant to cross horns with Jake, but his obsession to own the ranch rankled her. Hero or not, he had no right coveting her home.

After a few moments, Kit followed after Jake. She found him helping Johnny unsaddle Treasure and rub her down. He gave Kit a startled look, then turned his attention back to Johnny. She scooped a handful of oats into Treasure's feed box and waited for Jake and Johnny to complete their task.

"Always remember that your horse's well-being comes before your own," Jake said to Johnny. "He's been the one working to carry you all day while all you've done is sit on his back. So before you eat or sleep, you take care of your horse."

"Even if I'm really tired?" Johnny asked. "Ma says I get crabby when I'm tired."

Jake smiled down at the boy. "Even if you're really tired and crabby. Because without your horse, you'll be alone and on foot. And believe me, you don't want that to happen."

With Johnny serving as a buffer between them, Kit and Jake walked back to where Zeus was tied.

"I'd best get back to town," Jake said, unwrapping the reins from the post.

"Do you have to?" Johnny asked, his face downcast.

Jake hunkered down beside the boy. "Don't look so sad, kid. I'll be back in a few days."

"That's forever. Why don't you stay here, like Charlie and Ethan? There's room for him, isn't there, Ma?"

Jake glanced up at Kit's gaping mouth. "I've got my own room at Freda's, and I've got a job in town. You think about what I taught you, okay?"

"Okay," Johnny agreed reluctantly, then he brightened. "Thanks for teaching me how to ride. I had lots of fun, and I think Treasure liked it." He frowned. "But I don't think Toby did. He doesn't like to be locked up in the shed."

"Until you've had a few more lessons, Toby will have to stay there when I'm teaching you." Jake straightened, and smiled at Johnny. "You're a fast learner, kid."

Jake mounted Zeus, and looked down at Kit. "No hard feelings?"

She shook her head. "Not on my side."

"Good. Next time you're in town, drop by my office." He waved, then wheeled his palomino about, and headed back toward Chaney.

Kit dragged her attention away from his receding figure. "It's past chore time, Johnny."

"I did good, didn't I, Ma?" Johnny asked excitedly.

"You did better than good."

With a grin, the boy scurried off.

Unease rippled through Kit. Her son liked Jake; he liked him too well. If Jake was using Johnny and his riding lessons as an excuse to try to talk her into selling the ranch, Johnny was bound to get hurt. The Jake she'd known wouldn't have done something so underhanded, but there was a sharper edge to this Jake. She had no idea how far he would go to acquire his father's former ranch.

Charlie joined her, banishing her somber thoughts. "I seen Cordell with Johnny. Watchin' them, a person might think they were father and son," he remarked.

Kit opened her mouth, then abruptly closed it. "A person *might* think that."

"Iffen you're hiding something from Cordell, I'd think twice about it," Charlie said. "A man like him ain't gonna take kindly to secrets involvin' him."

Kit studied her observant hired man a moment and sighed. "Jake would be miserable if he had to settle down in one place."

"Why don't you leave that up to Cordell? He doesn't seem to be in a big hurry to shake Chaney's dust from his boots."

Kit's muscles tensed. "What happens to Johnny if he does decide to leave? I won't lose him, Charlie. Johnny's all I have."

"Don't you be frettin', Miz Thornton. Mr. Cordell won't be hearin' anything from me. You got my word on that."

Kit squeezed his work-roughened hand. "Thank you."

She turned away from the corral and walked toward the copse of trees that hid the house from view. Her steps as heavy as her heart, she followed the worn trail.

Was the resemblance that obvious? Shaking her head, Kit hoped not. She couldn't keep Johnny away from town, where keen-eyed folks might spot the similarities. Neither could she deny Jake the chance to get to know his son, even if he didn't realize Johnny was his flesh and blood. At least that would assuage her guilt for keeping silent.

She couldn't figure out Jake's preoccupation with his father's former ranch. Why did it have to be this specific place? Why couldn't he buy another parcel of land and raise horses, if that's what he truly wanted to do?

The more she saw Jake, the more she realized how much her girlish infatuation had colored her perception of him. She suspected he hadn't given up on the ranch, despite her flat refusal to sell. One thing she did know was that Jake Cordell had a stubborn streak a mile wide.

She rested her hand against the cheek he'd cupped and imagined she could still feel the heat of his palm. It would've been so easy to give in to temptation and let him hold her like he'd done years ago. When one of her animals had died, Jake had dug a hole for the lifeless bunny; he hadn't laughed when she'd cried over the tiny grave. Instead, he'd wrapped his arms around her, understanding her grief.

She and Jake were adults now—strangers who'd shared a friendship years ago. The only connections between them were the ranch and the son whom Jake didn't even know existed. And the dime novels.

Kit wrapped her arms around her waist and shivered. It was safer to keep her distance. Safer for Johnny.

And safer for her.

The following afternoon, as Jake pounded the last nail into his new bookcase, his first visitor knocked at his door. His hammer slipped, slamming his thumb instead of the nail head.

"Son-of-a—"

"Mr. Cordell?" A blond man entered Jake's law office.

"I already have insurance."

The stranger blinked, and a red flush started at his neck. "Are you Mr. Cordell?"

Pulling his sore thumb from his mouth, Jake glared at the man. "Who're you?"

"David Preston, owner and editor of the Chaney *Courier*," the man introduced himself.

Jake's scrutinized him, noting his fashionable blue and black striped trousers and the stiff, overly starched shirt cuffs showing below the sleeves of his elegant wool overcoat. He could see why Johnny didn't want the dandy for a father. "Did your mother dress you?"

Flustered, Preston blinked and glanced down at his clothing. "No, my mother doesn't even live here."

Jake sighed in mock relief. "Good thing."

Preston flushed. "Mr. Cordell, I didn't come here to be insulted."

"Then why *are* you here?"

"I was hoping to interview you."

Jake set his hammer on his desk, then studied his completed bookshelf. "Where do you think I should put this?"

"I have one suggestion."

The strutting rooster had a backbone after all. "All right, Preston, ask your questions."

The reporter appeared surprised by Jake's acquiescence. He fumbled with his buttons and removed the heavy coat. Reaching in a side pocket, he pulled out paper and a pencil. Preston licked the lead and stood poised to write. "Why did you become a bounty hunter, Mr. Cordell?"

"Because I believe in upholding the laws of our great country even at the considerable risk to my own life," Jake answered with a straight face, though it was difficult to keep the sarcasm from his tone. "Besides, I'm the hero and defender of justice."

Preston narrowed his shifty eyes.

"I read that in one of my books," Jake retorted with feigned indignation.

"I feel you're not taking this interview seriously,"

Preston said, lowering his arms to his sides. "Let me be frank—"

"You can be anyone you want to be."

A bead of sweat rolled down Preston's cheek. Insinuating two fingers between his stiff collar and thin neck, he tugged at the constricting cloth, then drew back his shoulders. "I believe you are a fraud, Mr. Cordell. The man in the dime novels is a caricature, a character created by a deluded writer. You are nothing but a hired gun with no morals who kills without conscience, drinks without reason, and has no regard for anyone but himself."

Jake considered his words, then nodded. "You got that right, newspaperman. Now, if you can convince everyone else that I'm not the person in those dime novels, I'd be obliged."

Again Preston appeared startled by Jake's candidness. "Most men would like to have your reputation."

"Next time you see them, tell them they're welcome to it."

The reporter studied him for a moment. "I understand your father was a lawman, then a judge."

"That's right."

"Is that why you're hanging up your gun and setting up this practice? To follow in your father's footsteps?"

Jake turned away from Preston to move the bookshelf against the wall nearest the door. He brushed his hands together and lowered himself to the chair behind his desk. "My father and I were not what you'd call close. What I've done with my life has nothing to do with him."

"Didn't you originally become a bounty hunter when you went after the man who killed him?"

Painful memories of the day he'd received the news of his father's death assailed Jake. Recently graduated from college, he'd been working as a clerk in a law office in Boston when he'd gotten the message. He'd left immediately after receiving the telegram, and he'd barely made it home in time for the funeral.

It was while he'd stood at the edge of his father's grave, with the north wind chilling him to the bone, that he'd sworn to get Jonathan Cordell's murderer. The killer had taken something away from him that could never be regained: the chance to make peace with his father.

"Did you hear me, Mr. Cordell?" Preston asked with a twinge of impatience.

"I heard you," Jake replied with a scowl. "The man was my father, and some son-of-a-bitch killed him. What was I supposed to do—walk away?"

"Most law-abiding people would have."

Jake leveled an angry gaze at Preston. "I never was very good at letting other people take care of my business."

The reporter's face remained impassive. "I see that even though you proclaim yourself a lawyer, you continue to wear your gun. It is nearly the twentieth century, Mr. Cordell. People do not need to carry weapons on their person anymore. We've progressed beyond those days of violence and barbarism."

"Ah, but with all life, there are throwbacks, beings who refuse to advance with the future," Jake began in a professor-like tone. "And those lowlifes are the reason I keep my gun close at hand."

"You're an intriguing man, Mr. Cordell. On one hand, you behave like an uncivilized boor, while on the other, it is obvious you are well educated. Who is the real Jake Cordell?"

Jake leaned forward in his chair and planted his elbows on the pockmarked desktop. "That, Mr. Preston, is a very good question."

The two men parried gazes for a long moment. Preston looked away first, then shrugged into his overcoat. He opened the door, but paused and glanced over his shoulder at Jake. "I hear you've been over to Kit Thornton's place."

Jake crossed his arms. "I'd forgotten how fast gossip travels in a small town."

"Stay away from her, Cordell. She's not for the likes of you."

"I suppose a fine gentleman like yourself is more her type?" Jake scrutinized him from his pomaded hair to his shiny shoes.

Preston's jaw muscle twitched. "Stay away from her." He started to leave.

"Mr. Preston."

The reporter stopped.

"Take my advice and get yourself some tooth powder."

Puzzled, Preston left and Jake listened to his footsteps descend the rickety wooden stairs. Scrubbing his face with his palms, Jake considered the man's parting shot. Although he shouldn't care if the newspaperman was courting Kit, his gut twisted in protest. Kit and Johnny deserved better than a stuffed shirt who couldn't see beyond the tip of his imperious nose.

He cursed under his breath. He couldn't afford this surge of protectiveness he felt toward Kit. Besides, she didn't seem like she needed anyone's help anymore, and she had managed fine on her own for this long.

But she's never come up against a bastard like me, either.

Not liking the direction of his thoughts, he stood and grabbed his hat and sheepskin jacket. After donning them, he left the oppressive silence of his empty office.

He headed over to the Red Bird, a saloon across the street, and ordered whiskey.

As he downed his second shot, he overheard the

mayor and Alford Mundy, the bank manager, conversing behind him. Snagging the bottleneck in hand, he joined the two men.

"Hope you don't mind," Jake said with a quick smile.

"It'd be an honor," Mayor Walters replied magnanimously. "I heard a rumor that you're fixing to set up a law practice here in town."

Jake filled his shot glass, and held it up to the light to admire the amber color. "It's not a rumor. It's a fact."

If Walters' grin grew any wider, Jake was certain his round face would bust open. "That's good news, Jake. Your father would've approved."

Jake shrugged. "I'm glad someone thinks so. Speaking of the wonderful Judge Cordell, either one of you know why I didn't get his ranch?"

Walters' pig eyes narrowed, and he looked at the banker. "Why don't you tell him, Alford?"

Mundy smoothed a hand across his bald pate. "His will gave explicit directions concerning the ranch."

"And?" Jake prodded.

The banker glanced at Walters, who nodded. "If you didn't take residence within six months following his death, it was to be offered to Theodora Thornton for a fair price."

Jake glared at Mundy. "Why her?"

The diminutive man shrugged. "I was not privy to that information. Only Miss Thornton can tell you that."

"Why wasn't I told about this stipulation?"

Mundy pulled a starched handkerchief from his breastpocket and wiped the sweat from his upper lip. "You never showed up at the reading of the will."

Jake came forward in his chair and planted his elbows on the table. "That's because I'd gone after my father's killer."

Mundy shook his head. "No, it was because you were too busy with your saloon friend. At the time of the reading, you and Miss Maggie Summerfield were 'visiting.' "

Jake thought back to the evening after the funeral. Mundy was right; he *had* been with Maggie. At the time, Jake hadn't wanted to hear the will. He didn't want to believe his father was truly dead.

He took a deep breath and settled back. "You're right, Mr. Mundy. So you sold the ranch to Kit?"

The banker nodded. "She was more than willing to purchase it, and with the sale of her father's newspaper, she had a good down payment."

Jake frowned. "She had to take out a loan?"

"That's right."

"Has it been paid?"

Mundy tugged at his lapels. "That is confidential, Mr. Cordell."

"For God's sake, it was his father's ranch, Alford," Walters said impatiently. "Tell him."

Mundy's tongue darted across his lips, and he lowered his voice. "When Miss Thornton bought some horses two years ago, she borrowed against the ranch. She was delinquent with her last payment, and if she doesn't pay off the balance, the bank will begin foreclosure."

Jake kept his expression blank as he digested the information. The solution to his problem had just fallen into his lap. He could buy the loan, and if Kit missed her payment, the ranch would become his. "When's it due?"

"Three and a half weeks," Mundy replied, a note of reluctance in his voice.

Jake's excitement was tempered by his concern for Kit and her son. Where would they go if she lost the place? She'd worked hard to make a go of it, and Jake didn't want to be the bad guy. He could offer her a partnership. The idea had merit, but what would Jake do with her and Johnny?

He drank another glass of whiskey. No, it was simpler to take possession of the ranch. He would offer Kit a fair price for her horses so she could move far from Chaney and start a new life with her son.

He rose. "Thank you for the information, Mr. Mundy. I'll be in to the bank soon to see you with a business proposition."

Jake walked out of the saloon, wishing he'd brought the bottle of whiskey with him. He could've used it to keep his conscience at bay.

Chapter 5

Kit turned to help Johnny down from the buck-board seat but found him already on the ground, smacking the dirt from his knees. She reminded herself that Johnny was growing up and becoming more independent. And although she encouraged his independence, a part of her was fearful he would turn out as footloose as his father.

"Are we going to see Mr. Cordell?" Johnny asked as he skipped onto the boardwalk.

Kit joined him. "How about if we visit Aunt Freda first?"

"Okay," he agreed.

She turned to Ethan, who'd come into town with them. "Do you need some help with the supplies?"

The young man tugged his hat brim low on his forehead and shook his head. "I can get 'em, Miz Thornton. First I'll go on over and pick up the bridles."

"Thanks. We'll meet you in front of the general store in a couple hours."

Ethan nodded, then strode across the street to Harvey's Leather Shop.

"Good morning, Kitty."

She turned to see Will Jameson standing behind her.

"You come to town to visit your hero?" he asked with heavy sarcasm.

She wrapped a protective arm around Johnny's shoulders and drew him behind her. "What do you want, Will?"

He leaned, hip-shot, against a hitching rail. "How long we known each other, Kitty?"

"Too long," she shot back. "And stop calling me Kitty."

Feigned indignation claimed his expression. "Long enough for me to worry about you all alone on that ranch with that breed and nigger. I hear you can't trust 'em around white women, even ones like you."

Swallowing back white-hot rage, Kit restrained herself from punching him. "You're still the same ignorant bully you were back when we were kids. Go back to playing lawman and leave us alone."

Jameson's smile faded and his eyes slitted. "Just because Cordell's back in town doesn't mean he's going to stand up for you like he done before."

Kit lifted her chin. "I don't need Jake or anyone else protecting me. If you haven't noticed, I'm not a child anymore."

"Anything wrong here, Kit, Will?" O'Hara asked.

"Uncle Patrick," Johnny exclaimed, and threw himself at the Irishman.

O'Hara scooped the boy up in his arms and grinned. "Hello there, lad." He looked at Will, his smile fading. "What mischief are you up to, Jameson?"

An oily smile spread across the younger lawman's face. "Kitty and I were discussing old times."

O'Hara's eyes narrowed as he looked at Kit. "That so, lass?"

She pressed her lips together. "You could say that."

"Be seein' you around, Kitty." Jameson tipped his hat in a mocking salute and swaggered away.

Kit's shoulders slumped. She thought she'd gotten past her childish timidity, but a part of that self-conscious little girl remained.

Johnny stuck out his tongue at Jameson's back. "I don't like him."

"Why not?" Patrick asked.

"He smiles a lot, but it's a mean smile. And he says things that make Ma mad."

Kit laid a hand on his back. "That's because he never grew up, sweetheart."

"You sure there's nothin' I can do?" Patrick asked.

Kit shook her head. "I can handle him."

"So, where were you headed?"

"We were going to Aunt Freda's for doughnuts," Johnny said.

Patrick winked at Kit. "I was just headin' there myself."

With the Irishman carrying Johnny, they walked to Freda's neat whitewashed house. Stepping into the warmth of her kitchen, Kit breathed in the comforting aroma of fresh baked goods.

"Hello, Freda," she greeted. "I hope you don't mind us dropping in like this."

Freda clucked her tongue. "Take off your coats, and I will fill a plate with donuts."

A few minutes later, Kit poured coffee for herself, Patrick, and Freda, then joined them at the table. Johnny had already begun eating and had a white moustache from his glass of milk.

"What is it between you and Jameson, lass?" Patrick asked Kit.

She grimaced and pressed her spectacles up. "When we were children, he was one of the boys who used to tease me. Fact is, he was the worst of the lot."

"Iffen you like, I'll have a talk with him," Patrick volunteered.

"Thanks, Patrick, but he's only a mean-minded little boy in a man's body. I can handle him," Kit reassured him. She paused, lost in years-old memories. "My mother died when I was born. Father raised me the best way he could, but I think he unconsciously blamed me for my mother's death. He loved her very much. I started wearing glasses when I was very young, and I was chubby, to say the least." She grinned ruefully. "I think I was a disappointment to him. He found fault in every-thing I did. Anyhow, because I was different, the other children made fun of me."

Freda laid a veined hand on Kit's arm. "Cruel chil-dren can be, without realizing it."

"I know that now, but back then, when they called me Fatty Four-Eyes and Tubby Kitty, all I know is that it hurt."

"I wouldn't have been mean to you, Ma," Johnny stated.

Kit squeezed his hand, and smiled. "I know you wouldn't have, sweetheart. Jake wasn't mean, either." She glanced at Freda and Patrick. "He used to chase the other children away when they teased me."

"He could not remember you the day you brought him here," Freda said with a frown.

"I know, but I wasn't surprised. We've both changed. How is he settling in?"

Freda shrugged. "Nightmares he has. Last night I heard him call out so I went to his room and knocked on his door, but it was quiet. This morning, he looked like he did not sleep at all."

Kit's throat tightened. She traced the cup handle over and over with her forefinger. "I guess it's not surprising. He's led a violent life."

"Will you go visit him?"

"I promised Johnny we would," Kit replied.

"He's teaching me how to ride," Johnny mumbled through a mouthful of doughnut.

"Sounds like Jake might be thinkin' of settlin' down in more ways than one," Patrick teased.

"Don't bet on it," Kit said lightly, although disappointment flickered in her. Seeing Jake every day was a tempting thought.

Yet how could they be friends when lies stood between them? Lies of omission, lies of deceit. Every instinct told Kit Jake would tolerate a lot of things, but deception wasn't one of them.

Johnny washed his hands and face. "Can we go see Mr. Cordell now, Ma?" he asked excitedly.

Kit nodded. "All right. Did you finish your milk?"

"Yep."

"What do you say?"

Johnny turned to Freda. "Thank you for the milk and doughnuts. They were damn fine."

Patrick guffawed and slapped his knee.

"What was that?" Kit asked her son, struggling to keep her voice stern.

"Pete says that all the time," Johnny defended. "He says it's the highest complaint a body can give."

Freda coughed, choking back laughter, her eyes dancing with merriment.

"Damn is still a cussword, and you will not use that type of language, young man," Kit scolded. "And that's compliment, not complaint."

Sulking, Johnny tossed the towel on the counter. "I don't see why it's all right for Pete to say it and not me."

"Because I'm your mother, that's why."

Still grumbling, Johnny tugged on his jacket.

"Do not be strangers," Freda said.

"Be seein' you," Patrick said.

Echoing their farewells, Kit ushered Johnny out of the comfortable kitchen.

Freda thoughtfully watched them leave.

"Now, what would you be thinkin' about that?" Patrick remarked.

Freda studied the burly Irishman. Her Hans had been a small man, and when she'd first met Patrick, his massive size had frightened her . . . until she'd learned his heart was as big as his body. She smiled. "Happiness Kit deserves, and I think Jake could give that to her."

"I wouldn't be arguin' with you there, but I'm not certain how Jake would take to gettin' hitched. Men like him are sometimes better off alone."

Freda clucked her tongue. "Alone he is unhappy. With Kit he would be better off. And a family he would have." She shook her head. "I know what it is like to have no one."

Patrick stood and wrapped his arms around Freda, resting his chin on her braided coronet. "You aren't alone anymore, lass."

She laid her cheek against his solid chest, aware of how tiny she was in his embrace. Freda had earned her hard-fought independence, but sometimes she missed a man's strength and protection.

"So when are you goin' to be sayin' yes?" Patrick asked softly.

"When you stop drinking." She gave the same answer she'd given him a dozen times since he had asked her to be his wife.

Patrick sighed. "Askin' an Irishman to give up his ale is like askin' a banker to give up his money."

She drew away from him. "Then my answer will not change."

He shook his head. "I'm thinkin' you Prussians are even more stubborn than we Irish." He clapped his hat on his red hair. "I'll be over this evenin' to finish that game of checkers."

"And for supper?"

Leaning over, he kissed her cheek. "Wouldn't miss it."

Alone in her kitchen, Freda questioned her reason for not becoming Patrick's wife. Liquor had destroyed her Hans; she refused to see that happen to another man she loved. It was better she remain alone than bear that pain again.

Despite her hope that Kit and Jake might find happiness together, she worried about Jake's penchant for whiskey. She wouldn't wish such heartache for Kit, either.

Tucking a strand of loose hair into her braid, Freda took her rolling pin in hand. Her mother had said work was the cure for anything that ailed her, and Freda often found solace in her kitchen. Today would be no different.

Johnny led Kit down the boardwalk toward Jake's new office, and Kit wondered if she'd made a wise decision in seeing Jake again. But when she saw the carved wooden sign hanging over the door, new resolve filled her. If he was going to become part of the town, she would have to get used to seeing him.

Johnny opened the door, and the first thing she saw was Jake sitting on the floor, surrounded by boxes of books and odds and ends.

Jake scrambled to his feet, brushing the dust from the seat of his pants. "Kit, Johnny—you're a sight for sore eyes."

"Having a little trouble getting organized?" Kit asked, as she gestured toward the mess on the floor.

He grinned sheepishly. "I never was very good straightening up."

His boyish expression warmed Kit, and she found herself laughing softly. "That's pretty obvious." She looked beyond the piles of books and journals and found the rest of his office had been scrubbed clean and the walls newly painted pale blue. She nodded her approval. "It already has your touch."

Jake hooked his thumbs in his belt loops and stood with his feet planted, a totally masculine stance that drew Kit's appreciative gaze to his muscular legs.

"Kinda reminds me of the wide open sky," he said. "I already miss getting on Zeus and riding over the next hill. But I have to get this straightened up before I can start taking on clients."

"Your room looks like mine before Ma makes me clean it up," Johnny interjected.

Jake ruffled the boy's hair. "I doubt if your room has ever looked this bad."

"I wouldn't bet on that," Kit said. "How about if we give you a hand?"

"You don't have to."

"I know, but we want to. Right, Johnny?"

"Yep!"

They removed their jackets, and Kit set to work organizing law books on the newly made shelves. Jake and Johnny sat on the floor, and together they opened boxes and arranged the supplies that were inside.

"Hey, Ma, Mr. Cordell's got all his books," Johnny exclaimed.

Puzzled, Kit turned to see which books her son referred to. Stacked in front of him were all the dime novels she'd written.

She licked her lips nervously. "I thought you didn't like those."

Jake shrugged. "Patrick lent me one, and I was curious to read the others."

"This one's my favorite," Johnny said, holding up *Vengeance Rides a Black Horse*.

Jake took it from him and riffled through the pages. He frowned. "Whoever this T. K. Thorne is, he sure knows a lot about me."

Kit held her breath; her palms grew moist.

"Did anyone ever come around town asking about me and my father?" Jake asked.

She shook her head, afraid to speak lest her voice betray her nervousness.

Jake opened the novel to the first page.

"Read it to me, Mr. Cordell," Johnny urged, moving close to Jake.

"I thought you heard this one already."

"I did, but only five times."

Jake chuckled. "I guess we can take a break. Is that okay, Kit?"

"Fine," Kit squeaked out.

He stood. "C'mon, let's sit by the desk." Jake lowered himself to the chair, and Johnny eagerly moved to sit on his knee. Jake put an arm around Johnny's waist and held the book up on the desk. He began to read.

" 'Jonathan Cordell rode tall in the saddle of a prancing black stallion as his son rode beside him, equally as prideful as his sire. The two men were a matched team, a deadly duo who courted danger as most men courted a lady. There had been a robbery in their town while they had been tracking down the notorious Ace Hardy. When they returned with their prisoner in irons, Deputy Logan greeted them with his arm in a sling.' "

Kit continued shelving the law books, listening as intently as her son to Jake's rich, mellow voice. It gave her a strangely unsettled feeling, hearing Jake's voice speak the words she'd written in tribute to him.

Ten minutes after he'd begun reading, Jake stopped and Kit glanced up to find Johnny asleep. His head rested against Jake's shoulder, his mouth open as he breathed deeply in slumber.

"He must've been tired," Jake said softly.

Kit gazed at Jake and noted the softening of the lines in his forehead. He seemed truly fond of Johnny, and the observation brought a recurrence of guilt. "He's been up since before sunrise," she said.

Jake settled Johnny in the desk chair, and Kit turned back to the books she was organizing by author. She sensed Jake's nearness a moment before he pulled a book from her hands. "You've done more than enough, Kit."

She tried to look away but found his brown eyes too alluring, his face too easy to admire. A small, crescent-shaped scar near the corner of his sensuous lips caught her attention. No whiskers grew in the slight mark, accentuating it further. He wasn't classically handsome like David Preston, but Kit found his rugged looks compelling. Jake had matured, his features carved by the rivers of experience.

Kit curled her fingers into her palms to keep from touching his whiskered jaw or the tousled strand of hair across his forehead. How often had she dreamed of being this close to him? But in her dreams, it had been the dime novel hero, not the man in front of her, who she'd fantasized about. Could she risk learning if the hero existed only in her mind? His rejection would hurt her more than any mean-minded comment from the townsfolk.

Her hand trembling, she took the book from him and slipped it on the shelf in proper alphabetical order. "I don't mind. Besides, you're so good with Johnny, and I feel as if I should repay you for your kindness."

"You don't owe me anything. I like having Johnny around. He's a good kid." Indignation lent a wounded note to his voice.

"I'm sorry. I didn't mean it to come out that way. I just wanted to help you as my thanks for taking Johnny under your wing. He misses having a father."

"Where is his father?"

"Gone."

"Oh."

Knowing what he was thinking, Kit didn't allow herself to set the record straight. It was better to have him believe she was as unvirtuous as everyone else thought, even if it lowered his opinion of her. Kit set the last book on the shelf.

"Looks like you're ready for business."

Jake straightened. "You wouldn't happen to be looking for a job, would you?"

"The ranch keeps me too busy the way it is."

"You know how to solve that problem," he said. Kit tensed, and Jake held up his hand. "I know, you won't sell no matter what."

"That's right," she said stiffly.

He stood, then offered her his hand. After a moment, she curled her fingers around his and he pulled her to her feet. Kit straightened and found herself pressed against the length of his hard-muscled body. Heat suffused her cheeks, and she tried to move away, but Jake held her close.

His gaze roamed across her face and down her neck and settled on the pale skin where the top shirt button lay undone. After a moment, he lifted his eyes to hers. "No wonder I didn't recognize you. You're not that same little girl I used to know." He traced her jaw with his forefinger, creating a shivery sensation that tripped her heart. "You're beautiful, Kit."

She swallowed. "Maggie was beautiful, Jake. I'm just plain old Kit."

His rakish smile started a tingle in the pit of her stomach. "There's nothing plain about you," he said in a husky voice.

She'd wanted Jake to notice her as a woman, but now that he did, Kit didn't know what to say or do. Her pulse skipped through her veins, and she told herself to move away, to protect herself and her secrets. But her muscles refused to obey her commands.

The wild yearning in her blood was nothing like the innocent infatuation of a ten-year-old. Her body had matured, and along with it, her passion. She burned with a need to touch him, and for him to touch her.

Johnny mumbled in his sleep, jerking Kit back to reality. She looked away from Jake's bold gaze and stepped back.

Jake raked his fingers through his hair and rubbed the back of his neck. "You wouldn't happen to be hungry, would you?"

Startled, she glanced at him.

"For lunch," Jake clarified, and his twinkling eyes told Kit he knew exactly what she'd been thinking.

She coughed to cover her embarrassment. "I don't think so. It's time we headed back to the ranch."

"What's another hour?" Jake pressed. "You have to eat sometime."

Johnny, awakened by their voices, joined Jake. "Please, Ma."

"It's two against one. We win," Jake proclaimed.

She couldn't fight them both, and Kit surrendered to the inevitable. "Ethan came to town with us. Would you mind if he joined us?"

Jake shook his head. "The more the merrier."

Johnny whooped and shrugged on his jacket.

Jake reached for his coat and pulled it on. Kit blinked, noticing the absence of his holster. "You're not wearing your gun."

Jake finished buttoning his brown wool jacket. "I noticed I was the only one in town besides the police who was wearing one. I doubt there's any need for it anymore.''

"What about your reputation? What if someone comes looking for you?''

"If I'm truly going to put my past behind me, I have to start sometime.'' Jake settled his hat on his head. "I gotta admit, it feels strange without it, like I'm missing a part of me.''

Mixed emotions filled Kit. Although she was glad he was giving up his violent past, she was fearful he would be gunned down in cold blood by someone wanting to build his own reputation. Still, his decision to leave his gun behind told her he might be serious about staying in Chaney. The possibility that he'd be there permanently sent her heart into a stampede.

"I guess the so-called wild West has been tamed,'' Kit said softly. "Maybe someday guns will never be needed by anyone.''

Jake shook his head. "There will always be violence. It's just that it'll take place in the cities instead of the frontier. You cram too many people in too small an area and tempers are bound to flare. It's human nature.''

Kit cocked her head, once again realizing how little she knew him. She had thought of him as being only a man of action, doing good deeds and dealing out justice to lawbreakers. She was learning there were many more facets to the man.

Jake led them down the stairs to the boardwalk, which bustled with activity. People greeted Jake with a familiarity that told Kit he'd reacquainted himself with most everybody in town. As they passed one of the many saloons lining Main Street, the sound of men's hoots and hollers and breaking furniture caught their attention.

A moment later, a man came flying out of the saloon's batwing doors and landed in the mud on the street below. Two burly men followed and pulled the fallen man to his feet. A few cowboys, beer in hand, stumbled out of the saloon to watch the fight.

Disgusted by the drunken brawling, Kit tried to maneuver around the onlookers.

"Show the breed he ain't welcome here," one of the men on the boardwalk called out.

Kit halted and peered through the growing crowd at the man being beaten. "Ethan!" she called, recognizing his dark hair and jacket.

The young man's attention wavered from his attackers, and one of the men landed a solid blow to Ethan's midsection.

"Stop hurting him," Johnny screamed.

"Let him go," Kit shouted, starting forward.

Jake grabbed them to stop them from jumping into the fray. "Stay put, both of you."

Kit wrapped an arm around her son and bit her knuckles as Jake charged into the uneven fight.

He jerked the biggest attacker away from Ethan, twisted him around, and punched him in the jaw. The man shook his head like an angered bull and charged Jake. He caught Jake around the chest with his trunk-sized arms and began to squeeze. Jake butted the man beneath the chin. The man's head snapped upward and he stumbled back. Taking advantage of his opponent's weakness, Jake drove his fist into his face, felling him like an oak tree.

Ethan lay on the ground as the other man raised his boot to kick him in the ribs. Jake grabbed the bully's leg and shoved him back. The man's head hit the edge of the boardwalk with an audible thud, and he lay on the ground unconscious.

The crowd booed but began to disperse, shaking their heads.

Kit and Johnny hurried to Ethan's side, and Kit knelt beside him. "Are you all right?"

Blood dripped from Ethan's nose and from a corner of his mouth. He nodded and grimaced as Kit helped him to a sitting position.

Johnny placed his small hand on Ethan's shoulder. "Why'd those men hurt you?"

Jake hunkered down beside Kit. "Because they're ignorant fools," he stated forcefully. He laid a hand on the younger man's shoulder. "Are you all right?"

Ethan sent Jake a guarded nod. "I guess I owe you one, Cordell."

"You don't owe me anything. I never could abide bullies," Jake said, helping Ethan to his feet.

Kit glanced at Jake, startled to see the anger darkening his expression. "Thank you."

Patrick crossed the street. "What's goin' on here?"

"You've got a couple of overnight guests," Jake said. He pointed to the unconscious cowhands. "They assaulted Ethan."

"Let 'em go," Ethan muttered.

"No," Kit argued. "You didn't do anything wrong."

"Those men broke the law," Jake added. "They should be tried in court."

Ethan smiled humorlessly. "And the judge is going to take a half-breed's word over two white men's? Forget it."

The young man stumbled away toward the wagon, and Johnny handed him his hat, which had fallen off during the skirmish.

One of the attackers stirred and struggled to his feet.

Kit glared at him, then looked at Patrick. "Can't you arrest them anyhow? I'll testify against them."

Jake shook his head. "It wouldn't do any good, Kit. We need Ethan's testimony and some collaborating witnesses from the saloon. And I have a feeling no one's going to testify on Ethan's behalf.''

"Jake's right, lass," Patrick said apologetically. "I can't be arrestin' them if there's no charges brought against them.''

"So they're just going to get away with it?" Kit asked in disbelief.

"There's nothing you can do, Kit," Jake said gently. "Why don't you take Ethan over to Dr. Lewis's and have him check the boy out?''

Bitterness galled Kit. "He won't go. I'll take him back to the ranch and take care of him myself.''

"The squaw's goin' to take her breed home," the burly attacker mocked, swiping the back of his hand across his bloodied lips.

Kit glared at him and her temper spiked. She strode up to him and planted her hands on her hips. "Ethan didn't do anything to you. Go back to the hole you crawled out of, and take your friend with you.''

The man spat a gob of blood. "He's a half-breed. We don't need no other reason.''

Kit charged toward him. Jake caught her around the waist and pulled her back. "Take Ethan and Johnny home, Kit," he said close to her ear. "There's nothing else you can do here.''

Sickened, she closed her eyes for a moment and opened them to give Jake a pleading look. "Isn't there something *you* can do?''

Anguish hollowed his features. "I can't make things all right this time, Kit.''

Her throat aching with bitter disappointment, Kit spun away. She hurried after Ethan and Johnny, her tears nearly blinding her.

Chapter 6

J ake watched her leave, his insides twisting with guilt.

"She's only upset, Jake. She'll get over it," Patrick reassured him.

"She had a right to be upset." He strode over to the bully struggling to his feet and grabbed him by the collar, jerking him upright. Jake planted his face a couple of inches from the man's bloody features. "You ever call Kit a squaw again or beat up on that boy, and it won't matter that the sergeant here can't arrest you. After I'm done with you and your friend, you'll wish he had thrown your carcasses in jail."

Jake shoved him away, and the man's partner caught him by the shoulders. Grumbling, they turned and shambled back into the saloon.

"You'll be makin' a few enemies," Patrick warned.

"That's nothing new," Jake said grimly. "Why the hell does Kit stay around this town? If I were her, I'd be long gone."

"Why'd *you* come back?"

Jake blinked. "I grew up here."

"Aye, and so did Kit." Patrick clapped him between the shoulder blades. "See you later."

Jake adjusted his hat and stepped onto the boardwalk. He studied the mountains, how the sun slanted off their granite- and pine-covered slopes. A few clouds moved over the peaks, obscuring the highest ones and creating irregular shadows that slid across the rocky faces.

He breathed deeply of the spring air. Much as he'd despised the town when he was younger, Jake couldn't think of any other place he could call home.

He returned to his office but found he couldn't concentrate. Wandering over to the window that faced the front street, he noticed a buckboard laden with supplies leaving town. A boy sat between the two adults on the buckboard, and Jake recognized Kit's blond hair. He'd let her down. Frustration stung him. He balled his fingers into tight fists at his sides.

His gaze followed them until they disappeared from view, and he turned back to his desk, once again amazed at the work Kit had done so efficiently. It explained why his former home looked so well kept. If there was a lazy bone in her body, he'd have to look pretty close to find it. And while the idea had merit, Jake knew he'd end up with a black eye if he tried.

He hadn't imagined Kit would turn into such a determined woman. He admired her willingness to defend Ethan, knowing her stand would be an unpopular one. Flopping into his chair, Jake wished he could have had charges brought against the two troublemakers. Closing his eyes, he saw the hurt in Kit's eyes when he'd told her he couldn't make things right.

He slammed his fist on the chair arm. What did she expect? He wasn't like the hero in the books. He was only a man who wanted what was rightfully his. He wanted his father's former ranch.

Why hadn't he gone over to see Mundy at the bank that morning?

The ranch was the reason he'd returned to Chaney,

and he meant to get it. Despite his growing fondness for Kit and her son, he couldn't allow them to sidetrack his plans.

Rising from the chair, he grabbed his hat and headed out the door. A few minutes later, he stood in Alford Mundy's office.

"Have a seat, Mr. Cordell," Mundy said.

Jake lowered himself to the worn chair in front of the desk.

"Now, what can I help you with?" the banker asked, folding his pale hands together and resting them on the uncluttered desktop.

"When we talked at the saloon, you said that Kit Thornton had a loan out against the ranch," Jake began.

"That's correct."

"How much is it?"

"That's confidential."

Jake perched on the edge of the chair. "I want to buy the papers."

Mundy leaned back, steepling his fingers. "That's highly irregular."

"So was my father's will. That ranch should've been mine."

"Does Miss Thornton realize your intentions?"

Jake worried the brim of his hat. "She knows I want the ranch. I've offered to buy it."

"And she's refused to sell?"

Jake fought the impatience rising within him. "Would I be here if she'd accepted?"

Mundy shifted nervously. "I suppose not." He stood and moved to a cabinet against the wall. He searched through the files a few moments, then withdrew one. Seating himself behind the desk, he handed the papers to Jake.

He perused the official document, noting Kit had borrowed $1,300 to purchase horses nearly two years ago. She'd used the ranch as collateral. He could imagine her optimism, her hopes that she'd be able to build a thriving business. Her only problem was that she hadn't taken into account the length of time it took to build up salable stock. It would take at least five years to see the returns in foals.

She'd paid back $800 and the balance was due in a few weeks.

"Has she talked to you about extending the due date?" Jake asked.

Mundy nodded. "I told her I couldn't."

"Why not?"

"I run a business, Mr. Cordell, not a charity. Miss Thornton knew the risks when she signed the document."

Kit had put her faith in those horses, and her gamble had failed. Jake understood her drive to succeed, but he seriously doubted she'd be able to meet her payment. That would leave him holding the deed. And it would all be legal.

"I want to buy her loan," Jake stated.

"I assumed that would be your decision." He took the papers back from Jake. "I want to remind you that this is not the way I usually run my business, but since you are Jonathan Cordell's son, I believe there is sufficient reason to overlook the ethics."

"As long as it's legal, I don't care," Jake said.

"I assure you, it's all perfectly legal." Mundy pulled a sheet of parchment from his desk drawer.

Half an hour later, Jake exited the bank, the document in hand. The elation he should've felt didn't surface, though. Instead, all he could imagine was the betrayal in Kit's face when he took possession of the ranch.

Self-reproach soured his mood. He didn't want to take away Kit's dreams, but he had no choice. He would prove that he was a better man than his father.

He glanced at the saloon across the street. Maybe a

few shots of whiskey would silence his conscience so he could celebrate his victory.

The few days following the disastrous trip into town, Kit tried to work at her typewriter, but words seemed lost to her. The hero she'd written about no longer existed. It left her with a desolate feeling, not unlike the time after Maggie had died.

Fortunately, the horses gave her something to take her mind off Jake Cordell. Kit, Charlie, and Ethan kept busy training the horses and cleaning out the stalls. Ethan refused to take any time off to allow his injuries to heal, and did his chores as usual, albeit slower than normal.

As Kit made lunch, her son burst into the kitchen.

"It's been four days since Mr. Cordell said he'd come back," Johnny whined.

Kit wiped her hands on her apron and filled a bowl with soup for him. "Sit down and eat, before it gets cold."

Johnny dropped into a chair but didn't begin eating. "He won't ever come again, will he?"

Kit placed slices of bread and jam on the table and joined her sulking son. "I don't know, sweetheart. Maybe things got busy at his office."

Johnny swung his feet back and forth and picked up his spoon. "Maybe he doesn't like me anymore."

"I doubt that." Kit kept her voice light. "What about if I give you your next riding lesson?"

Johnny shrugged. "It won't be the same."

Kit leaned forward, placing her hand on his arm. "We can't count on Mr. Cordell, Johnny. He comes and goes as he pleases."

"But he promised!"

He shoved a spoonful of soup in his mouth, and propped his chin in his other hand.

Kit's appetite fled.

Even though Jake had saved Ethan from a vicious beating, she'd repaid him by releasing her wrath on him. She realized now that it hadn't been his fault Ethan didn't want to press charges. But she'd unfairly expected her hero to make things right, as he'd done when they were children.

Kit studied her son's—Jake's son's—glum expression. If she was why Jake hadn't come back for Johnny's next lesson, she had to apologize. And although her mind told her it would be better to keep them apart, her heart couldn't abide the disillusionment in Johnny's eyes.

"As soon as we finish eating, I'll help you saddle Treasure and you can ride her a little in the corral. Then when Jake comes, you can tell him you got to practice," Kit said, injecting enthusiasm into her voice.

Johnny's long face brightened. "Okay."

After the dishes were done, they went out to saddle Treasure. Kit helped Johnny onto the horse's back and tried to imitate Jake's steadfast calm, but her instinct to protect her son wouldn't allow her to relax. Afraid he'd fall from Treasure's back, Kit refused to release the bridle despite Johnny's pleadings.

Half an hour later, she helped Johnny down.

"Mr. Cordell woulda let me ride by myself," he complained.

"Probably, but I'm not Mr. Cordell," Kit said.

Grumbling, Johnny led Treasure back to the barn.

Kit wiped her sweat-dotted forehead with a shaky hand and removed her spectacles to wipe them with her blouse. She replaced her glasses and folded her arms across her chest. Looking in the direction of Chaney, she spoke aloud. "If you think you're going to get out of this, Jake Cordell, you're sadly mistaken."

It was late afternoon when Kit rode into town.

She hadn't told Johnny the real reason for the unscheduled trip to Chaney. She didn't want him to get his hopes up only to have them dashed. With any luck she'd be home before Johnny's bedtime. But if she wasn't, she knew Charlie and Ethan would take care of him.

She directed her horse to Freda's and dismounted.

Freda opened the door as Kit approached and motioned her into the house. "Heard about Jake, did you?"

Puzzled, Kit stopped in the foyer. "What about him?"

"For two days he has been in that saloon," Freda replied disgustedly. "Tried to get him out, Patrick did, but Jake would not leave. Now that you are here, he will listen to you."

Kit absorbed the shocking news. "Why do you think I can get him out?"

Freda narrowed her eyes and folded her arms. Despite her diminutive stature, she appeared as immovable as the Rock of Gibraltar. "Respects and likes you, he does."

"What gave you that idea?"

"He bothers me with questions about you and Johnny."

Kit stiffened. "What kind of questions?"

Freda shrugged. "Why you hide yourself with men's clothing; why you never married Johnny's father—"

"What did you tell him?"

"That I do not know." She narrowed her perceptive gaze. "What I think, I do not tell him."

"And what do you think?"

" Johnny is his son."

Kit's composure slipped. "Why would you think that?"

"A feeling." Her voice softened. "I will keep your secret."

Kit's heart thumped against her breast. First Charlie, now Freda had guessed the truth. She couldn't deny it and lie to her friend. "I promise to tell you the whole story sometime, but now I should go see if I can talk some sense into Jake.'' She sighed. ''I had hoped the incident when he first arrived in Chaney was the exception. It's beginning to look like it might be the rule.''

''This I do not tell you so you will feel sorry for me, but because it is something you should know,'' Freda began in a low voice. ''My Hans, he was a good man, unless he drank; then he would become mean. Toward the end, he was drunk more than he was not. Coming back from the saloon one night, he was so drunk he fell off his horse and broke his neck. That is how my Hans died.'' She closed her eyes for a moment, then opened them, new strength in their depths. ''So you get Jake before he becomes like my Hans.''

Empathy filled Kit, and she squeezed Freda's hand. ''I'll try, but Jake may not want to listen.''

Freda studied Kit a moment. ''Maybe if you tell him of his son.''

Kit shook her head. ''No! I won't risk losing Johnny. He's all I have.''

Stifling silence cast a pall over the parlor. ''Which saloon is he at?'' Kit asked.

''The Red Bird.''

Kit nodded. ''Hopefully, I'll be back soon. With Jake.''

Freda followed Kit to the front door, then stopped her before she left. ''Turn out, it will. You will see.''

Kit tried to smile, but failed. Hunching her shoulders under her coat, she trudged across the rutted street. She paused outside the Red Bird's closed door as uneasy doubts pursued her. It wasn't too late. She could still turn around and go back to the ranch. Then the image of Jake all alone assailed her. Had her novels contributed to his drinking? Did she owe him for turning his life into something like a P.T. Barnum sideshow?

Forcing aside her reluctance and swallowing her anxiety, she entered the salon. Ribbons of smoke curled upward from kerosene lamps, cigars, and cigarettes, and her nostrils twitched from the thick odor. Bluish-gray clouds drifted close to the lights to form wispy shadows, adding to the oppressive atmosphere of the low-ceilinged room. A few poker games were in progress, and many of the players glanced up at Kit curiously.

Where was Jake?

The knights of the green tables studied Jake Cordell, noting his tied-down holster and the danger in his hawk eyes. Those men who gambled their lives away knew that even their biggest game could never match the stakes Cordell played for. He played the odds with death every day, betting his own life against a pot filled with murderers and all those opposed to justice.

Kit shook aside her thoughts. She finally spotted Jake sitting in a corner, his back to the wall, a nearly empty bottle of whiskey in the middle of the table. A scantily clad saloon gal was perched on Jake's lap, one arm draped around his neck. He whispered something in her ear, and she giggled like a lovesick schoolgirl.

Jealous despair struck Kit like a lightning bolt, but she squared her shoulders and approached them. "Hello, Jake," she greeted him in a husky voice.

The painted woman stared at Kit as if she had two heads, and Kit met her gaze without flinching.

"Miss Thornton, nice of you to join us," Jake slurred. "Let me introduce you to Louise."

Kit sent her a stiff nod. "Hello, Louise."

She batted blackened lashes. "So you're Kit Thornton. You don't act no different than all them other high-falutin' women who think their privies don't stink."

Maggie had worked in a bar, too, but she didn't harbor the spite that oozed from Louise.

Jake shook his head, a trace of impatience in the gesture. "Pull in your claws, Louise. Kit's my friend."

Kit was gratified to see the other woman glower at Jake and remove herself from his lap.

"Then I'll leave you with your *friend*." Louise's sarcasm was sharp enough to skin a squirrel. She stomped away, her faded red satin skirt flouncing about her knees.

Kit lowered herself into the seat, shocked at Jake's appearance. His brown eyes, usually so clear and steady, were now glassy and bloodshot. His cheeks held a three-day whisker growth and his shirt was spotted with stains.

"Sorry if I interrupted anything," Kit said, without a hint of contrition.

The smile Jake gave her was anything but pleasant. "Louise'll be back. She likes me."

Kit's anger rose to the surface. "What the hell do you think you're doing here?"

Jake reached for the bottle but missed and tried again, this time nearly spilling it before he clasped the neck.

"I am pouring myself some whiskey," he enunciated carefully.

Kit leaned forward and wrapped her fingers around his hand. "I think you've had enough, Jake. Why are you doing this to yourself?"

With an effort, Jake focused on Kit and smiled inanely. "I'm not doin' it, the whiskey is."

Kit scowled. "Freda told me you haven't stopped drinking in two days."

"But I have. I can't drink when I'm in the privy." He wiggled his fingers. "Need these for other things."

Kit ignored his coarse humor. "What do you think Johnny would think if he saw you like this?" she asked softly.

The question seemed to bring a moment of sober clarity to Jake. He sat up straight, grabbing hold of Kit's wrist. "Don't you let him see me. Don't let him near me!"

She settled back in her chair, forcing nonchalance. "I

was beginning to wonder if you cared about anyone or anything. C'mon, let's go back to Freda's."

He shook his head slowly. "Nope. Don't want to."

"Why not?"

"The dreams."

Kit's calm evaporated. "What dreams?"

"I keep seein' them," Jake explained.

Puzzled, Kit asked, "Who?"

His eyes clouded with nightmares. "Men I killed; men I brought in to be hanged."

The anguish in Jake's voice cut a ragged wound in Kit. "Listen to me, Jake. Those men were murderers and robbers and God knows what else. You were doing decent folks a favor by bringing them to justice."

He took a deep breath and lifted the whiskey bottle to his lips, but Kit pulled it away before he could drink from it.

"You've had enough. It's time to go," she stated firmly.

Jake stared at the bottle for a full minute. "All right," he finally said.

Kit went and put an arm around his shoulders, helping him to stand. She took most of his weight as his feet shuffled about, doing more to throw Kit off-balance than propel him forward. They finally managed to make it past the gawkers and Louise's hostile glare, and out onto the boardwalk.

They were nearly to Freda's when Jake tripped, taking Kit down with him. They ended up in an undignified heap with Jake on top of Kit.

A devilish smile claimed Jake's lips. "This is kinda fun."

Kit's face grew hot as her body responded to Jake's lean muscles pressed tightly against her. What was wrong with her? His breath reeked of whiskey, and his unwashed clothes were saturated with stale sweat and acrid smoke. She was disgusted by his drunkenness, yet she had no control over the searing desire that stole through her defenses.

"Well, well, well. What do we have here?"

Kit recognized the voice, and humiliation and dread thrummed through her. She managed to get Jake to roll off her so she could scramble up to face Jameson. Glancing down at her ex-hero, who floundered about, trying to get to his feet, Kit felt a pang of sympathy.

Resolve filled her, and she placed herself between the men. "This isn't any of your business, Will."

Behind her, she could hear Jake struggling to rise.

Jameson sneered. "Some hero! Who would've thought the great Jake Cordell was a drunken bum!"

"He just had a little too much to drink." Kit leaned down to help, but it took three attempts to get Jake in an upright position.

She looked up to find Jameson directly in their path. Her heart slammed against her ribs, and she felt like she was ten years old again.

The lawless Jameson cornered the heroine, leaving her no escape. She pressed the back of her lily white hand to her smooth ivory forehead. "Please don't hurt me. I beg you."

"Unhand her, you evil brute," Jake Cordell commanded.

The outlaw laughed, a harsh grating sound that left no doubt Jake would have to shoot him to save the innocent maiden. He eased his Colt 45 from its holster, and leveled it at the bad guy. "Don't make me kill you, Jameson."

The villain stared down death's dark tunnel, then into the unyielding eyes of Jake Cordell. Jameson's hand shook and his true colors emerged. "Please, Mr. Cordell, don't shoot. I was only joshing."

The cold air had begun to stir Jake out of his stupor,

along with the harsh words between Kit and the police officer. He tried to straighten, and only partially succeeded. "I think the lady wants you to leave her alone."

His words, slurred, didn't come out as forcefully as he'd intended.

"And what are you going to do if I don't?" Jameson taunted.

"Jake, leave it be," Kit murmured.

"Jake Cordell, hiding behind a woman's skirts." Jameson snorted with derision. "Even if the woman doesn't wear a skirt."

Lucid enough to know his masculinity was being challenged, Jake took a wobbly gunman's stance. "I don't have to hide behind anyone."

He focused on Jameson's face, on the gray eyes that seemed as brittle as the cold evening. As he stared into them, Jameson's features began to run like a wet painting, transforming into another face filled with merciless angles and shadows. His father's murderer had returned!

Jake growled deep in his throat. "You bastard!"

He launched himself at the younger man, and the two of them rolled to the street below the boardwalk. Jake was able to dodge a few of Jameson's blows and land a couple of his own, but too much liquor and not enough food had weakened him. The policeman got in an uppercut to his jaw and Jake fell back, shaking his head clear of the colored spots in his vision. Before he recovered, Jameson went on the offensive, sending another punch to his face. Warm, sticky moisture rolled across Jake's lips and down his chin.

"That's enough!" Sergeant O'Hara's voice boomed out above them, and Jameson was jerked out of Jake's line of sight. "What's goin' on here?"

"Cordell is drunk and disorderly. I was going to arrest him."

"You liar," Kit exclaimed.

Her angelic face, surrounded by a tangle of hair, swam into Jake's view. Gentle hands eased him into a sitting position and he glanced down at his shirtfront, stained scarlet from the blood that flowed from his nose.

"Jake and I were going to Freda's." Kit's sweet breath cascaded across his throbbing face.

"I'm believin' the lass, Jameson. Go on with you, and leave Cordell and Miss Thornton be," Patrick ordered with a wave of his hand.

Jameson glared at Jake, then mockingly tipped his hat at Kit and sauntered away.

Kit breathed a sigh of relief. "Thanks, Patrick. Could you help me with Jake?"

He nodded and slipped a brawny arm around Jake's waist, helping him up. Jake tried to escape the helping hands, but what little strength he had had disappeared.

"I see you have brought him home," Freda commented, as she moved aside to allow them in the house. "Take him into the kitchen. We can clean him up there."

They propped Jake in a chair by the table, while Freda poured water from the pot on the stove into a tin basin. Patrick got himself a cup of coffee with a familiarity that showed this wasn't the first time he'd been in Freda's kitchen.

Kit removed her jacket, then rolled up the sleeves of her wool shirt. Taking a cloth from Freda, she began the chore of cleaning up Jake's face.

"What happened?" Freda asked.

"Will Jameson." Disgust reflected in her tone. "You'd think he'd grow up some day."

She dabbed at Jake's swelling nose.

"Damn it, that hurts," he cussed, grabbing her wrist and halting her ministrations.

"Mr. Cordell, what have I said about swearing under my roof?" Freda reminded sternly.

"You'd best be listenin' to her, Jake. You'd hate to be missin' out on her apple pie," Patrick added with a wink.

With a muttered oath, Jake released Kit. Her lips settled into a grim, disapproving line, but she carefully wiped the blood from his face. Her clean, soapy smell tantalized Jake, and her flushed cheeks tempted his fingers to touch her, to learn if her skin was as peachy soft as it looked. But it was her mouth, only inches from his, that held his rapt attention. What would her lips feel like? He imagined her soft compliance as he kissed her lush ripeness, and his groin tightened in response.

Settling the damp cloth on his nose, Kit said, "Lean back to stop the bleeding."

He eased his head back until he gazed at the white-washed ceiling.

"I don't think it's broken," Kit said.

"It's not," Jake said. "I've had it broken a couple times, and it didn't feel like this."

"That's reassuring," Kit said dryly.

As he waited for the bleeding to cease, Jake tried to remember exactly what had happened. The fact that Jameson would've beaten him sent humiliation shafting through him. If he'd been sober, Jameson wouldn't have been more bother than a mosquito. But because he'd indulged in a good case of self-pity, he hadn't been able to protect Kit from the officer's taunts. Some hero he was.

Slowly, Jake brought his head up, then closed his eyes as dizziness assailed him. Once the nausea passed, his eyelids flickered open and he found a steaming cup of coffee on the table in front of him.

And he and Kit were alone.

"Where'd they go?" he asked.

"Into the parlor." Her curt reply did nothing to assuage his guilt.

Sighing heavily, he took a long swallow from the mug. He immediately slammed the cup down and swore, glad Freda had disappeared. "Did she boil it twice?"

Humor glinted in Kit's eyes. "Three times. She figured you'd need it."

Stubbornly, Jake drank the coffee, though this time he sipped it. He set the empty cup on the table. "There! I'm done."

Kit stood and refilled the cup. "You haven't even begun."

Jake grumbled, but emptied the pot. By the time he was finished, he needed to make a trip to the privy. He felt more sober than he had in two days, and he pushed back his chair only to have the floor tilt beneath him. He threw out a hand, slapping the table to keep from falling flat on his face.

"Aren't quite as sober as you thought, are you?" Kit asked softly.

Jake turned to find Kit within a few inches of him, and her arm curved around his waist. It was decidedly the only benefit of being so drunk he couldn't stand on his own feet. Without his asking, she helped him down the muddy path.

"I'll wait for you," she said in a tone that brooked no argument.

A minute later Jake emerged, carefully holding onto the door frame. Kit moved toward him, but he shook his head. "No, I'll do it myself."

Slowly, Jake returned to the house on legs that wobbled like a two-bit chair. He leaned against a counter, trying to regain his equilibrium. As he waited, he studied Kit's stance, the arms crossed below her breasts, her booted feet planted twelve inches apart, and her expression curtained.

"What were you doing in town today?" he asked.

"Trying to talk some sense into that thick skull of yours."

He frowned. "How did you know——?"

"I didn't. Johnny was upset that you hadn't shown up for his next riding lesson. I thought it might've been my fault."

Shame clogged his throat. He imagined the sparkle in Johnny's eyes disappearing, replaced by disenchantment, and his heart lurched. He hadn't meant to disappoint the kid. "I forgot."

"Damn it, Jake, I don't want to see Johnny hurt. Either you keep your promises to him, or you keep away from him." Kit's eyes blazed with righteous anger. "It's up to you."

For years he hadn't answered to anyone but himself, and he'd liked it that way. The boy, however, had stolen past Jake's defenses. He found himself wanting to see Johnny again, to teach him not just how to ride, but the other things a boy should learn.

Exhaustion crept up on him, and he pushed away from the counter. He stumbled slightly, but Kit didn't try to help him. For some reason, disappointment flared within him.

Once in his room, Jake plopped down on his bed and removed his shirt with clumsy fingers. He lay down and his eyelids fluttered shut. Even when he felt Kit remove his boots and socks, he found he didn't have the will to open his eyes. She tucked a blanket around him.

"I don't want to hurt him," he murmured. "Or you."

"I know, Jake."

Immediately before slumber overtook him, Jake realized that was a promise he couldn't keep. When he'd bought the loan papers for the ranch, he'd sealed his fate. And theirs.

Chapter 7

❦

Kit left Jake's room and joined Freda, who had returned to her kitchen to make supper. Exhausted, Kit slumped in a ladderback chair and took a sip of the lukewarm coffee left in her mug. She grimaced and set the cup aside. "Did Patrick leave already?"

Freda nodded. "He wanted to speak to Jameson." She vigorously mixed dough for dumplings. "How is Jake?"

Kit shook her head. "I don't know. He seemed to sober up some."

Freda nodded, bitter experience in her expression. "Tomorrow morning, sick he will be. I will watch him so he does not hurt himself."

"That's not necessary." At the older woman's questioning look, Kit went on. "I plan on staying with him all night. That is, if you don't mind."

Freda shook her wooden spoon at the younger woman. "As long as there is no panky-hanky."

Kit's face flushed with heat. "He's drunk, Freda." A chuckle slipped past her embarrassment. "And that's hanky-panky."

"A man can still want a woman even if drunk he is." Her stern features eased, revealing an uncharacteristic vulnerability. "This is true, I know."

Remembering the feel of Jake's lean body atop hers on the boardwalk, Kit understood what she meant.

She straightened in her chair, determined to ignore the humiliating image. "He's not anything like I thought he'd be, Freda. The Jake Cordell in the books doesn't drink or cuss or cavort with prostitutes, and he's a sight more gentlemanly, too."

"Maybe he is not like the man in the books, but a good man he is. All he needs is a good woman and family."

Nervous agitation brought Kit to her feet, and she paced back and forth across the well-swept floor. "Nothing is that easy." She paused, recalling the blond hussy on Jake's lap. "Besides, Jake doesn't care for me like a man cares for a woman." She ignored the remorse that flickered deep within her. "We're friends, that's all."

"Maybe so, maybe not. You are a very pretty woman."

Kit shook her head. "No, he doesn't think that way about me." She forced a smile past her regrets. "Let me help you."

Despite Freda's protests, Kit helped get supper on the table. After they'd eaten and the dishes were done, Kit filled a cup with coffee and bade Freda goodnight. Entering Jake's room, she sat in the rocking chair next to the bed.

Kit studied the faded bluebell wallpaper. She scrutinized a crack in the side of the maple armoire. She perused the faded block quilt. Then she imagined Jake's muscular form beneath the blanket. Closing her eyes, Kit tried to think about something, anything, besides the man who lay on the bed. But she couldn't ignore him any more than she could turn a deaf ear to her heart.

"Oh, hell," she swore softly, and indulged herself in an unhindered examination of him. She leaned forward, placing her forearms on her thighs. Sweeping her gaze across his sleep-slackened features, she yielded to the temptation of brushing aside an errant curl from his smooth brow. Her hand lingered, enjoying the sensuous feel of its silky texture. It reminded her of Johnny's hair—which produced unwanted guilt. Perhaps Maggie had been wrong. Maybe Jake should be told he had a son.

Kit suddenly sat back. She couldn't allow herself to weaken. Johnny was her son; Jake had no right to him. He hadn't raised him since he was a baby.

Closing her eyes, she listened to the evening sounds of the town: the faint tinny tinkling of a piano, voices that grew louder, then faded as people passed by the house, and the eerie cries of two cats fighting in a nearby alley. The ceiling creaked as Freda prepared for bed in the room above.

Kit's eyelids fluttered open, her gaze once again settling on the dim oval of Jake's face. Even with three days of whisker growth, he appeared as vulnerable as a child, without any trace of the cynicism she'd witnessed in the saloon. What kind of demons chased him? What did he hope to escape from when he lost himself in a bottle of whiskey?

And where did her hero go?

Kit wasn't sure what woke her, but when she opened her eyes the evening had changed to night and the town had grown silent. The lamp she'd lit earlier was still burning, though it was turned low. When she glanced at Jake, she realized what had awakened her. He muttered unintelligible words and moved about restlessly.

She leaned forward and laid a hand on his shoulder. "Shh, it's okay, Jake." His motions became more violent and Kit moved to the side of the bed. "Jake, wake up. Jake!"

"No!" he shouted, then sat bolt upright, his face drenched with perspiration.

"It was only a dream, Jake," Kit reassured.

Awareness filtered into his sleep-rumpled features. "Kit?"

She breathed a sigh of relief as she let go of him. "That's right. Are you awake now?"

Jake blinked. "I think so." He laid a hand on the side of his head and another on his stomach. "What did you put in that coffee?"

"Don't blame the coffee," Kit said.

She poured some water from the chipped china pitcher into the matching bowl, and wet the corner of a towel. She sat on the bed beside Jake, sponging his face like she'd done for Johnny when he'd been sick with influenza.

"Would you like a drink of water?" she asked.

He nodded.

She returned a moment later with a glass and helped Jake sit up to swallow the contents. Gently she eased him back on the pillow.

"Any better?" Kit asked.

"Yeah." He looked at her as if seeing her for the first time. "What're you doing here? I thought you went home."

She busied herself with smoothing imaginary wrinkles on the quilt. "I decided to stay and make sure you didn't do anything stupid."

Jake's smile appeared more of a grimace. "You don't have a lot of faith in me."

Kit lifted her gaze to his lantern-lit face. "You haven't given me much reason."

A self-effacing grin tugged at the corners of his dry lips. "I guess you've got a point, lady. Am I going to live?"

"Unfortunately for you, you are. Why don't you go

back to sleep? It's the middle of the night."

He shivered. "If I'm going to have another nightmare, I'd rather stay awake."

"Do you want to talk about it?"

Jake closed his eyes a moment, as if summoning his courage. "Did you know I was almost killed back when I first started hunting Frank Ross?"

Kit's stomach churned as she shook her head.

"He shot me. I thought I was going to die."

"What happened?"

A few beads of sweat appeared on Jake's forehead. "Ross had left a trail a tinhorn could've followed, and I got cocky. Only problem was, he was smarter'n me, and he'd set a trap." He rubbed away the perspiration with a trembling hand. "My father would've seen it, but I was too sure of myself. I went down with a bullet in my side, figured I was a goner. But before Ross could finish me off, this family came by in their wagon, and they got me to a doctor. If those farmers hadn't shown up when they did, I would've died."

"Is that what your nightmare was about?"

"Partly." He took a deep breath. "In my dream I was lying on a rough wood floor, and splinters were jabbing me. But all I could feel was this burning in my gut. I looked down and saw this bright red seeping through my fingers and down my side. It gathered in a puddle on the floor, and the sun that shone through one of the dirty windows made it glitter like a ruby."

He paused, as if living through the nightmare. "I started to shiver and I closed my eyes. There was this long black tunnel, like the kind a train goes through in the mountains, but it had a light at the other end. I walked toward it and there was my father. I called out to him, but another voice answered."

"Maggie's?" Kit asked softly.

He shook his head, then pierced her with an intense

gaze. "It was you. You told me I couldn't go yet."

A cold hand fisted in Kit's stomach. "What happened then?"

He pinched the bridge of his nose with his thumb and forefinger. "I just wanted the pain to go away, but you wouldn't let me go. You said I had too much to do yet."

Although shaken by what he'd told her, Kit managed a reassuring smile. "I'm sure it was just brought on by everything that you've been through. When Johnny has nightmares, I sit with him to keep the monsters away while he sleeps."

"Who's taking care of Johnny?" Jake suddenly asked.

"Charlie and Ethan," she replied, and lifted her chin. "They're like family."

Jake's silent examination disconcerted her. "I told you, a person's skin color never did make much difference to me."

Kit nodded ruefully. "You've already proved that." She paused, drew in a deep breath, and said, "I'm sorry, Jake."

"For what?"

"For getting mad at you. Since Ethan wouldn't press charges, it wasn't your fault those two men couldn't be charged."

Jake touched her hand. "I wish I could've done something, Kit, but real life isn't like those stories. Sometimes the law isn't on the side of justice."

His feathery strokes were turning her insides as soft as melted butter. "That's a strange thing for a lawyer to say."

"Maybe so, but it's true more times than not." His bloodshot gaze pierced her, and his finger ceased its unsettling caresses. "Someday you'll know exactly what I mean."

Unease rippled through her. Kit already knew that the

law and justice were not one and the same, but there seemed to be a deeper meaning to Jake's words.

"Go back to sleep. I'll be here if you have another nightmare," she said softly.

His eyes closed, and Kit pulled the blankets up around his broad shoulders. Standing over him, she laid her palm against his whiskered cheek, enjoying the foreign, soft-bristled texture. "I've never known anyone quite like you, Jake," she whispered.

She lowered herself into the nearby chair and began rocking. A quiet creak accompanied each backward motion.

"I never noticed how comforting the sound of a rocking chair can be," Jake remarked in a low voice.

Surprised he was still awake, Kit paused a moment, then continued her rhythmic back-and-forth motions. "Did your mother ever rock you when you were a child?"

The sound of his husky voice broke the long silence. "I remember one time when I was younger than Johnny, Pa was gone and there was a bad thunderstorm. I remember being scared, then hearing my mother's voice, soft and gentle, and she put me in her lap while she sat in the rocking chair in front of the fireplace."

"When did she go back East?"

He shifted below the pile of blankets. "A long time ago."

"Why'd you get drunk, Jake?"

She could see his eyes open in the moon's slanted light.

"Because I wanted to."

His flippant reply startled Kit. Hurt by his offhandedness, she snapped, "I think you were only feeling sorry for yourself. Well, Mr. Cordell, I'll have you know life is not a bed of roses for anyone. But the rest of us don't hide in a whiskey bottle and wallow in self-pity.

We make the best of what we have. I suggest you do the same.''

She stalked out of the room, then leaned against the wall in the hallway, trembling from her outburst.

A touch on her shoulder startled her, and she peeled her hands away from her face to find the man in her thoughts standing directly in front of her. With his dark hair mussed and his feet bare, Jake hadn't taken the time to pull on a shirt. Curly black hair covered his chest and tapered down to his flat stomach to disappear beneath his waistband. In spite of his appearance, or because of it, languid heat flowed through her limbs.

''Are you all right, Kit?'' Jake's voice was low, intimate in the darkened hallway.

''Fine.'' Kit focused on a spot on the wallpaper behind him. ''I shouldn't have lost my temper. Especially with the way you're feeling.''

Jake gazed intently at her, searching for a sign of—what? With a deliberate motion, he raised his hand and touched her peach velvet cheek. Her eyes widened behind her spectacles. Expectation displaced her surprise, and she leaned into the palm of his hand.

Using his thumb, Jake traced light whorls on Kit's cheek, and she wrapped a hand around his wrist. He didn't know if she wanted him to stop or continue; he chose the latter.

''You're right, Kit. I *was* feeling sorry for myself, and I couldn't just get on Zeus and ride away this time,'' Jake confessed in a low voice. ''You've got everything I ever wanted—a home and a son—and you get to do what you love, raise horses. I envy you, Kit.''

Her eyes widened behind her lenses. Abruptly she moved away from him. ''I've envied *you* nearly all my life, Jake.''

Jake sensed the sadness in her words. ''I'm not some

perfect made-up hero, Kit. And I can't change who I am.''

''I know that now. You should get back to bed. You're white as a sheet.''

They returned to the room, and Jake fell on the mattress and closed his eyes, his dark lashes shadowed against his pale cheek. The moon's silvery rays glinted across his bare skin, revealing a puckered scar on his side. A mark of the violent life he'd led, the life she'd foolishly glorified.

Kit squeezed his hand reassuringly, and he clung to her.

''You won't leave me, will you?'' Jake asked in a low, raw voice.

His vulnerability undermined her defenses, clogging her throat with emotion. ''No.''

A sigh escaped his lips, but he didn't release her. Keeping her fingers curled around his, Kit pulled the chair closer to the bed with her free hand. She sat down, still imprisoned by his grasp. A few minutes later, the steady rise and fall of Jake's chest told Kit he finally slept.

Jake awoke a few hours after sunrise and looked around, disoriented, his head pounding. Pressing a hand to his temple, he turned to find Kit curled up in the rocking chair, a blanket wrapped around her. He thought it had all been a dream—waking in the middle of the night and talking to Kit, and nearly losing himself in her compassionate eyes. And asking her to stay with him. She had done so, and not for any gain on her part, but because she was his friend and she trusted him.

He swallowed, not liking the taste of deception. The hell of it was, he wanted her friendship—yet he couldn't have both the ranch and Kit.

As if sensing his gaze upon her, Kit awakened. He

studied her sleep-tousled expression and smiled affectionately. "Morning."

"Good morning," she said quietly. "I see you survived."

"Barely." He rubbed his brow. "I'm getting too damn old for this."

A hint of a smile graced her face. "I hope that means you're swearing off liquor."

"I'd swear to anything right now if it meant my head would stop feeling like a stomping ground for a herd of buffalo."

Disappointment sent her smile scurrying away.

"Don't worry," Jake went on. "I don't plan on repeating that episode."

Kit appeared relieved. "Good. You need to get on with your life, Jake. Get your law practice going. And if you have some spare time, Johnny would like to have you continue his riding lessons." She paused. "He likes you a lot, Jake."

"I never had much use for kids before. I used to think they should be locked away until they were grown up." His smile faded. "But I like Johnny, and I don't want to disappoint him."

Gratitude glowed in Kit's eyes. "You won't. I'll get you something to eat. You're going to need some strong coffee, too."

"You've done more than enough, Kit. Why don't you go on home?"

"Because you were there when I needed you. The least I can do is be here for you."

He studied her a moment, noting the gentle tilt of her chin, the upswept brows, and the compassion brimming in her eyes behind the round lenses.

His groin tightened with awakening desire. What he wanted was her, but he couldn't speak the words aloud. Not after what she'd done for him. He couldn't make love to her, then forget about her as he'd done with all the other women in his checkered past. Or worse, use her and then take away her beloved ranch. Even he wasn't that lowdown.

"You don't owe me anything," he said.

"Maybe, maybe not, but I plan on staying until you're up on your own two feet."

If he'd had any morals, he'd have told her to run as far away from him as she could. But her concern for his welfare was as intoxicating as a bottle of twenty-year-old scotch whiskey. He'd never had anybody worry about him before.

"Are you up to eating in the dining room, or should I bring you a tray?" she asked.

"I can eat at the table, but I need a bath first."

She wrinkled her nose impishly. "Good idea. I'll see what I can do."

Kit strode out the door.

An hour later, Jake entered the kitchen. The smell of fried ham and baking bread plunged his stomach into a rapid descent. He choked back the nausea and took the coffee cup Kit offered him.

His square-tipped fingers brushed Kit's hand, and she fought the urge to prolong the contact. Noticing his clean-shaven jaw, she caught a whiff of soap. His damp hair glistened like a blackbird's wing, and the dark strands were tamed back from his forehead.

He actually resembled the hero she'd written about for the past five years.

Fastidious to a fault, Jake Cordell adjusted his four-in-hand and tugged his vest down. The black broadcloth jacket fit his expansive shoulders like a leather glove, snug but flexible across his muscles. His trousers, pleated to perfection, covered his long sturdy legs, and his knee-length ebony boots had been polished until he

*could see himself in them. He'd even cleaned his Colt
and oiled his holster.*

*Surveying his handsome image in the mirror, he
added the crowning touch with his freshly brushed black
Stetson.*

"Good morning."

At Freda's words, Jake started and turned to see the
no-nonsense German woman enter the kitchen with her
usual briskness. Kit watched him focus his bleary eyes
on his landlady. "Morning, Freda."

"Good to see you are sober this morning," she stated.

"And that's about all I am," he retorted.

Kit crossed her arms, leaning a hip against the
counter. "Don't let him fool you, Freda. He's doing
much better. Or he will be, as soon as he eats."

Jake grimaced but didn't comment as Kit filled a plate
with the hash browns, ham, and eggs she'd made. Freda
set a pile of bread on the table, along with a bowl of
cinnamon apple butter.

Jake picked at his food, chewing only small bits at a
time. After a couple of minutes, however, he began to
eat with more enthusiasm.

Relieved, Kit joined him at the small table.

"No wonder Johnny says you're the best cook in Wyoming," Jake commented, as he rewarded her with a
smile and wink. He glanced at Freda, who was rolling
out pie crusts. "Make that one of the two best cooks in
Wyoming."

"Will you be havin' any coffee for a poor policeman?" Patrick asked, as he entered the back door.

Freda wiped her hands on her apron. "Men. Always
they bother you at the worst time."

Patrick wrapped his arms around her small waist and
nuzzled her neck. "Now, is that any way to be greetin'
your favorite admirer?"

"Flattery will get you nowhere." The twinkle in her hazel eyes belied her brusque tone.

Patrick sank into a chair and took a sip from the cup of coffee Freda poured for him. He sighed blissfully. "I can always count on you to be makin' the best coffee in all of Chester County." He glanced at Jake. "I was beginnin' to wonder if you'd ever join the livin' again."

Jake ducked his head self-consciously. "I wondered myself."

"So what were you thinkin'?"

He kept his gaze aimed at the tablecloth. "I'm not so sure practicing law is what I want to do the rest of my life, but bounty hunting is a thing of the past." He shrugged. "I guess I was just feeling sorry for myself."

Patrick narrowed his eyes. "Now, isn't that too bad? Excuse me if I'll not be extendin' my sympathies to you, Cordell."

Kit swiveled her shocked attention to the Irishman. "You can't blame him, Patrick."

"Then who am I to be blamin', lass? Maggie, for up and dyin' on him? Or maybe Frank Ross, for lettin' himself get caught? Or maybe even you, lass, for buyin' his pa's place instead of lettin' it go to ruin?"

"That's enough, Sergeant." Anger threaded through Jake's low words.

"I'm not done yet. You want all of us to be feelin' sorry for poor Jake Cordell because things didn't go as he planned? Well, Mr. Cordell, maybe your da didn't spend enough time with you when you were a lad, but at least you had enough to fill your belly."

"I said knock it off, O'Hara!"

Kit saw in Jake's eyes a spark she hadn't seen since he'd returned home. His whole body seemed to grow, his shoulders became straighter, his chin was held higher. Damn, Patrick knew exactly what he was doing!

"Who's goin' to make me? The great Jake Cordell?

He can't even see straight, not after takin' the coward's way out in a whiskey bottle.'' Patrick offered the final taunt.

Jake exploded out of his chair and grabbed the lapels of Patrick's jacket, hauling the beefy Irishman out of his seat. ''Nobody calls me a coward.''

The two men stared at one another for a long moment, neither giving an inch.

''Now *there's* the Jake Cordell from the books,'' Patrick said, a twinkle in his green eyes.

Confusion edged Jake's features. He glanced at Kit and she sent him a slight smile. After a few moments, Jake relaxed his hold on Patrick and offered the police officer his hand. ''Thanks, Patrick. I guess I needed that.''

The two men shook on it.

''That you did,'' Freda stated. ''No good comes from wallowing in self-pity, my mother used to say.''

Kit stood and gathered the dirty plates. ''If you two are finally done with the manly posturing—''

''Now, that's not the way for a decent lass to be talkin','' Patrick said with a red face.

Kit laughed and shared a knowing look with Freda. ''Sorry, Patrick. Now that you two gentleman have come to an understanding, would either of you like more coffee?''

They shook their heads.

''Jake, I'll be needin' to talk to you,'' Patrick said.

Jake groaned. ''I didn't pay for the whiskey?''

The sergeant pursed his lips. ''I wouldn't be knowin' about that.''

Kit moved to the sink to wash the breakfast dishes.

''Do you need any help, Kit?'' Jake asked.

She turned, surprised, and shook her head. ''That's all right, but thanks for the offer.''

Noting the somber expression on Patrick's rough-hewn face, she chilled. What did he need to talk to Jake about? What had happened? Had a gunslinger come into town looking for Jake?

Patrick led the way into the sitting room and Jake followed with a black foreboding that grew with every step. He stopped by the fireplace, one booted foot braced against the hearth. Patrick stood at the other side of the mantel and faced Jake. The sergeant glanced down, tracing a crack in the stonefront hearth with a blunt finger.

"So what's this news you have to tell me?" Jake asked, impatience and anxiety making his voice curt.

Patrick took a deep breath and raised his grim gaze. "Frank Ross cheated the hangman's noose."

Chapter 8

Jake's whole body tensed, and his stomach lurched. "What the hell happened? He was supposed to be under guard until his hanging!"

Patrick raked a hand through his thick red hair. "Aye, he was, lad. He killed the poor soul deliverin' his dinner. But Ross was shot before he even got out of the building."

Jake scrubbed his jaw. "So he's dead?"

Patrick nodded. "Aye, but not at the end of a rope."

"At least he's dead." Jake should have been relieved, but all he felt was a pervasive disappointment. He'd made a point to bring Ross in alive to face a trial and be hanged legally. Jonathan Cordell would've approved of that.

"Are you all right, lad?"

He nodded in resignation. "Ross got what he deserved."

A soft knock at the door interrupted their conversation. Kit stuck her head through the doorway.

"I'm going to head back to the ranch now," she announced.

"Wait, I want to talk to you a minute," Jake said.

"It's time I got back to the station." A grin kicked

127

up the corners of the Irishman's lips as he left the room.

Gently, Jake tugged Kit into the parlor, closing the door behind them.

"What did you want to talk about?" Kit asked, her voice thready.

Jake glanced down at the worn rug, wondering how to thank someone for picking him up off the floor. Especially when one of the reasons he'd taken to drinking concerned her. "I'm grateful for all you did for me. I don't know how long I'd have stayed in that saloon if you hadn't shown up."

Kit crossed her arms. "I'm sure Louise would've taken care of you."

For a moment, Jake couldn't figure out who Kit referred to, then he remembered the blue-eyed prostitute—the one who'd resembled Kit through his whiskey-hazed vision. He lifted his hand and swept a strand of hair behind a dainty ear. "I don't think so. You were right, you know. It's time I started looking ahead instead of back."

"You could have a good life here, Jake," Kit said, equally as quiet.

He would when he got his father's ranch back, although that thought now filled him with mixed emotions. "I hope so."

Kit stepped back. "I'd best get going." She paused at the door. "Is there anything you want me to tell Johnny?"

"Tell him I'll be there tomorrow."

A radiant smile lit her face. "He'll be thrilled."

Jake approached her, holding her gaze. He gently placed his hand on her shoulders. Caught like sunlight in a spangled spiderweb, she nearly melted beneath his feathery touch.

"What about you? Will you be happy to see me again?" he asked in a husky voice.

His soft breath cascaded across her lips like an angel's caress. Instinctively she leaned forward, and the tips of her breasts grazed his hard-muscled chest. A spark with the heat of a wildfire raced through her. He wrapped his strong arms around her, drawing her against him. Kit wanted to curl up inside his embrace and have him build the embers he'd stirred into a consuming blaze.

"Kiss me, Kit," Jake whispered.

Moaning, she met his lips with a fervor that matched the fire in her blood. The fierceness of their possession eased into a tender exploration as she tasted Jake's sweetness. Her thoughts spun into a maelstrom of colors, and the tangy scent of Jake wrapped around her like a quilt in winter.

Jake drew away from her slowly. Her mouth burned for more of his tantalizing mastery.

"Thank you for everything you've done for me," he said.

His words, like a bucket of cold water, dashed the lingering passion. She drew away from him and hated herself for the tears that threatened.

"You're welcome." Before she could humiliate herself, she scurried out of the parlor.

She paused a moment in the hallway to wrap a cool facade around her shattered emotions. Why had she thought the kiss was more than a mere expression of gratitude?

Because I wanted it to mean more.

For Jake it had been nothing more than a thank you. For her it had been a wondrous discovery. She'd been kissed before, but she'd never experienced such a soul-stirring reaction. Why did it have to be Jake? Why couldn't she have felt that when David Preston had kissed her?

Because he had bad breath and slobbery lips, she thought peevishly. Shaking her head, Kit retrieved her coat from the rack by the door. With trembling fingers she buttoned her jacket.

She went to the kitchen to say good-bye to Freda and found her friend selling a few loaves of bread to the mayor. Kit wished she could turn around and leave, but Walters had spotted her.

"Doesn't Mrs. Walters bake?" Kit asked, deciding it'd be better to get in the first word.

Walters' florid face flushed a deeper red. "She's busy with her many women's groups."

Kit arched her brows. "Which?"

"None you would be interested in, Miss Thornton."

She shrugged. "How do you know? I can be very sociable when I want to be."

Walters tried to draw up his diminutive height, but succeeded only in sticking out his rotund belly even further. "Her organizations wouldn't approve of your ilk."

Kit laughed. "I've never had my ilk maligned before."

Walters harrumphed and grabbed his bread loaves, then scuttled away.

"You should not make fun of the mayor," Freda scolded. "He is an important man."

Kit tried to appear contrite, but failed. "I'm sorry, Freda, but he makes it so darned easy."

Freda chuckled. "A scamp you are, Theodora Katherine."

"I just wanted to thank you for letting me spend the night. I think Jake'll be all right now."

Freda tucked a strand of gray-peppered hair into her braided coronet. " He has feelings for you, Kit."

She shook her head, her smile disappearing. "It's not what you think. I'd better get back to the ranch. Thanks again, Freda."

Kit gave the woman a quick hug, then left. The air was crisp and clear as she walked down the boardwalk.

Engelbertina Wellensiek, the minister's wife, sent her a disapproving glance and drew her skirts aside so they wouldn't be contaminated by her. Although she was accustomed to such snubs, Kit hated the woman's sanctimonious attitude. If the reverend had been as hypocritical as his spouse, Kit would've stopped attending services. But the Reverend Wellensiek had a generous nature and had always welcomed Kit in his flock.

She crossed the street to the livery and entered the relative warmth of the barn. The barn smelled of hay, horse, and manure, a familiar odor that acted as a balm for her stormy thoughts.

"Ned, are you in here?"

Silence. Shrugging to herself, she found Cassie's stall and saddled the appaloosa mare. She spoke soothingly to the animal as she placed the hackamore bridle on her.

"Did you have a nice night?"

Kit jerked, startling Cassie. Turning, she spotted David Preston approaching her. Relieved it wasn't Will Jameson, she pressed a hand to her chest to still her rapid heartbeat. "You scared me, David."

"I'm sorry, Kit. When I saw you come into the livery without stopping by, I thought I'd check and see if everything was all right." The newspaperman's apologetic smile didn't seem to touch his eyes.

Suddenly irritated by his overprotectiveness, Kit turned to tighten the saddle's cinch. "I'm fine."

David brushed the front of his jacket with a fastidious hand. "How is Jake Cordell?"

She glanced up sharply. "How should I know?"

Disgust twisted David's thin lips. "It's common knowledge that you escorted him from the saloon yesterday." He narrowed his suspicious eyes. "And it's been speculated that you stayed at Freda Finster's last night to be with him."

Kit glared at him. "You sound more like a reporter than a friend."

He shrugged shoulders encased in an expensive wool suit. "Jake Cordell is a drunken has-been. He can't give you what I can, Kit."

She thought of the kiss Jake had given her and knew Preston was wrong. "Look, David, I thought I made my feelings clear. I think of you as a friend, nothing more."

He took a step toward her, and fear wisped in Kit. She shook the absurd emotion aside. David wouldn't hurt her.

"And I thought I made my feelings clear," he began. "I would like you to be my wife, and move into town. Forget your foolish fantasy of being a horse breeder." Distaste emanated from his tone. "Or of marrying your hero, Jake Cordell. He'll only disappoint you."

Kit's mouth gaped at his bluntness. "I have no plans to marry Jake. And raising horses isn't a whim I'll lose interest in—it's my dream. I've told you that."

David reached out, grabbing Kit's shoulders. "I can give you respectability and security. It's more than you'd ever have with him."

She jerked out of his grasp, shaking her head. "I have all I want. You of all people should know respectability is as fickle as Fanny Walters' opinions."

David's jaw muscle twitched. "She has no say in what I put in the paper."

Wryness brought a sad smile to Kit. "The mayor does, which means Fanny does." She shook her head. "I'm sorry if I hurt you, David, but I can't be someone I'm not. When I was a young girl, I tried. I won't change for you or anyone else."

"You in here, Miz Thornton?" Ned's creaky voice called out.

"Over here," Kit replied. She glanced at David. "Please try to understand."

His face seemed to be carved of stone, and he studied her with a cold scrutiny that chilled her. Then his expression eased into a smile. "All right, Kit, if that's what you wish."

She nodded, relieved. "Thank you."

David turned away, and passed the livery owner without acknowledging him.

"You need any help there, Miz Thornton?" Ned asked.

"No, thanks. I've got Cassie saddled and ready to go," Kit answered. She led her horse out of the stall, pausing beside the wizened old man. "How's your rheumatism, Ned?"

He rubbed his back with a knotty hand. "Not so good. This weather ain't no good for us old-timers."

"Next time I come to town, I'll bring some more of Two Ponies' concoction."

Ned grimaced. "See if you can have 'im sweeten up the smell a mite. Stuff stinks like a two-week-dead possum."

"I'll mention it to him. Did Cassie give you any trouble?"

"Nope, she's got a real sweet temperament. You ever want to sell her, you let me know."

The realization that she might have to give up her beloved mare to save the ranch brought a chill to Kit's heart. She wouldn't do it unless there was no other way. "Selling Cassie would be like selling part of my family."

Ned sighed. "Figured as much. You take care, Miz Thornton."

"You too. Bye."

She guided her mare out of the barn and mounted. Keeping a firm hand on the reins, she held Cassie to a walk until they reached the outskirts of Chaney. There she loosened the leather and urged the mare into a ground-eating gallop.

But Cassie couldn't run fast enough to escape the financial problems that plagued her with increasing intensity. Or the newly discovered feelings Jake had awakened within her.

The following afternoon, Jake dismounted in front of Kit's porch. Johnny flew out of the house and launched himself at Jake, throwing his arms around his waist.

"Ma said you were coming today, but I wasn't so sure," Johnny said.

Jake patted the boy's back awkwardly. "Didn't you know, kid? Jake Cordell always keeps his promises."

He glanced up to see Kit studying him from the top step, her arms folded beneath her breasts. He read her dubious expression as easily as if she'd spoken aloud, and he couldn't blame her for being skeptical. Without her interference, he would still be guzzling whiskey at the Red Bird.

"Are you all ready for your next riding lesson?" Jake asked.

Johnny's eyes sparkled with excitement. "Yep! Ma isn't nearly as good at teaching me as you are, Mr. Cordell."

Jake glanced at Kit questioningly.

"A couple days ago Johnny rode Treasure around the corral a few times," Kit explained.

"Ma wouldn't let go of the bridle," Johnny complained. "I'm not a baby anymore. I can ride alone. You'll let me ride by myself, won't you, Mr. Cordell?"

"We'll see how you're doing," Jake replied. "Let's go get started."

"Be careful," Kit said.

"Aren't you coming to watch?"

"I can't," she replied.

"Why not?" Johnny demanded.

Kit turned her gaze to her son. "I have work to do."

"You always have work to do," he grumbled. "You never have time to do anything with me anymore. You're always in your office or working with the horses."

"That's because there are things that have to be done before——" She broke off, glanced at Jake, and finished lamely. "Before I can relax."

Jake noticed the dark circles partially hidden by Kit's wire spectacles. She was probably spending sleepless nights worrying about the loan. Kit wasn't one to take the easy way out, and she'd fight for the ranch until the end.

"Maybe your ma can stop by the corral after she's done her chores," Jake suggested.

Kit cast him a grateful look. "I'll be down to watch you later, sweetheart." She drew an imaginary X on her chest. "Cross my heart."

Johnny nodded, appeased by her promise. He grabbed Jake's hand and pulled him toward the barn. "Are you gonna teach me how to gallop today? I bet it'll be easy. I seen Ma and Charlie and Ethan ride fast, and it don't look so hard."

Jake glanced back at Kit helplessly, and the smile she gave him was one that two people exchanged when they shared a secret. A funny feeling curled in the pit of his stomach. For a moment he felt like they were a family, like he belonged instead of being an outsider.

An hour later, Jake stood in the center of the corral, watching Johnny trot Treasure around the perimeter.

"Okay, go ahead and gallop," Jake called.

Johnny touched his heels to the horse's sides, and Treasure slipped into a rocking gait. The boy stayed in the saddle like his backside was glued to the leather. Jake shook his head and smiled. Johnny was a natural rider, just as he'd been. The only difference was that Jake, having given up on his father, had taught himself.

"All right, you're doing great, kid. Slow down and bring her over here," Jake said.

Johnny eased back on the reins, and the mare responded instantly. With sparkling eyes, Johnny halted Treasure beside Jake.

He laid a hand on the boy's leg. "I don't know what you needed me for. I think you were just pretending you didn't know how to ride."

Johnny shook his head, his dark bangs spilling across his forehead, his eyes bright with excitement. "No, I wasn't. I used to think it'd be hard to ride, but it's not. It's fun, funner than chasing squirrels with Toby."

"Where is that hound, anyhow?" Jake asked, glancing around.

"Ma made me put him in the shed so he wouldn't scare Treasure. She's scared that I'll fall off and get hurt." He wrinkled his nose. "But I won't fall off. I ride too good, don't I, Mr. Cordell?"

Jake spotted Kit walking toward the corral, the wind molding her blouse against her rounded breasts, and he nodded absently. "That's right, kid."

"Did you see me, Ma?" Johnny called out.

She slid her hands into her back trouser pockets, causing her chest to jut out more prominently. Jake's groin responded to her innocently provocative stance.

"I sure did," Kit said. "Looks like you caught on real fast. What do you think, Jake?"

He swallowed, drawing his reluctant gaze away from her tempting attributes. "Yeah, that's right, he did real good. In fact, he's done so well that I think we should all go for a ride."

Kit's smile fled. "Even if I didn't have work to do, I don't think Johnny's ready to leave the corral yet."

"Why not?" Johnny asked.

If he hadn't been on horseback, Jake figured the boy would've stamped his foot for good measure.

"You said yourself he's doing well," Jake said.

She flashed a concerned look at her son's flushed face. "Anything could happen out there, Jake. Are you certain he's ready?"

Jake nodded grimly. "A lot readier than I was. Go get Cassie, and Johnny and I'll meet you by the barn."

"What about my work?"

Jake sauntered over to where Kit stood and leaned over the corral's top rail. "Sell me the ranch and you won't have to worry about all that work," he stated, intentionally keeping his voice pitched low so Johnny wouldn't hear.

Kit's lips thinned to a grim slash, and fire leapt into her blue eyes. "I'll go get Cassie."

Fuming, Kit saddled her appaloosa. Her father had once said Judge Cordell's son was as wild as a March hare and twice as stubborn. Kit hadn't believed it—until now.

She joined Jake and Johnny, and they rode three abreast down the road. With Treasure between Zeus and Cassie, Kit felt a small measure of comfort for her son's safety. She glanced at Jake and silently cursed him for his apparent lack of concern.

Jake turned and caught her eye, then sent her a wink. "Relax, Kit, and enjoy the beautiful spring day."

His dangerously charming smile melted her insides. She deliberately shifted her attention to Johnny, who held the reins in his gloved hands like he'd done it for years. Kit consciously untensed her shoulders, determined not to be an overprotective mother hen. Besides, nothing would happen with Jake there.

Jake Cordell sat atop Zeus like he was a part of the stallion, rocking in the saddle as relaxed as a farmer in his favorite chair after a long day's work. Jake glanced at his wife riding sidesaddle beside him, her maroon velvet split skirt and jacket the height of fashion. Blond strands that had escaped the confines of her hat curled about her smooth peaches-and-cream face. She turned to him, casting him a knowing half-smile.

She alone knew the great sacrifice he'd made in settling down and leaving the exciting life of a bounty hunter behind. He'd turned in his guns for this woman, and he'd gladly do it again. She and their son were the center of his life now.

He clasped her hand, and they both gazed at the boy their love had created.

Kit breathed in the uncommonly warm spring air, redolent of damp soil and wildflowers. A gentle breeze brought the faint scent of Jake's bay rum wafting past her, triggering the memory of his kiss and the slumbering feelings he'd awakened within her. It was like the time her father had taken her to the mercantile to buy an Easter dress. She'd fallen in love with a yellow and pink one with flounces and bows, but her father had disapproved of it. He had said that the dress was made for little girls, not big girls like her. She'd secretly pined for that dress every time she'd gone into the store, until one day it was gone. Fifteen years later, Kit still thought about that dress.

Fifteen years from now, would she be wondering what it would've been like to have had more than a kiss from Jake?

Kit spotted a brown blur out of the corner of her eye. A moment later, Toby's bark broke the peaceful silence. Cassie danced around, tossing her head, and her muscles flexed and quivered beneath Kit's legs.

"Whoa, easy, girl," she spoke in a low, soothing voice.

Toby raced around them excitedly, spooking the horses. Kit noticed Jake had tightened his hold on Zeus's reins, but he was struggling to keep the animal in check.

"Whoa, Treasure, whoa," Johnny said, a frantic note in his voice.

Using one hand to keep Cassie under control, Kit reached for Treasure's reins with the other. But the usually gentle mare bolted away at a full gallop, and Kit's fingers closed around air.

Without thought, she spurred Cassie after the frightened runaway. Branches whipped at her and tugged at her shirt sleeves. She barely registered the stinging pain when a twig slashed her cheek. Through tearing eyes, she saw that Johnny was still atop Treasure. She urged Cassie faster, and the powerful mare closed the distance.

Startled, she saw Jake and Zeus move up beside her, then overtake her. The black stallion caught up to Johnny quickly, and Jake leaned out of his saddle to grab Treasure's reins. He began to slow both horses. Without warning, Treasure stumbled, and Johnny flew over her neck to land on the ground ten feet in front of her.

"Johnny!" Kit screamed.

Jake managed to get Zeus and Treasure under control and Kit jerked Cassie to a halt, springing from the saddle before the mare had stopped completely.

Her limbs trembling like an aspen, Kit fell to her knees beside Johnny's still body. His pale face was a stark contrast to his usual ruddy complexion. She reached down to turn him onto his back, and Jake grabbed her wrist.

"Don't move him," he said curtly. "He might have a broken bone."

Kit nodded numbly and laid her clenched hands on her thighs. She watched in silent horror as Jake threw off his hat and lay his ear against Johnny's back.

"He's breathing good," Jake announced.

Toby lay on the ground a couple of feet away, his

front paws crossed and his tongue lolling. After escaping the shed, he must've followed their scent.

Jake checked the boy's legs and arms, and breathed a sigh of relief. "Nothing's broken. I'm going to turn him over slowly."

Kit reached out to help him, and the warmth of Johnny's body through his heavy shirt reassured her. As they rolled him onto his back, Johnny's eyes fluttered open and he dragged in a ragged gulp of air.

Jake raised him to a sitting position. "I think he just had the wind knocked out of him." He wiped perspiration from his forehead. "He'll be all right."

"Ma," Johnny said hoarsely. Color filtered into his pallor, and tears trailed down his red-splotched cheeks.

Kit gathered him in her arms and rocked him back and forth. She savored the familiar scent of his downy soft hair and his welcome weight in her embrace. "You're going to be fine, sweetheart. Everything's all right now."

Her quaking abated, and she glared at Jake over Johnny's head. "He could've been killed!"

"But he wasn't," Jake said.

"No thanks to you," she snapped. "If you hadn't insisted on taking him out for a ride, this wouldn't have happened."

"You can't protect him forever, Kit." Jake stood and stared down at her.

"He's only a little boy!"

"And someday you're going to wake up and find he's a man. Then what?"

Kit stroked Johnny's hair. "He's all I have. If something happened to him . . ." She gulped back the sobs that tore at her throat.

Jake hunkered down beside her. "When I was a boy, I used to wish I had a mother who cared for me as much as you care for Johnny." He raised her chin with his crooked finger, and said softly, "Sometimes loving someone means you have to let them go."

Kit thought of Maggie, and how she'd been able to release Jake despite her love for him. Maggie was a stronger woman than Kit could ever hope to be.

"We should get back to the ranch," Kit said, her voice hollow.

Jake helped Kit and Johnny to their feet.

"Johnny can ride with me on Zeus," Jake volunteered.

Kit didn't want to release her son, but something in Jake's voice caught her attention. She studied him, noting the worry etched in his brow, and regret pierced her. He'd been afraid, too, when Johnny had been thrown, but she'd been oblivious to anything except her own fears.

"All right," she agreed.

Jake picked Johnny up, and the boy threw his arms around Jake's neck.

"I'm going to lift you onto Zeus so you can ride with me. That okay with you, kid?" Jake asked.

"What about Treasure?"

"I'll lead him back," Kit assured.

"Did she get hurt?"

"No. She's fine."

"Good. I want to ride her again."

"But not now," Jake said firmly. "Next time I'll teach you how to stop a runaway horse." He gazed at Kit.

All her instincts screamed that there wouldn't be a next time, but Jake was right: she couldn't protect Johnny forever, and her little boy would grow up. What kind of man would he become? What kind of role model could she be for a boy? For the first time, Kit questioned her ability to raise Johnny on her own. Maybe a boy did need his father.

Jake deposited Johnny on Zeus's back, then stuck his boot toe in the stirrup and settled in the saddle. When Johnny was safely ensconced between Jake's arms, Kit mounted Cassie and secured Treasure's reins to the saddlehorn.

She urged Cassie beside Zeus, and they rode back to the ranch with a subdued Toby following behind.

"Don't be mad, Ma," Johnny said. "It wasn't Mr. Cordell's fault that I fell off Treasure."

Kit mustered a weak smile. "I'm not mad. I was afraid that you'd been hurt."

"I don't hurt, except for maybe my butt," Johnny admitted.

"That's normal, kid. Even as much as I've ridden Zeus here, my butt gets sore sometimes, too."

Johnny giggled, and Kit couldn't help but smile.

They rode in silence for a few minutes.

"I'm sorry, Mr. Cordell," Johnny said softly.

Jake frowned. "For what?"

"For not learning better."

"Don't go blaming yourself, Johnny," Jake said, his voice rough. "Sometimes things just happen and it isn't anybody's fault."

Johnny gazed up at Jake. "Then why are you blaming you?"

Startled, Kit looked at Jake. He tugged at his hat brim and smoothed the leather reins.

"Who says I'm blaming myself?" Jake asked, not meeting Johnny's eyes.

"Me," Johnny replied. "I can tell."

A smile tipped up the corners of Jake's lips. "You can, huh?"

"Uh-huh. You got this funny look on your face, and you're being real quiet."

"Anyone ever tell you that you and your ma are a lot alike?"

"No."

"Well, you are."

He was also a lot like his father, Kit thought with more than a shred of guilt.

Entering the yard, Kit led them to the barn and they dismounted. Johnny walked toward the door.

"Hey, Johnny, what's the rule about taking care of your horse?" Jake called out.

"Take care of him before you eat or sleep," Johnny replied.

"That's right."

Kit bristled. "After what happened to him, don't you think you can make an exception?"

Jake shook his head firmly, and said in a low voice Johnny couldn't hear, "He's got to learn that rules can't be arbitrarily broken."

She stared at Jake, hearing Judge Cordell's nononsense tone in his son's voice.

Jake moved away to help Johnny unsaddle Treasure, and Kit mechanically went through the same motions with Cassie. Kit had always believed she could do as good a job alone raising Johnny as a mother and father together. She thought that her love could make everything right, but maybe there was more to being a parent.

She hung the saddle blanket she'd used to rub down Cassie over the stall door. Looking into Treasure's stall, she saw Jake examining the mare's legs. Johnny leaned close to Jake, their heads nearly touching.

A suffocating weight settled on her chest. They'd taken to one another as if an invisible thread had drawn them together. Who gave her the right to deny them the truth?

"She looks fine," Jake announced, straightening.

Johnny nodded. "I'm glad she wasn't hurt."

"And I'm glad *you* weren't hurt," Jake said, ruffling the boy's hair.

Jake opened the gate and they joined Kit. Silently the trio left the barn.

Kit wrapped her arms around her waist. "Do you have plans for Easter dinner, Jake?"

"When's Easter?" Jake asked.

"Sunday," Johnny answered. "Don't you know that?"

Jake smiled down at the boy. "I haven't been to church in a while. I'm not even sure if God remembers what I look like."

"Ma says that He knows everyone, and it don't matter what they look like."

"Maybe so, but after all the things I've done, if I set foot inside a church, I'd probably get struck by lightning."

Johnny frowned, puzzled. "You're a hero. God would like you."

"Besides, it's too early in the year for thunderstorms," Kit added mischievously. She sobered. "Maybe it's time you and He got reacquainted."

"I'll have to think on that," Jake replied. He mounted Zeus with an easy, fluid motion. "The dinner part sounds good, though."

"Then we'll see you in a couple days," Kit said.

"Count on it." He glanced down at Johnny. "Now, you don't be taking Treasure out on your own, or bother your ma to take you out. I'll take you for a ride next time I come by."

"Okay." Johnny rubbed his backside and grimaced. "That'll be time enough for my butt to get better."

"We'll see you Sunday, then." Jake glanced at Kit and tipped his hat, "Kit."

She drew her son back and together they watched Jake leave.

"It wasn't Mr. Cordell's fault, Ma," Johnny said with uncanny perception.

Kit wrapped her arm around Johnny's shoulders. "I know that, sweetheart." She paused. "Do you miss having a father?"

Johnny glanced down and kicked at the ground with his boot toe. "Sometimes," he admitted in a tiny voice.

Kit's heart knotted at the anguish in his single-word reply. "Did you think I'd be angry if you told me you wanted a father?"

He shrugged his thin shoulders. "I dunno. Maybe." He lifted his gaze to her. "You never talk about him. Didn't you like him?"

Moisture hazed Kit's vision. "I liked him very much, and I know you'd like him, too."

"Is he dead?"

A few lies came to mind, but Kit couldn't deceive her son. "No, he's alive."

"Then where is he? Doesn't he like me? Is that why he doesn't live with us, because he doesn't want me?"

Kit struggled to come up with answers to his rapid-fire questions. "He never knew about you. Your mo— I didn't tell him because I didn't think he was ready to be a father."

"Why?"

"Because he said he wasn't the settling-down type, and I respected that." She felt as if she were sinking in quicksand, unable to do anything but continue to be sucked down. Squatting beside Johnny, she met his bewildered eyes. "Not having a father has been hard on you, hasn't it?"

He stared at her a long minute and laid his smooth palm against her cheek. "It doesn't matter. I got a real good ma."

Kit hugged him, hiding her sheen of tears.

It *did* matter. If she was a good mother, she'd do what was best for Johnny and give him the father he desperately craved: the man he already idolized.

Chapter 9

Easter morning dawned bright and cheery, with a clear azure sky to greet Jake as he readied himself for the church service. Staring at his image in the small mirror hung crookedly on a wall, he tried to straighten the black string tie about his neck, but had little success.

"Why am I doing this?" he asked his reflection. "I haven't set foot in a church in ten years. Dinner wasn't contingent on my going to Easter service."

Still, Jake had vowed to make a new start after his binge. Swearing off alcohol, he'd put his energies into his law practice. He'd already negotiated a business contract for the mercantile owner; he also had four clients for whom he'd drawn up wills. His biggest case had involved a broken window and the fourteen-year-old boy who'd thrown the rock. Unfortunately, it hadn't gone to court, so Jake still hadn't gotten any courtroom experience. However, he had enough to keep him busy.

Attending Sunday service would be another step in rebuilding his reputation.

Giving up on his tie, he pulled his black broadcloth jacket over his snow-white shirt. He grabbed his Stetson and left the room only to nearly bowl over his petite landlady in the hallway.

"Sorry, Freda," he apologized.

"Why are you dressed up?" she asked curiously.

He surveyed her brown print dress and the practical rust-colored hat perched on her head. "Same reason you are."

Surprise flickered across her unlined face. "To church you go?"

He nodded. "Kind of shocked myself."

"Yes." Her shrewd eyes narrowed. "Kit and Johnny will be there."

Jake smoothed a finger over the worn material of his hat. "I know. She invited me over for Easter dinner."

"Surprise me not."

"Would you like me to walk you over to the church?"

She shook her head, a pink flush staining her cheeks. "Patrick will be here soon."

Jake shook his head in mock disappointment. "So Patrick is my competition—I should've known."

"Friends only we are."

"And a bee doesn't buzz, either." He laughed. "Why, Freda, I do believe you're blushing like a schoolgirl!"

She slapped his arm lightly. "Off to church you go."

Still chuckling, Jake strode outside and fell in step with the small throng of people moving toward the steepled building at the edge of town. He greeted the men and tipped his hat to the ladies, hiding his nervousness behind a pleasant facade.

At the door to the church, he paused with hat in hand. His palms were moist and he questioned his reason for being there. Was it only Kit who drew him to the place of worship, or did he really want to reacquaint himself with God?

Hell, he didn't know. Mumbling an apology for his silent curse, he backed away from the entrance.

"My goodness, did you hear that thunder?"

Startled, he found himself gazing into teasing blue eyes behind glass spectacles. His perusal swept down Kit's cream-colored dress with little pale blue flowers scattered all over like a field of bluebells. He'd never seen her in anything but trousers, and the transformation stunned him.

"I didn't hear no thunder, Ma," Johnny remarked, puzzled. He looked skyward. "There isn't even any clouds."

Jake laid a hand on Johnny's shoulder. "Your ma was just trying to be funny."

"And succeeding quite well," Kit said, laughter brightening her voice.

Jake tossed her a don't-bet-on-it look and turned to the boy. "How's your backside?"

"All better. And I'm ready to ride Treasure. This time I promise I won't fall off."

"I think Treasure's the one who should be promising not to throw you," Jake said. "You look downright dapper in that suit, Johnny."

He wrinkled his nose. "Ma made me wear it."

Jake took her hand and threaded it through the crook of his arm. Extending his other hand to Johnny, he said, "Shall we?"

"I don't think—"

"Don't think," Jake said firmly. "It'll be fine."

Stiffening her spine, Kit allowed Jake to lead her and Johnny into the simple chapel. He passed the back row where she usually sat. Keeping her eyes focused on the altar, she looked neither right nor left. Condemning gazes scorched her, and she wished she'd hadn't invited Jake to attend Easter service. She didn't want him to experience the repercussions of being seen with her.

As if reading her thoughts, he squeezed her fingers

gently. She glanced up at him and he smiled encouragingly.

Jake Cordell gallantly swept the imperiled young woman up in his virile arms and dodged the shower of bullets that kicked up dust around his feet. He spotted shelter from the lead rain that poured down upon them from the evil Chaney gang. He dashed toward the sanctuary, the woman's slight weight hardly noticeable.

Sinking behind the rocky outcropping, Jake lowered the woman gently to the ground. "Don't worry, ma'am; you're safe here."

"Why do they want to kill me? What have I done?" she asked, her voice trembling with wretched despair.

"You stood up to them," Jake replied. "I'll stand with you, ma'am, and make sure no harm comes to you."

She sighed a breathy little sigh and snuggled tightly against his muscular torso. She trusted him, her hero, Jake Cordell.

"Is this okay?" Jake asked uncertainly.

He'd escorted them all the way to the front. She blinked. No, it wasn't okay, but they couldn't turn around without garnering even more attention.

"Fine," she whispered, keeping her gaze directed forward so she wouldn't have to see the stares that pierced her back.

Kit sat with Johnny between her and Jake like they were a real family. The irony of the situation brought a bubble of laughter up to Kit's throat and she swallowed it before it slipped past her lips.

Then the Reverend Wellensiek entered and the hushed conversations ceased. He took his place at the front of the room, glanced around at the gathered congregation, and blinked when he spied Jake. After sending him a welcoming smile, the minister began the service.

Although she tried, Kit couldn't seem to concentrate

on his words. She studied Jake out of the corner of her eye, and remembered the kiss they'd shared. Her face grew warm, and she shifted on the hard plank seat. She'd tried hard to forget the desire he'd invoked within her, and she thought she'd succeeded. But her wayward thoughts told her otherwise.

Jake turned toward her and caught her studying him. Knowing her cheeks flamed scarlet, she fought to concentrate on the words from the pulpit. How could she be thinking such scandalous thoughts, in church no less? Besides, the desire had been one-sided—for Jake, it had simply been a gesture of gratitude.

After what seemed an eternity, the final hymn was sung and the congregation dismissed. She stood and glanced at Jake.

"You seemed to be woolgathering," he said in a low, teasing voice.

"I was just reflecting upon the scriptures." She sent God a quick petition for forgiveness.

"What were they again?" he asked with too-innocent a look.

Caught in her lie, she thought quickly. "So you didn't listen?"

"Touché, Miss Thornton." Gallantly, he extended his arm. "Shall we?"

One look at his devilishly handsome features dashed her objections. "Thank you, kind sir."

Outside the church, Johnny joined a couple other boys to play a quick game of tag.

The minister greeted Jake and Kit with a cordial smile. "Hello, Miss Thornton." He extended his hand to Jake. "And Mr. Cordell, it's nice to see you have returned to the flock."

"At least for a visit, anyhow," Jake amended. "I'm not sure how God feels about ex–bounty hunters."

"You were doing the work of the Lord, bringing criminals to justice for their evil deeds."

"You sound like you're quoting one of Jake Cordell's dime novels instead of the Good Book, Reverend."

The minister's self-conscious smile creased his narrow face. "Perhaps I was, but I'm sure I'll be forgiven for my misdeed."

Kit cleared her throat. "It was a wonderful service, Reverend Wellensiek."

"Thank you, Kit, and I must say it was nice to see you at the front instead of hiding in the back as you usually do."

"That was Jake's doing," she replied.

"I hope he does it every Sunday."

"Karl, come speak with the mayor and his wife," Engelbertina Wellensiek said, tugging on her husband's arm.

"Have you met Jake Cordell, Bertie?" the minister asked.

"I've seen him about town," she replied with a tone that would've frosted the devil's tail. "Come along, Karl, the Walterses don't have much time."

"Excuse me, folks. Have a happy Easter," the Reverend Wellensiek said, as his stout wife pulled him away.

Humiliated by Mrs. Wellensiek's insulting behavior toward Jake, Kit stalked toward her wagon.

Jake grabbed her arm before she'd gone far. "Hey, where are you going so fast?"

"I have to get home and check on our dinner." She glared at Bertie and the mayor. "Besides, if I stay here, I may do something that will only add more fuel to Bertie's gossip."

Taking her chin between his thumb and forefinger, he turned her face toward him. "Don't let that old battle-ax get to you. I've met too many clucking hens like her to be insulted by her pettiness.'' He forced his voice to be light, though anger thrummed through him. Seeing Kit upset stirred his dormant sense of protectiveness. ''If you want, I'll call her out.''

She laughed and grasped his hand. ''Thanks, Jake, but I don't think that will be necessary.''

He squeezed her fingers gently. ''Your wish is my command, madam.''

''You said the exact same thing to me fourteen years ago.''

In his mind, Jake saw the chubby little girl with the same sky blue eyes that peered at him now. ''I'm surprised you remembered.''

''Would you be shocked to learn I still have the bandanna you gave me to wrap around my knee?''

He studied her a moment, bewildered. ''Why?''

She began to walk toward her wagon, and he fell in step beside her. ''You were my hero, Jake.''

''*Were?*''

''Little girls grow up.''

Sweeping his gaze down her figure, he smiled. ''I'm glad they do.''

She blushed and called to her son. Red-faced from his game, Johnny joined them.

''Good morning, Kit,'' David Preston greeted. He leaned close to the boy. ''Hello, Johnny.''

The boy said hello and then turned his head away, waving a small hand in front of his nose. Jake coughed to smother a chuckle.

''And Mr. Cordell. I didn't realize you were a church-going man,'' Preston said with infinitely less warmth.

''I didn't see you in there,'' Jake said.

''David is an agnostic,'' Kit interjected.

''Egg-what?''

Preston smirked condescendingly. ''Agnostic, Mr.

Cordell. Surely a big-time Yale lawyer like yourself would know what that means.''

''It means you prefer your eggs sunny side up, right?''

Preston's face reddened with anger, while Kit fought her laughter. Johnny didn't try to restrain his giggles.

The newspaperman turned away from Jake to face Kit. ''Will you and Johnny join me for dinner at the cafe?''

''It's Easter, David,'' she replied.

''You don't have plans, do you?''

''As a matter of fact, she does,'' Jake interrupted. ''I'm going over to her place to have dinner with her and Johnny.''

Preston's shoulders stiffened, but Jake couldn't see his face.

''Is that true?'' he demanded of Kit.

She nodded. ''That's right.''

''Why are you doing this? I thought you understood what kind of man Cordell is.''

Jake grabbed the reporter's arm, gaining his undivided attention. ''Maybe you should tell me what kind of man I am.''

Kit leaned close to Jake, and the flowery scent of her hair filled his senses. She laid her palm on his rigid forearm. ''Let him go.''

He'd have preferred to beat the hell out of him, but Kit's imploring voice cooled his temper. He pushed Preston away, and the dandy stumbled, stepping in a pile of fresh horse droppings.

Preston glared at Jake and looked back at Kit. ''See what I mean?''

Lightning flashed in Kit's eyes. ''You deserved it for making such a fool of yourself, David.''

The reporter shook his head. ''You're making a mistake, Kit.''

''Maybe, but it's my mistake to make.''

Preston's lips flattened and he hurried away, dragging his foot as he tried ineffectually to scrape the smelly mess off his leather shoe.

Kit stared after him, a pensive expression on her delicately sculptured face. "He's changed."

"Does that mean he won't come around anymore?" Johnny asked hopefully.

Kit ruffled her son's burnished hair. "Probably. Do you mind?"

He wrinkled his nose. "Nope."

"Smart boy you got there, ma'am," Jake said with a wink.

"Takes after his father," she retorted.

Abruptly she turned away, but not before Jake noticed the color drain from her cheeks.

"We'd best get home and get dinner ready," she said stiffly. "Are you going to ride over?"

He nodded. "I'd like to run over to my room and change out of this suit first."

"Don't be late, or there won't be any food left," Johnny exclaimed as he climbed up into their wagon.

"I'd better hurry then," Jake said. "I'd hate to miss out on your ma's cooking."

Kit urged her team into motion, and Johnny turned to wave.

Jake returned the gesture absently. The mention of Johnny's father had seemed to upset Kit, and for the first time, Jake wondered about the man. He must have been a smooth talker to get into her bed.

If Jake ever met the son-of-a-bitch, he'd give him a taste of his fists. Any man who deserted a woman who carried his child was as worthless as a bucket of spit.

Especially when that woman was Kit.

"Charlie and Ethan are coming, Ma," Johnny shouted.

"I think the horses down in the south barn heard you," Kit teased.

The boy grinned unrepenitently and grabbed a slice of still-warm bread, taking a monstrous bite from it. "When's Mr. Cordell gonna get here?" he mumbled.

"Pretty soon. Did you sweep off the porch, like I asked you?"

"Yep. Then me and Toby cleaned up the tack room."

"Toby must've been a big help."

"I taught him how to hang up the bridles."

Kit laughed. "I'll believe that when I see it."

Footsteps at the front door alerted Kit to the entrance of her hired men, and a few moments later Charlie and Ethan stepped into the kitchen.

"I hope you're hungry," Kit said.

Ethan nodded. "I could eat a horse, Miz Thornton."

"I hope you didn't have any specific one in mind." She winked at Charlie.

A blush reddened Ethan's ruddy complexion, and deepened the purplish bruise on his high cheekbone. "Oh, no, ma'am, I was just—"

"I was just teasing you, Ethan." Kit stepped forward and straightened the bow of his string tie. "Could you get the plates down for me?"

Ethan seemed relieved to have something to do, and he retrieved five plates from the oak china hutch.

"You'll need one more," Kit said.

"For who?"

"Jake Cordell will be joining us."

Ethan scowled.

"That was mighty neighborly of you," Charlie said. The twinkle in his coal black eyes told Kit he suspected more than a simple act of hospitality.

Kit narrowed her gaze at her old friend, but Johnny and Ethan's presence kept her silent.

"Why'd you do a fool thing like that?" Ethan demanded.

Johnny tugged on the young man's white shirt sleeve. "Why don't you like Mr. Cordell, Ethan? He helped you when those bad men were hurting you."

"It ain't that I don't like him, Johnny. I just ain't sure I can trust him, is all."

"You don't trust nobody," Charlie stated. "How many times have I told you, you can't measure everyone with the same stick. Cordell proved he ain't like all them folks that done those things to you."

Kit's heart constricted. Besides Ethan's recent cuts and bruises, she'd seen scars on both him and Charlie, and she couldn't fathom how a human being could treat another so cruelly.

"Mr. Cordell wouldn't hurt you, Ethan. He's nice," Johnny interjected.

"And he's fair," Charlie added.

Ethan didn't appear convinced, and Kit touched his forearm lightly. "I wouldn't have invited him if I thought he was like the others."

The young man's expression eased, and he treated Kit to one of his shy smiles. "I know that, Miz Thornton."

Kit gave his hand a slight squeeze. "Why don't you and Johnny set the table?"

Ethan nodded, and he and Johnny disappeared into the dining room to do as she'd asked.

"You think Cordell might finally lose his blinders?" Charlie asked in a low voice.

Kit frowned. "What do you mean?"

"With them clothes on, Johnny looks a lot like his pa."

Kit studied her son, who'd returned to the kitchen to gather napkins from a drawer. He'd changed clothes as soon as they'd arrived home from church. He had insisted on wearing tan pants and a navy shirt, just like his hero, Jake Cordell. He even wore a light blue kerchief around his neck.

After Johnny left the room, Kit glanced at Charlie nervously. "Maybe I should have Johnny change clothes."

The burly black man shrugged. "What're you gonna tell him? That he can't wear them 'cause he looks like his papa?"

Kit nibbled her lower lip. "You're right. But Jake knows I couldn't be Johnny's mother if he was the father, so it probably won't even occur to him that he and Johnny share some similarities."

"You probably got a point there."

Kit leaned over and pulled the ham out of the oven. The heat steamed her glasses, and she waited a moment for them to clear. "Do you think I'm wrong not to tell Jake about Johnny?"

Charlie crossed his brawny arms, and leaned against the counter. "That ain't for me to say."

She heard the censure in his deep rumbling voice. "You think I should tell Jake."

"I think you'd best be knowin' what you're gettin' into by bein' so friendly with him."

Kit basted the savory ham with the juices from the bottom of the pan, then did the same to the sweet potatoes tucked around the meat. She slid the roaster back into the oven and smoothed back a damp strand of hair that lay against her forehead.

Turning back to Charlie, she said softly, "There's a part of me that wants Jake and Johnny to know each other as father and son. But there's this other part that's scared to death I'm going to lose Johnny if I tell Jake."

Charlie settled his broad work-roughened palm on her shoulder. "No one said lovin' someone was an easy thing, Kit. Sometimes a person just got to listen to their heart."

"We got the table all set, Ma," Johnny announced, as he and Ethan reentered the kitchen.

Kit sent Charlie a grateful smile and turned to her son. "You used the good silverware?"

"Yep."

"And put them on the right sides of the plates?"

Johnny glanced at Ethan. "We did, didn't we?"

"Just the way your ma taught us last Christmas."

Kit observed the two of them with a fond smile. When Ethan had first arrived at the ranch, broken and bloody, she'd cared for his physical injuries. It had been Johnny, however, who'd begun healing Ethan's spirit. Since that time, Ethan had taken on the role of older brother to Johnny. After the hatred the younger man had endured, Kit was determined to give him the security and acceptance he'd been denied for nineteen years.

The back door opened and Pete Two Ponies limped in. "You got any food left, or did you heathens eat it all?"

Kit smiled. "You're in luck. We haven't started yet." She glanced at a kettle on the stove. "Charlie, could you stir the gravy, please? And Johnny and Ethan, I need you two to run down into the root cellar and get me the milk and a jar of pickles."

Everyone moved to carry out their assigned tasks, and Kit neared Two Ponies. "Did you get the eggs hidden?"

He nodded his gray-haired head. "Seems like a stupid thing to do with perfectly good eggs."

"That's what you said last year, and the year before that. Did you hide all two dozen?"

Pete shrugged. "Got hungry while I was doing it, so I had me a couple."

"I guess that's better than last year."

Indignation crossed Pete's wrinkled face. "I didn't have any breakfast that morning and them eggs tasted mighty good. Don't understand this thing you call

Easter, anyhow. Whoever heard of someone rising from the dead? According to us ignorant savages, once some-one's been sent to the happy hunting ground, he's gone.''

Accustomed to Pete's irreverence, Kit grinned wryly. "You know darn well what Easter is all about. In fact, you told me it was a lot like one of the ceremonies in your tribe.''

"I told you that, huh?''

"Yes, you did.'' She lifted serving bowls down from the cupboards, mentally counting the number of side dishes she had made.

"Gotta watch what I say around you. You remember everything.'' Pete crossed to the stove and examined the abundance of food. " 'Course, anything that makes you cook up a feast like this can't be all bad.''

Johnny and Ethan returned with the milk and pickles, and she handed Ethan a shallow square bowl. "Could you put the pickles in there?''

He nodded and opened the jar. The sweet-sour scent of vinegar and pickling spices wafted up to mix with the rest of the food's aromas.

Kit could barely move in the crowded kitchen, but contentment swelled within her. Charlie and Pete argued about the saltiness of the gravy; but if they hadn't been quibbling, Kit would've worried. Ethan surreptitiously passed Johnny a pickle, and he popped it into his mouth and puckered his lips.

"Give me a ride, Ethan,'' Johnny begged.

Ethan squatted down, and Johnny climbed onto his shoulders. Ethan galloped about the room, nudging Pete and Charlie aside. Johnny's giggles echoed in the rafters.

Surrounded by her closest friends and Johnny, Kit wanted to savor the sense of well-being that imbued her. The only person missing was Jake.

The ranch house seemed abandoned, but Jake Cordell

knew appearances were often deceiving. He fought the urge to turn around and return to town. He paused, listening intently, and heard voices from inside.

Taking a deep breath, Jake knocked on the door.

A moment later, the door swung open. A gruff man dressed in black studied him.

Jake's palms sweated under his scrutiny. He'd faced down murderers without blinking an eye, but this man was different—this man was his fiancée's father.

"So you're Jake Cordell," he finally said.

"Yes, sir, I am."

Kit jumped as she spotted Jake standing hesitantly in the kitchen entrance, and her heart lifted. "Hello, Jake."

"Nobody answered the door, so I just walked in. Hope you don't mind," Jake said.

"Not at all. Here, I'll take your coat and hat."

He handed her his Stetson and jacket, and she whisked down the hallway to hang them up.

Jake nodded at Charlie, then met Ethan's brooding countenance. "How're the bruises healing?"

"Fine." Ethan lowered Johnny to the floor.

"I wish you'd have filed charges against them."

"It wouldn't have made no difference. No court's gonna take the word of a—" Ethan glanced at the boy. "Of me against them."

Jake took a step toward him. "You don't know that. You have to give the law a chance."

"Laws weren't made for people like me."

"They were made for everyone," Jake said vehemently. "Kit and I would've testified on your behalf."

Ethan shook his head. "Look, I owe you my thanks for stepping in and helping me, but I don't owe you anything else."

Jake sighed. "I wish you'd reconsider, Ethan. The courts are changing, and judges aren't as narrow-minded as they used to be. You have the same rights as anyone else to bring charges against those who violate your liberties."

"Better look out Jake, you're beginnin' to sound like a lawyer," Charlie teased.

Jake paused. He *had* spoken as a lawyer, but he believed every word he'd said. Glancing at Ethan's obstinate expression, he also knew he had little chance of changing his mind.

"I'm glad you're finally here, Mr. Cordell. We've been waiting forever," Johnny said earnestly.

"Sorry I'm late," Jake apologized.

Kit returned to the kitchen, her heart-shaped face flushed. "You aren't late, and we haven't been waiting forever. I think you know everybody but Two Ponies. Jake Cordell, Pete Two Ponies."

Jake eyed the scraggly-haired Indian curiously. "Nice to meet you."

Jake stuck out his hand and Two Ponies ignored it, holding up his own hand, palm out. "How."

"Pete," Kit said, reproval in her voice.

Pete glanced at her. "Isn't that the way I'm supposed to greet the famous white-eyes hunter?" Two Ponies turned back to Jake with a smile etching his creased face. "We got to sit down and talk sometime about the way you tracked down those outlaws in your books. Were you trained by a Pawnee?"

Startled, Jake shook his head. "My father."

Pete nodded in understanding. "That's right. Jonathan Cordell had the gift. He could track a snake across dry rock."

"Did you know him?"

"We shared a couple of campfires."

"Do you like my clothes?" Johnny tugged at Jake's pantleg.

Examining the boy's outfit, Jake was startled to see

Johnny had copied his own clothing down to the neckerchief. "They look mighty good, kid."

"They're like the clothes you wear."

"I would have never guessed." Jake sniffed appreciatively. "Something sure smells good."

"Wait until you taste it," Johnny said.

"The gravy needs more salt," Two Ponies interjected with a pointed look at Charlie.

"Just because you're made of jerky don't mean the rest of us are, old-timer," Charlie retorted.

"You can always add your own salt, Pete," Kit said tactfully. "If anyone wants to eat, you're all going to have to get out of my way so I can dish it up."

"Mr. Cordell can give you a hand," Charlie volunteered, then looked at Jake. "That okay with you?"

"Fine by me."

Everyone else disappeared into the dining room.

Kit turned away from Jake to open the oven door, and as she bent over, her skirt outlined her curvaceous bottom. He took a few moments to admire the pleasant sight, then cleared his throat and shifted his gaze. He spotted a partially eaten piece of bread on the counter. "You must have awfully big mice."

She straightened and followed his gaze. "Johnny grabbed it right after I sliced the loaves."

"I've got a weakness for fresh baked bread myself. What do you want me to do?"

"Why don't you cut the ham?" She held up a wicked-looking butcher knife.

He took the sharp-edged blade from her. "Yes, ma'am."

"I'm glad you could make it, Jake."

"I didn't know it'd be a full house."

Her pleasant expression sobered. "Does it bother you?"

"No, but I can imagine Bertie might be a little scandalized.'' He leaned close to Kit's ear. ''Personally, I think Bertie needs to have her knickers shocked off.''

Kit laughed. ''That's terrible, Jake.''

''That is a terrible picture, isn't it? I'll bet the Reverend Wellensiek would think so, too.''

Kit's cheeks reddened, but her eyes sparkled behind her spectacles as she filled the serving dishes and took them out to the table.

By the time Kit had carried the last item out, Jake had slices of ham piled high on the platter.

''Thank you,'' Kit said. ''I hope you're hungry.''

Jake gazed down into her heat-reddened face, thinking not of his stomach, but of another appetite.

She glanced away as if reading his thoughts.

Studying her profile, he found himself wishing things could've been different. He truly liked her son, and he admired her. More than that, he wanted her.

When she learned of the steps he'd taken toward regaining his father's ranch, she'd be hurt and angry. And he didn't want to lose the kinship he had with Johnny, or the friendship he shared with her.

''I think that's everything,'' she said, reaching for the plate of ham.

''I'll take it,'' Jake offered.

Kit smoothed back her hair from her temples and opened the door to the dining room. Finding an empty space on the linen-covered table, Jake set the platter down, then held Kit's chair for her. He lowered himself to the last chair, between Kit and Johnny.

As the food was passed around, Jake inspected the china dishes with vining flowers etched around their edges. Matching cups and saucers rested beside each setting except Johnny's.

Blue lilies: the image struck Jake with the force of a thunderclap. His mother had had a fancy set of dishes with painted lilies that she'd used only when guests ate with them. She'd taken them back East with her. He hadn't remembered them until now.

"Jake, did you want some potatoes?" Kit asked.

He forced himself to answer. "Yes, please."

As he spooned mashed potatoes on to his plate, he pictured his mother setting this very same table with her china. Past and present seemed to merge. Instead of Kit, he saw his mother; and in Johnny he saw himself.

Chapter 10

⟨᪲⟩

"**J**ake, are you all right?"

Kit's face came into focus as her concerned voice penetrated his thoughts. He glanced at the curious faces surrounding him.

"I'm fine," he reassured. "I was just thinking how long it's been since I've eaten a holiday meal in this house."

Compassion shone in Kit's eyes. "I'm sure this house holds quite a few memories for you."

"Some, but I spent most of my time staying with other folks. With my father gone so much..." He shrugged.

Her gentle hand covered his. "You're welcome here anytime, Jake."

Kit's heartfelt offer brought a stab of self-reproach.

After everyone had eaten their fill, Kit supervised clearing the table and getting the leftovers packed away.

"I'll help wash the dishes," Jake volunteered.

Kit shook her head. "Thanks, but I'll take care of those later. We've got something much more fun to do."

As Jake stared at Kit in puzzlement, she grabbed his hand and pulled him out of the kitchen. "Come on, before Johnny finds all the eggs."

Kit led Jake outside into the warm spring afternoon, to the corral where Pete, Charlie, Ethan, and Johnny stood. Toby danced around their legs.

"Are you ready?" Kit asked her son.

Johnny's dark eyes lit up. "Yep."

"All right. There's twenty-two eggs hidden around the yard," Kit said.

"Twenty eggs," Pete corrected.

Kit groaned. "I thought you only ate two."

He shrugged his thin shoulders. "I'm old. I forget."

She rolled her eyes. "Make that twenty eggs. Whoever finds the most wins."

"Wins what?" Jake asked curiously.

"Twenty hard-boiled eggs."

"Maybe I can sell them to Liam at the Red Bird and he can put them in the pickle jar."

"You can help me, Mr. Cordell," Johnny said. "I bet we'll find all of them."

"That wouldn't be fair. It's everybody for himself," Charlie stated. "Besides, you already have Toby helpin' you."

"Any other rules?" Jake asked.

"No stealing from another person's cache," Pete replied. "And since I'm the official overseer, I say the penalty for taking someone else's eggs is cutting off a couple of fingers."

Johnny giggled.

Kit's eyes twinkled. "Sounds fair to me." She glanced at Jake. "This is serious business."

"I'm beginning to get that impression."

"Get ready," Pete began. "Set. Go."

Kit hurried away in the direction of the shed. Johnny, with Toby at his heels, trotted away toward the woods. Ethan and Charlie moved with a bit more decorum, but Jake could see the enthusiasm in their faces.

"Why're you standing here making like a fence-post?'' Pete exclaimed. ''Put some of your pa's tracking skills to good use.''

Jake wondered how his stern father would feel about hunting Easter eggs. He followed after Kit and spotted her around the corner of a barn.

''I found one,'' she announced excitedly. She opened her hand and in her palm lay a reddish egg.

''Do you do this every year?'' Jake asked.

She tucked her prize into her skirt pocket. ''Ever since Johnny was two years old. Pete hides the eggs and the rest of us look for them.''

Kit continued her search, and Jake fell in step beside her.

''Have you ever gone on an Easter egg hunt?'' she asked curiously.

''Once or twice when I was around Johnny's age. It was always while I was staying at someone else's place, though.''

She stopped and studied Jake with a piercing gaze. ''It wasn't your father's fault. He had a job to do.''

''Yeah, I know, and that job was more important than me.'' He hadn't meant to sound bitter, but the words left a caustic taste in his mouth.

''Your father would rather have stayed with you than chase down outlaws, but he had a responsibility to the people of Chaney,'' Kit said.

''After Ma left us, I was passed around from neighbor to neighbor whenever Pa was out of town. I never felt like I belonged anywhere.''

''At least you had people to talk to.'' Kit lifted her gaze to the cloudless sky. ''My father was working most of the time, too, but I was left alone. And since I wasn't the most popular girl in school, I didn't have any friends to visit. The thing I remember most about my childhood is taking care of sick animals and talking to them like they could understand me. God knows my own father never did.''

Kit's confession pierced Jake's self-pity with an arrow of guilt. He'd been so wrapped up in his own misery, he'd forgotten how alone she'd been.

''But now you have Johnny,'' Jake said.

She smiled, the gesture lighting her features like the sun's rays after a thunderstorm. ''Yes, I have Johnny, and Charlie, Ethan, and Pete, too. I knew your father, Jake, and he wouldn't have wanted you to stay so embittered. He loved you. He just didn't know how to show it.''

''You must've known him a lot better than me.''

''Only because I made the time to get to know him. Something you never did.''

Jake pinned her with a sharp gaze, but he found no condemnation in her expression. The knowledge that she'd known his father better than he did bothered and bewildered Jake. ''Why did you get the ranch?''

''Your father gave me first buyer rights in his will,'' she replied defensively.

''But why did he have that stipulation in there at all? Why didn't he just leave it to me free and clear?''

''Your father knew I wanted to raise horses, and he didn't think you wanted the place. You never came home to visit after you left for college, and your letters were few and far between.''

''He didn't even bother to write and ask me what I wanted.''

''Would you have written back?'' Kit asked.

Jake thought for a moment, then shook his head. ''Probably not. I was more interested in drinking with my fellow classmates and meeting women.''

''Why doesn't that surprise me?''

A rueful grin tugged at Jake's lips. ''Sometimes I think you don't have a very high opinion of me.''

"Sometimes you might be right."

A breeze kicked up, blowing some of Kit's hair across her cheek. Jake leaned forward and smoothed the stray strands back. She trembled beneath his touch.

"You don't have to be afraid of me," he said softly.

Her eyes wide and luminous, she shook her head. "I'm not. You'd never hurt me."

"Maybe I'm not the man you think I am."

"It's true that I was disappointed in you when I first saw you in the jail cell, and later in the saloon. You weren't like the hero in the books. But the more I learn about you, the more I've come to admire the man rather than the hero."

The naked honesty in her face twisted the knife deeper into his conscience. He didn't deserve the adoration in her eyes. He didn't deserve the trust in her voice. He didn't deserve this strong, compassionate woman.

The only problem was, he wanted her with an intensity that frightened him.

He turned his face, kissed her palm, then curved his hand around the back of her slender neck. Drawing her close, he feathered a caress across her parted lips. Her heart thundered against his chest.

He tasted the sweetness of her mouth. Shyly she reciprocated, sweeping her tongue across his, dancing and retreating like an inexperienced lover. Jake wrapped his hands around her hips, drawing her flush against his rigid desire.

"Ma!"

Johnny's scream ripped through passion's ensnaring web.

Kit's face drained of color. "*Johnny.*"

Her frightened voice was a mere whisper, and Jake grabbed her hand, pulling her in the direction of the boy's cry. His blood pounded through his veins, fearful of what condition they'd find Johnny in.

He crashed through the underbrush, thorns tugging at his shirt and arms. Before he even spotted the boy, Jake stumbled into him. He instinctively put out a hand to steady the boy, whose mouth and nose were covered with his palm.

Then the stench struck Jake, nearly knocking him over with its potency.

"A skunk sprayed me," Johnny managed to spit out, nearly gagging from the odor.

Kit reached down to hug Johnny, then drew back, coughing. "I thought something terrible had happened to you!"

"It did!" Johnny exclaimed, pinching his nose. "I think I'm gonna die."

Color seeped back into Kit's pale face, and she looked at Jake with relief. "I kind of doubt that."

A moment later Ethan and Charlie burst into the clearing, fear clouding their expressions.

The burly black man seemed to grasp the situation immediately. "Whew heee! Smells stronger'n a ten-hole privy."

Kit put her hand over her mouth and nose. "I thought Toby was with you."

"He ran after a rabbit," Johnny said in disgust. "If he'd been with me, this wouldn't have happened. I didn't see him until it was too late, then the stupid thing sprayed me."

Jake tried to breathe in shallow spurts. Some of the skunk's stink had been transferred to him when he'd run into Johnny. "He was only protecting his home," Jake managed to say, in between miserly breaths. "Besides, I'm sure he was more afraid of you than you were of him."

Johnny held up his arms, wrinkled his nose, and looked down at his damp clothes. "Do you think you can get them clean?"

Kit shrugged helplessly. "I'm not even sure I can get *you* clean."

Johnny scowled. "I woulda won the egg hunt, too." He pulled a couple of cracked eggs from each of his two front pockets. "See?"

The scathing smell seemed to intensify, bringing tears to Jake's eyes. "Anyone have any ideas how to get this odor off him and me?"

"When I was a young'un, a friend of mine got sprayed by a polecat. They scrubbed him with tomatoes," Charlie suggested.

"Do they have to be fresh?" Kit asked.

Charlie shook his head. "I think canned ones'll do."

"You and Ethan go bring up all the jars of tomatoes from the root cellar. It's a little cool to bathe out here, so we'll have to put the tub in the kitchen. I'll get the water started heating up for the bath." She glanced at Jake, a twinkle in her eyes. "Baths."

He shot her a pointed glare.

Jake and Johnny walked side by side, following in the wake of the others who'd gone ahead to begin their tasks. Toby the traitor had returned, but retreated with a yelp after getting a whiff.

"Are you mad at me, Mr. Cordell?" Johnny asked in a low voice.

"For what?"

"For getting you all stinky."

Jake laid a hand on Johnny's shoulder. "It wasn't your fault. In the spring all the critters are a little more excitable."

Including people, Jake thought as he remembered his interrupted dalliance with Kit. Hell, maybe it was for the best.

They passed the corrals, and the horses snorted in annoyance at the sharp odor. At the house, Kit made Jake and Johnny stay outside until she had everything organized. After twenty minutes, Kit opened the kitchen door and allowed them inside. A round wooden barrel stood empty in the center of the kitchen, with opened jars of tomatoes sitting beside it. A tin tub a few feet away was filled with steaming water.

"Strip first, then wash with the tomatoes in the barrel. After that, rinse off in the water," Kit explained. She wiped the moisture from her tearing eyes. "Take off your clothes, Johnny."

"In front of Mr. Cordell?"

Jake grinned. "Don't worry, Johnny, I used to be a boy, too."

Humor twinkled in Kit's eyes as she gazed at Jake. "So what are you now?"

"Odiferous," Jake shot back.

Kit laughed, then coughed and waved a hand in front of her nose. "That's for sure."

"I ain't takin' off my drawers," Johnny said stubbornly.

"I suppose giving them a tomato bath wouldn't be a bad idea, anyhow," Kit said with a helpless shrug.

Johnny removed his shoes, then his shirt and trousers, leaving on his lightweight woolen drawers. Kit used a wooden stick to pick up his clothing.

"Could you help him?" Kit asked, as she moved toward the back door.

"Where are you going?" Jake asked desperately. He wasn't averse to sharing a hot sudsy tub with a willing woman, but he'd never given a child a bath before.

"Pete says he knows a way to get the smell out of clothes. I'll be back in a little while."

She disappeared, leaving him with a near-naked kid and ten jars of squashed tomatoes. Sighing, Jake removed his own shirt, and rolled up the sleeves of his undershirt.

"Step right up," Jake said with a dramatic flourish.

With a boyish grimace, Johnny got into the barrel and stood with his arms crossed. "Now what?"

Jake lifted one of the jars and held it up. "Here goes, kid."

Jake poured the gloppy substance over Johnny's head, and the boy yelped. "That's cold!"

"Start rubbing it around like it's soap," Jake ordered.

Johnny complied as Jake continued to pour more jars of tomatoes over him. The reddish juice cascaded down his face, leaving pulp and seeds in his hair and on his shoulders.

The boy grimaced. "It feels kinda like a wet frog."

It'd been a long time since Jake had caught frogs, but he didn't have any trouble recalling the slimy texture. It wasn't one of his favorite memories.

Once the boy was saturated, Jake grabbed a cloth and began to scrub Johnny. Tomato droplets got onto Jake's trousers, and he cursed aloud.

Johnny giggled at the profanity. "Ma'd wash your mouth out with soap if she heard you."

"It'd be better than tomatoes." Muttering under his breath, Jake stripped down to his drawers. "If you can't beat 'em, join 'em. Move over, kid."

The barrel barely accommodated both of them, and when Jake emptied a few more jars over himself, Johnny was splattered, too. A gleam in his eyes, the boy leaned over, cupped his hands, and filled them with juicy tomatoes. He tossed them at Jake, who sputtered under the onslaught.

"So you want to play tough? All right, you got it." Jake smushed a tomato against Johnny's neck, and the boy laughed and counterattacked.

Kit paused outside the kitchen, listening to them hoot and holler.

Jake Cordell had always been a clean man, favoring a bath more than once a month, as was customary

*among his colleagues. Arriving in Holyoke, Kansas, he
found the nearest bathhouse and entered its clean,
steamy interior. A pretty, plump-cheeked girl worked at
the counter and quickly led him to an open copper tub
filled with hot water.*

*After the young woman had left, Jake removed his
clothing, folding each article carefully, leaving his revolver on the top of the pile within easy reach. He didn't
plan on any interruptions, but it was those unplanned
intrusions that he always expected.*

*Sinking his saddle-sore body into the hot, sudsy water,
Jake sighed in ecstasy. He leaned his head back and lit
a cigar, savoring the silence and the tobacco.*

Kit pressed her palms against her heated cheeks. Her
overactive imagination had little trouble envisioning the
picture she painted with her words.

"I don't think that little scene would make it past my
editor," she said, fanning her face.

Taking a deep breath to regain her composure, she
opened the door and stepped into bedlam. Her eyes widened at the scene that greeted her, and her nostrils re-
belled under the onslaught of tomatoes and skunk odor.
Jake and Johnny, looking like bloody ghouls, were involved in a tomato fight. Red sauce splattered everything
within ten feet of the barrel, including Jake's clothes,
which lay scattered on the floor.

She lifted her gaze to Jake, whose drawers stuck to
his body like a second skin. Following the line of his
back down to his rounded buttocks and muscled thighs,
Kit swallowed hard.

"Hi, Ma!" Johnny broke the spell.

Kit blinked, and she felt a hot flush crawl up her neck.
"Ah." Her voice cracked, and she cleared her throat.
"It looks like you and Mr. Cordell have been busy."

Jake turned to her, and his dark eyes twinkled devilishly. Did he suspect her unladylike thoughts? Oh, Lord, how could she look him in the eye?

Jake arched a saturated brow, where a glop of tomato had dripped down from his hair. "Care to join us?"

She quickly turned her back and moved to the sink, where she fiddled with the dirty dishes. "That's all right. You seem to be doing fine without me."

"The more the merrier," Jake pressed.

The suggestive note in his voice brought a tremble to her insides. If she was going to retain any shred of dignity, she had to leave. Immediately.

"Why don't you and Johnny go ahead and rinse off in the tub? I'll just take your clothes out and put them with Johnny's," she said quickly.

Using a broomstick, she picked up his clothing.

"What am I supposed to wear when I'm done?" Jake asked. "Not that I'm ashamed of my body; it wouldn't bother me to run around naked as a jaybird until my clothes are dry."

Startled, Kit twirled around to stare in openmouthed amazement. "That would be . . . improper."

"I thought you didn't care about things like impropriety," Jake challenged.

"Even I have my limits," Kit replied stiffly.

Valiantly she tried to keep her line of sight fastened on his seed-littered hair. In spite of her effort, though, Kit's uncooperative gaze drifted to his chest and lower, and found the tomato-soaked woolens had stuck to everything in the front, too.

"I can see that," Jake remarked with a knowing grin.

She pivoted on her heel and fled the kitchen, Jake's laughter tumbling after her. Kit ran until she arrived at the barn. Leaning against a post, she struggled to regain her breath.

"Good to see a man get the better of you," Pete remarked, emerging from the shadows.

Drawing her shoulders back, Kit tried to regain some semblance of control over her tumultuous thoughts. ''Jake Cordell did not get the better of me. He simply—'' The outline of his masculinity beneath the soaked drawers slipped into her mind. ''Surprised me.''

Pete chuckled. ''That's one way of putting it.''

Kit pursed her lips, and thrust the broomstick with the skunk-smelling clothing at him. ''Here's Jake's clothes. They need to be soaked, too.''

''You know where the tub is,'' Pete said. A sly grin crossed his leathery face. ''I figure the stream's right cold this time of year, if you're interested in a quick dip.''

Kit tried to muster up a degree of outrage, but failed. She shook her head, giving in to her embarrassment. ''What am I going to do, Pete?''

He shrugged. ''What do you want to do?''

Heat flooded her cheeks. ''Something I'm sure Bertie Wellensiek wouldn't approve of.''

The old Indian snorted. ''Who gives a rat's turd what she thinks? Besides, you're raising Cordell's son already.''

''So you saw the resemblance, too?''

''They both take after Judge Cordell.'' Pete rubbed his prominent jaw.

''What am I going to do?'' she reiterated plaintively.

''Marry Cordell and give Johnny some little brothers and sisters.''

Kit's heart leaped at the fantasy. If only it were that simple. ''There's a little matter called 'love' that enters the picture. I don't love Jake, and he doesn't love me.''

''You marry Cordell, and the rest'll happen in its own time.'' The Indian's wizened face gentled. ''I can see you have feelings for him, Kit, and Cordell isn't blind to you. His pa was a fair man, and I'd say Jake's cut from the same cloth. He looks to be a good one to ride the river with.''

Kit contemplated Pete's words. Though she respected his advice, there was too much to lose if he was wrong.

She glanced down at the smelly bundle. ''I'm going to take care of these, then get Jake and Johnny some other clothes to put on after their baths.''

A quarter of an hour later, Kit handed Ethan a pile of folded clothing for Jake and Johnny. Fortunately, her father had been close to Jake's size, and Kit had found a pair of pants and shirt for him. ''Could you take these in to them?'' she asked.

Ethan nodded. ''Sure, Miz Thornton.''

As he disappeared into the kitchen, her stomach flipped nervously. How could she face Jake now, with her imagination conjuring up visions of what lay beneath his clothes?

Ethan returned. ''They're almost done.''

''Thanks,'' Kit said with a weak smile.

''I'd best get started on chores.''

The young man left, leaving Kit to wait alone. A couple of minutes later, Johnny and Jake emerged.

''How do we smell?'' Johnny demanded, stepping up to her.

Kit sniffed tentatively, but only the faint scent of lye met her nostrils. ''Much better.''

She glanced at Jake nervously. Her embarrassment fled when she noticed the fit of her father's old clothes. The trousers stopped above his ankles, and Jake clung to the waistband to keep them from falling down.

''I guess they don't fit you as well as I thought they would,'' Kit said, then burst into laughter. ''I think I can find you a pair of suspenders.''

''Oh, I don't know.'' He leaned close to her, his brown eyes twinkling. ''Jake Cordell lives for danger.''

Kit crossed her arms. ''I doubt if T. K. Thorne had

that type of danger in mind.'' She noticed Jake and Johnny's matching cowlicks in their damp hair. "Looks like both of you need your hair combed.''

Upstairs in Johnny's room, she handed Jake a brush. "Here. I'll go see if I can find those suspenders.''

When Kit returned, she found Jake sitting on the bed with Johnny standing between his knees, trying to tame the boy's mussed hair. She paused in the doorway, watching and listening to their conversation.

"I never knew my pa,'' Johnny said. "Ma says he was a good man, though.''

"Do you ever wish he was here?''

Johnny shrugged. "I got Ethan and Charlie and Pete. I figure that's like having three pas.''

"I hadn't thought of it that way." Jake licked his palm and smoothed Johnny's cowlick. "There, that oughta pass your ma's inspection.''

Johnny turned to face Jake. "You can be my pa, too, if you want.''

Jake studied the boy for a long moment, his expression unreadable. "I'd be proud to be your pa.''

Kit's breath caught in her throat. Maggie had told her Jake Cordell wasn't meant to be a father, and if he learned he had a child, he'd end up being miserable. Maggie had said Jake didn't want to be tied down, and she'd made Kit promise not to burden him with the news of his son.

Had Maggie been wrong? Could Jake be ready to settle down?

Kit rubbed her eyes. She didn't have to make a decision this moment, but she couldn't keep ignoring it either. Later . . .

Pasting on a smile, Kit entered the bedroom and held out the suspenders. "Here you go, Jake.''

"Thanks.'' He stood and took them from her, his fingertips brushing hers. "Could you give me a hand?''

She seemed to approach timidly, as if afraid to touch him. Afraid of him? Or of herself? He'd have to be blind and a hundred years old not to notice her reaction to his body in the kitchen. Since he was neither, he knew his attraction to her wasn't one-sided. She wanted him as badly as he wanted her.

He turned around, passing the suspenders over his shoulders. She clipped the ends to his waistband as he listened to her uneven breathing. It took her longer than he thought it should, and he imagined her fingers trembling. Glancing down, he noticed his own hands weren't exactly steady. And he was suddenly glad the trousers were too large.

"There." Her husky voice feathered across him.

"Thanks," he replied, and was surprised by his own raspy tone.

Her gaze flitted from his face and down to his toes, and her cheeks pinkened. "At least you won't lose them now."

At least, not unintentionally.

"When do we get pie?" Johnny asked.

"Oh, I forgot. I'll have to get the kitchen cleaned up first," she said, flustered.

"We alre—"

Jake clamped his palm over Johnny's mouth. "We already, uh, digested our dinner."

Kit looked at him quizzically, then shook her head and hurried out of the bedroom.

Jake lowered his hand.

"Why didn't you let me tell her?" Johnny demanded.

"Because I want to see her face," Jake replied. "Come on, let's go."

Johnny grinned and followed Jake down the stairs. Despite the suspenders, Jake kept a firm hold on his trousers. He paused by the door.

"Ready?" he whispered to the boy.

Johnny nodded eagerly.

They burst into the kitchen.

"Surprise," Jake exclaimed.

Kit stood in the middle of the spotless kitchen.

"When did you have time to clean it up?" she asked, her eyes round behind the spectacles.

"While we were waiting for our clothes," Johnny answered. "It was Mr. Cordell's idea. He said it would shock your drawers off."

Kit's pretty face flushed with embarrassment. "He does have a way with words, doesn't he? How did you get the tub and barrel out?"

"Ethan and Charlie did it," Johnny said.

She glanced questioningly at Jake.

"When Ethan brought our clothes in, I asked him if he and Charlie would take care of them," Jake explained.

"Thank you," Kit said sincerely.

"You're welcome." Jake rubbed his palms together. "Now, where's the pie?"

"Give me a few minutes to put some fresh coffee on." She turned to Johnny. "Run out and get the others."

The boy dashed out the back door, leaving Jake alone with Kit.

She bustled about pumping water into the metal pot. After adding some ground coffee, she set the pot on the stove. Leaning over, she reached into the pie pantry and pulled out four tins.

"I want to thank you for taking care of Johnny," Kit said, as she cut into the first pie. "He adores you, Jake."

"I like him, too," he said. "Reminds me of me."

"Oh?" she commented, her voice breathy.

"Only Johnny's got his mother. By the time I was his age, Ma had left Pa and me."

Kit's heart clenched. "I can't imagine leaving Johnny

behind.'' She met Jake's eyes. "I'd want to crawl away and die if I couldn't be with him.''

"I wish my mother had felt that way." A long-abiding sadness showed on his face. "She must've really hated me."

Kit finished slicing the last pie into fourths, then wiped her hands on her apron. "I can't imagine a mother hating her own child. It seems so unnatural."

"Pa told me one time that some women weren't made to be mothers, and that my ma was one of them." He shrugged nonchalantly. "It was probably for the best, anyhow."

The solicitude and understanding in Kit's eyes made him wonder why his mother couldn't have been more like Kit. It was that all-consuming unconditional love that Jake had searched for all his life and never found.

Kit reached out and laid her slim hand on his arm, her warmth scorching Jake through his shirtsleeve. "You don't believe that, and neither do I." Her gaze became unfocused, as if looking at an image in her mind. "A child needs his mother."

Jake settled his hand over hers, enjoying the silky skin beneath his touch. "Maybe I would've turned out differently if I'd had mine."

The front door opened, and Kit drew away from Jake. Johnny entered the kitchen with the hired men following closely.

"I got 'em, Ma," Johnny announced.

While Kit dished out thick slices of pie, Jake poured coffee. After everyone had eaten their fill, Kit picked up the empty plates.

"We'd best go check on the horses," Charlie said as he stood.

Ethan and Two Ponies also got to their feet, and Kit walked the three men to the door. Jake and Johnny remained sitting by the table.

"Thanks for dinner and all, Miz Thornton," Ethan said bashfully, as he worried his hat brim in his hands.

"You're more than welcome," Kit replied with a smile.

She watched Ethan and Two Ponies walk away, the older Indian speaking to Ethan in his native language. She turned back to Charlie. "Do you need any help with the horses?"

He shook his head. "We can take care of it. Me and Ethan'll take turns sleepin' in the barn in case one of the mares start foalin'."

"All right, but remember to come get me."

"Don't we always?" Fond exasperation colored his words.

Kit grinned ruefully. "Sorry." She sobered, staring off into the growing dusk. "The note's due in a couple weeks. If I don't sell a few horses before then, I'll lose the place."

"You got any buyers?" Charlie asked somberly.

She shook her head. "Sam Roberts from Cheyenne said he was looking to buy more horses. I sent him a telegram a couple of days ago, but I haven't heard from him yet."

"You got a few others that are always interested in your stock. Maybe you should wire them."

"I have. Nobody's ready to buy yet." She took a deep shuddering breath. "After all the sweat that's gone into this place, I can't lose it now. It's all I have to give Johnny."

"You got a lot more to give to that boy than a piece of land. But I know how much this place means to you, and I ain't gonna let anyone take it away from you."

Kit squeezed Charlie's hand. "Thanks, but we might not have any choice. Hopefully things will work out."

"They always do," he reassured. " 'Night, Kit."

"Good night, Charlie."

Closing the door behind him, Kit returned to the front room. "Have you fed the animals, Johnny?"

He shook his head, and pushed himself to his feet. "They're probably hungry."

"What animals?" Jake asked curiously.

"Orphaned and injured ones," Kit replied. "It's Johnny's job to make sure they're fed and watered every day. I check those that have been hurt and make sure they're healing all right."

"You wanna help me, Mr. Cordell?" Johnny asked.

"I'd be glad to give you a hand." Jake glanced at Kit. "Just like I used to help your ma. Back when she was just a few years older than you, I used to help her feed her animals, too. Remember, Kit?"

She nodded and said teasingly, "I seem to recall you bothering me when I was trying to take care of them."

Mock indignation appeared on Jake's face, and he turned to Johnny. "I'll have you know your mother used to put me to work filling the water dishes and cleaning out the cages. I even helped her set a few bones."

"Did he really, Ma?" Johnny asked.

Kit smiled. "Yes, he did, sweetheart—and *he* never complained."

Jake winked at Johnny. "At least, not where your ma could hear. How many animals do you have?"

Johnny began to count them off on his fingers. "There's Salty and Pepper—my two cats—two rabbits, a squirrel, a possum, and Jasper." He glanced at his hands. "That makes seven all together."

"Who's Jasper?"

"A raccoon," Kit supplied. "His leg was caught in a trap."

After Johnny and Jake had left the house, Kit tied an apron about her waist and washed and dried the dishes. The afternoon waned, and Kit went to check on Jake and her son. She entered the barn, closing the door behind her.

As she waited for her eyes to adjust to the relative dimness, she heard Johnny's childish giggles and Jake's deeper chuckles. Before Jake had returned to Chaney, Kit had not allowed herself to imagine father and son together. Now it was all she could think about. It amazed her how quickly Jake had taken to Johnny, since the man had had little contact with children in his line of work.

Jake Cordell faced the biggest challenge of his career. Upon arriving in town, he'd had a feeling, a sixth sense, that something would happen, something he wouldn't like, something he'd never imagined could happen.

He checked his rugged face in the beveled mirror one last time, then slapped his Stetson on his recently trimmed hair. Adjusting the holster on his hip, he hoped he wouldn't have to use his Colt. Its weight gave him a sense of security, and he strode out of his hotel room down to the street below. His spurs jingled with each confident step, reminding him he was the fearless bounty hunter who never flinched from danger.

Reaching his destination, he paused, his courage floundering for a moment. Then, valiantly, he squared his broad shoulders, entered the schoolhouse, and came face to face with twenty bright-eyed, awe-filled children.

Kit moved deeper into the barn. Spying Jake sitting on an overturned bucket, Kit stopped. Salty was leaping up to try to snag Jake's too-short trousers to climb his leg, while Pepper had planted himself on Jake's wide shoulder.

Coming to his rescue, Kit tugged Salty off his leg and cuddled the small animal close to her chest.

"Looks like you've got your hands full," she said mischievously.

Jake grimaced as Pepper bumped its tiny head against his chin. "I think they know I don't like cats."

"I wouldn't be surprised. They seem to have a sixth sense about things like that. Besides, in their own way, they're trying to convince you they're not so bad."

Johnny lifted Pepper from Jake's shoulder. Salty purred in Kit's hands, his eyes closing, and Kit lowered herself to the hay-covered floor beside Jake.

"Why do you still collect them?" Jake asked curiously. "I would think you'd have more than enough to keep you busy."

"They needed help."

Jake thought for a moment. "Nobody helped you when you were a child, did they?"

Kit blinked, startled by his observation. "*You* helped me."

"I didn't do that much, just made sure you were okay and gave you a hand with your pets once in a while," Jake replied.

"That was more than anybody else did." She buried her face in the kitten's fuzzy coat to hide the moisture in her eyes.

Jake laid his hand on Kit's bowed back. "If it's any consolation, I kept an eye out for you after those boys tripped you that day."

She raised her head slowly and nodded. "I know." She frowned quizzically. "I was only a chubby little girl with crooked glasses. Why would the handsomest boy in town help me?"

He shrugged. "I don't know. Maybe I saw some of me in you."

Kit laid her palm on the kitten's warm body, and his loud purrs vibrated against her hand. "I had a crush on you."

He appeared surprised, then chagrined. "I never knew."

"You weren't supposed to. I would've been mortified." She attempted a rueful smile. "Besides, Jake Cordell and Kit Thornton had nothing in common.''

Jake cupped her cheek, studying her with sympathetic eyes. ''Yes, they did.''

Kit's skin tingled beneath his caress. ''What?''

''We were both lonely.''

Chapter 11

~~~~~~~~~~

K it's crystal-clear gaze glimmered with disbelief, then acceptance of his words. Jake wondered if she realized how telling her eyes were.

"I never thought of you as lonely," she said. "Everyone liked you, and you were always smiling."

"You can get away with a lot more if you smile." He didn't tell her a smile could also hide a world of hurt; he suspected she already knew.

"Why did you go to college?"

Jake thought a moment. He remembered the endless arguments, the angry words he'd exchanged with his father. "Because Judge Cordell ordered me to."

"He was your father, Jake. He only wanted what he thought was best for you." She studied him with a probing, unsettling gaze. "Besides, if you truly didn't want to go to college, you wouldn't have."

Taken aback by her matter-of-fact comment, Jake kept his face impassive as he shrugged. "Hell, maybe I thought he'd finally notice me." A harsh laugh escaped him. "He was killed right after I graduated, before I could find out."

She curled her long slender fingers around his forearm. "You always had his respect and love, Jake."

187

The conviction in her tone unbalanced him. "If that's true, why didn't he tell me?"

"He wasn't a man prone to flowery words. He probably thought you knew how he felt."

Knowing he shouldn't, but unable to stop himself, Jake covered her hand with his. "I knew what he thought of me, all right."

The lantern's subdued arc softened her features, blunting her wire-rimmed spectacles. Her concern, like a candle's glow, swirled around him, encompassing him. He thought of his nightmares, filled with violence, and shuddered. "You don't know what kind of man I am, the things I've seen and done—things you can't even imagine."

She shook her head. "I know more than you think. When you're on the outside looking in, you watch everything, all the time wondering what made you so different from everybody else. And you learn a lot about people."

Sadness reflected in her eyes as she gazed at him, her deceptively delicate chin tilted upward as if daring him to shut her out, too. Strong yet fragile, bold yet tentative, a mother yet an innocent. Kit Thornton was a bundle of contradictions that both intrigued and irritated Jake.

Unlike other women, she refused to take him at face value, and the chance that she'd find the man beneath the facade disturbed him. The real Jake Cordell was no legend, no herald of justice, and definitely no gentleman.

"Do you know why it took me six years to hunt down my father's murderer?" Jake asked.

Kit shook her head.

"Because I was afraid I'd fail. My father would've tracked him down in a month or two. I took six years. The whole time I could feel my father standing over me, judging me."

"But what about all the other outlaws you brought in?"

"Whenever I lost Ross's trail, I would concentrate on a different bounty. Then I'd hear my father's voice, telling me I'd never amount to anything, and I'd get back to looking for Ross."

The white kitten in Kit's lap climbed up to perch on her shoulder. Jake reached forward to lift it down, but she stilled his motion with a shake of her head. "Maybe it wasn't your father's voice, but your own," she said softly. She gazed up at him, a few pieces of straw scattered across her lap and in her flaxen hair. "Why do you really want the ranch, Jake?"

"I told you—to raise horses," he replied irritably.

She shook her head. "If that were the reason, you could buy another place and do the same thing. Your father's gone, Jake. You don't have to prove anything to him; it's only yourself you have to prove something to."

Unwilling to examine her words too closely, Jake said, "You don't understand." He glanced over at Johnny, who dangled a string in front of a playful Pepper, then looked back at Kit. "Who was Johnny's father?" he asked in a low voice.

Defensiveness sprang to her features. "Why do you want to know?"

He shrugged. "Curiosity, mainly. You don't seem the type to put the horse before the carriage."

Her wariness eased, replaced by a twinkling of humor. "Or to give the milk without selling the cow?"

Jake felt unaccountably embarrassed. "Something like that."

She stared at her son, who sat on the straw-littered floor out of earshot. Affection glowed in her face as she turned back to Jake. "I adopted him."

The unexpected answer shocked Jake. By the love that

she showered on the boy, Jake hadn't even considered they might not be blood kin.

"What happened?" Jake managed to ask.

"His mother died shortly after he was born. There was no other family, so I took him in." She paused, absently petting the mewling kitten curled around the back of her neck. "Johnny doesn't know. Someday when he's old enough to understand, I'll tell him."

"So he's just another stray?"

She stabbed him with a piercing look. "Even though I didn't bring him into this world, Johnny *is* my son."

He held up his hands, palms out in surrender. "Sorry. Anyone ever tell you you're too soft-hearted, Kit?"

Anger changed her eyes to a stormy gray. "You make caring for someone sound like a curse."

"No, not a curse, more like a millstone around your neck."

Her defensiveness slid away. "Loving someone isn't a burden, it's a blessing."

Jake wanted to believe her, but he knew from experience she was wrong. "Tell my mother that."

"At least you had your father."

"The *town* had my father."

She pursed her lips like a tart-tongued spinster.

"I'm not like you, Kit," Jake said. "I can't forgive and forget."

"I'm not asking you to. That's something you'll have to decide to do for yourself," she said softly.

How could a woman her age be so naive? Didn't she realize there were some things a person couldn't forget? Or forgive? He thought of the loan papers hidden in his room at Freda's. She wouldn't be so understanding when he took her beloved ranch; she wouldn't be able to forgive and forget.

Jake smothered the unwanted guilt. "Didn't you know? I'm a selfish bastard."

She laughed. "You don't have to try and convince me. I already know what you are."

So she already thought he was a bastard? Hadn't he wanted her to see him without the damned blinders? However, it didn't mollify Jake like it should've, and sarcasm oozed from his tone. "Thanks."

"What I meant was, I know you're *not* that kind of person, so there's no reason to berate yourself."

"How about when I was drunk? I was a bastard then."

She nodded thoughtfully. "That's true enough. And don't forget—when you met Freda the first time, you weren't a gentleman then, either."

Bewildered, Jake raked his fingers through his hair. "It sure didn't take much to convince you."

She leaned forward. "Look, Jake, you're not the same man who rode into Chaney a month ago. I think you might finally be figuring out you're not as bad as you thought you were."

"Damn it, Kit, do you always have to see the best in people?"

"Yes."

Her direct answer and unflinching gaze melted a corner of Jake's heart. She laid a hand on his knee, and her touch sent a jolt of heated pleasure up his leg to settle in his groin.

"Johnny, come get Salty and put him in with Pepper," Kit said.

Johnny deposited the protesting kitten in the cage and played with the animals through the chicken wire.

Jake stood and held out his hand to Kit. Tentatively, she reached out, placing her cool fingers in his palm, and he grasped them snugly to pull her to her feet.

"You'd better be careful, Jake; someone might think you *are* a gentleman," Kit teased.

He studied her flushed expression, the sparkling blue

eyes behind her spectacles. She trusted him. He could see it in her candid expression. Unexpected resentment welled within him. "You don't know me any better than T. K. Thorne."

She drew out of his grasp and met his gaze evenly. "Because I see the good in you?"

"Because you won't see me for who I really am," he refuted. "T. K. Thorne built the reputation of Jake Cordell. It's his fault I keep looking over my shoulder, and it's his fault people think I'm a damned hero."

Kit's face drained of color. "I'm sure he never meant to hurt you, Jake. He wrote them as a tribute to you, to show everyone your bravery as you fought to bring justice to the lawless frontier."

"How would you know why he wrote them?" He shook his head. "He did it for the same reason people rob banks: to get rich at the expense of another person."

"That's not true. He did it because he admired you."

Jake grabbed her upper arms. "Damn it, Kit, open your eyes." He glanced down at her full lips. "I'll show you I'm not like that make-believe hero."

He drew her willowy body against his. Her full, rounded breasts flattened against his chest and brought a flare of arousal. His gaze fastened on her rosy lips, sending his blood on a reckless journey through his veins. He had to teach her she couldn't trust him.

"Are you going to kiss my ma?"

Johnny's innocent question doused him like a bucket of cold water, and Jake released Kit. She stepped back, her bosom rising and falling with her ragged breaths.

"No, he isn't," Kit replied, her voice husky. "We're going to the house to have some supper."

Her spine as stiff as a pitchfork handle, she turned, leading the way out of the barn. Jake grabbed the lantern and followed, Johnny walking beside him. His appreciative gaze followed Kit's backside as it moved enticingly beneath the layers of skirts and petticoats, and his arousal grew painful. He swore to himself and mentally reviewed torts and writs and habeas corpus to distract his lecherous thoughts.

"You want to play with me?" Johnny asked.

"Sure." Anything would be better than keeping images of Kit at bay with a mental law exam.

Jake took the boy's outstretched hand and allowed himself to be tugged along to the house. He blew out the lantern and left it on the porch, then followed Johnny inside. The boy disappeared into the front room.

Jake noticed Kit's flushed cheeks. "Are you warm?" he asked too innocently.

Kit lay her palm against the side of her face. "It must've been the walk from the barn."

Jake moved closer to her. "Or maybe you're disappointed we got interrupted."

She blinked. "Of course not."

He smiled rakishly, using the persuasive skills he'd perfected with countless women. "I think you're lying."

"I thought we were friends."

"We are, but not as close as we could be." Jake played his game well.

Her pupils dilated, and she moistened her lips with the tip of her tongue. "Don't do this, Jake."

He leaned closer until he could feel her moist breath on his neck. "I haven't done anything. Yet."

She took a step back, her whole body poised to bolt like a frightened doe. "I have to get supper on. Are you hungry?"

Jake placed his palms against the wall on either side of Kit, effectively trapping her between his arms. "Ravenous."

"Then let me go to the kitchen."

She ducked under his arm, but he caught her around the waist, the underside of her breasts resting on his forearm. With her back against his chest, he could smell her fresh-scented hair as it tickled his nose. "Who said anything about food?"

She trembled like a frightened bird, and the image brought a pang of conscience. He thrust the emotion aside, instead giving in to the passion that flowed and ebbed within him. With his free hand he swept her hair aside and nibbled her velvet-soft earlobe. Moving downward, he tasted the sweet saltiness of her skin. He felt more than heard her throaty moan, and the sound unleashed an answering need within himself.

As her stiff body relaxed, her curved bottom pressed against his rigid desire. He closed his eyes, giving in to the tortuous pleasure she unwittingly gave him.

"Jake . . ." Kit's voice made him drag his lids open. "Yes?"

"We can't . . ."

Her pulse throbbed in her slender neck, and he skimmed his lips across the satiny skin. Trailing kisses along her jaw, he turned her in his arms until they faced one another. The scent of cinnamon invaded his senses, and he smiled slightly. He'd never lain with a woman who didn't smell like cheap liquor or cheaper perfume—usually both.

"Johnny—"

"What about him?" He buried his fingers in her golden hair, trapping the silky strands in his palms. Leaning forward, he lightly pressed his lips to a corner of her mouth, and moved downward to the top of her starched collar.

She gasped, her hands moving to his back, touching, sweeping across his shirt. Her movements were at first tentative, then bolder as she became an active participant in the game he'd instigated.

Lust coursed through his body, erasing all reason, all thought of teaching her a lesson. He wanted her lying below him, crying out his name as he pleasured her body.

"Johnny might see us."

Her husky words made it past the thunder that filled his ears. Reluctantly he drew back, his body aching with frustrated need. If the boy hadn't been there, he wasn't sure if he would've been able to halt his lesson before he went too far. "One of these days, it'll just be you and me."

Her face crimson, Kit said, "I don't think that would be wise."

Studying the alarm in her wide eyes, he asked, "Did I scare you?"

She shook her head. "No."

There wasn't even a hint of hesitancy in her tone. He'd failed to show her the real Jake Cordell. With an impatient hand, he rubbed his whiskered jaw. "I want you, Kit, but I can't promise you anything, because I've got nothing to give."

She reached out and laid her hand on his arm. "Love isn't something you choose to give or keep, Jake. It either is or it isn't."

He frowned. "You sound like you speak from experience."

After a moment, she nodded thoughtfully. "Maybe I do."

Unexpected jealousy snared him abruptly and painfully. The alien emotion stymied him. Why should he care if she'd loved someone else?

"Johnny's waiting for you in the front room," Kit said. "I'll call you when I have supper ready."

She hurried away like hell's hounds were nipping at her heels.

"Well, Jake, you went and did it this time," he muttered, raking his fingers through his tousled hair. "Good thing she's got more sense than you."

He joined Johnny in the front room. The boy motioned him over, and Jake settled gingerly on the rug beside him, grateful his trousers were too large. He studied the layout of the stick corrals and assorted wooden horses. "This looks like Ki—your ma's ranch."

Johnny nodded. "It's going to be mine someday. Ma said so."

Guilt punched Jake in the gut. He hadn't considered Johnny in his scheme to regain his father's ranch. Getting the place from Kit was bad enough, but robbing a boy of his future didn't set well on Jake's mind.

Since Johnny wasn't actually Kit's flesh and blood, though, it wasn't like he was stealing the boy's heritage. If Jake's father hadn't thought so little of him, he would've left it to his own son, and the land would've remained in the Cordell family. The ranch rightfully belonged to Jake.

"Don't you want to leave Chaney and see the rest of the world?" Jake asked.

Johnny picked up a black toy horse and trotted it into a corral. "I wouldn't want to leave Ma alone. She needs me."

"She'd have Charlie and Ethan and Two Ponies."

The boy planted his elbow on his knee and propped his chin in his hand. "Yeah, but I think she'd miss me. I wouldn't want her to be sad."

Jake figured that was an understatement. Johnny meant the world to Kit. "Would you miss her?"

Johnny rearranged a toy corral. "Maybe a little."

Johnny was trying so hard to act grown up. "I know what you mean. So, what are the names of your horses?"

Kit moved about the kitchen in a daze, her body still tingling in all the spots Jake had caressed. And some he hadn't. She leaned against the counter and crossed her arms below her breasts, which ached with a wanting she'd never experienced. However, it was more than her physical reaction to Jake's masterful caresses that bothered her. Something much more devastating.

She thought she'd overcome her girlhood infatuation with him, but her racing heartbeat as he'd nearly seduced her belied that notion. This time, however, she saw him as he was, instead of as the shining knight she'd seen him as since she'd been a child. He was right. He wasn't the perfect man she'd portrayed in the dime novels, but neither was he the prodigal he believed himself to be. He thought he was incapable of loving or being loved, but she'd watched him with Johnny and she knew otherwise.

And therein lay the danger. Now she was an adult, with the desires of a woman. She'd thought loving Johnny would be enough. Now she knew it wasn't.

Although naive, Kit recognized her own awakening passions in Jake's arms. Yet, understanding why Maggie had taken what he'd given without asking for more, she couldn't give herself without his love.

And even if Jake found this love he swore he didn't possess, there also lay the truth of Johnny's parentage between them. Jake would be angry at first, but she suspected he would be able to forgive her.

The last and largest stumbling block was her identity as T. K. Thorne. If she confessed to being the infamous author, she feared she'd lose his friendship.

Burying her face in her hands, Kit gave in to her self-pity. Her attraction to Jake couldn't be allowed to flourish. The insurmountable obstacles between them couldn't be overcome.

She tried to forget how Jake's muscles had felt beneath her hands, and the burning trail his sensuous lips had forged across her jaw and neck. She tried to forget how his masculinity had been plainly outlined when she'd seen him standing in the tub.

She tried to forget her body's traitorous reaction to his long-dreamed-of kisses.

Straightening, she squared her shoulders and placed the meal on the table, then walked to the front room.

In the doorway, she paused to watch Jake and Johnny bent over the toy animals, overcome with melancholy.

Jake Cordell had never missed one before, and he wasn't about to miss one now. He leaned low over Zeus's neck, urging the powerful stallion into a ground-eating gait. Laying a hand on the saddlebags, Jake was reassured that the precious package still lay inside. He'd taken an extra day to find the famed carver, but the man's work had been well worth it.

The ranch came into view, and Jake slowed his trusty steed. Drinking in the familiar picture, Jake wished he could hang his gun up for good. All he ever needed or wanted was found here behind the sturdy log walls of the Cordell home.

Despite his impatience, Jake cared for Zeus's needs first with a rubdown and an extra helping of fresh hay. His tasks completed, Jake threw his saddlebags over his shoulder and strode to the house. He opened the door and breathed deeply of the comforting smells of meat frying on the stove and cedar crackling in the fireplace.

"Pa!"

Jake caught his young son in his arms, tossed him in the air, and caught him as the boy laughed with glee.

"Jake, you made it." His beautiful wife's melodic voice washed across him and made him glad he'd pushed himself to exhaustion to return home in time.

He shifted his boy to one arm and gathered his wife close in the other. He'd missed them more than he'd thought possible.

"It's my birthday, Pa," the boy exclaimed, his cheeks rosy. "And Ma made me a cake!"

"I was afraid you'd miss it," his wife said softly.

Jake shook his head. "Not as long as I have a breath of life in me."

He set the boy down and hunkered down beside him to open his saddlebags. Jake drew out a package tied with string, and handed it to him. "Happy birthday, son."

Jake stood and wrapped his arm around his wife's tiny waist, drawing her flush against his lean-angled body. Together they watched as the boy tugged on the string to open the present.

He held the horse carving up to them. "It's Zeus."

"That's right," Jake said. "Do you like it?"

"I love it, Pa. Thank you." He threw his arms around Jake's waist and hugged him.

Jake's throat ached with raw emotion. The joy in his son's face erased all the aches and pains of five days of hard riding. He swore he wouldn't leave them again.

He wouldn't chance missing his son's birthday ever again.

Misty eyed, Kit shook herself free of her fantasy.

"Supper's ready," she announced,

Identical pairs of brown eyes looked up, and Jake and Johnny got to their feet.

She led the way to the dining room. "Would you like to say the blessing, Johnny?"

He nodded and clasped his hands. "Thank you for getting all the skunk smell off me and Mr. Cordell. And thanks for the food. Amen."

"I like your style, Johnny—short and to the point," Jake said.

Kit smiled. "God listens to everyone."

Jake forked a few pieces of ham onto his plate. "You really believe that?"

"Of course. Don't you?"

He shrugged. "I used to, until I grew up."

Whether Jake knew it or not, there was a part of him

that still believed. If he didn't, he wouldn't have re-turned to Chaney.

Toward the end of the meal, Johnny's eyelids began to close.

"It looks like you're ready for bed, young man," Kit said.

"But me and Mr. Cordell haven't gone riding yet," he protested in a sleepy voice.

"I'll make you a deal," Jake said. "I'll tuck you in, and next time I come, we'll take twice as long a ride."

"Promise?"

"Jake Cordell's word is as good as gold, kid." He stood and came around to steer Johnny up the stairs. Kit remained seated, feeling guilty for enjoying watching father and son together.

Upstairs, Jake tugged Johnny's nightshirt on the boy.

"There you go. Now, hop into bed," Jake said.

Johnny plopped onto the mattress, his eyes closing before Jake had the blankets tucked in around him. He rested a light hand on Johnny's hair. The vulnerability in the boy's serene face brought a stab of self-contempt. When Johnny looked at him with idolizing eyes, he saw someone who didn't exist. For the first time, Jake wished he was the hero Johnny thought he was.

How could he take the ranch from Kit, knowing he'd also be taking away the only home Johnny had ever known? If she didn't make the last payment, Jake could legally seize the place, but Johnny wouldn't understand that was his right.

Jake was a lawyer, not a minister. So why did he feel lower than a flat frog in an empty well?

"Good night, kid," he said softly.

Stomach churning, he quickly retreated from the moonlit room.

Kit met him at the bottom of the stairs. "Here's your clothes. They're still a little damp, but I'm sure you'd rather go back to town in these than in what you have on.''

Jake glanced down at the ridiculously short trousers and snug shirt. Taking the pile of clothing from her arms, he looked around for a place to change. Kit pointed to the kitchen. "Go ahead and change in there. I'll wait in the front room."

"How do I know I can trust you? You seem to like seeing me in my unmentionables."

"That wasn't the first time I'd seen you in your unmentionables." She crossed her arms, her eyes twinkling impishly. "Do you remember how you and Harvey Olson used to go skinny dipping?"

Incredulous, Jake said, "You watched us?"

Kit shrugged. "Let's just say, that summer I learned what made boys and girls different."

"Miss Thornton, you should be ashamed of yourself."

"You're probably right, but I'm not."

"Don't ever stop surprising me, Kit."

He hurried into the kitchen, humming "Buffalo Gal" as he went. After changing into his clammy clothes, he rejoined Kit in the parlor. She rose from a spindle-legged chair.

"I'd best get back to town," he said.

She nodded, averting her gaze. "Yes, I suppose you'd better."

Temptation urged him closer. "I'd prefer to stay."

"No. That wouldn't be a good idea." Boldly, she met his eyes. "I'm not like the people in town think I am. I don't give my favors freely or otherwise."

"I know."

She shuffled her feet. "Well, I suppose this is good night, then."

"Actually, *this* is good night."

Cupping her face between his palms, he tilted her

head upward. Her wide, luminous eyes followed his descent, and he drew his tongue along her sweet lips, coaxing her to open them. She complied, allowing his tender invasion, and he explored her satiny softness. Wrapping her arms around his neck, she twined her fingers through his hair to draw him closer.

Jake tried to tell himself this was a continuation of her lesson, a delicious game. His body, however, had other plans, and his mind filled with Kit's intoxicating innocence. He had to stop before he got carried away.

But her slender curves fit against his jagged planes as if made to complement him, and with one hand he followed the indentation of her waist and skimmed down her hip, which was camouflaged by the dress's gathers.

As his breath grew ragged, he drew away from her. A gasp escaped Kit's parted lips, and Jake wanted more than a kiss. He wanted to remove her clothing one article at a time. He wanted to see her quiver below him in the throes of ecstasy, her golden hair fanned about her head. He wanted his name to be on her lips when he buried himself in her welcoming heat.

Taking a step back, he managed to say, "I'd better go."

Kit cleared her throat. "I'll get your coat."

She returned with his jacket draped over her arm and his hat in her hand. "Here you are."

He nodded, uncertain he could voice a coherent sentence, and slipped on his coat. Taking his Stetson, he held it between his hands, spinning it around. "Goodnight, Kit."

"I liked the other goodnight better," she said softly.

"Me, too, but they're a helluva lot more dangerous."

Saucy impertinence lit her face. "It's a good thing Jake Cordell lives for danger."

Shy, yet brash. Another contradiction.

"Thanks for dinner, Kit." Jake lifted a hand in farewell, then slipped into the cool night air. Toby greeted him with a wet tongue, but Jake enjoyed the company as he strolled to the barn where Zeus awaited him.

"Well, fellah, I almost did it this time," he said, as he saddled his palomino. "But even I'm not low enough to bed her, then take her ranch."

Zeus snorted and swished his tail.

Jake tightened the cinch. "Okay. Maybe I could've done something like that when I was younger, but not now. And sure as hell not to Kit."

Jake led Zeus outside and swung into the saddle. He took a last lingering look at the house. Yellow light spilled out of two windows, then only one.

"Think she's watching?" he asked in a low voice.

Zeus pawed at the ground and tossed his head.

"No one's ever worried about me before," Jake said thoughtfully.

Shaking aside the unfamiliar emotion, he urged Zeus out of the yard and down the long, dark road. His thoughts centered on the day, from Johnny's skunk incident to his near-seduction of Kit. His lesson in trust had backfired. Kit's willingness had scattered his wits and sharpened his hunger for her. Drawn to her tenderheartedness, yet not understanding her belief in him, Jake was torn. He wasn't capable of caring for a woman like her. He belonged with saloon gals who didn't ask for anything more than a good time in bed and a few well-earned dollars.

Then why didn't he just relieve the frustration in his groin with one of those women?

Because he didn't want them. He wanted Kit.

Shaking aside his disturbing thoughts, he pondered his decision to take the ranch. Imagining the adoration in Johnny's dark eyes changing to anger and disappointment, Jake wasn't sure he could live with that on his conscience. He didn't know anymore if the ranch was worth a little boy's trust.

An idea sifted into Jake's mind. If he married Kit, Johnny would be able to grow up in the only home he'd known. And Jake could satisfy his body's cravings for Kit. Even though she was inexperienced, her response to his caresses told him she'd be a passionate bed partner.

"What do you think, Zeus? How would you like to live in that nice, warm barn? All the oats you could eat? You'd get fat and lazy in no time."

Zeus neighed.

Jake laughed. "Are you saying if I married her, I'd get fat and lazy, too?" He patted the horse's neck. "I have a feeling I'd be busier than I've ever been, both during the day and at night, if you get my drift."

Zeus snorted and sidestepped nervously.

Jake sobered instantly. "What is it, boy?"

Barely registering the gunshots, he felt Zeus stumble. Jake instinctively kicked free of the stirrups. Then pain exploded in his skull as he tumbled to the ground with a bone-jarring jolt that sent awareness fleeing into darkness.

Chapter 12

Kit watched Jake until the darkness swallowed him, then dropped the curtain back in place. Loneliness invaded her, surprising her with its sharp pang. It had been a long time since she'd felt so alone.

A pounding on the door startled her; irrationally thinking Jake had returned, she threw it open.

Ethan stood in the entrance. ''The roan is gettin' set to drop her foal.''

Her disappointment was quickly replaced by a surge of excitement. Grabbing her old coat from a hook, she followed Ethan across the yard. Halfway to the barn, faint gunshots broke the evening's silence.

Kit grasped Ethan's arm. ''Where'd those come from?''

He shook his head. ''Sounded like a ways down the road.''

''It wouldn't be hunters after dark,'' Kit said. Her blood ran cold. ''Jake left about ten minutes ago.''

''Don't you go thinking something happened to him. Those shots could've been anything,'' Ethan reassured.

''Like what?'' Kit demanded.

The young man shifted nervously. ''Like anything.''

205

"Were those shots I heard?" Charlie called from the barn door.

Kit and Ethan joined him.

"Sounded like it," Ethan said.

"I'm going to find out if it was Jake," Kit said, her voice hoarse with apprehension. She closed her eyes a moment to gather her disarrayed thoughts. "You two stay here and deliver that foal."

"That don't take two of us," Charlie stated. "Ethan, you go on with Miz Thornton."

The young man nodded curtly. Five minutes later, Kit and Ethan raced down the hard-packed path leading to town. Kit tried not to think about Jake lying dead on the side of the road. She trembled uncontrollably, and Cassie stumbled as if sensing Kit's anxiety.

"We'll find him even if we have to go all the way into town," Ethan said.

Kit glanced up at the boy's resolute face and mustered a smile for his sake.

She tried to convince herself that they'd find Jake safe and warm at Freda's. After all, he was the infamous Jake Cordell.

Gunshots rang out all around Jake. He dived behind a water trough, pulling his trusty Colt from his holster as he moved with a grace few men could equal. Raising his head cautiously above his protective barrier, he fired in the direction of the ambushers.

A bullet kicked up dust beside him and he rolled over, but he couldn't see any sign of his attackers. His sixth sense told him they surrounded him, waiting to pick him off like a tin can at a turkey shoot.

Sunlight glinted off a rifle barrel sticking out from a rooftop across the street, and Jake lifted his revolver. Before he could fire, a burning pain exploded in his back. He fell forward, facedown on the dusty street.

He had to move, to get away, but his muscles wouldn't

obey his commands. The sun grew dimmer, the pain more intense, and Jake knew he had little time left on this world.

Backshot by a craven coward. It wasn't the way Jake Cordell had figured on dying.

He gazed up at the sky, wishing he'd had one more day, one more hour, to prepare. Ruby red blood poured from his wound, saturating his shirt and disappearing into the thirsty earth beneath him.

His lungs rattled, struggling to prolong the inevitable a moment longer. Regrets haunted him, and moisture hazed his vision. There would be no one to mourn his passing, and no son to carry on his name.

Jake Cordell took his last breath and lay still, dying as he'd been destined to do: alone.

Kit sobbed, then shook her head fiercely. What if she'd brought about Jake's death?

Suddenly Ethan halted his horse and took hold of Kit's reins.

"There's something up ahead," he said in a low voice. "You stay here. I'll go check it out."

"I'm going with you," Kit stated firmly.

Ethan gazed at her a long moment, and sent her a quick nod. "All right, but stay behind me."

As Kit followed him, she swallowed the bitter bile rising in her throat. *Dear God, what if Jake was dead? What if he died not knowing he had a son?*

Ethan dismounted by the body lying on the dirt road, and Kit joined him. She recognized Jake's coat immediately, and at the sight of the bloodstains soaking the collar, blackness crowded her vision as the world spun around her.

"He's still alive," Ethan said, his voice sounding far away. "Looks like a bullet grazed his head. That's why there's so much blood."

Jake came back into focus, and with shaking fingers,

Kit touched his marble-cold cheek. "We have to get him back to the ranch."

Ethan nodded shortly.

Working together, Kit and Ethan managed to lift Jake into Ethan's saddle. Kit held the horse steady while the young man got up behind him and put his arms around Jake's chest to keep him from tumbling to the ground.

The ride back to the ranch seemed to stretch into hours. Charlie came out to help Ethan carry the wounded man into the spare bedroom and Kit scrambled about the kitchen, heating water and gathering clean rags and bandages. In her haste, she splashed hot water on her hand, but ignored the pain.

He couldn't die, not before he knew Johnny was his son. How could she live with herself if that happened?

Kit entered the bedroom carrying a pan of steaming water. Her gaze fell on Jake's blood-smeared face, and her stomach dipped. "Any change?"

Ethan shook his head.

Kit squeezed the excess water out of a cloth, and began to dab at the drying blood on Jake's forehead. "Ride into town and get Dr. Lewis."

Ethan grabbed his hat and hurried off to do as she'd bid.

"How's it look?" Charlie asked.

"He's bled a lot, but that's normal with head wounds," Kit replied. She cleaned the shallow furrow on the side of his forehead.

"You need any help?"

Kit shook her head. "I can handle it. How's the mare doing?"

"Should have a new foal in a few hours," Charlie replied.

"Good," Kit said. "As soon as I can, I'll come out to see her."

Charlie laid a hand on her back. "You stay with Jake. I can deliver the foal by myself."

The hired man left the room, and Kit wrapped a bandage around Jake's wound to staunch the trickle of blood. Completing her task, she rested her elbows on her thighs. Her body trembled with exhaustion and concern.

It was past midnight when the sound of hooves alerted Kit to Ethan's return with the doctor. A few minutes later, Dr. Lewis trudged up the stairs, his shirttails haphazardly tucked into his pants. His unshaven face and rumpled hair told Kit that Ethan had gotten the doctor out of bed.

"What's this about someone getting shot?" Dr. Lewis demanded.

Kit pointed to Jake lying on the bed. "Somebody ambushed him as he rode back to town."

"Damned inconsiderate of him," Lewis muttered.

"It wasn't Jake's fault," Kit defended.

He leaned over Jake and lifted the bandage, then examined the wound. "Looks like he was shot."

Kit glanced at Ethan, who stared at Lewis like he was a few pickles shy of a barrel. She reminded herself of the doctor's eccentricity and kept her voice calm. "That's right. A bullet grazed his forehead."

"Well, if you knew that, why'd you drag me out here?"

"I want to be sure it didn't crack his skull."

Dr. Lewis re-covered the injury. "No such luck. He's got a head harder'n my late wife's flapjacks. She was a good woman, just couldn't cook."

"So he'll be all right?" Kit asked.

"Why wouldn't he? Keep that wound cleaned good." He reached into his bag and gave her a bottle. "When he wakes up, he'll have a whale of a headache. Give him some of this powder mixed in a glass of water, or whiskey would work, too."

"I think I'll stick with the water," she said dryly.

He shrugged. "It doesn't matter none to me."

Kit sighed. "Thanks, Dr. Lewis. I really appreciate your coming out to check on him."

"No problem, Miss Thornton. Been proven folks get too much sleep, anyhow. Me, I try to keep it to about four hours a night."

She wondered if she should suggest he get a few more, but thought better of it. "Why don't you go down into the kitchen with Ethan and have a cup of coffee before you head back?"

"You got tea? Coffee gives me the jitters."

"I'm sure we can find you some tea," Kit assured him.

She watched Ethan escort Dr. Lewis out of the room.

Relieved that Jake wouldn't suffer any lasting effects, Kit allowed herself to relax. She lowered herself to the edge of the bed and studied his pallor. Smoothing back the burnished hair from his forehead, Kit rested her palm against the side of his face. His whiskers rasped her skin, sending liquid heat spiraling through her veins.

She'd never really thought about the differences between men and women, until Jake. Her face was smooth, while his was rougher, more rugged. She took hold of his hand, clasping it between hers, willing him to wake up. Her fingers were long and slender, his blunt and callused. Brushing a fingertip across the back of his hand, she felt a light dusting of hair. The sensation triggered a tingle in her stomach.

"What happened to Mr. Cordell?"

Johnny's frightened voice startled her, and she turned to see her son standing behind her, his eyes wide with fear as he stared down at Jake.

Kit gently rested Jake's hand on his chest, then put

an arm around her son's shoulders. "He was shot, honey, but Dr. Lewis said he'll be all right."

"Is he sleeping?"

"In a way," she replied. "It's his body's way of trying to make him better."

Johnny moved closer to Kit, wrapping his arm around her neck. Settling the boy on her knee, Kit rested her cheek against his soft, thick hair, so much like his father's.

"When will he wake up?" Johnny whispered.

"I don't know. Remember when Ethan got thrown by Midnight?"

Her son nodded. "Charlie said he'd be okay because he had a hard head."

Kit smiled. "That's right. Well, Mr. Cordell has a hard head, too, but just like Ethan, he'll sleep for a while until his body heals some on its own."

She tightened her hold around him. "Don't worry; he'll be all right." *He has to be.* She eased Johnny down to stand and released him. "Why don't you go back to bed? I'm sure Mr. Cordell will be better in the morning."

Reluctantly, Johnny did as she'd said.

Sometime later, Charlie came up to let her know the roan had had a healthy colt. Pleasure mixed with sadness. It was the first foaling Kit had missed, and it might be the last one she'd have a chance to witness on her ranch.

Remaining beside Jake all night, Kit dozed lightly in the chair a few times. By early morning some color had returned to his cheeks, and he seemed to be resting easier.

Johnny joined her in the coral glow of the sunrise, and he reclined on her lap quietly. It was as if he sensed her need to hold him, and ease his anxiety.

As she stroked Johnny's downy hair in an absent caress, her thoughts centered on Jake. He deserved to know the truth about Johnny. Maggie had known the young hellraiser, not the man he'd become. Though he was a man who said he didn't know love or want a family, Kit had seen what lay behind his defensive shield. He'd been searching for a place to call home his whole life, and she had it in her power to give him his family, a reason to plant roots.

She listened to the even breathing of father and son, able to admit she'd done wrong by both of them. After Jake recovered, she'd tell him the truth and face the consequences. She only hoped they both could forgive her.

The buzz in Jake's ears increased to a dull roar, and he pressed his hand to his temple. Pain exploded at the point of contact, and he grunted. Opening his eyes, he blinked at the dimness surrounding him. Disoriented, he tried to distinguish anything that would give him a clue as to where he was. He wasn't lying on the hard ground, but it didn't feel like his bed at Freda's, either.

Frowning, he attempted to push back the opaque veil that hid the events following his departure. He'd spent Easter day at Kit's, and had left in the evening. His memory surged back. He'd been shot.

Gingerly, he touched the bandage on his forehead. The bullet must've grazed him. No wonder his head throbbed like a hangover. Of course, if his ambusher had had better aim, a headache would be the least of his worries. He'd have been busy trying to talk his way out of an overdue appointment with Old Nick.

Shifting his position, he could make out a figure sitting in a chair beside the bed. He blinked and the image coalesced into two persons, a child on a woman's lap.

Kit and Johnny.

They must've found him and brought him back to the

ranch. His eyelids drooped, demanding more rest for his injured body, but Jake kept his gaze focused on Kit and her son. Nobody had ever sat with him, worried about him. Now twice in less than a month, Kit had given him her concern without any strings attached.

His breath caught in his throat. He didn't want to contemplate a life with her always caring for him, a life with Johnny as he watched him grow to become a man. He didn't want to think about those things, but his mind was too weary to hold the images at bay. Giving in to his body's need for rest, he closed his eyes and dreamed of living in a real home.

When he awoke again, light streamed in the uncurtained window and he lifted his hand to shield his eyes from the bright sunshine. The chair where he'd seen Kit and Johnny earlier sat empty.

Kit breezed into the room, dressed in her customary trousers and man's shirt. A bright blue kerchief around her neck added a splash of color and enhanced the warmth of her eyes.

She glanced at him, then looked again. A relieved smile lit her features as she leaned over him. "Good morning. I was beginning to wonder if you were ever going to wake up."

Jake licked his dry lips, his mouth as arid as a desert. Kit poured him a glass of water from the pitcher on the dresser. She slid her cool hand behind his neck, raising his head so he could drink. After a few swallows, she withdrew the cup.

"You might get sick if you don't go slow," she said.

Jake peered up at her solicitous expression.

With a nervous gesture, she swept back a strand of hair. "How're you feeling?" she asked.

"Like hell," he replied in a raspy voice.

Her laughter washed across him like a gentle rain.

"You can't be too bad. You're sounding like your old self."

"Did you and Johnny sleep in the rocker?"

Her smile faded as a trace of sadness haunted her expression. "How did you know?"

"I woke up earlier and saw you. I thought I might've been dreaming."

Her cheeks pinkened. "Johnny was worried about you."

"I'm sorry he had to see me like this."

"Why? You didn't ask to be shot." Anger threaded through her words.

Surprised by her defensive tone, Jake said, "No, but at his age he shouldn't have to see what men are capable of doing to each other."

"For a selfish bastard, you're awfully concerned about Johnny," Kit commented with a wry smile.

"Even us selfish bastards have our weak moments." His memory clicked into motion, and he remembered the gunshots, Zeus's stumble and scream . . . "Zeus—where is he?"

"He wasn't with you. Could he have run off?"

Jake grasped her forearm. "No, he would've stayed with me. You have to find him!"

Kit laid her hand on his. "I'll send Ethan out looking for him. He'll find him."

"Hurry. I think he was hurt."

She nodded and slipped out of the room.

Jake closed his eyes against the pain thudding in his temple. Zeus had been with him for over six years; Jake couldn't have asked for a more loyal horse. He'd spent hours in the saddle trailing outlaws with only Zeus as his companion, and Jake had taken to conversing with him out of sheer boredom. Though Zeus couldn't understand the words, often he seemed to understand his tone.

What if Zeus had been killed by the ambusher? Anger roiled in Jake, and he tried to sit up. The room rolled and pitched and turned his stomach inside out. He fell back against the pillows with a groan.

Johnny entered the room with a tentative step. "Can I come in, Mr. Cordell?"

Jake fought the lingering nausea. "Sure."

The boy hurried to his side, laying a light hand on Jake's bare shoulder. "Are you better now?"

Jake focused his gaze on Johnny's worried face. "Don't you be worrying about me, kid, I'll be just fine."

Johnny heaved a sigh. "I'm glad. Ma said you'd be all right, but I wasn't sure. You looked pretty sick."

"You listen to your ma," Jake said. "She's a smart woman. The smartest I ever met, but don't you tell her I said that. It'll be our secret."

A conspiratorial smile lit Johnny's face. "Cross my heart." His grin vanished. "Do you know where Ma went?"

Jake nodded. "She was going to ask Ethan to look for Zeus."

"What happened to him?"

"I don't know." He debated whether to tell the boy the truth or not. "Zeus might've been hurt."

"By the bad man that shot you?"

"That's right."

"I'll put some fresh straw in a stall for him," Johnny volunteered. "When Ethan brings him back, he'll have a clean place to stay and get better."

Touched by the boy's offer, Jake couldn't speak for a moment. "Thanks, kid. I'm sure Zeus would like that."

"I'd best go get it ready," Johnny stated solemnly. "And I'll tell Pete, too. He knows all about how to take care of horses. He'll know what to do."

"I'm sure he will."

Johnny scurried out of the room and Jake listened to the muffled thud of his boots down the stairs. His chest tightened with an undefinable emotion. What had he done to deserve the boy's affection? He'd enjoyed teaching Johnny how to ride and spending time with the kid, but he'd not gone out of his way to gain his friendship. Somewhere along the way, the kid had formed an attachment.

Even more surprising, Jake reciprocated that feeling. He'd always figured children were a necessary evil, something to be tolerated until they grew up into interesting adults. The bond he shared with Johnny was something he'd not anticipated.

Weariness overtook him, and despite his worry for his horse, he fell asleep.

Some time later, a touch on his shoulder awakened him.

"Jake," Kit said.

"What is it?" he asked with a sleep-graveled voice.

"Ethan found Zeus."

Her words shoved the effects of slumber aside. "How is he? Is he hurt?"

Kit nodded somberly, and dread filled him. "It's pretty bad."

Jake threw back his covers. "I want to see him."

She grabbed his arm. "You shouldn't get up yet, Jake."

He shook himself free of her hold, and swung his feet to the floor. "I'm going."

Kit pressed her lips together. "All right, but let me help you."

She handed him his clothes and turned her back while he struggled into them. The floor tipped, but he gritted his teeth and pulled on his boots. He stood and took a shaky step.

Silently, Kit moved to his side and slipped an arm

around his waist. Jake draped his arm across her shoulders and they left the room together.

His head pounding and his stomach churning, Jake kept his sights focused on the barn where Kit guided him. She didn't speak, and Jake was relieved. He wasn't ready to hear how badly hurt Zeus was.

They went into the barn and Kit led him to a stall where her hired men and Johnny gathered around. Ethan and Charlie moved apart to allow Jake through. Steeling himself, Jake looked into the lantern-lit pen and saw Pete Two Ponies bending over Zeus, who lay on his side in the fresh straw.

"How bad?" Jake asked, not caring that his trembling voice betrayed his feelings.

Pete turned and shook his head slowly, then returned his attention to the palomino.

Jake opened the gate, and Kit stepped back, leaving him to negotiate the last few feet by himself. Oblivious to everyone's presence, Jake dropped to his knees beside Zeus's head. He laid a shaking hand on the stallion's sweat-coated neck.

"Hey there, fellah. You look like I feel," Jake said softly.

Zeus snorted, the sound a faint echo of his usual whinny.

Jake spotted the blood on Zeus's chest, and his heart tightened painfully. He didn't need Pete to tell him Zeus was dying in slow, suffering degrees.

"I don't know how he made it back here," Ethan said quietly.

Jake tried to smile and failed. "He always was a stubborn cuss."

Pete touched Jake's arm. "There's nothing anyone can do," the old Indian said.

"Yes, there is." He stared into Pete's wisdom-filled eyes.

Pete nodded, and straightened, then walked over to Ethan. "Jake needs your gun."

"No!" Johnny's cry ripped through Jake's sorrow.

Kit grabbed hold of her son to keep him from running into the stall.

"Let him in," Jake said to Kit.

She hesitated a moment, then released the boy. Johnny stumbled to Jake's side.

"You have to make him better. Zeus can't die," Johnny pleaded.

"Everyone has to die sometime, Johnny. We can't make Zeus better. He's hurt real bad," Jake explained, even as his own grief threatened to choke him.

"But the books say he's your best friend. There has to be *something* you can do."

Jake took a shaky breath. "Do you want me to keep him alive a little longer, even though it means he'll be in a lot of pain?"

Johnny leaned over Jake, and stroked Zeus's forehead. "No."

"As Zeus's best friend, it's up to me to stop his suffering. Do you understand?"

A tear splashed on Jake's arm, leaving a damp circle on his shirtsleeve. "Yes," the boy whispered.

"Come on, Johnny," Kit said huskily.

Jake glanced up to see her standing above them. The light reflected off her spectacles, but he noticed the bright sheen of moisture in her eyes.

"Go with your mother," Jake said, urging the boy to his feet.

Johnny sniffled and laid his small hand on Zeus's forehead. "Bye, Zeus."

Kit guided Johnny out of the stall, and Pete handed Jake a revolver. With a nod of understanding, the ancient Indian followed Ethan and Charlie out of the barn.

Jake hefted the weapon's weight in his palm, wanting

to fling the gun aside. Instead, he tightened his hold on it.

"I'm sorry, Zeus, but I can't let you suffer." Jake took a deep shuddering breath, and tears stung his eyes. "You've been a loyal friend—the best a man could ask for."

He laid one hand on Zeus's neck, and aimed the pistol with the other. His finger curled around the trigger. "Good-bye, old friend."

The gunshot sounded like an explosion, and Kit jumped. Tears ran unheeded down her cheeks. Though sobs tore at her throat, she kept them inside. Taking a tentative step toward Zeus's stall, she saw Jake leaning against the top rail. His head hung down, and he held the revolver loosely in one hand.

Silently Kit walked over to him and took the gun from his grasp. She didn't dare look into the pen, knowing she'd lose control if she did. She laid her palm on Jake's back. "Come on. Let's go back to the house," she said softly.

Jake didn't move. "He was a good horse, Kit. The best a man could ask for."

She nodded. "I know."

Silence surrounded them.

Jake pushed himself upright and came out of the pen. In the barn's meager light, his pallor gave his face a haunting skeletal appearance. Kit stayed close to Jake's side but didn't attempt to help him as they walked out of the barn.

Pete and Charlie stood by the corral, but Ethan and Johnny were nowhere in sight. Kit suspected the young man had taken her son to see the new foal, hoping to assuage the boy's grief.

She handed Charlie Ethan's revolver and followed Jake to the house, feeling Jake's sorrow as keenly as if it were her own.

Jake negotiated the stairs slowly and dropped onto the bed in his room. He lay on his back, staring at the ceiling.

"I'm going to get the bastard that killed him," he vowed.

Kit removed his boots and covered him with the blanket. By the time she was done, he was asleep.

"I know you will," she whispered.

Jake awakened around suppertime, weak and hungry. Kit brought him a tray laden with food and set it on the nightstand.

He sat up, but a bout with dizziness forced him to close his eyes until her face stopped spinning like a roulette wheel.

"Do you want me to feed you?"

Jake scowled. "I can do it myself."

She shrugged and set the tray across his lap, then sat down in the chair. "I'll stay in case you change your mind."

"I won't."

"I'll still stay."

Jake managed to eat most of the potatoes and beans, as well as the beef. He drank two glasses of water, then sipped his coffee.

"Did someone take care of him?" Jake asked abruptly.

Kit nodded. "Charlie and Ethan did."

"They didn't let Johnny help, did they?"

"No. He stayed in the house."

Jake breathed a sigh of relief. "It was hard enough on the kid."

"It was harder on *you*." Her chin trembled. "I'm so sorry about Zeus, Jake. I know how much he meant to you."

Her sympathy reopened his own grief, and he forced

his voice to remain even. "I couldn't let him suffer."

Kit remained quiet a moment, then asked, "Do you have any idea who shot you?"

He pressed his head back against the pillow. He had gotten sloppy. The most likely suspect was someone who thought gunning him down would bolster his own fame. He'd been thinking about Kit and Johnny, and that lapse had nearly cost him his life. It *had* cost Zeus's life.

"I didn't see anything."

"Whoever it was knew you were spending Easter at my place," she mused aloud.

"Maybe Bertie Wellensiek was trying to save my soul."

"That's not funny. Somebody wants you dead."

"Or maybe they were just scaring me. Maybe it was your boyfriend Preston."

"I doubt it. The newspaper is the only weapon he uses." Her frown deepened. "Do you think it was someone trying to cash in on your reputation?"

Jake considered easing her worries but decided she deserved to know of his suspicions. "More than likely."

Her complexion paled. She stood and picked up his tray. "Get some rest, Jake. We can talk more later."

Jake clasped her wrist. He could more than encircle it with his thumb and forefinger. "Don't worry, Kit. This isn't any of your concern."

"Yes, it is."

"What happened wasn't your fault," he reiterated. "I'm the one in your debt."

"You don't owe me anything, Jake. It's me who owes you."

He studied the green flecks in her compassionate eyes. "Why are you doing this?"

"Doing what?"

"Taking care of me. What do you want from me?"

She tilted her head. "You're my friend, Jake. I don't want anything from you."

Kit left the room and a hollow yearning opened in Jake's chest. Maggie had never asked anything of him, either, besides a good time in bed. He had proposed to her, but that had been during one of his weak moments after he'd sated his needs with her willing body. He'd been young, and his offer had been a spontaneous one without a thought to the consequences.

Experienced Maggie had known he didn't love her like a man should love a woman. She'd turned him down, bruising his fragile pride. Later, Jake had been glad she had. They would've ended up hating one another.

His feelings toward Kit were different. He wanted Kit in his bed, but he also admired her compassion and fiery spirit. No longer a painfully shy wallflower, Kit had grown into an independent woman with strong beliefs and the courage to stick to them.

He squeezed his eyes shut, flinching when an arrow of pain streaked through his head. Grateful for the distraction despite his discomfort, Jake allowed the familiar sounds of the spring day to lull him to sleep.

Jake pulled on his trousers, glad to see that they were his own and they were clean. His temple still pounded, but much of his strength had returned and he'd grown bored soon after he'd awakened in the afternoon. After tucking his shirt into his waistband and easing into his boots, Jake carefully walked downstairs and out onto the porch.

The sky had been particularly generous to the sun, allowing it to shine unhindered by clouds. The bright rays warmed the air, bringing the pungent smell of spring, earthy and fresh, to the land. Jake was glad he was alive to experience it.

A horse nickered, drawing his attention to the corrals. He squinted, studying the slight figure in the enclosure who worked with a yearling. Sunlight glinted off glass, and Jake recognized Kit.

Stepping off the porch, he wandered down to the corral. Kit spotted him, and he caught her quick, welcoming smile in a flash of white. He rested his forearms on the top rail and watched her take the bay gelding through its paces. Holding onto the rope fastened to the horse's halter, Kit had the animal trot around the perimeter of the fence as she turned slowly with its progress. A subtle movement of her wrist, and the horse slowed to a prancing walk.

He shifted his gaze from the bay to Kit. Her low voice carried to him on the slight breeze, and he shivered as her mellifluous tone curled inside him. He'd never felt jealous of a horse before, but for a moment Jake wished she'd turn her attention to him and forget about the yearling, who couldn't appreciate her seductive voice.

As he continued to observe, he noticed how well she worked the gelding. How at ease she appeared. Her love for her horses was as evident as stars on a clear night. When he regained his ranch, she'd be left with no place for herself or her horses to go. She'd be forced to sell them to him or to someone else, leaving her with nothing but her adopted son and the clothes on her back.

He balled his hands into fists. Why did this have to be so damned complicated?

He glanced up to see Kit release the gelding. The animal tossed his shimmering mane, then trotted to the trough and buried his muzzle in the water. With a loose stride, Kit walked toward him. The breeze molded her shirt across her breasts, and her trousers outlined the delicious curves of her hips and thighs. The dull throb in his head was forgotten as another, more insistent ache deposed it.

"You shouldn't be up yet," Kit scolded.

"I was bored," he admitted. "Besides, all I got is a headache. Not even as bad as most of my hangovers."

Kit ducked through the fence, and stood in front of him, and Jake studied her sun-kissed face—the perspiration sheening her brow, the vitality shining in her sparkling eyes.

"Can I ask you a question?" she asked unexpectedly.

Kit's solemn tone brought Jake's defenses into place, but he shrugged nonchalantly. "Sure."

"Did you work at being the opposite of the hero Jake Cordell?"

He forced a chuckle. "You like to hit below the belt, don't you?"

Kit shook her head. "I'm just curious." She shifted her weight from one foot to the other. "The man I saw in jail and the saloon was nothing like the Jake Cordell I saw yesterday morning with his horse."

Her steady gaze flustered him, as did her comment. "I never did like anyone telling me what I could and couldn't do," he admitted. "And when T. K. Thorne created this person who was supposed to be me, I figured I'd prove him wrong. My drinking and whoring wouldn't fit the hero image."

"Maybe T. K. Thorne didn't realize heroes were only normal people doing the best they could," Kit said.

Her soft words caressed him, fanned a need within him that craved her gentle honesty and steadfast confidence in him. Lifting a hand, he traced the curve of her jaw with a light finger. She closed her eyes and parted her sensuous lips invitingly.

His blood burned with now-familiar desire. The top button of her shirt was undone, exposing creamy skin that hinted at what lay hidden from his greedy gaze. He clasped her slender neck between his palms, allowing his fingers to slip under her collar and splay across the satiny skin of her shoulders.

She breathed a moan and opened her eyes. "Jake."

The way she spoke his name could have been a prayer or a curse. He swept his tongue across her parted lips, then kissed the tip of her nose.

She leaned forward, her silky crown tickling his chin, and rested her forearms against his chest. Jake accepted her invitation to continue, nuzzling the side of her neck, kissing a fiery trail down inside her shirt's collar.

His blood stampeded through his veins, growing more tumultuous with each sample of Kit's sweet charms. He cupped her face between his palms, swooped down to capture her lips with his, alternately coaxing and demanding. Drawing back, he breathed deeply to cool the flames that burned within him. She stared at him with heavy-lidded eyes, and Jake could see the answering desire in their smoky depths.

"I want you, Kit," he stated, his voice so husky with need he almost didn't recognize it as his own.

Chapter 13

ow often had she dreamed Jake would speak those words to her? Although aching to feel Jake's tender caresses once more, Kit stepped out of his intoxicating embrace. She trembled with suppressed desires and surrendered to the need to remain in physical contact. Curving her fingers around his hand, she gazed up at his dusky heart-robbing eyes and nearly lost her resolve.

She touched the stark white bandage around his forehead, reminding her how unpredictable life could be.

"There's some things I need to tell you," she said, her voice breathy with anxiety. She glanced down at his hand, clasped in hers, then brought her attention back to his strong-jawed face. "Have you ever thought about settling down, Jake?"

He studied her with a twinkling gaze. "Is that a proposal?"

Startled, Kit shook her head. "No, of course not."

"That's too bad. I might've been tempted to say yes."

Could he be serious? Kit thrust the thought aside. "You haven't answered my question."

Jake drew away, his expression sobering. "I've come back to Chaney and set up a law office."

"That isn't what I meant. I'm talking about a family, children." Her heart pounded like she'd run a mile.

"Last I heard, I'd have to have a wife first, and you know how I feel about that."

Kit's stomach twisted with apprehension. He wasn't making this easy.

His grip tightened on her hand, and he squeezed his eyes shut.

"What is it?" she asked anxiously.

"I should probably get back to the house," he replied with a failed attempt to smile.

His complexion matched the bandage around his forehead, and concern sent Kit's confession scurrying back to its hiding place.

"I told you it was too soon for you to be up," she scolded.

Jake managed a lopsided grin. "You sound like a nagging wife."

Kit bit her tongue to keep her sharp retort unspoken. As she led him across the yard and up to his room, her impatience evaporated. She shouldn't have allowed herself to get carried away by his skilled touches.

She eased him down on the bed. With her back to him, Kit leaned over to tug off his boots and dropped them to the floor with a loud clump. He chuckled and she turned, propping her hands on her hips. "What're you laughing about?"

He arched a dark brow. "You give me another view like that, and you'll be sharing this bed with me."

Kit's face burned with mortification. "I thought you were too weak to do anything but sleep."

"It's my head that's hurting. Everything else works just fine." With gingerly movements, he folded his arms behind his head. "What is it you wanted to tell me?"

Kit's gaze swept down his broad chest to his narrow waist and hips, pausing on the telltale sign of his arousal.

He was right; nothing seemed to be wrong with that part of him. Flustered, she spun away. "We can talk about it later."

Kit hurried out, not stopping until she came to the corral. Leaning against the fence, she gathered her breath and her wits.

Her fiery response to his kisses had astonished her. If her conscience hadn't bothered her, she'd have surrendered to his seductive invitation. That realization didn't shock her as it should have. She'd fought her attraction to him ever since he'd returned, but he'd been etched upon her heart for years.

She rested her arms on the fence and laid her flushed cheek on her folded wrists. She was tired of doing the right thing. Jake's roguish smile alone had the power to set her heart fluttering and her insides tingling with an ache only Jake could appease.

Raising her head, she gazed upward at the sky that was so blue it almost hurt her eyes. She could no longer deny what every fiber in her body already knew.

She loved Jake Cordell.

"Can I say good night to Mr. Cordell?" Johnny asked.

Kit finished buttoning his nightshirt. "If he's still awake."

Johnny dashed out of his room, and Kit lowered herself to the edge of his bed. She heard Jake's low voice and Johnny's answering childish tones. Imagining Jake tucking his son in every night brought a lump to her throat, and the thought of sharing Jake's bed every night brought another kind of wistful longing.

"He was awake," Johnny said, and threw himself on the mattress beside Kit. "He's feeling a lot better."

"Did he tell you that?"

Johnny shook his head. "No. I could just tell." He

knelt on the bed. "I wish he didn't have to leave."

"Me, too," Kit answered honestly. "But he can't stay with us forever."

Johnny slumped against her back, wrapping his arms around her neck. "I'm going to miss him."

The dejection in Johnny's voice brought a haunting sadness to Kit. She squeezed her son's small hands and whispered, "Me, too."

Johnny knelt beside the bed and folded his hands together. "God bless Ma and Charlie and Ethan and Pete and Mr. Cordell. And please, God, take care of Zeus in heaven. Amen."

Guilt settled like a rock in her stomach. There was a strong possibility that Zeus's death was her fault.

Johnny crawled into bed, and Kit covered him.

"Do you think we could give the new colt to Mr. Cordell? I know it wouldn't be like having Zeus back, but I think he might like him," Johnny said.

Her son's suggestion gave Kit a means to appease her conscience slightly. She smiled. "I think that's a good idea. How about if we talk to Mr. Cordell tomorrow and see what he thinks?"

"He'll like Smoky, and he can train him to be as smart as Zeus was." He frowned. "Who would want to kill Zeus?"

"I don't know, but whoever it was, he had to be a very bad man." She leaned down and kissed his forehead. "Good night, sweetheart."

"Good night, Ma."

Kit paused in the doorway, her gaze lingering on Johnny's beloved face.

Lightning split the night sky, and thunder rumbled off in the distance, heralding the first spring storm. A shiver shimmied down her spine. Despite the possible repercussions, she had to tell Jake about his son. The boy ached for a father, and he already cared for Jake. Johnny would be ecstatic to learn his hero was also his father. And Kit had no doubt Jake wouldn't leave his son, the way he believed his own father had deserted him.

Where would that leave her? She hoped that because Jake knew what it was like to grow up without a mother, he wouldn't separate Johnny from her. Did she dare hope that her dream of a family could be fulfilled?

Leaving the door ajar, she moved toward Jake's room, but her courage failed her. It was late. She'd tell him tomorrow. Feeling like a coward, Kit retreated to her bedroom.

Three hours later, sleep remained elusive. With an impatient tug, Kit unrolled the blankets that had twisted around her. Staring at the ceiling, she recalled Jake's kisses and the light touch of his fingertips on her bare shoulders. She groaned in frustration and sat up.

Throwing back her covers, she swung her feet to the woven rug and stood. She might as well do something constructive and work on the last Jake Cordell dime novel. Maybe she'd forget the taste of his sinfully delicious lips. Maybe she'd forget his tangy scent that invaded her senses. Maybe she'd forget the masculinity that had been outlined by his damp drawers.

Kit slipped on her spectacles and pulled on her robe, tying the sash around her waist. Tiptoeing down the hall, she heard a muffled groan and stopped by Johnny's room to peer at his peaceful features. With a frown, she crossed to Jake's bedroom, where murmured words met her ears.

Opening the door, she spied him tossing and turning, his blankets draped to the floor. As he muttered unintelligible phrases, Kit's compassion overcame her prudence. She glided across the floor to his bedside and leaned over to shake his shoulder.

"Jake, wake up," she said.

"No, he's dead . . . the blood . . ."

Jake thrashed about and Kit grabbed his flailing hands. "Shhh, it's all right, Jake. You're safe here."

Jake clasped her wrists and jerked her toward him. She tumbled onto his long, lean frame. Too surprised to move, Kit remained in his grasp, her cheek pressed against the curling dark hairs that covered his chest and her legs straddled on either side of his.

"Kit?" His deep-timbered voice sounded confused. "What're you doing here?"

She raised her head and found his whisker-shadowed chin a couple of inches from her face. "You were having another nightmare. I was trying to wake you."

Jake stared up at her, the slumber disappearing from his eyes as a fire kindled within their dark depths. "Or maybe you couldn't resist me any longer?"

She struggled to escape his hold, but he wouldn't free her. Glaring, she tried to hide her fluttering pulse. "I think you overestimate your charm. Let me go."

"Not until you kiss me." Impudence curved his lips upward.

Not that smile! Longing spiraled through her, but deceptions still remained between them. Staring down at his devilish grin and sparkling eyes, she felt her resolve waver. After she told him the truth, Jake might never look at her that way again. This might be her last chance at claiming a piece of her dreams.

She snuggled closer to the masculine angles that were covered only by a thin pair of drawers. "What do I get if I kiss you?"

He blinked as if startled by her acceptance of his terms. "A surprise."

"I like surprises," she replied in a husky voice.

Allowing instinct to guide her, she let her mouth settle on his. He didn't move a muscle, and Kit drew her tongue along his sensuous lips. They were velvety smooth to her inexperienced touch, and she grew bolder with the new adventure. She nibbled at the corners of his mouth, and he moaned.

Kit drew back. "How was that?"

Jake gazed at her with an astonished expression. "Where the hell did you learn that?"

Giddy excitement gave Kit a sense of smug confidence. "From you."

"You're a helluva pupil. I think you deserve a reward."

He removed her wire-rimmed glasses and set them on the nightstand. Wrapping his arms around her, he drew her flush with his hard contours, her breasts flattening against his chest. His tangy scent intoxicated her, making her dizzy with wanting him.

He stroked her upswept brow with his thumbs, and guilt knifed through him. If he possessed an ounce of honor, he would force her to leave before he shattered her illusions. But he wasn't a hero, and he wanted Kit with a deep, abiding ache that begged to be sated. He wanted her gentle acceptance. He wanted the gift she offered more than he'd wanted anything.

With a savage growl, he crushed his mouth to hers. A whimper escaped Kit. He tamed the fierce kiss, turning it into a gentle caress. He traced her swollen lips, feasting on her honey-sweetness.

With clear, love-lit eyes, Kit spoke in a low voice. "Love me, Jake."

His breath stumbled in his throat. He had no right taking what she offered freely and without conditions, yet he knew he would. Nothing on earth could have prevented him from surrendering to the molten heat that coursed through his blood.

"Are you sure?" he asked, giving her one last chance to leave with her fairytale hero still intact.

Drawing a light finger across his lips, she nodded. "I've waited for you all my life, Jake."

He stared into her moonlight-gilded features, wondering what he'd done to deserve such adoration. He tipped her angelic face upward, and their breaths blended into a single sigh.

Kit slid her fingers into his silky hair and met his exploring tongue with hers. His uneven breaths matched her own, and she felt his erection pressing into her abdomen. Answering instinct's summons, she moved against his aroused flesh.

A breathy moan broke from Jake's lips, and he nibbled her earlobe, teasing it. Unexpected moisture dampened the core of her desire, and she closed her eyes, shocked by her potent reaction to his touch. He inched up her gown and cool air swirled around her legs. Curving his hands around her buttocks, he slid his fingers upward, leaving a trail of fiery heat halfway up her spine. Stroking downward, he grasped her hips, pulling her snug against him.

Kit licked a salt ribbon that glided into the coarse hair at the base of his neck. His pulse quickened beneath her tongue, fluttering like a hummingbird's wings. Awed by her power over him, Kit continued her moist trail along his neck to the tender skin beneath his ear.

Jake removed the sash of her robe, then fumbled with the ribbon at the top of her nightgown. "I want to see you, Kit."

She rose, kneeling above Jake's waist. For a moment, uncertainty gripped her. Passion warred with apprehension. She gazed down at Jake and recognized the desire in his eyes. Her trepidation dissolved and she removed her robe, dropping it to the floor. She grasped the hem of her lacy white nightgown and lifted it over her head, allowing it to drift to the floor with a whisper.

Jake's deliberate gaze moved over her, devouring every detail of her slender, willowy body. The moon's glow brushed her full breasts with silver strokes, and her tight nipples beckoned him. Her narrow waist flared to curved hips that framed the triangle of honey-gold curls at the juncture of her thighs. As if afraid she would vanish, he reached out with a tentative hand to touch her breast. He brushed her pillow-softness with his finger-tips, then moved downward over the hardness of the crest. He weighed one blushing breast in his palm, then leaned forward and drew the crowning nipple into his mouth. Kit's sharp intake of breath sent blood surging through his veins.

He followed the gentle indentation of her waist with his work-roughened hand, and moved lower, pausing at the golden tangle of hair. She moaned and shifted slightly. She was hot and slick, and he caressed her tenderly.

Desire pierced Kit like a hundred tiny arrows. Jake moved to her other breast, and a tremor seized her. She grabbed Jake's arms, forcing him back, away from her chest.

"No, I want to make you feel this good, this special," she said.

He stared at her, his thick, inky eyelashes unflickering. He stretched out his hand, brushed back a strand of hair from her forehead. "When I touch you like this—" He pressed his lips against the heated valley between her breasts. "It makes me feel good." Pausing, he kissed one satiny slope, then the other. "Special."

"But I want to touch you, too. I want to make you feel the way I feel."

He'd never known anyone like Kit. Studying her passion-lit features, he foundered in the loving concern displayed in her wide blue eyes.

"By pleasuring you, I will feel the same way," he assured her. He drew a blunt-tipped finger along the curve of her jaw. "Do you like that?"

She closed her eyes, nodding with a jerky motion.

"Every time you touch me, I feel like I'm going to shatter into a million pieces."

"Soon, darling. Soon," Jake promised.

He eased his fingers back into her damp heat, opening her like rose petals unfurling beneath a summer sun. Exploring the silky folds, he found the core of her pleasure and stroked it with infinite patience.

Kit threw back her head, shuddering, and arched up to meet his exploration. Her bosom jutted out, and Jake laved each turgid center with greedy kisses. Her scent surrounded him; cinnamon and musk and sweetness swirled through his senses, making him grow harder. He squeezed his eyes shut, determined to hold back until Kit was ready to follow him over pleasure's pinnacle.

She pressed against his hand, urging him, directing him, but Jake instinctively knew. Her tiny gasps tugged at his control, and sweat soaked the bandage around his forehead.

"Please, Jake."

Her whispered plea spurred his passions to the breaking point. Clasping her waist, he rolled her onto her back in one swift motion.

Kit gazed up at him with wide, questioning eyes as her knees bracketed his hips.

With only a slight hesitation, she reached for the band of his drawers and slipped her fingers between the material and his skin. Her warm hands slid the clothing down his hips, releasing his masculinity.

Kit had never seen a naked man before, and at the sight of his rigid length, an ache throbbed in her loins. He removed his underwear completely, dropping them to the floor to join her gown and robe.

She held out her arms, beckoning him to return.

He moved back over her, his hardness poised at her hot, pulsing entrance. The curling hairs that covered his chest and tapered down to encircle the base of his erection tickled Kit's sensitive skin. Her stomach coiled, the tension spreading outward like spokes on a wheel.

She raised her hips, soundlessly urging Jake to complete their joining, to give her the relief her body craved but her innocence couldn't comprehend.

He gazed down with smoldering eyes and eased himself into her demanding heat. Forcing himself to move slowly, he pressed forward and met the evidence of her virginity. Even though she'd told him Johnny wasn't her child, part of his mind reeled with the knowledge. He couldn't hold back any longer.

He grasped her hips and plunged deep inside her with a single thrust. Her whimper of surprise and pain tore at his gut, and he wished he could've spared her and taken the discomfort into himself. For a moment, he lay still. Her sheath was so tight and hot around him, he was afraid it would end too soon, before Kit could learn the pleasures of lovemaking.

After a few moments, she relaxed and he began to move with long, easy strokes, stoking the fires to an uncontrollable conflagration. He clutched her hips in his hands, and increased his tempo.

Kit threaded her fingers through his hair and pressed her lips against his stubbled chin. Sweat slicked between their joined bodies and Jake's tingling nerves grew taut.

Lightning flashed outside, illuminating every curve and hollow of her rose-flushed body. Thunder rumbled, reverberating through Jake, merging with the wild storm that raged inside him. Another jagged line of white light washed through him, followed by nature's rampant repercussion.

Jake buried his face in Kit's hair, and his harsh breathing roared in his ears. Desire gusted through him like the wind that tore at the shutters.

"Come with me, Kit," he whispered hoarsely.

Her body stiffened beneath him, and she exclaimed, "Jake!"

Kit's joyful cry filled his mind, and his body shuddered with release. A wave of uncontrollable ecstasy crashed through him, and he sought her bow-shaped lips with fierce possessiveness.

Jake dropped his forehead to the pillow beside Kit. Her heart pounded so hard, he could feel its rapid beat against his breast. He could taste her on his lips, and her musky scent curled in his nostrils. No other woman had made him feel so replete, so contented.

Only Kit, whom he trusted as he trusted few others.

He tried to roll to her side, but she tightened her embrace around him. "No, don't."

"I'm too heavy."

"I like being so close to you." She peered up at him. "I've dreamed of this for so long, Jake."

"What do you mean?"

She glanced away as if embarrassed, then returned her artless gaze to him. "I never looked at another man without comparing him to you. Even after I thought I was over my infatuation, I still found myself thinking, 'Jake wouldn't do it that way,' or 'His smile isn't nearly as handsome as Jake's.'"

He hadn't realized the depth of her feelings. How could a man like him, who'd squandered his time on whiskey and whores, have gained the affection of a woman so generous, so unblemished by life's harsh lessons?

Unable to articulate his thoughts, he feathered a tender kiss across her passion-swollen lips. As if she were made of exquisite china, he framed her face in his hands, and her lashes swept downward.

Kit wanted the moment to last forever, to be inscribed upon her heart like her unspoken love. Now she understood why Maggie had accepted Jake's lovemaking without demanding anything in return. Kit had never known anything so glorious, so eclipsing. Instinctively she knew it would be that way with no other man.

He'd known she was the only woman for him the first time he'd laid eyes upon her angelic face and perfect feminine figure. Jake Cordell had never allowed another person into his soul as he'd allowed her to infiltrate his heart. It was as if she had been made for him alone, just as Eve had been made for Adam. And equally as tempting.

Her shy, gentle demeanor begged for protection, and Jake delighted in playing the role of Sir Lancelot, her knight in shining armor. Only for her would he consider hanging up his guns and settling down to a quiet, anonymous existence, content to bask in the brilliant light of her adoring eyes.

As tentative as a speckled fawn, she touched his hand with her kidskin-encased fingers. Her love radiated through the demure contact, and pink blossomed her cheeks. He brushed the side of her face lightly and whispered his undying love to his beautiful maiden.

Kit sighed dreamily, still feeling the aftershocks of breathless rapture. Although her thighs were tender, she shifted her body beneath Jake's welcome weight.

"Let me pleasure you this time," she whispered.

Jake gazed down at her, puzzled. "You did, honey."

She shook her head. "Not the way you did." She pressed her palms against his broad shoulders. "Roll onto your back."

Jake eased off her and lay on the mattress, and Kit stretched out next to him, her breasts pressed close to his side. Remembering the wondrous melody he'd played upon her body, Kit tried to repeat the refrain. She coaxed his nipples to pebble hardness. Awed that his body reacted in a similar fashion to hers, she leaned forward and drew a nipple into her mouth.

Jake moaned, a deep, primal sound that rumbled through her, and he wrapped his hands around the back of her head. "Kit."

Encouraged by his passionate response, she trailed a moist line to the other crest and licked the tip with slow, measured motions. The dark, springy hairs tickled her nose, and she slid her fingers through the whorls moving downward, over his navel, and paused. Did she dare touch him *there*? He'd caressed her in ways she'd never dreamed a man would. Would it be unseemly for her to reciprocate?

Her heart thudded against her ribs, and her palms dampened with anxiety. Curiosity and desire urged her on. She continued her journey, and his masculinity grazed her knuckles. Jake's quick intake of breath told Kit he didn't find her actions too bold.

Growing more confident, she curved her fingers around him. Jake's muscles grew taut and he seemed to swell within her grasp. She'd never imagined a man could be so hard, yet the skin remain as smooth as silk. Exploring him as he'd done to her, Kit felt her stomach clench and her lungs struggle for air as her passions escalated.

Abruptly Jake grabbed her wrist, halting her motions. Startled, Kit feared she'd incited Jake's disapproval.

"Are you trying to kill me?" he demanded in a harsh voice.

Afraid to look into his face, Kit kept her gaze focused on his chest. She shook her head. "I'm sorry. I didn't think—"

He raised her chin with a crooked finger, and she was forced to look at him.

"Oh, Kit," he breathed. "You have nothing to be sorry about." A chagrined smile lit his features. "It's just that I didn't expect . . . well, I didn't expect you to do what you did."

Puzzled by his embarrassment, Kit tipped her head. "You mean a woman shouldn't—"

Jake chuckled, although there was underlying tension in his tone. "No, honey, it's just that I've heard so-called good women don't do things like that."

She drew her stilled hand away from his masculinity, her cheeks burning. "I only wanted to make you feel the way I do."

"I do, believe me—and I'm glad to learn that what I heard about good women was wrong." His sensuous lips curved upward, his eyes twinkling with deviltry. "Fact is, I liked it too much."

Relieved, she grinned with saucy insouciance. "Good. Can I shock you again?"

He blinked and nodded, his expression both wary and excited.

"Does the man always have to be on top?"

Jake tried to choke back his laughter, but failed. "Oh, Kit, what did I do to deserve you?"

She trailed her fingertip along his stubble-laced jaw. "What did I do to deserve *you*?"

Her heart swelled with love for this man who could see others as they were but was blind to his own goodness and generosity. His hands spanned her waist, urging her to complete their joining. Needing no other invitation, Kit swung her leg over him. As she sank down upon him, she closed her eyes in expectation of a twinge of pain—but only pleasure coursed through her nerves.

Her eyes flickered open and she found Jake's heavy-lidded gaze upon her. She raised herself slightly, and Jake's palms slid to her hips. He directed her motions as Kit settled into a rapturous rhythm, her thighs slick with excitement. Keeping her eyes on Jake's pleasure-filled face, she covered his hands with hers and reveled in her feeling of completeness.

Their crescendo built to a crashing climax, and Kit

followed Jake's plunge over the edge. Collapsing onto him, she laid her cheek on his muscled chest, which rose and fell with deep breaths. Her heart thumped against her breast, merging with his rapid pulse. His muskiness swirled around her, imprinting his unique scent upon her senses.

He wrapped his corded arms around her, hugging her close and kissing the top of her head.

She pressed her lips against the springy hairs at the base of his neck, then gazed up at him. "Is it always this good?"

He swept a few damp tendrils from her face with a gentle hand. His pensive expression pierced Kit. "No. This was special."

She believed him, and the knowledge warmed her. "I'm glad."

Lying within the circle of his strong arms, Kit could almost forget another world existed . . . a world where she had less than two weeks to get the mortgage money or lose the ranch. A world where Jake didn't know the woman he held was the hated T. K. Thorne.

A world where Johnny's parentage was still a secret.

She clenched her hands into tight fists.

"What is it?" Jake asked.

She was surprised and dismayed he'd noticed her distress. Realizing that now was the time to reveal her secret about Johnny, she prayed for strength.

"Remember when I was trying to tell you something earlier today?" Kit began.

Jake nodded, and mock outrage filled his features. "Don't tell me you've never done this before!"

Kit tried to smile, but her lips wouldn't cooperate. She swallowed, her blood thundering in her ears. "It's about Johnny."

Jake's expression sobered. "Is someone trying to take him away from you?"

She shook her head. "It's about his parents."

His eyes narrowed, but he remained silent.

Kit's breath stuttered in her throat, and she shivered with apprehension. "Johnny's mother was Maggie."

Jake grew motionless as he stared at her with an expressionless mask. "Who's his father?"

Kit licked her lips and stammered her husky reply. "You are."

Chapter 14

❦

Jake's world tipped, throwing him off-balance.
Johnny was *his* son. His and Maggie's. His mind
reeled with the revelation.

He rolled Kit off him and scrambled out of bed.
Oblivious to his nakedness, he stalked around the room.
He stopped in front of Kit, who, with white-knuckled
fists, held a sheet over her chest. "Does Johnny know?"
he demanded.

Kit shook her head. "I thought I'd tell him when he
was old enough to understand."

He stared down at her, noting she didn't meet his
gaze. Johnny hadn't known, but *she* had. "Why didn't
you tell me before? Didn't you think *I* was old enough
to understand?"

She swallowed, hesitantly raising her eyes. "I didn't
think you wanted to be tied down."

Unexpected fury lashed through him. "*You* didn't
think I wanted to be tied down. Who the hell do you
think you are, making that decision for me?"

She trembled. "Maggie said—"

"I don't give a damn what Maggie said. She's been
dead for over five years. You had no right keeping
Johnny from me." Jake choked on his anger.

243

"I wanted what was best for him."

"And you figured you were best for him?" Jake paced from one end of the room to the other. "A son has a right to know his father. And a father sure as hell has the right to know his own son."

Kit rose, replacing the sheet with her robe. A pink splotch stained each cheekbone, the only color in her pallid face. "You were out gallivanting around the country, drinking and sleeping with who knows how many other women. Maggie knew that, though I didn't want to believe it. Then, when you came back, you told me yourself you didn't know how to love, how to be part of a family."

Her breasts rose and fell, and the glimpse of her shapely legs threatened to scatter his senses, but he clung to his bitter resentment. He forced himself to look into her battle-lit eyes. "That doesn't mean you had the right to withhold my son from me."

"I've raised him by myself. I'm the only family he's ever known."

He stepped up to her, aiming his index finger at her. "And whose fault is that?"

Her gaze faltered, and for a moment, Jake thought he detected moisture glimmering in her eyes. He thrust the image aside. Spinning away, he moved to the window. A spear of lightning split the night. "Go to your room, Kit."

"I won't be treated like a child."

His gentle-hearted Kit had hidden claws. "Seems to me if you act like one, you should be treated like one."

He heard her pulling on her gown, and the sound of the material sliding over skin conjured up visions Jake didn't want to imagine. But his body had no such scruples. He didn't hear her approach, but his skin tingled with awareness of her, and he remained facing the window.

"I guess it takes one to know one," she said, her quiet voice slicing his soul.

The harsh whisper of her flurried footsteps told Jake she'd left the room. He turned, shivering in the chill that seemed to seep into his bones. Pulling on his trousers, he tried to keep his gaze averted from the sheets that lay in disarray from their lovemaking. Kit's betrayal cut deeper than anything since his mother had deserted him. He'd trusted Kit as he'd trusted few others, and she'd turned out to be like everyone else.

He flattened his forearm against the window and leaned his forehead against his wrist. *My God, I have a son.* The knowledge overwhelmed him, shook him to the core. Even though he hadn't known of Johnny, guilt washed through Jake. He had promised himself that if he had a son, he wouldn't ignore him the way his own father had deserted him. And he'd confided that to Kit. Why hadn't she told him then?

Raising his head, he curled his fingers into a tight fist. Could he forgive her? Maybe. Could he ever trust her again? No.

The image of Kit's slender curves and passion-filled expression as she'd ridden him brought a heaviness to his loins. His reaction to the memory only increased his anger. How could his body still crave her when his mind was sickened by her deceit? He drew back his fist, wanting to smash something, anything, to relieve the bitter betrayal that soured his gut.

Struggling against his anger, Jake unclenched his fingers and rubbed his bandaged forehead. He had a son to consider.

"Johnny is my son," he stated in the darkness.

Speaking the words aloud sent a frisson of fear racing up his spine. What was expected of him? How would Johnny react to the news? When should he tell him? How should he tell him?

Jake's mind swirled with helplessness. Who could he confide in and ask for advice? An hour ago, his answer would've been Kit, but now she was the last person he'd turn to.

The room seemed to close in around him. He had to leave this place until he sorted out his tumultuous thoughts and figured out how to claim his son. Glancing out the window, he noticed the storm had passed and only a light drizzle remained.

He finished dressing and stalked out to the barn. Once there, he paused. Without Zeus, he had no way to get back to town.

Charlie entered behind him. "Iffen you need a horse, I'm sure Miz Thornton wouldn't mind you borrowin' one. Just leave it at old Ned's livery."

Jake nodded. "Much obliged."

He picked out a piebald mare and began to saddle her.

"Any special reason you're leavin' in the middle of the night?" Charlie asked conversationally.

"Yep."

Charlie continued to watch him, and Jake had the uncanny feeling the hired man could read his mind.

"Sometimes her heart gets in the way of her head," Charlie said quietly.

Jake stopped to peer at the dark man in the lantern-lit barn. "That doesn't give her the right to decide what's best for everyone."

"No, but it might explain why she done what she did."

Jake returned to his task. "There's no excuse to keep a man's son from him."

"Try lookin' at it from her side before you be castin' the first stone."

Jake led the horse out of the barn and settled in the saddle. Looking at Charlie, he said, "I'll be back for my son."

Riding into town, he began to plan his strategy. When he returned to Kit's, it would be to assume his duties as a father.

Kit peered into the mirror and tried to pinch some color into her pale cheeks. Her eyes, puffy and swollen from crying long into the night, were red-rimmed. How could she face Jake after all that had happened? One moment her life seemed complete in Jake's arms, and the next the illusion was shattered into a million jagged splinters, each fragment shredding her heart.

She didn't blame Jake for being angry. She'd deserved his wrath and had expected it, but she also hoped he would overcome his fury and do what was best for Johnny.

She inhaled and let out her breath in a steadying gust. Would Jake insist on telling Johnny immediately? Kit imagined herself in his position and knew she'd want her child to know as quickly as possible. She'd have to be prepared. How did a mother prepare to lose a son?

Blinking back tears, she ran a brush through her hair and ventured into the hall. She stepped over to Jake's room and found it empty.

Had he taken Johnny away in the middle of the night? The blood drained from her face, and she pressed her hand against the wall to steady herself. Her heart pounding like a smithy's hammer, she forced herself to move across the hall. Using every ounce of courage she possessed, she looked into her son's room.

His dark head showed above the blankets, and his chest moved up and down with sleep-steady breaths. Relief flowed through her, as intense as her terror had been moments before. She crossed the bedroom to Johnny's bedside and knelt on the floor burying her face in the bedcovers.

What if Jake never allowed her to see Johnny again?

Surely he wouldn't be so cruel as to separate her from her son. He wasn't that cold-hearted.

And she wouldn't let him! No one would take Johnny from her, not even his own father.

Kit left Johnny's room with reluctant footsteps and went downstairs in search of Jake. Not finding him, she went outside into the rain-freshened morning. The pungent odor of damp earth greeted her, followed closely by Toby, who skipped around her in excitement.

She scratched behind his ear. "Have you seen Jake?"

The dog yipped in reply and dashed toward the barn. Kit followed him at a more sedate pace, her body sore from the glorious lovemaking with Jake. She forced the sweet memories aside, unable to deal with them without remembering his angry words afterward.

She entered the barn and spied Charlie standing by the stall that held the new mother and her colt. She went to join them.

"Mornin'," Charlie greeted her. "Both mama and baby appear to be doin' just fine."

Kit smiled, glad to find one ray of sunshine in her dreary mood. "That's good. I hope I can see that colt grow up."

Charlie turned to face her, his expression solemn. "Is it the loan?"

"Partly," Kit admitted. "I have only ten days to come up with five hundred dollars."

"Somethin' will come up. It always does."

Kit wasn't so certain. The small income from her dime novels had pulled her through a couple of times, but even that had dried up. "Have you seen Jake this morning?"

"He rode out in the middle of the night."

Shock robbed Kit of her voice for a moment. "He must've left right after I told him about Johnny."

"Can't say as I blame him."

"I was only doing what I thought was best."

"Did you ever wonder what was best for Cordell and Johnny?"

Kit pressed her spectacles up with her forefinger and turned her attention to the nursing mare and her hungry foal. "I thought I was doing the right thing." She sighed.

Charlie studied her a moment. "You went and done it, didn't you? You fell in love with him."

Kit wanted to deny his words, but she'd had enough of lying to last a lifetime. "I didn't mean to."

"Ain't no one ever *means* to fall in love. So is he gonna do right by you?"

"I doubt he ever wants to see me again. He was so angry, Charlie." A sob escaped her. "What am I going to do if he takes Johnny away?"

Charlie put his muscled arms around her, and Kit accepted his awkward hug, grateful for the shoulder to lean on. Her body trembled as tears rolled down her cheeks, dampening Charlie's rough-spun shirt.

"It'll be all right," the burly man soothed in a gravelly voice. "Cordell strikes me as a man who ain't goin' to shirk his duty."

"But what if he figures his duty is to take Johnny home with him? First I lose Johnny, then I lose the ranch. I won't have anything left." Kit wept, her voice muffled.

"Hush, now; nobody's gonna be takin' Johnny or your ranch, not as long as you got me and Ethan."

"I ain't too old to take a scalp or two myself." Pete Two Ponies stepped out of the shadows.

Kit moved away from Charlie, brushing her sleeve across her damp cheeks. She managed a smile. "I don't think that'll be necessary, but thanks anyhow." Her smile faltered. "I'm not sure what's going to happen, but I want you both to know that I'm grateful for everything you've done for Johnny and me.''

''Ain't nothin' gonna happen,'' Charlie assured her. ''Leastways, nothin' we can't handle.''

Kit wished she could be as certain. ''I'd better get back to the house and put breakfast on.''

As she left a rustle of footsteps behind her made her turn to see who'd followed.

Pete's creased face glanced upward, then to the east and west. Remaining silent, the gray-haired Indian closed his eyes a moment as if in supplication.

He opened his eyes, and Kit asked in a low, reverent voice, ''Was that your morning prayer?''

He shook his head. ''Naw. I was trying to decide if it'd be a good day to go fishing.''

''What'd you decide?'' She kept her tone as dry as tinder.

He nodded with a slow, measured motion. ''I think the fish will bite today. Mind if I take Johnny? Been a while since me and him been down to the creek.''

A grateful smile touched Kit's lips. ''And if Jake comes back to get Johnny, he won't be around.''

Pete shrugged his thin shoulders, a picture of innocence. ''If the boy isn't here, Cordell can't take him, can he?''

''I appreciate the offer, but ignoring the problem won't make it go away.''

Pete stepped closer to Kit. ''I ain't saying to ignore Cordell, all I'm saying is that Johnny won't be around when you two start arguing. That wouldn't be good for the boy to hear.''

Pete was right; there was no reason to put Johnny in the middle. She nodded. ''All right. I'll get a lunch basket put together.''

Pete studied her with an impenetrable gaze. ''Send Johnny down to the barn when he's ready.''

Without another word, he limped away. Kit wondered what thoughts he hadn't spoken. Did he disapprove of what she'd done? Did he agree with Charlie's view that she should've told Jake earlier?

Straightening her back, she moved to the house. She'd get Johnny fed and away for a little while. Then she'd prepare herself for the inevitable confrontation.

An hour later, she handed Johnny a basket filled with sandwiches, pickles, boiled eggs, and an apple pie. "I hope you and Pete catch lots of fish. We haven't had fried trout in a long time."

Johnny lifted the checkered cloth covering the picnic meal and peeked at the pile of food. An enthusiastic smile lit his boyish face. "I can't wait for lunch."

Despite her worries, Kit smiled. "You'd better. That's all you and Pete are going to get until this evening." She took hold of his shoulders and steered him toward the open doorway. "Have fun, sweetheart."

"I will."

Kit watched him trot outside and across the yard.

"Johnny," she called out.

He paused, glancing back.

The sun cast filaments of fiery reds and golds in his hair. Kit swallowed her fearful premonition and crossed her arms. "I love you, Johnny."

His young face appeared puzzled, but he waved. "I love you, too, Ma. Bye."

Pete stepped out of the barn with two fishing poles in hand and met Johnny. They fell into step, walking toward the trees that hid the creek from view.

Kit watched the slight figures until they disappeared in the shadows of the oaks and aspens, then she returned to the silent house. As she considered how to appeal to Jake, memories of the previous evening intruded, derailing her thoughts. She couldn't even envision him without her pulse quickening and desire shallowing her breathing. How could she be in the same room with him without remembering what they'd shared? Without wanting to curl into his embrace and spend another night in his arms?

She had to think of Johnny. She had to think of a life without her son. She had to think of a way to convince Jake to allow Johnny to continue living with her. If she didn't, she'd have nothing left.

The morning crawled by as Kit scrubbed floors until her hands were red and wrinkly and her back ached. Though the physical activity kept her busy, her idle mind refused to set aside thoughts of Jake. After lunch, she escaped the suffocating confines of the house and continued training the bay gelding she'd begun to work with earlier in the week.

While she put the horse through its paces, she could dismiss from her mind worries about the ranch and Johnny. The familiar leather between her fingers and the warm spring breeze wafting across her face lifted her spirits.

An hour after she'd begun working with the yearling, Kit spotted a rider approaching the ranch. Sunlight slanted off the horse's spotted coat, giving horse and rider an ethereal glow against the greening backdrop of budding trees. Kit's stomach fisted, and for a moment all she could do was stare at Jake. Sweat slicked her palms, and her anxiety seemed to telegraph itself to the young bay, who skittered sideways. Kit forced her attention back to the colt and soothed it, unstrapping the lead from its halter. The animal trotted away, shaking its mane.

Kit looped the leather strap around her hand and elbow, watching Jake out of the corner of her eye. He drew his horse up by the corral, dismounted, and loosely wrapped the reins around a pole. He wore his hat with the brim pulled low over his eyes, shading his features, but Kit could see the anger in the stiff set of his broad shoulders and the flexing of his fingers. The return of the tied-down holster around his hips added to his aura of danger.

With deliberate motions, she strolled across the enclosure and swung the gate open. She stepped over to Jake, stopping a few feet in front of him. Her traitorous gaze noticed his long, muscled legs and thighs encased in snug tan trousers, and the dark blue shirt taut across his chest with his customary brown vest worn over it. A few curling hairs peeked out above the V at the base of his neck, and Kit remembered too clearly how they'd tickled her nose when she'd caressed him.

Passion careened through her like a runaway stage, and she fought the urge to touch him. "Hello, Jake."

"Where's my son?"

His terse question plummeted her hopes that he might have forgiven her. She lifted her chin. "He's not here."

"Where is he?" His tone snapped with impatience.

"He's with Pete. Let's go up to the house and talk." She turned away, and Jake grabbed her arm, spinning her around to face him.

"I came for my son," he said flatly.

Panic threatened to overwhelm Kit's carefully constructed facade. She breathed deeply, pressing the hysteria into a corner of her mind. "We need to talk first."

Kit parried his smoldering glare, and with a muttered curse, Jake released her. Her heart threatening to strangle her, Kit led the way to the house. Even though she didn't glance behind her, she felt Jake's hostile gaze drilling a hole into her back. Once inside, Kit went into the kitchen and poured them each a cup of coffee. She handed Jake a mug, and after a moment's hesitation, he accepted it silently.

"We don't have anything to discuss," Jake stated.

Kit sipped her coffee, burning her tongue on the hot

liquid. She allowed the silence to grow as she gathered her turbulent thoughts.

"Where do you plan on taking Johnny?" she asked, her voice breathy with nervousness.

"To live with his father," he answered, in a crisp tone that cut to the core of her mother's heart.

Kit flinched. "What about me? Are you going to tell him that the woman he believes is his mother isn't really? That he has no mother, and he can't ever see me again?"

Doubt flickered in Jake's granite visage, but he quickly masked it. "He'll understand once I tell him."

"He's only five years old, Jake. All he'll understand is that you've taken him away from the one place he's always felt loved and secure. What's that going to do to him?" Kit pressed.

"You should've thought of that five years ago."

Defiance surged through her, and she plunked her cup down on the table. She took a step toward him, aiming an accusing finger at him. "Tell me, Jake, where were *you* five years ago? Even if I'd wanted to tell you, I wouldn't have been able to find you."

Jake kept his gaze locked with hers. "You didn't even try."

She leaned forward, his face only inches from hers. "Where would I have started? And even if I had found you, would you have come back? When you left Chaney, you were hell-bent on revenge."

Jake glanced away. His conscience mocked him, reminding him what kind of person he'd been back then. Would he have returned to care for a child he hadn't even known he'd fathered? He swallowed hard and shoved his doubts aside. "He's my son, my own flesh and blood."

"What would you have done with a baby? What kind of life could you have given him?" she persisted.

Kit's words hit too close to the truth. While he'd hunted his father's murderer, Jake had raised enough hell to give even the devil pause. What kind of life was that for a child?

Drawing on a heavy dose of anger, Jake refused to give in to Kit's arguments. He wouldn't allow her to sway him from his objective. "I checked the court records. You never legally adopted him."

She drew back as if she'd been slapped, and the color drained from her face. Then she shot back fiercely, "I don't need a piece of paper to prove he's my son."

"The court does."

Her lips thinned in irritation. "I'm not talking about legalities, Jake, I'm talking about the heart. I love him. Isn't that enough?"

"Love didn't keep my mother here." The words tumbled out before Jake could stop them.

She studied him with an intensity that seemed to bore straight to his soul. "So you want your son growing up thinking his mother never loved him, either? Do you want your son to feel that same pain you've felt every day since your mother left you?"

Jake slammed his cup down on the table, and coffee sloshed over his hand and across the scarred wood surface. "You're *not* his mother!"

"I'm the only mother he's ever known," she said, her voice gut-wrenchingly soft, her eyes glimmering with moisture.

A lonely black pit yawned within Jake. For a moment he was six years old again.

"Why are you packing, Ma?" young Jake asked curiously.

"I'm going to take a little trip, sweetheart," she replied.

"I want to go with you."

She paused in the middle of folding a dress, and sat

*on the bed. Patting the mattress, she urged Jake to join
her. He scrambled up, and his mother grasped his small
hand.*

*"I wish you could, Jake, but your father needs you.
He loves you very much," she said.*

"Don't you love me?"

*She pulled him close to her chest, kissing the top of
his head. Her familiar flowery smell soothed him. "Of
course I do, more than you'll ever know. But I have to
go away for a little while."*

*Jake's bottom lip quivered. "I'm going to miss you,
Ma."*

*"And I'm going to miss you. If I could take you with
me, I would. You have to believe me, Jake." His
mother's tone sounded funny, like when he cried after
he got hurt.*

"When will you be back?"

*"I'm not sure, sweetheart, but remember, I'll always
love you, no matter what. Please promise me you'll remember that."*

*Jake eased out of her embrace and gazed up at her.
Tears rolled down her cheeks, frightening him. "I promise. I love you, Ma."*

For months he'd waited for her to return, but she
never did. Finally, he'd given up on her and his promise.
He'd also learned how women's tears were used to hide
their lies.

He swallowed the bitter hurt. No, he didn't want
Johnny to know that kind of torture.

"What do you suggest we do?" Jake demanded.

Kit blinked as if surprised. "I don't think you should
take Johnny into town to live with you."

Anger returned, giving his tone a sharp edge. "You
think he should stay living with you like nothing's
changed?"

She glared at him, her eyes flashing behind the round

lenses. "You can't expect him to accept so many changes at once. We can tell him you're his father, and let him get used to that first."

"And when do I get to see him if I'm in town and he's here?"

She drew back. "You can ride over here whenever you'd like."

"What if I want to put him to bed every night? You expect me to ride out here every day, then ride back after dark?"

"You certainly can't live here."

Jake snorted. "I thought you didn't care about your reputation."

Her blush deepened to scarlet. "I don't, but . . ."

He crossed his arms. "But what?"

She pressed her spectacles up on her nose, and defiance sparked her tightly drawn features. "It wouldn't be right."

He clenched his teeth, his jaw muscle flexing. Should he bring up the ranch loan? If she didn't pay her mortgage, it would be she who wouldn't belong there, not him. It would be her breaking society's rules, not him. It would be her all alone, not him.

Guilt pierced Jake's stubborn wrath. He didn't want to relegate her to living the lonely life she'd known as a child. For all her deceit, Jake didn't want to shred her tattered reputation any more than it had been by the gossipmongers of Chaney. And he *had* taken her virginity. She hadn't lied about that.

Her steady gaze remained unflinching, her lips thinned to a grim line. She resembled a she-cat protecting her young, ready to attack at the slightest provocation. He admired her grit; her bookish appearance had fooled him into thinking she'd back down.

Kit *was* Johnny's mother—if not by blood, then by love—and she didn't want to leave her son as his mother had left him. He admired her for that while at the same time wanting to damn her for keeping Johnny from him.

Kit relinquished her glare and picked up her cup. Studying him silently, she leaned against the counter and sipped her coffee. Although she appeared calm and resolute, Jake spotted a fluttery pulse point in her neck.

He considered his options the way he would approach a client's defense. With any luck, the ranch would be his in a short time and he would legally move into the house he'd grown up in. Johnny wouldn't even have to leave the only home he'd known. But there still remained the problem of Kit.

Without her, Johnny would be miserable. Jake couldn't do that to his son. The only way to ensure Johnny had both his parents would be for Jake to marry Kit.

Having seen his parents' failed marriage, he hadn't planned on falling into the same trap. He breathed deeply to dispel the suffocating impact.

Unbidden, the memory of Kit holding the kitten in the barn surfaced. He remembered her gentleness with the tiny creature, and the way the lantern's light had bathed her hair with a golden halo. He had thought it an angel's halo.

In spite of her duplicity, he wouldn't be able to look at himself in the mirror if he cast Kit out of the home she'd worked so hard to possess. Infinitely worse would be the loss of her son.

As he considered marrying Kit, the idea didn't disturb him as much as it originally had. Of course, he'd already tasted her charms and knew she'd be able to assume her wifely duties. And enjoy them.

Warming to his plan, he had to admit marriage wouldn't be such a bad trade-off. She'd remain Johnny's mother, and Jake would have her to himself every night.

Because he could no longer trust her, the marriage bed would be the only thing they shared.

He glanced at Kit. "I think I've come up with a solution to our problem."

She tipped her head to the side, a lone curl straying across her creased forehead. Wariness crept into her eyes. "What's that?"

"Marry me."

Chapter 15

❧ ⟲⟳ ❧

Jake Cordell slicked back his thick, autumn-touched hair and slapped bay rum on his neck. Squaring his hat on his head, he picked up a small black velvet box. He flicked open the container's lid and gazed down at the glittering diamond, a token of his love for the woman he would spend the rest of his life with.

"For richer or for poorer, in sickness and in health, 'til death do us part," Jake quoted softly.

He'd made his decision. No more would he strap on the instrument of death around his hips. No more would he risk his life against murderous outlaws. No more would he be alone.

His heart swelled with an emotion he'd lived without for most of his thirty-one years. No matter what hardships came upon them, Jake knew he and his bride would face them together; side by side for all time. She who knew him as no other woman did and who gazed at him with loving adoration . . .

From this moment forward, he'd be her hero alone.

Kit stared at Jake's emotionless mask. He'd proposed marriage the way she proposed a horse deal. She, however, displayed more enthusiasm to a prospective buyer.

Hurt indignation swelled in Kit, igniting her temper. "The hell I will."

Surprise flickered in his eyes, then he narrowed his gaze. "Before you turn me down, think of Johnny. What would he think if his father and mother got married and he had a real family?"

Kit knew Johnny's response: he'd be overjoyed. "That's not fair!"

A scowl curled his upper lip. "Life isn't fair. Besides, you're the one telling me to think of Johnny, to think how all this will change his life. If you marry me, it's going to be a lot easier on him."

"And if I say no?"

His expression turned to stone. "Then I take Johnny with me."

Kit spun away from Jake to stare unseeing out the small kitchen window. To be Mrs. Jake Cordell had been a childish dream she'd clung to for years, but not this way. Not without Jake's love. How could she marry him, knowing the marriage was a sham, a blackmail scheme she'd agreed to only to stay with her son?

Closing her eyes against waves of anguish, Kit lamented she had no choice. She would remain Johnny's mother, but she wouldn't have Jake's heart. And if she became Jake's wife, she also relinquished all rights to her ranch to him. Surprisingly, that didn't bother her. She loved the ranch, but deep down she'd always thought of it as Jake's. One of the reasons she'd bought it was to ensure Jake's son would inherit the Cordell home.

But what of Charlie, Ethan, and Pete? This was their home as well. If she agreed to his plan, she had to make sure her friends would have a place here if they wanted to stay.

If she accepted his proposal, it wouldn't be much different than the way she and Johnny lived now. Surely

Jake expected her to be a wife in name only. He'd made his disgust for her obvious. She swallowed her disappointment and was angry at herself for her treasonous reaction.

She forced herself to think of Johnny. How would Jake explain he was Johnny's real father? Would the five-year-old understand? Or would it lead to more questions, questions Kit feared to answer?

Turning slowly, Kit met Jake's rock-steady gaze. "I have some conditions."

Suspicion lit his maple-colored eyes. "What are they?"

Kit scrubbed her damp palms across her trouser-clad thighs. "What do you plan on doing about Charlie, Ethan, and Pete?"

Jake shrugged. "As far as I'm concerned, they'll continue working here like they've always done. I plan on keeping my law office for a little while, and I'll need some men I can trust to take care of the horses."

Gratitude tightened Kit's chest. "Good, that was one of my conditions. This is their home." She took a deep breath. "And I don't want you to tell Johnny about Maggie."

"Why?"

"It'll be confusing enough for him when you tell him you're his father. When he's older, he'll understand the situation better."

A muscle flexed in his jaw. "All right."

Kit sighed in relief as she nodded. Only one problem remained: the mortgage on the ranch. Unwilling to deceive him any further, she wanted to have everything in the open between them. If she had been honest when Jake had arrived home, maybe things would've worked out differently.

"There's one more thing," she said.

"What's that?"

"If we marry, the ranch becomes yours," she began.

Jake's features became like marble, his eyes curtained to hide his thoughts. "That's right."

She swallowed the pride blocking her throat. "In ten days, the mortgage comes due. It's five hundred dollars, and I only have two hundred. I'm not proud of the fact that I don't have the money, but you have a right to know what you're getting into."

An unidentifiable emotion flickered across Jake's face, and he looked down at the floor, hiding his expression. Kit's palms grew moist from nervousness. His estimation of her must have taken another steep plunge.

Raising his head, Jake met her eyes with a steadfast gaze. "I've got some money saved from my bounty hunting. The mortgage'll get paid."

Both elated and humiliated, Kit didn't know how to respond. "All right." The only secret she harbored was her identity as T. K. Thorne. She looked at his flinty expression and her courage failed her. "I guess that's it, then. I'll marry you."

"When?"

She shrugged, surrendering to the inevitable. "Whenever you want."

"Sunday."

Shock robbed Kit of her voice for a moment. "That's in four days!"

He nodded. "The sooner we get married, the sooner I can start being a father to my son."

Although his voice was steady, Kit could hear regret echo in his tone. He'd already lost five years with Johnny; Kit couldn't deny him any longer.

"We'll have to talk to the minister," she stated.

"Tomorrow morning we'll go visit with him. Where's Johnny?"

Kit hesitated a moment. "Pete took him fishing down at the creek."

Jake's expression grew pensive. "My father took me fishing a couple of times. Those were the only times I really felt like he cared for me a little." He started, as if he'd revealed too much. "I want to take Johnny fishing, and I want him to remember those times after he grows up."

Kit resisted the urge to touch him, to assure him he would be a good father. She turned toward the door. "I'll take you to him."

She led him out of the house, and they walked in strained silence through the trees. At the edge of the clearing, Jake paused and clasped Kit's wrist, halting her. "I'll tell him we're getting married."

She remained silent a moment, seeing anxiety in his eyes. "Do you want me to?"

He seemed to ponder her question. "We'll both tell him."

Hope flickered in Kit's breast. He'd said *we*. Maybe there was a chance Jake would come to care for her like a real husband. Pleased by his concession, she smiled. "Good idea."

His features eased as a smile ghosted his lips.

Jake glanced down at his hand, which banded Kit's slender wrist. He liked touching her. He admired her courage in standing up to him for the sake of her friends, instead of trying to ease her own plight. But it was her divulging the news about the ranch's mortgage and her inability to pay it that had nearly shattered his resolve. He'd been certain she'd hide that from him, as she'd hidden Johnny's identity.

Confused by her candor, he didn't know what to think of Kit. This time she'd been honest. This time it was him keeping the secret.

He released her reluctantly, and they crossed the remaining distance to the creek's high bank.

"Hi, Mr. Cordell," Johnny hollered, scrambling to his feet.

Pete rose also and laid a firm hand on the boy's shoulder, holding him back protectively. Jake glanced at Kit, who sent the gray-haired Indian a nod. Pete removed his hand, his creased face relaxing. Had Kit thought he'd steal Johnny away? Her distrust struck a discordant note in Jake. It was one thing for him to distrust her, but another for her to distrust him.

Jake turned back to his son. *His son.*

"Hello, Johnny." Jake could hardly speak past the lump in his throat. He hadn't even been this nervous at his first gunfight.

Like the focusing of a blurry picture, Johnny's image cleared and Jake could suddenly see himself in the boy. Why hadn't he recognized his own flesh and blood? He took a deep breath. "Catching anything?"

Pete held up a stringer with five medium-sized trout. "Got us a start on supper." He latched his shrewd gaze on Jake. "How about you?"

Jake glanced at Kit, who seemed to be studying the fish with more attention than necessary. He turned back to the aged Indian. "You could say I caught more than I bargained for."

Kit speared him with a sharp look.

Jake hunkered down beside Johnny, who stood holding his crude fishing pole. "Remember when you asked me if I would be your father if I married your ma?"

Johnny nodded. "Yep, but you said you had to love each other first."

Kit straightened and turned away, but not before Jake spotted her trembling lips. His own stomach clenched with regrets. He pasted on a smile. "What if I told you that even if I didn't marry her, I'd be your father?"

Johnny appeared puzzled. "What do you mean?"

"I'm really your father."

Johnny turned to Kit. "Is it true, Ma? Is Mr. Cordell my pa?"

Her smile appeared strained. "Yes, he is, sweetheart."

Johnny squealed with delight and wrapped his skinny arms around Jake's neck. "You're my pa!"

Unexpected tears burned in Jake's eyes, and he hugged his son close. Glancing up, he noticed Kit's gentle gaze upon them, and his heart skipped a beat. Never knowing what he'd missed all these years, he hadn't longed for a home and family. Now, however, a fierce protectiveness rose in him. No one would harm Johnny, or Kit, as long as he lived.

Johnny drew back, but kept his hand on Jake's shoulder. The boy frowned slightly. "How come you never came to see me before?"

Jake licked his suddenly dry lips. How could he tell Johnny he'd been too busy drinking and whoring?

"He had a job to do, Johnny. He was hunting down outlaws who belonged in jail," Kit replied.

Surprised by her defense for him, Jake cast her a grateful look, and she nodded in acknowledgment.

His son's beaming smile returned. "But now you're going to stay here with us, right?"

"As soon as your mother and I get married."

The boy looked at Kit. "When is that?"

"Sunday," she replied.

"Then we'll all be a family," Jake added.

Johnny's whoop nearly deafened him. "You hear that, Pete? I got a real family."

The sage Indian nodded, his obsidian eyes twinkling. "It's about time. I figure if a man and a woman is going to get married, they may as well do it without a lot of fuss."

"Believe me, there isn't going to be a lot of fuss for this one," Kit said, bitterness ringing in her words.

Jake's light mood evaporated. In spite of the circumstances surrounding the wedding, his pride didn't want others to know he'd used extortion to gain Kit's agreement.

Johnny suddenly grabbed his fishing pole. "I got one," he shouted, drawing Jake's attention.

He turned back to the boy, and together he and Johnny landed a flopping fish on the bank.

"Thanks, Pa," Johnny said, holding up the twisting trout by the line.

Jake ruffled his dark hair, his heart expanding into his throat. "You're welcome, son."

The next morning, Kit reined in Cassie in front of Freda's neat whitewashed fence. After dismounting, she wrapped the leather straps around the hitching post and brushed the dust from her burgundy split skirt.

Opening the gate, she followed the hard-packed dirt path to the front porch. Her knock was answered a few moments later by her petite friend.

"Come in," Freda greeted with an expansive wave of a flour-covered hand. After Kit stepped across the threshold, Freda closed the door behind her. "What brings you here this early?"

"Do you have a fresh pot of coffee?"

Freda's smile faded. "In the kitchen. There you can tell me what bothers you."

After pouring them each a cup of coffee, Kit lowered herself to a ladderback chair. The older woman wiped her hands on her apron and joined her.

"This is about Jake Cordell," Freda stated.

Kit glanced at her friend, startled. "How did you know?"

" I wasn't born yesterday." She shrugged her narrow shoulders. "Jake has been as grouchy as a fox."

Kit bit back a smile. "As grouchy as a bear." She

sipped her coffee, appreciating the strong, bitter brew. "At least Jake's not enjoying this any more than I am. We're getting married."

Freda's eyes widened as her mouth dropped open. "Serious you are?"

Kit nodded. "I'm afraid so. I told him Johnny was his son, and he threatened to take Johnny away from me if I didn't marry him."

The German woman sighed. "I am not surprised. Jake will do anything to keep his son happy."

Kit laughed without humor. "And here I thought nobody knew Johnny was Jake's son. I guess everyone but Jake saw the resemblance." She paused, a sob welling in her throat. "How can I go through with it, Freda? He doesn't love me."

"But you love him."

"That's why it hurts so much."

Freda reached across the table and grasped Kit's hand. "In the old country, arranged marriages were common. It was with Hans and me, but we came to love each other. For Jake, it will happen also. He already cares for you. If he didn't, your feelings for Johnny would not have mattered to him."

Freda's words pulled Kit out of despair, but did she dare hope that Jake would someday love her as much as she loved him? "How did you make your husband love you?"

Freda smiled, and her gaze seemed to turn inward to unseen memories. For a moment, Kit could see how Freda must've looked as a young woman, before time's trials had furrowed her brow and shadowed her eyes. "After we were married, those were good days. My Hans would work in the fields and I would take him his lunch. We would sit and talk beneath a big oak tree. We fell in love during that time." She blinked and focused on Kit. "I did nothing but be with him. Often we did not even talk, but just sat quietly in front of the hearth. I would mend and Hans would smoke his pipe. Sometimes when I close my eyes, I can still smell the tobacco.'' Freda shook her head, the years stamping their mark on her features once more. ''If only he had stayed away from the liquor.''

Kit squeezed the woman's work-roughened hand. ''Did you still love him after he started drinking?''

''Yes, even though I hated what he became,'' Freda admitted. She leaned forward, capturing Kit with the intensity of her hazel eyes. ''But Jake, I think he is different. A good father he will be, and a good husband.''

Hope flickered in Kit's breast. Could she make the marriage work? Determination kindled within her. There really was no choice. She loved him, and she'd have the rest of her life to make him love her. ''I pray you're right, Freda, or this may be the biggest mistake I ever made.''

''Or the best decision,'' Freda said softly.

The door swung open and Jake halted inside the kitchen. ''Am I interrupting anything?''

Kit glanced up, startled by his appearance, and even more surprised by his businesslike attire. A dark broadcloth suit hugged his broad shoulders, and a dazzling white shirt made his complexion appear darker. Black trousers fit his muscled legs like a second skin, and shiny boots molded his calves. He appeared rakishly handsome, and Kit's desire flared. She forced herself to look away from the tempting picture.

''Visiting we were,'' Freda replied. She stood and resumed kneading the bread dough on the counter. ''Congratulations.''

''Kit must've told you the news,'' he said, pouring himself a cup of coffee.

He took Freda's vacated place at the table across from

Kit, and the unsettling scent of bay rum cut through the pleasant smell of baking bread and pies.

"Who's watching Johnny?" Jake asked, concern written in his features.

"Pete took him fishing again," Kit replied.

Jake nodded in satisfaction. "Did she tell you about Johnny, Freda?"

The older woman's eyes twinkled. "I already knew."

Jake groaned. "Why didn't anybody bother to tell me?"

Kit noticed the bandage was gone from his forehead, although the wound was surrounded by a fading yellow-ish bruise. Her irritation cooled, replaced by a muscle-tightening dread that the bullet could've killed him instead of only wounding him.

"Did she tell you when?" he asked.

Freda shook her head.

"Sunday."

The woman's accusing glance scolded Kit. "So soon? A dress you must have, and food, and music, and a dance."

"No," Kit said firmly. "I'll wear one of my old dresses and it'll just be Jake and me and Johnny. And you and Patrick can be the witnesses."

Jake studied her, his expression unreadable. "I thought this was my wedding, too."

Kit's agitation increased. She wanted to shield Jake from the sharp-edged tongues of those who would won-der why he married Chaney's shunned spinster. And her pride didn't want those same people to witness his hol-low vows. "Don't make this any more of a mockery than it already is."

"It's you who's not taking it seriously," Jake said in a dangerously calm voice. He glanced at Freda, then leaned close to Kit and lowered his voice. "I plan on keeping my wedding vows."

Kit stared at him, trying to read the meaning behind his intense words. Which vows was he referring to? If he didn't love her, how did he expect to keep his vows?

Did he plan on exercising his husbandly rights? Her pulse quickened at the thought, and she admonished herself for her weakness. He couldn't possibly plan on sleeping with her.

He continued to stare at her, and Kit searched for a response to his veiled challenge. "And you think I won't keep my part of the bargain?"

His gaze slid down her face to her chest and back to her eyes. "You will."

Heat flooded Kit's cheeks. What little she knew about men she'd only recently learned, but she recognized the arrogant hunger in his deliberate scrutiny. If he demanded she come to his bed, would she be able to deny him? She shoved the question from her mind, unwilling to examine the answer too closely.

"You look like you're going to a funeral," she stated dryly, anxious to change the subject.

He chuckled, a full, masculine sound that sent sensual awareness skittering through her. "Reverend Wellensiek is expecting us this morning."

Freda remained silent, but Kit knew she'd heard most of their conversation.

He stood. "Are you ready?"

Kit swallowed her reservations and nodded. "Thanks for the coffee and the advice, Freda."

"You're welcome," she replied. Stepping over to Kit, she embraced her and whispered, "All will work out, you will see."

Kit closed her eyes prayerfully. "I hope so, Freda, I truly hope so."

As they walked outside, Jake asked, "What's this advice she gave you?"

Kit shrugged. "Nothing you'd be interested in."

Jake glowered in irritation, and Kit hurried ahead of him, repressing a childish urge to stick her tongue out at him. He might soon as be her husband, but she wasn't about to lose all of her hard-won independence. With his long-legged stride, he caught up to her by Freda's whitewashed fence. He blocked the gate and crossed his arms.

"Is that any way for a fiancée to act?" he asked in a deceptively soft voice.

Kit glared at him, wondering what game he was playing now. "How should I act?"

He reached for her hand and guided it through the crook of his arm. "Like we can't stand to be apart."

She attempted to pull away from him, but he held tight. "Why do you care? You're only marrying me so Johnny will have a mother."

He glanced over her shoulder, then returned his shuttered gaze to her. "After my mother left, I got sick and tired of everybody's pity. I don't want folks treating Johnny like they treated me. As far as everyone is concerned, it was love at first sight between us."

Kit tried to think, to ignore the warmth of his body through the layers of clothing. Didn't she worry about the same thing? And besides, for her, love at first sight wasn't far from the truth. "All right."

Jake nodded, his taut expression easing. "Good. Now let's stroll over to the reverend's house like a happily engaged couple."

She allowed him to lead her down the boardwalk. He matched his pace to hers and greeted each person they met. Kit managed to paste a pleasant smile on her face even as she fought to ignore the allure of Jake's hard muscles beneath the civilized veneer.

"Top o' the mornin'," Patrick greeted them.

"Morning, Patrick," Jake replied with a wide grin.

"Hello," Kit said, genuine warmth in her welcome.

The burly Irishman pressed his hat off his forehead with his thumb. "What're you two doin' up and about this beautiful mornin'?"

"We're on our way to see the minister," Kit replied.

Patrick's eyes rounded. "Don't tell me you're gettin' hitched!"

Jake patted the back of her hand as though she were an obedient little girl, and Kit resisted the urge to kick his shins. "That's right. Kit's agreed to become my wife."

Patrick's smile almost split his broad face. "That's fine news to be hearin'." He shook Jake's hand and dropped a light kiss on Kit's cheek. "Congratulations to both of you. I'm thinkin' you two'll be a grand couple."

"Just grand," Kit repeated, and sent Jake a syrupy smile.

Jake telegraphed a warning with a narrowed gaze, then spoke to Patrick. "The wedding is Sunday, and you and Freda are invited to be our witnesses."

"I'd be honored," Patrick said. "You be lettin' me know the time and I'll be there."

"We will," Jake assured him, then lowered his voice. "Did you find anything?"

Patrick's expression sobered as he shook his head. "Nothin', except a few .32-30 cartridges."

Jake rubbed his fresh-shaven jaw. "Doesn't prove a thing. Every man jack and his brother owns one."

Kit frowned. "Prove what? What're you talking about?"

Patrick suddenly found something interesting to study on his boot toe, and Jake sighed. "I told Patrick where I'd been ambushed and he went to have a look around. We figure it was someone trying to make a name for himself."

Kit's throat ached with dismay.

"I'll be lettin' you know if I find anything," Patrick said.

"Appreciate it."

Patrick's footsteps faded away.

"Come on, Kit, we have an appointment to keep," Jake said.

Her mind numb, Kit allowed him to escort her to the parsonage. He knocked on the solid oak door, and Bertie Wellensiek answered the summons a moment later.

"Good morning, Mr. Cordell," the rotund woman greeted, not acknowledging Kit's presence.

"Hello, Mrs. Wellensiek. We have an appointment with your husband," he said, a brittle edge to his polite words.

"Oh?" Her voice vibrated with perverse curiosity.

Calm down, Bertie, or your stays will come undone, Kit thought peevishly.

"Could you let him know we're here?" Jake asked, keeping his voice courteous but cool.

After a moment, Bertie nodded and motioned them inside. Kit and Jake waited in the drab foyer as Bertie scuttled down the hall. Unease settled in Kit, and she forced herself not to fidget.

"You can go in," Bertie announced stiffly a few moments later.

"Thank you," Jake said.

The Reverend Wellensiek rose from his chair behind the scratched desk and leaned over to grasp Jake's hand. "Hello, Mr. Cordell." He turned to Kit. "Miss Thornton, nice to see you."

His friendly greeting eased Kit's misgivings slightly, and she lowered herself into the offered chair. Once everyone was seated, the Reverend Wellensiek clasped his hands and rested them on the cluttered desktop. "What is it you wished to talk to me about?"

"Kit and I want to get married Sunday," Jake stated without preamble.

Kit remained silent, listening to the two men work out the details of her wedding. Jake sounded convincing and held her hand, his thumb rubbing the back of her hand. She tried to concentrate on the plans, but Jake's absent caresses inflamed her senses, reminding her of their one night of passion. Her body grew languid, her mind conjuring visions of Jake in the moonlight and how beautiful he'd appeared.

"Is that all right with you?" Jake asked.

Kit blinked aside the sensual images, her cheeks heating with embarrassment. What in the world was she doing thinking about such things in the minister's house?

"Whatever you say, Jake," Kit stammered.

He glanced at her like she'd lost what few wits she'd possessed. With what she hoped was an angelic smile, Kit turned to the Reverend Wellensiek. "Is there anything else we need to do?"

He shook his head. "I believe everything has been taken care of."

Kit rose, eager to escape. "Then Jake and I won't take any more of your time."

After a round of farewells, Jake escorted Kit out to the bustling street. He leaned close to her. "What were you thinking about in there?"

Kit recalled his tantalizing touch and her unbidden reaction to it. "I'm sure you and the Reverend Wellensiek have everything worked out."

He studied her a moment longer, and a knowing grin captured his lips, bringing a new wave of embarrassment to Kit. Had her thoughts been that evident? He brought his mouth close to her ear. "Be patient, Kit. Just a few more days."

Startled, she glanced at him.

His suggestive wink answered her earlier question. After they were married, he expected her to occupy his bed.

Chapter 16

⁓⟨◎◎⟩⁓

Today was Kit's wedding day, and a bittersweet ache panged beneath her calm facade. She had made her choice to marry Jake and to work to make the marriage a real one. However, her earlier optimism had faded in the reality of the wedding preparations. Jake had been polite but distant, and the friendship that had blossomed between them had seemed to wither.

Kit stared at her reflection in the mirror. She had chosen to wear her cream-colored dress with tiny bluebells scattered across the material, and a garland woven from early spring flowers encircled her crown of ringlets. Dark smudges lay beneath her eyes, partially hidden by her wire spectacles.

Was she naive to think she could bring love into a marriage that had been born of distrust?

A light knock sounded.

She took a deep breath and pinched some color into her pale cheeks. "Come in."

Freda slipped inside. "It is time."

Kit studied the woman who was as close to a mother as she'd ever had. "Am I doing the right thing?"

Freda raised herself on her tiptoes and hugged Kit. "Be patient. He will love you in time."

Closing her eyes, Kit breathed a prayerful "I hope you're right."

The off-key organ notes announced the start of her wedding.

Freda released her and stepped back. Laying a palm against Kit's cheek, she said softly, "You deserve this happiness. It will work out. You will see."

Kit nodded, swallowing her fears. Taking a deep breath, she followed Freda out of the back room of the church. Wearing a formal black broadcloth suit, Patrick met her at the entrance.

She placed her trembling hand through the crook of his arm, patted her hair into place one last time, and wrapped her fingers around the small bouquet of blue-bells.

Patrick laid his palm over her white knuckles. "Relax, lass. 'Tis your wedding, not your funeral."

A nervous laugh escaped her lips. She gazed up at his familiar florid features and slicked back auburn hair. "You're a good friend, Patrick."

The Irishman's face flushed. "Just as you are, Kit. 'Tis time to meet your intended."

Much to Kit's chagrin, the small church overflowed with people. It seemed everyone in Chaney had shown up to see if the great Jake Cordell would actually marry the town's social outcast. Even the mayor and his wife, Fanny, had turned out for the occasion.

As Kit walked down the aisle gripping Patrick's comforting arm, the hair at the back of her neck prickled. Through lowered lashes she sought the source of her disquiet. She spotted him a few moments later. Halfway down at the end of a pew sat David Preston, a glower marring his classic handsomeness. She pressed closer to Patrick's solid side and slid her gaze away from David's disturbing stare. Spotting Charlie and Ethan, Kit felt her apprehension ease, and she smiled at her two friends.

She knew what courage it took for them to come to Chaney and face the silent and not-so-silent snubs . . . especially Ethan, who still bore fading marks from his last visit to town. Charlie stood proudly and winked at her. Her heart lifted and she squared her shoulders.

As she glided to the front beside Patrick, Kit spotted Jake, and her breath caught in her throat. He looked more handsome than her imagination could ever conjure. Resplendent in a worsted gray suit with a red vest, he appeared every inch the hero of her dime novels. Standing by his side, Johnny looked like a miniature of Jake, his clothing matching his father's down to the black tie and shiny shoes. If there'd been any doubt that Johnny was Jake's son, it was dispelled by the similarities made more obvious by their attire.

Patrick stopped, and she took Jake's offered arm with more than a little trepidation.

Kit tried to imagine the hero Jake Cordell and his bride at the altar, preparing to pledge the rest of their lives to one another. She tried to imagine a scene full of love and happiness. She tried to imagine touching dialogue and an exchange of yearning gazes.

However, the words refused to be written in her imagination. The truth was too painful, too far removed from the fanciful tales she'd woven into dime novels.

Afraid Jake would see the tears brimming in her eyes, she focused on the reverend as he began the ceremony.

An hour later, Kit stood beside her husband and accepted good wishes from the same people who'd shunned her a week earlier. As she kept a frozen smile in place, she tried to remember the ceremony, but all she could recall was the kiss Jake had given her to seal their vows. Her knees still trembled in the aftermath of the soul-stealing caress, and she dared not look at Jake lest he see the undisguised love in her eyes.

Jake was her husband in name only now, but she *had* to believe someday he would be her true husband.

If she didn't have that hope, she had nothing.

The wedding and celebrating were finally over.

Jake heaved a weary sigh as he guided the wagon's team down the bumpy road toward home. *Home.* It had been a long time since he'd thought of anyplace as home. The word conjured up visions of Jake teaching Johnny how to work with the horses, and reading a story to his son after he'd tucked him into bed.

He cast a sidelong glance at Kit's stiff expression, the pallor so unlike her usual glow. Images of her sharing his bed brought a tightness to his groin. One night with her had only whetted his appetite for more. Knowing the passionate fire that blazed beneath her placid warmth, Jake wanted her even more than he had the first time.

Since he'd blackmailed her into marrying him, he wondered if she'd allow him in their room. If she refused, he had every right to force her into his bed, but Jake had never forced himself upon a woman, and he wasn't about to start with his own wife. Despite her deception, he cared for her as much as he could care for any woman. Maybe someday he'd even forgive her deceit.

He steered the horses into the ranch yard and halted them in front of the barn. Hopping down from the wagon, he reached for Kit's hand to help her to the ground.

As soon as she stood on the hard-packed earth, she pulled out of Jake's grasp. "Thank you," she mumbled.

His conscience tugged at him, but Jake ignored it. The fact that she appeared miserable on her own wedding day bothered him more than he cared to admit.

Johnny climbed down by himself and leaned over to give Toby a quick hug. The dog wagged its tail gratefully, then nudged Jake's hand with its damp nose. Jake scratched behind the animal's drooping ear and was rewarded with a moist tongue.

Johnny laid his palm on his pet's back. "This is my pa, Toby." The boy gazed up at Jake with adoration brimming his eyes.

Paternal pride swept through Jake, stunning him with its force.

Kit coughed, drawing his attention. He studied her for a moment, noting her pale face. The dark circles beneath her eyes attested to a lack of sleep. Knowing he was the cause, Jake took hold of her arm gently. "Why don't you go on into the house and lie down for a little while? It's been a busy day."

She lifted her chin in a familiar defiant gesture. "I'll go put supper on. Johnny can help you put up the horses."

Kit spun around and flounced toward the house, her cream-colored dress dancing around her long legs.

Johnny frowned. "Ma seems mad."

Jake stared after Kit a moment, then tousled the boy's thick hair. "She's just tired. Let's put the horses in the barn."

They removed their jackets and set to work. Jake unhitched the traces from the horses and had Johnny lead them into the barn. After hanging up the gear in the tack room, Jake joined his son in giving the animals a quick rubdown.

Watching Johnny's intent expression as he worked, Jake could tell the boy was eager to please him—yet he supposed it was he who should be seeking approval. The loose-moraled life he'd led the past few years wouldn't have been conducive to raising an impressionable boy. Kit had done an admirable job raising his son, and much as he hated to admit it, he was indebted to her.

Jake tossed the damp saddle blanket he'd used over

the fence slat and stepped out of the stall, closing the gate behind him. He leaned against the upper rail to observe Johnny. His son. The child Kit had raised without asking for anything in return.

Startled by his thoughts, Jake straightened. Kit *hadn't* demanded any recompense for giving five years of her life to rear a boy who wasn't even kin to her. And she had taken Maggie in to stay with her until Maggie had given birth, just as she'd given Charlie and Ethan jobs when nobody else would.

The truth glared at him, proclaiming *him* the villain, not her. Jake shifted uncomfortably. He'd run away and left Maggie and his son alone. He'd blackmailed Kit into marrying him. He'd bought the note to the ranch behind Kit's back.

He scrubbed his whiskers with his palms. Maybe *he* was the one who needed forgiveness.

"I'm done," Johnny announced.

Startled out of his somber reverie, Jake smiled at the boy. "You did a fine job. Let's go see your ma."

Jake held out his hand, and Johnny wrapped his small fingers around it. Leaving the barn, Jake pushed the bar into place across the door, and they crossed the dusky yard to the house.

"I hope Ma's got supper ready," Johnny said.

Jake sent his son an expression of mock incredulousness. "After all that food you ate this afternoon, you're hungry again?"

Johnny shrugged. "Ma says I'm a bottomless pit." He gazed up at Jake with inquisitive eyes. "What does that mean?"

"It means you're a growing boy, and growing boys never run out of room in their bellies."

"Did your ma call you a bottomless pit, too?"

Anguished pain shafted Jake's chest. "My ma left me when I was about your age."

"Were you bad?"

Jake paused and glanced down at Johnny. "Why do you say that?"

He shrugged his thin shoulders. "Sometimes I'm scared Ma might leave me if I'm bad."

"Has she ever said that?"

Johnny shook his head. "No, but Ethan's ma done that to him."

Jake hunkered down in front of his son, placing him at eye level with the boy. "You listen to me, Johnny. Your ma loves you, and she'd never leave you, no matter what you did."

The boy studied Jake for a long moment, his dark eyes nearly swallowed up by the black pupils. "Would you leave me if I was bad, Pa?"

Jake's throat clogged with an emotion so powerful that for a moment he couldn't speak past the lump. Instead, he gathered Johnny in his arms and pulled him close. "I promise I'll never leave you, Johnny. No matter what," he whispered in his ear.

Johnny wrapped his short arms around Jake's neck.

After a few moments, Jake released his son and drew an arm across his eyes, glad for the darkness that hid his features. Yellow light spilled out of the windows, beckoning Jake, and he and Johnny hurried to the house.

The smells of fresh coffee and frying meat brought a smile to Jake's lips. Many nights as he'd lain under the stars, he'd imagined coming home to this ranch and stepping inside to be welcomed by a family and mouthwatering scents of supper. He glanced down at Johnny, his chest tightening at the sight of his son.

Kit entered the hall and he noticed she still wore her wedding dress, although she'd donned an apron which accentuated her enticing curves. The flower garland on her crown had disappeared and her hair danced about her shoulders. She glanced at him, her expression cool, and disappointment fell across Jake like a condemning shadow. He couldn't blame her for being so distant.

Her gaze shifted to Johnny, and her expression eased into a smile. "Why don't you go upstairs and change your clothes, Johnny? When you come down, you can have something to eat."

"Doesn't Pa have to change, too?" he asked.

Kit pressed her spectacles up on her nose, a gesture Jake had come to recognize as a sign of nervousness. She glanced at him, her smile vanishing. "He doesn't have to if he doesn't want to."

Johnny scowled. "Then *I* don't have to if I don't want to."

Kit opened her mouth, but Jake held up his hand to stave off her reprimand. He hardened his features, hoping he looked stern. "You heard your ma. Go and change, or you won't get any supper."

Johnny stared at Jake in surprise, then with only a slight grumble, stomped upstairs. Once the boy was out of earshot, Jake turned to Kit. "Did I do all right?"

The corners of Kit's bow-shaped lips tilted upward. "You did fine. When he gets tired, he gets crabby."

"It'll be an early night for all of us," Jake commented.

Kit's cheeks reddened, and her gaze stumbled around the foyer. "I'd best go finish getting supper on."

She hurried away, leaving Jake alone. He debated whether to follow her or not. What would he tell her— that there'd been no hidden meaning to his words? He'd be lying. He wanted her with an intensity that almost frightened him.

Suddenly restless, he roamed into the front room and stood in the center. Turning slowly, he tried to picture the room as it had been when he was a child. Stark and cold. He shuddered with the bleak memory. His father had removed every visible reminder of his wife after she'd abandoned them. Kit, however, had transformed four barren walls into a place filled with warmth and life.

He sank into a wingback chair and rubbed his brow. He had his rightful home and an heir to pass on the Cordell legacy. He should've been content.

A few minutes later, Kit called them to supper, and although Jake wasn't hungry, he joined his new family in the dining room. Her usual place, at the head of the table, lay vacant. Kit had seated herself across from Johnny, and Jake stared at the new arrangement. He glanced at Kit, who regarded him with an expectant tilt of her head. Behind her lenses, her eyes appeared as bright as a summer sky, and equally as alluring.

Feeling like an impostor, Jake took his place. He frowned. "Where are Charlie and Ethan?"

Keeping her gaze averted from Jake, Kit adjusted the napkin in her lap. "They usually eat in the bunkhouse."

"I guess I'll talk to them tomorrow."

"About what?"

"I'm going to tell them they have a job here as long as they want. I gave you my word on that."

"Thank you."

She and Johnny bowed their heads, and Jake followed their example, folding his hands together.

"Thank you for all the blessings you've bestowed upon us," Kit prayed aloud. "Amen."

Johnny echoed her amen, and Jake mouthed the word silently. As Johnny began chattering about the wedding and all the nice people he'd met, Jake tried to concentrate on his excited words, but Kit's presence kept drawing his attention. She picked at her food, and her face appeared carved from white marble.

He missed the Kit who'd sat on the floor alphabetizing the books in his office. He missed the Kit who'd convinced him to leave the saloon, then who'd stayed with him while he'd suffered through a massive hangover. He missed the Kit whom he'd kissed behind the barn on Easter Sunday.

Maybe tonight when they were alone, he could coax the Kit he'd known out from behind her cool mask. He didn't understand why it was so important to him that she smile at him again; he only knew he wanted to see that woman once more.

After they'd finished eating, Kit rose and glanced at Johnny, whose eyelids drooped sleepily. ''Jake, could you put Johnny to bed while I take care of the dishes?''

Jake stood and moved to his son's side. ''C'mon, Johnny, it's time for bed.''

After a token resistance, the boy surrendered to Jake and allowed him to guide him upstairs to his room. Although Jake often experienced a wispy déjà vu when he visited Kit's house, this time the sensation overwhelmed him. As Johnny readied himself for bed, Jake pictured himself as a boy in this same room. Jake's own father, however, had never tucked him into bed. Another memory, like a vague dream, spilled across his thoughts. One night after he'd gone to sleep, something had awakened young Jake. He'd opened his eyes, and at first he thought a bear was sitting in the rocker beside his bed. Then he'd recognized his father watching him silently, puffing on the ever-present pipe that created a cloud of smoke around him.

Go back to sleep, son. I'll always be here for you.

Jake heard his father's gruff yet gentle voice as if he stood behind him. Jake turned, but no apparition greeted him. Irrational disappointment filled him. Had he imagined that night so long ago?

Instinct told Jake the memory was real. Why had he remembered it now, so many years later? Was it because Jake now had a son, and he could understand a father's concern?

Maybe Kit was right—maybe Jonathan Cordell *had* loved his son, but didn't know how to express his feelings. Maybe the only way his father had known how to show his concern was to sit with him late at night while Jake had been asleep. Only then could his father lower his guard and display his true feelings.

"You gonna tell me a story, Pa?"

Jake blinked, startled out of his reverie by Johnny's request. He lowered himself to the edge of the boy's bed and tucked the blankets in around Johnny. "What kind of story do you want to hear?"

"Tell me what you did when you were my size."

Expecting a request for his exploits as a bounty hunter, Jake was surprised. Surprised, but pleased.

Jake began to tell him about the time he'd gone fishing with his own father, but only a few minutes into the tale, Johnny fell asleep. Gazing down at his son's innocent features, a wave of love and protectiveness crested through Jake. This must have been what Jonathan Cordell had felt as he'd watched over young Jake's sleeping figure. Now, six years after his father's death, Jake experienced a kinship with the elder Cordell, and he grieved for what had been lost between them. Studying Johnny, Jake vowed never to be only the midnight shadow his father had been.

He owed Kit his gratitude for giving Johnny the nurturing the boy needed. He owed her for not turning his own son against him as she'd raised Johnny alone. And he owed her for agreeing to become his wife to ensure Johnny the love of both parents.

Jake leaned down and kissed his son's untroubled brow. Reluctantly he stood and left the room with silent footsteps. At the bottom of the stairs he paused. The muted clatter of metal against metal told Jake that Kit was in the kitchen, finishing the supper dishes.

Would she want him to join her? What was expected

of a husband on the wedding night? A husband who'd coerced his bride into marrying him. He bit the inside of his cheek. He might not love her, but he cared for her and wanted to make amends.

He'd been wrong about his father, and he'd allowed his bitterness to affect all aspects of his life. He couldn't afford to allow that same resentment to influence his relationship with Kit and Johnny—especially since he wasn't so certain Kit had been completely at fault. He couldn't blame her for wanting to protect Johnny.

In spite of everything, she had given him his son. She could've kept silent, but she'd taken the chance of losing Johnny so Jake could know his flesh and blood.

Self-disgust twisted his stomach into knots. He'd accused her of deceit, when it was he who'd lied to her. Kit, with her tender heart, deserved better than him.

He ached with the need to hold her, to ask her forgiveness. Somehow, he'd convince her he cared for her as much as he could for any woman. And if he was capable of love, maybe someday . . .

Stiffening his spine as if he was readying himself for a showdown, he strode to the kitchen.

Kit glanced up at Jake's abrupt entrance. She turned away, afraid he'd see her heart threatening to gallop out of her chest and the desire his mere presence conjured.

"Is Johnny asleep?" she asked, and realized her voice sounded as if she'd just raced her son from the corrals to the house.

Jake nodded, a dark curl spilling across his forehead. "The little guy was all tuckered out."

The fondness in his tone brought a lump to Kit's throat. Avoiding his gaze, she folded her dish towel and hung it over a chair. She lifted the pan of soapy water out of the sink and turned to take it outside. Jake took hold of the basin with steady hands.

"I'll take care of this," Jake said softly. "Why don't

you go get ready for bed?'' His crooked smile could've charmed a spinster out of her corset.

Heat flushed Kit's face and desire pooled in her stomach.

"Well, are you going to let me take it?'' he asked, with a provocative arch of his dark brow.

Flustered, Kit realized she still held fast to the metal pan. His hands were so close to hers, she could feel the heat of his skin. She let go her hold abruptly, and the water splashed up to dampen Jake's shirtfront.

"I'm sorry,'' she exclaimed, grabbing a towel to dab at the wet material. Embarrassment heated her cheeks.

"Don't be,'' Jake said softly. He leaned close, his balmy breath spilling across her neck. "I'm not.''

Kit jerked back, and gazed up at his liquid brown eyes. If she wasn't careful, she would drown in their inviting depths.

"Go upstairs, Kit. I'll join you in a few minutes.''

Jake took the pan of water out the back door, and Kit scurried out of the kitchen. She raced up to her room. *Our* room, she corrected herself with a panicky thought. How did one prepare for a wedding night?

She surveyed her bedroom as if she'd never seen it before. No longer would she be sleeping alone in the four-poster bed with the double wedding ring quilt her mother had made before Kit had been born. From now on, she'd be sharing it with the very man she'd dreamed of many past restless nights. If only the marriage had been based on love instead of distrust and extortion.

Jake's movements downstairs spurred her into action, and she removed her clothing in record haste. Tempted to don her usual flannel nightgown with its button-up high collar, Kit instead opened a trunk at the end of the bed. She withdrew a creamy white gown made of foulard, a material so thin it appeared almost indecent. Her mother had worn it on her wedding night, but she and

Kit's father had loved one another. Kit hoped it wouldn't be sacrilegious to wear it when only the bride loved her husband.

The stairs creaked and Kit made her decision. She threw the nearly sheer gown on, and with trembling fingers, fastened the few buttons that closed the front.

The door opened, revealing Jake's heart-achingly familiar figure. He stood motionless, framed in the opening as his gaze caressed every part of her body. She shivered beneath his scorching perusal and her muscles seemed to melt beneath the fiery heat.

He entered, shutting out the world behind him. The room seemed dwarfed by his broad shoulders and six-foot-plus frame. His glorious maleness stole her breath, sending her chest into an energetic race for air. Jake's attention strayed to her breasts, and she consciously forced herself to keep her arms at her sides.

He approached her with an innate confidence, his powerful thighs flexing beneath his snug trousers. Held spellbound by the smoldering desire that darkened his eyes, Kit ignored the tiny voice that told her to move away, to escape before the web was complete.

She could run to the ends of the earth, but there'd be no fleeing the simple truth: she wanted him and he wanted her.

"You're beautiful, Kit."

His velvety voice wrapped its fine-spun words about her, cloaking her with warmth. She closed her eyes, trying to remember that Jake had forced her to marry him by threatening to take Johnny away. But his dizzying caresses and tender words melted her outrage.

Besides, she'd promised herself to make him love her, and actions spoke louder than mere words. She lifted a trembling hand and cupped his whiskered cheek. He turned into her palm, kissing the sensitive skin and sparking a trail of fire that led to the center of her desire.

Jake eased away and removed the spectacles she'd forgotten she still wore. Humiliated, she looked away, but he drew her back, raising her chin with his forefinger.

"Don't be embarrassed, honey." He flashed her a devilish grin. "I happen to like them."

She shook her head. "Don't patronize me, Jake. I know how ugly they make me look."

His expression sobered, and he held her face between his palms. "Whoever told you that is an idiot."

Did he really mean it, or was he only trying to ease his way into her bed?

"Do you believe me?"

Jake's quiet question startled her, forcing her to decide. Relying on her intuition, she nodded with a short, jerky motion. "Yes."

His shoulders seemed to relax, and she frowned, puzzled by his reaction. "Do you care what I think?"

He drew back as if she'd slapped him. "Yes."

If he cared even a little, someday that might turn into love. With a returned sense of hope, Kit raised her hand to the buttons of his shirt. She couldn't deny either of them what they wanted. Her feather-light fingers skimmed across Jake's chest, and then she leaned forward, taking one of his nipples between her lips.

He moaned with unexpected pleasure. If he hadn't taken her innocence himself, he'd wonder about her boldness. But with Kit, he recognized her giving nature. She wanted to please him, to give him as much delight as he'd given her their first time together. It humbled Jake to think she would still want to give so much of herself after all he'd taken from her.

Kit flattened her hands on his chest as she moved her mouth to lave his other nipple. Her slender body pressed against his, setting his nerves afire at every point of contact. She tested his rigid control, making him feel like a nervous boy lying with his first woman. Since he'd become a man, he'd never experienced a loss of self-restraint—until Kit.

Grasping what little control still remained, Jake stepped back and removed his clothing as Kit's luminescent gaze traveled down the length of his body. He stood motionless as he forced restraint over his rampant desire.

As he watched her in the shallow lantern light, Kit unbuttoned her nearly transparent gown and slid it off her shoulders. It whispered to the floor to gather like a gossamer pool about her delicate ankles.

Jake's breath caught in his throat. The wondrous woman before him was his wife, his mate. The thought brought no panic, only an overpowering urge to gather her in his arms and make her his wife in every way.

He held out his hand. Without hesitation she accepted his invitation. He led her to the bed and they lay down upon it. Jake smoothed her cornsilk hair from her brow and dropped a delicate kiss on her petal-soft skin where her shoulder met her neck. Kit gasped, her fingers twining in his hair, urging him to continue the light caresses. He complied, trailing kisses down to her full breasts, then continuing lower to the blond curls at the juncture of her thighs.

"Oh, Jake," Kit breathed.

Her womanly scent filled his nostrils, increasing his longing for her, but he held his passion in check. He wanted to pleasure her first, show her how much he cared for her. He teased the swollen nubbin with the tip of his tongue, and she arched her hips in answer to the instinctual summons.

"Jake, what are you doing?" Kit's voice contained more breath than sound.

He splayed his hand across her soft abdomen, which rose and fell with her agitated breathing, and moved upward to cup her breast in his palm. Her inarticulate sighs and the tightening of her fists at her sides told him she was near the edge.

"*Jake*," Kit cried.

Her body shuddered, and Jake tasted her sweetness on his lips. Unable to hold back any longer, he moved over her and she opened her willowy legs to accommodate him. Leaning forward, he kissed her and her tongue teased his, parrying and withdrawing in a sensual game of tag.

Kit wrapped her arms around Jake and ran her hands up and down his back. She shivered, enjoying the sensation of silken skin over steel muscle and his springy chest hairs tickling her sensitive nipples. He slid his palm down her side and rested his hand on her curved hip. His masculinity pressed against her thighs, seeking entrance, and her body stretched to accommodate him, welcoming him into her awaiting slickness. Kit marveled at how perfectly he fit, how perfect he felt.

Jake's heart pounded against her chest as he moved above her. Kit met each thrust with equal fervor, her nerves tingling, reaching again for gratification. Jake's motions became deeper, his breathing more laborious, then he crushed his lips to hers as he shuddered convulsively. Kit echoed his groan as a second release seized her, startling her with its intensity.

Gradually their breathing slowed, and Jake rolled to her side, although he kept a possessive arm around her waist. Kit turned on her side to face him and found his contented gaze upon her. Unable to stop herself, she brushed back an errant lock of hair from his sweat-slicked forehead.

He captured her hand and kissed the back of it. "I'm sorry."

She tilted her head, puzzled. "For what?"

"I shouldn't have blackmailed you into marrying me.

You took care of my son for five years, and I rewarded you by threatening to take him away. I had no right doing that to you, Kit.''

She saw the sincerity in his troubled expression. ''We both wanted what was best for Johnny.''

''And what about what's best for you, Kit? Would you have married me if I hadn't blackmailed you?''

''I always thought I'd marry for love,'' she replied evasively.

He drew the back of his forefinger along her jaw. She tried to ignore the little shivers that raced along her nerves, to focus on his abject expression.

''I don't know if I have any love inside of me to give you. All I know is that I want you—and not just here, in bed,'' he said.

Kit nodded, moisture blurring her vision. This was the tender, honest Jake she loved. ''I understand,'' she whispered. ''Do you regret marrying me?''

''No. I care for you, and I want to make a fresh start with you and Johnny.''

Her heart lifted, and she bent forward to kiss the corner of his mouth. He wrapped his strong arms around her, and drew her close.

Within her heart, Kit whispered her words of love to Jake and prayed for the day he would be able to reciprocate.

Chapter 17

Jake carried the breakfast tray into the bedroom, pushing the door closed with his shoulder. He stood for a moment, observing Kit as she slept peacefully, her hair fanned across her pillow and her cheeks rosy. Although she was covered to her neck with the sheet, Jake had no trouble envisioning her womanly curves. He'd explored every inch of her satiny skin throughout the long night of making love.

His wedding night had been more satisfying than he could have imagined. Kit's inexperience was compensated for by her unquenchable curiosity. She'd matched his passion with her own eagerness to learn and accept the pleasures he taught her.

In spite of the shaky beginning, Jake believed their marriage would work out—and if every evening proved as exhaustive as their wedding night, Johnny would soon have many brothers and sisters. The thought of a little girl with Kit's blond hair and startling blue eyes stirred something in him, something that squeezed his heart and sent a wave of wonder through him.

Taking a deep breath, he approached the bed and set the tray on the nightstand. He leaned over and kissed Kit's full lips. She stirred, wrapping her arms around his neck and drawing him down onto the bed beside her. The covers fell from her chest, exposing her breasts to his appreciative gaze.

Reluctantly, Jake drew away from her sweet mouth. "Good morning, darling."

Kit blinked the sleep from her eyes, and a saucy grin lit her features. "I know how to make the morning even better."

Despite the many times they'd made love throughout the night, Jake responded to her as if he'd been without a woman for weeks. "You've become insatiable."

She arched a winged brow. "You have only yourself to blame."

Half an hour later Jake sat with Kit on the wide bed, the empty breakfast tray between them.

"I didn't know you were such a talented man, Jake," Kit said.

He swept a deliberate gaze across her robe-covered body.

She laughed and her cheeks flushed. "I'm not talking about that talent, although I must admit you don't seem to be lacking there. I meant your cooking—even though the eggs were cold."

"And whose fault was that?" Jake teased.

Her twinkling eyes and mischevious tone warmed Jake. He wasn't accustomed to an easy camaraderie with women after spending the night with them. However, Kit wasn't someone he'd leave the next morning. She was his wife, and he found himself wanting to spend all his mornings with her.

She glanced out the window, at the sun climbing above the horizon, and sighed. "Johnny'll be up soon."

Although he'd married Kit for his son's sake, Jake found himself wishing he could have her to himself for the rest of the day. He grinned at the irony. "You're right. We'd better get up."

He pulled on his shirt, tucking it into his waistband, then tugged on his boots. Kit dressed in her usual tantalizing trousers, and Jake slipped around to hug her, his palms curving around her shapely backside. After kissing the tip of her nose, he whispered, "Those pants could make a man forget everything but what's beneath them."

Kit's cheeks flushed. After all they'd shared, he could still make her blush.

Taking her hand, Jake led her downstairs.

Johnny was already in the kitchen, eating a piece of bread with plum jam on it. "You musta been awfully tired," he said. "The sun came up a couple of hours ago."

Jake winked at Kit. "That wedding must've tuckered us out."

"I been waiting forever for you to get up," Johnny said. He glanced at Kit. "Can I give him his present now, Ma?"

She nodded, a gentle smile curving her lips.

"What present?" Jake asked.

"It's a surprise," Johnny replied.

Puzzled, Jake allowed the boy to tug him out of the kitchen. Kit took hold of Johnny's other hand and the three of them walked to the barn. Once inside, Johnny led him to a stall that held a mare and a young colt.

"He's yours, Pa," Johnny announced. "He probably isn't as smart as Zeus, but I'll bet he'll be nearly as good."

Jake turned to Kit, who nodded. His chest felt like an anvil rested on it.

"I can't take him," he argued.

"Why not?" Kit demanded. "Johnny's right— Smoky can't replace Zeus, but if you start with him this young, he might come close." She slid her hands into her pockets, and glanced down. "Besides, I feel responsible for what happened to Zeus."

"It wasn't your fault."

She lifted her gaze. "Please, Jake, take the colt. I'd feel better if you did."

"I'll help you train him, Pa," Johnny volunteered.

If he refused the generous gift, he'd hurt Kit and Johnny's feelings. "With an offer like that, how can I refuse?" He squatted down and hugged Johnny. "Thank you."

Looking past his son, he saw a tear trail down Kit's cheek. She understood how much Zeus's death had hurt him, and how much Johnny's gift meant to him.

Jake stood, picking Johnny up, and wrapping his other arm around Kit.

"Thank you both."

A month later, as Kit placed the last of the breakfast dishes in the cupboard, she heard Johnny's bright laughter and Jake's deep-timbered chuckles. She glanced out the window and saw them hitching up the horses to the buckboard for the trip into town. Crossing her arms, she smiled at the two people she loved most in the world.

Her marriage to Jake had given her more happiness and contentment than she could have believed possible. She'd spent the days side-by-side with Jake as they'd worked with the horses, and Jake had taken Johnny riding each day. Sometimes Kit accompanied them, but more often she allowed them the time alone to get to know one another. Watching Jake become more and more like a father to Johnny had convinced her she'd made the right decision to tell him of his son.

The nights, however, were for her and Jake alone. Thinking of the wondrous raptures they'd shared, Kit found herself wanting the evening to come more quickly. The only dark cloud in her perfect world was

Jake's inability to love her, or at least to speak the words. How could they share the things they did without him loving her? Often her own declaration would be on the tip of her tongue—and although her pride kept her from saying it aloud, it was getting more and more difficult to keep her true feelings hidden from him.

Mentally shaking herself, she brushed back the stray tendrils from her forehead and smoothed her skirt. Even though Jake had gone to town a few times each week to work at his office, this would be the first time they went into Chaney as a family, and Kit wanted to make a good impression.

She joined Jake and Johnny out by the wagon. With tail wagging, Toby greeted her, and she scratched him behind a floppy ear.

"Did you bring the list?" Jake called to Kit.

She nodded, patting her reticule. "Right here."

He walked to her side, dropping a kiss on her cheek. "I forget how well you remember things."

His eyes twinkled suggestively, and heat crawled up Kit's neck. Nonplussed, she turned to see Charlie leaning against the corral fence. "Is there anything you or Ethan need, Charlie?"

The ebony-skinned man shook his head, his eyes sparkling with humor. "We're just fine, thanks, Kit." He glanced at Jake. "You want me to keep workin' that paint?"

"Good idea. We've got a buyer coming up in a few days who's interested in her," Jake replied.

"Can we go now?" Johnny interjected.

Jake smiled and lifted the boy into the back of the wagon, then turned to assist Kit up to the springboard seat. He joined her and picked up the reins.

"We should be back this afternoon," he called out to Charlie.

The hired man waved his acknowledgment.

Jake drove the team down the road, his side pressed against Kit's. She enjoyed the feel of his firm muscles through the layers of clothing between them, and she relaxed against her husband's secure strength. Raising her face to the clear blue sky, she allowed the sun's hospitable rays to play across her cheeks. She couldn't remember a more splendid morning.

Jake Cordell removed his well-oiled gunbelt, then the Colt that resided within the holster. He'd killed men with the weapon, but he'd done so with a clear conscience. They'd been murderers and thieves with no sense of right or wrong, like wolves gone rabid.

But now it was time to hang up his gun. He no longer lived in a world filled with darkness and evil. Now his life revolved around his family: the woman he loved and the son she'd given him. He didn't want to go back to a dull, colorless world.

Jake slid the Colt back into its scabbard and wrapped the belt around it. Raising the lid of the trunk that held his family's legacy, he laid the gun on his wife's wedding dress. He closed the cover, locking away the past.

No longer would he be Jake Cordell, bounty hunter. All he wanted now was to be a good husband and father. Maybe it was all he'd ever wanted.

"Woolgathering?" Jake asked.

She glanced up to find him studying her, and she shrugged self-consciously. "I was just thinking how perfect the day is."

"Just the day?"

She smiled. "You, Johnny, me. We're a family."

He fixed his gaze on the road ahead, his expression pensive. "Have you been happy, Kit?"

The somber tone of his question startled her. "Yes, happier than I'd ever imagined."

Jake turned back to her, his hat brim nearly brushing

her forehead. "Me, too. Maybe it's because I finally have what I've always wanted."

Kit threaded her hand through the crook of his arm, and with his free hand, Jake clasped her fingers.

"I love you, Jake." The words slipped past her lips before she could censor them.

Surprise widened his eyes. "I—"

Kit shook her head quickly to stop him before he could tell her he didn't love her. "It's okay. You don't have to say anything. I understand."

Jake squeezed her hand. "That's all right. I just wasn't expecting it."

With a wry smile, she said, "I wasn't either. I didn't mean to."

"Say it, or fall in love?" he asked gently.

She stared into his mesmerizing eyes, straight into his soul. "Both."

He pressed his lips to the back of her hand. "I don't know if I deserve your love."

"I don't think love cares whether a person deserves it or not. It just happens."

He studied her as if trying to decide whether he believed her or not. She wished he would tell her what he was thinking, but he remained silent, his eyes not revealing his thoughts. Concentrating on regaining the euphoria she'd tasted minutes earlier, Kit turned her attention to the chattering birds in the budding trees and the greening hillside speckled with wildflowers.

She wouldn't lose her faith. Someday he would be able to say aloud what she knew was already in his heart.

Jake stopped the wagon in front of the mercantile, then hopped down. He swung Kit to the hard-packed street, his strong hands wrapped around her waist and his fingers grazing the underside of her breasts, sparking now-familiar desire with a single touch.

"I'm going to see Patrick, then I'll meet you back here in the store," he said.

Kit nodded. "All right."

Jake turned to Johnny. "You want to go with me to see Sergeant O'Hara?"

The boy scrambled to Jake's side. "Okay."

Kit crossed her arms in mock disappointment. "You mean you're going to leave your poor mother all by herself?"

Johnny blinked, and shuffled his feet. "I guess I can stay with you, Ma."

"I was just teasing you, sweetheart. Go on with your father."

"Thanks, Ma."

Kit winked at Jake, and waved after her son and husband. She entered the store, retrieving the list from her purse.

"Hello, Kit."

Startled, she stumbled and David Preston reached out to steady her. She pulled out of his grasp and said stiffly, "Thank you, David."

She studied the newspaperman, wondering how she'd ever thought him handsome. He was shorter than Jake, and less muscular, almost effeminate. His greased hair gave him a malevolent appearance. All he needed was a waxed moustache to complete the sinister picture.

"I assume you're finding marriage to that so-called hero suitable?" he asked with a sneer.

Kit resisted the urge to lower herself to his level. "We're very happy, thank you." She lifted her chin and attempted to stride past him. He caught her arm, spinning her around.

"Let go of me, or I'll scream," she said, pitching her voice low so the other customers wouldn't hear.

David released her and held his hands up. "I was merely going to tell you something."

"And why do you think I'd be interested in anything you have to tell me?"

"Still the same Kit, claws and all." He brushed an invisible speck of dust off his immaculate jacket. "I heard a disturbing piece of news the other day."

"News is your business," she retorted dryly.

"This news pertains specifically to you."

Despite herself, Kit found her curiosity was piqued. "And what was that?"

"Your beloved husband bought the loan papers for your ranch."

Kit's heart warmed at the thought that Jake would protect her like that. "Since it's *our* ranch now, I'm not surprised he'd want to keep it safe."

David shook his head, his close-set eyes narrowing. "He bought the papers two weeks after he moved back to Chaney. I checked."

For a few moments Kit was confused, then her vision darkened and the store blurred around her as the meaning of his words sank in. "You're lying. He'd have told me."

"I just can't figure out why he married you. Pity, perhaps. All he had to do was wait for you to miss the payment and the ranch would've been his," David pressed. "And he'd have had every right to throw you and that whelp of yours out into the cold."

Kit struggled to make sense of his words. If she hadn't been able to meet her loan deadline, he'd have gotten the ranch anyway—the ranch he'd offered to buy when he'd first come to visit.

The room seemed to close in around her, and she turned and scurried out the door. Standing on the boardwalk, she gulped in deep draughts of air. Sickness threatened her, and she choked back the bitterness.

Why hadn't Jake told her? Would he have taken it from her just as David had said, if she hadn't married him? And if he had bought the loan, why did he marry her? He could've had both the ranch and Johnny without tying himself to her. *Had* he felt sorry for her? Or duty bound, because she had raised his son?

She didn't want his pity, or to be a blemish on his conscience. All she'd wanted was his love. Was that so impossible? Was she so unlovable?

Despair overwhelmed her as her fleetingly perfect world shattered around her. She thought of her declaration of love, and humiliation burned her cheeks. She had laid bare her soul, her heart, and he'd been laughing at her the whole time.

She'd made her bed, and now she was damned to sleeping in it—but she'd sleep in it alone. She'd done it before; she could do it again.

Kit's paleness alarmed Jake. That, and her silence since they'd gotten the supplies and loaded the wagon. He'd asked her if anything was wrong, but she'd only shaken her head.

Something *had* happened, though. Something that had upset her badly enough that she wouldn't speak to him about it. Later, when they were in bed together, he'd get her to tell him what troubled her.

Supper proved to be a quiet affair, and even Johnny noticed his mother's uncharacteristic brooding.

"What's wrong, Ma?" the boy asked, his dark eyes anxious.

Kit blinked, and her lips turned upward in a caricature of a smile. "I'm just a little tired, is all, sweetheart."

Jake didn't believe her excuse, but he didn't want Johnny to worry any more than he already did. "It's been a long day, son. Once you're done eating, I'll tuck you in and tell you a story. How does that sound?"

Although not convinced, Johnny nodded. "Maybe you should tell Ma a story, too, so she can go to sleep."

"That's all right," Kit said. "I don't think your father has any stories I haven't heard."

Her sharp-edged tone surprised Jake. Had someone in town told her something about him? Something that would've upset her?

As soon as they'd finished eating, Jake took Johnny upstairs to his room. Half an hour later, the boy was asleep and Jake returned to the kitchen. The dishes had been washed and the lamp had been extinguished, but Kit was nowhere in sight. He went back upstairs to their bedroom. That, too, was empty.

Fear squeezed his heart. Where had she gone?

He flew down the steps and out into the cool night air. Pausing in the middle of the yard, he pivoted around, wondering where she would've gone. Jake hurried to the corrals, his heart thumping in his chest. Seeing a figure, he moved toward it, hoping it was Kit. A tall lanky form stepped out of the shadows into the moonlight.

Disappointed, Jake called, "Ethan, have you seen Kit?"

The young man nodded. "I seen her headed to the barn where her critters are. Is something wrong?"

Jake forced himself to smile reassuringly as he shook his head. "She didn't tell me where she was going, is all. Thanks."

He hurried to the barn, berating himself for not guessing her destination. Opening the broad door, he slipped inside the warm, hay-scented building. A kerosene lantern hung from a nail in a post, and Jake walked toward it. He spotted Kit sitting on a pile of hay, both kittens in her lap. She had her hands wrapped around the small animals, absently stroking them with her thumbs.

Her anguished expression halted his approach. She appeared so desolate that Jake's own heart seemed to tear in two.

What had happened in the short time they'd been separated in town? Had Jameson bothered her again? Jake's blood boiled, and he crossed the distance to Kit in three long strides. Hunkering down beside her, he took hold of her shoulders and gazed into her downcast eyes.

"What is it, Kit?" he asked, keeping his voice gentle against the rise of concerned anger within him.

She set the kittens aside and scrambled away from him. The loathing in her pale features struck Jake like a physical blow, causing him to fall back.

"Why didn't you tell me?" she demanded, her tone high-pitched.

Bewildered, Jake could only shake his head. "What're you talking about? Tell you what?"

"The ranch. The loan papers."

Panic seized Jake. "What about them?"

Her lips trembled. "You had them all along."

Kit's misery twisted his gut into knots. He'd planned on telling her, but the time had never seemed right. "I'm sorry, Kit. I figured it didn't matter, not after we were married."

She balled her fingers into fists at her sides. "You accused me of lying, of hiding the truth about Johnny. I was scared you'd hate *me*, that you'd never be able to forgive *me*, for deceiving you." She laughed, a sound filled with heartbreak and disillusionment. "And here you were hiding your own secret from me."

Jake held up his hands in supplication. "I can explain."

Kit shook her head vehemently, her hair falling across her face. "I should've known. The first day you came out to the ranch, you asked me if I'd sell. I should've known you wouldn't give up so easily." She stared at him like he was something to scrape off the bottom of her shoe. "I guess the only reason you married me was to stack the deck in your favor. You weren't sure I'd make that payment or not. Too bad you didn't wait a little longer—you could've had the ranch and Johnny *without* a wife you didn't want.''

Jake stepped toward her and she moved back, keeping the distance between them. Helplessness clawed at him. ''No, that wasn't the reason I married you.''

She folded her arms below her breasts. ''It sure as hell wasn't because you loved me.'' Kit blinked, and a tear slipped down her cheek. ''I thought you cared for me. This past month you almost had me believing you loved me in your own way.'' A convulsive sob escaped her. ''I was such a fool, thinking the great Jake Cordell could care for someone like me. But all you wanted was the ranch and Johnny. And now you have them, along with a woman to take care of your 'needs.' You should be real proud of yourself.''

''It wasn't like that,'' Jake nearly shouted in his frustration. ''I didn't tell you because I figured you'd take it wrong, just like you're doing.''

Kit's lower lip trembled and she swallowed. ''Are you getting tired of me yet? Or do I have a few more nights left in me?''

Jake looked away, guilty because he *had* had those thoughts, back when he'd been consumed by self-pity.

Before he'd fallen in love with her.

He felt the blood drain from his face, and he flattened his palm against a pole to steady himself. He didn't know how to love. Of course, he loved Johnny because he was his son, but did he love Kit?

The woman who'd seen past his drunkenness to the lonely man. The woman who'd taken in his son. The woman who'd given him her love, knowing she might never hear the words repeated to her.

He gazed at her proud stature, at the achingly familiar defiance in her raised chin. He could proclaim his new discovery, but she wouldn't believe him. Not now. He'd hurt her too badly. This time it was he who'd lost her trust.

Jake held out his hand and spoke softly, "I bought that mortgage before we became friends. Before I knew you."

She stared at him, bitter betrayal reflected in her eyes. "You may have your precious ranch and your son, but you'll never play me for the fool again."

She rushed past him and out of the barn. The silence was broken only by the kittens' mewling.

The door opened once more. Had Kit returned? The tall silhouette in the opening extinguished the glimmer of hope.

"What is it, Ethan?" Jake asked, suddenly weary.

"What'd you do to her?" the boy demanded.

"What're you talking about?"

"Miz Thornton was crying." Anger vibrated through Ethan's words.

Conscience-stricken, Jake couldn't even find the strength to remind Ethan Kit was now a married woman. "We had an argument. She'll be all right."

"I ain't never seen her cry before." A savage scowl marred his handsome features. "Not until you came here."

Self-recrimination filled Jake. All she'd been guilty of was being generous and loving, and he had turned her life upside down. He stepped toward Ethan. "Look, I know you care for her, but she's *my* wife."

The boy's eyes glittered like cut obsidian. "You hurt her."

Jake glanced down, shouldering the guilt of the accusation. He raised his head, meeting Ethan's damning gaze. "That's right, I did. I admire your loyalty to Kit, but this isn't any of your concern. It's between Kit and me."

"You ain't no good for her, Cordell." Ethan raised his fists.

Charlie entered the barn, laying a meaty hand on the young man's shoulder. "He's right, Ethan. Kit's his wife now. Ain't any of our business what goes on between them."

Jake could see the boy's struggle. After a few moments, Ethan's tense posture eased, and with a final glare at Jake, the young man spun around and strode out of the building.

"Thanks, Charlie," Jake said.

Charlie's eyes narrowed. "Don't thank me, Jake. Iffen any harm comes to that girl, it'll be both of us you'll be dealin' with."

Charlie left, leaving Jake alone with the kittens. He picked up the tiny creatures, cradling them against his chest. Salty rubbed Jake's chin with his white head, and Pepper curled up in his palm, purring in contentment.

Kit's friends, though few, were a stalwart group. Freda had staunchly defended Kit when Jake had first moved into her house, and Patrick was fond of Kit, too.

"Maybe they're right. Maybe I'm not any good for her or Johnny. Maybe I should go back to bounty hunting. Leave them and let them go back to how they used to be."

But he couldn't go back to his former life. He had a family now. He had a responsibility to them. A responsibility to make them unhappy? It would be so easy to shake Chaney's dust from his boots like he'd done six years ago. But he'd promised Johnny he wouldn't leave, and he'd promised himself he'd be a better father than his own had been.

A chilling thought struck him. What if Kit left?

How would he tell Johnny his mother had left them? Jake's breath caught in his throat. Had his father lost his mother's trust, too? Maybe Jonathan had driven her away, even though she had loved Jake and hadn't wanted to leave.

Was history doomed to repeat itself?

Chapter 18

~~~OO~~~

Kit fled to her room, the tears that filled her eyes blurring the walls surrounding her. She closed the door behind her and flung herself onto the quilt. Jake's musky smell filled her senses, bringing into crisp focus images of her and Jake making love in the four-poster bed.

She'd been naive to believe his flattering words and charming smile. But she'd wanted to believe him. Even when she'd confronted him in the barn, she'd wanted to believe the despair in his expression was genuine.

She curled her fingers into her palms, silently cursing her weakness. She'd married him knowing he didn't love her. Why did the proof hurt so badly? He'd made no secret of his desire to possess his father's ranch. Had he also used his position as Johnny's father to achieve that goal?

Kit hiccuped and sat up, drawing her hand across damp cheeks. She recalled how Jake and Johnny had laughed and wrestled together in the front room a couple of days ago. She'd peeked in Johnny's bedroom as Jake had tucked him in the night before. The tenderness in Jake's expression had been sincere. No, he truly loved his son: that much was certain.

But was he capable of loving her?

Faint rustlings from downstairs told Kit Jake had returned. If he demanded entry to their room, she wasn't sure she'd have the strength to deny him. She concentrated on the caustic taste of bitterness, willing the anger to fuel her resolve.

Perched on the edge of the bed, Kit awaited the approach of his footsteps, but the house grew silent once more. She mechanically changed into her flannel nightgown, then lay down and stared at the moonlit ceiling. Her heart thudded against her breast in a slow, steady rhythm. Although she'd spent numerous nights alone, Kit had never known the intense loneliness that now settled in her chest. Because she'd experienced passion's heat in Jake's arms, solitude became bitterly cold in comparison.

She closed her eyes, wondering if Jake had gone into Chaney to visit one of the saloon girls, since he no longer would be able to amuse himself with her.

A tear spilled down her cheek. If she hated Jake so much, why did the thought of him with another woman shatter the last remaining piece of her heart?

Jake awoke to the early morning sunshine shafting in the front room's window. He sat up on the sofa, groaning from the stiffness of having spent the night on the lumpy cushions. He'd tossed and turned throughout the long hours of darkness, falling into a restless slumber shortly before dawn.

Standing, Jake pressed his hands against his lower back and stretched, gratified to feel his backbone snap into place. He'd missed having Kit lying beside him, the warmth of her body pressed against him, comforting him with her tranquil presence and keeping away the nightmares.

He hoped she'd listen to reason this morning, but he

had his doubts. Once she had her mind set on something, even dynamite would do little good in displacing her notion. It was that same unbreakable moral fiber that made her do what was right, instead of what was socially acceptable.

He cursed as he remembered that he had to go see a client in Red Cliff, a town thirty miles south. He'd planned on telling Kit last night. The trip would take a couple of days and he hated to leave her and Johnny, but he had no choice.

The sound of light footfalls caught his attention, and he walked into the kitchen to find Kit starting breakfast. Her head snapped up in surprise.

"Good morning," Jake greeted her in a low voice.

She nodded shortly and went back to cutting side pork into long strips and placing them in the hot skillet. The meat sizzled and popped in the awkward silence, and the smell of frying bacon filled the room.

Jake straddled a chair, resting his forearms on the back. Kit looked like she'd gotten as little rest as he had. "How did you sleep?"

She tossed a curt answer in his direction. "Fine."

"So did I."

Glancing back at him, Kit said, "That's good."

Her tone told him she believed his reply as much as he believed hers.

"About the ranch—" Jake began.

"I don't want to talk about it now," she interrupted.

Irritation roughened his voice. "When *will* you want to talk about it?"

She pivoted to face him. "I've heard all I need to know."

"No, you haven't." He stood, taking a step toward her. Wariness veiled her eyes, and Jake had the impression she wanted to bolt from him. Remorse cut a wide swath through him. Jake fought the impulse to hold her and chase away the shadows he'd created.

"I planned on telling you about the mortgage," Jake began.

"That's easy enough to claim, now that your secret's out."

He lifted hands fisted in exasperation. "When I came back to Chaney, I planned to get my father's ranch back any way I could. I was going to become a successful horse breeder, the one thing Jonathan hadn't succeeded at. I was going to show everybody that I was just as good a man as the great Judge Cordell."

Her lips thinned to a grim line, and Jake could guess what she was thinking. She'd admired his father. He doubted her opinion of him was nearly as high.

"When you told me Johnny was my son, my priorities changed. Being a father to my son seemed a sight more important than owning a piece of land."

"You have both."

Her words were blunt, yet they sliced through him like cold steel.

Johnny burst into the kitchen, ending the conversation.

Dressed, but with his hair mussed, Johnny clambered onto his chair. "What's for breakfast?"

"Nothing until you wash up and comb your hair," Kit said, turning her back to Jake once more.

The boy grumbled.

"Have your father help you," she added.

Johnny grabbed Jake's hand and pulled him toward the lean-to where the pump and basin were. Torn between his wife and his son, Jake gave in to Johnny's urging.

Ten minutes later, fresh-shaven and with spirits lifted by Johnny's playful antics, Jake sat at the table. Kit laid plates covered with fried pork and eggs in front of him and Johnny, and a bowl of biscuits along with pale butter and orange marmalade in the center of the oilcloth-covered table. She remained standing, drinking a cup of coffee.

Jake frowned. "Aren't you going to eat?"

"I'm not hungry," she replied.

Unable to penetrate Kit's icy facade, Jake ate the meal she'd prepared. Johnny finished first and asked to be excused to go outside to play with Toby. After he'd gone, Jake stood and refilled his coffee cup. Kit cleared the table, sliding the dishes into a pan of soapy water.

"I have to go to Red Cliff for a couple days," he announced.

She jerked her head up, her eyes wide. Quickly lowering her gaze, she turned back to the sink. "Why?"

"I have a client up there who needs me to do some work for him," Jake replied.

"What kind of work?"

Puzzled by the uncharacteristic sarcasm in her voice, he considered how to respond. Keeping his tone neutral, he said, "He wants me to translate some business contracts into English. He wants to know what he's signing."

"Oh."

She continued washing the dishes, ignoring him.

Jake sighed, set his cup down, and stepped behind Kit. He laid his hands on her shoulders lightly, turning her around to face him.

She pressed her damp palms against his shirt front, and kept her gaze aimed at his chest. "I have work to do."

Jake disregarded her halfhearted attempt to escape. "And I want to say good-bye to my wife."

With his forefinger, he raised her chin and kissed her. Her lips remained stiff. He drew his tongue across their velvety softness, and a primal moan rose from her throat as she crushed his shirt between her curled fingers. Like a morning glory at sunrise, she eased open her mouth.

He pulled away before he succumbed to his burgeoning desire. Taking a shaky breath, Jake marveled at Kit's ability to excite him. If only his heart hadn't gotten involved, he could've finished what he'd begun without his conscience nagging him.

"I have to go," Jake said softly.

Kit turned away, but not before he saw the glisten of unshed tears.

"Good-bye," she said, her strong voice contrasting with the sadness he'd glimpsed.

He stared at her bowed neck. Although Kit was angry and hurt, the physical attraction between them couldn't be denied. If he wanted, he could seduce her into bed, but she would hate him even more afterward. And Jake was no longer satisfied with just her body; he wanted her heart and soul.

"I love you," he said, his throat aching with need.

Kit froze, but remained mute. He waited, hoping she'd acknowledge his declaration and reiterate her love. The silence expanded, threatening to choke him.

Without another word, Jake strode out of the kitchen and up to the bedroom. After throwing some clothes into his saddlebags, he went downstairs. Pausing, he debated whether to try to talk to Kit one more time. Although he didn't want to leave, he figured a couple of days apart might make Kit more willing to listen. He hurried out of the house and down to the barn.

As he saddled a piebald mare, Johnny joined him. "Where're you going, Pa?"

Jake tightened the cinch and dropped the stirrup into place. Facing his son, he said, "I have to go away for a couple days."

"Are you goin' to hunt down an outlaw?" Johnny asked, his eyes saucer-wide.

Jake smiled and shook his head. "I'm not a bounty hunter anymore, Johnny. I'm a lawyer."

The boy's eyebrows knitted in question. "What does a lawyer do?"

"Lawyers write contracts and wills, and they go to court to defend their clients."

Johnny's frown deepened. "That sounds boring."

Jake hunkered down, putting himself at eye level with his son. "Maybe, but it's a lot safer. And I won't be gone from home as often."

"What're your stories goin' to be about now?"

"I don't think there are going to be any more adventures." Disappointment filled Johnny's eyes. "Does that bother you?"

Johnny shrugged. "I dunno."

"If I kept on bounty hunting, I'd have to be gone a lot. You wouldn't want that, would you?"

"I guess not."

Jake studied his son's long face and tried to imagine what it would be like to learn your father is a famous hero, only to have him hang up his guns. He took hold of Johnny's arms. "I need you to do something for me."

Johnny canted his head. "What?"

"I want you to take care of your mother. I won't be here to do it, so I'm counting on you. Can you do that for me?"

The boy nodded somberly. "Yes, sir."

Jake gathered his son close and hugged him, and Johnny wrapped his arms around Jake's neck. "I'm going to miss you, Pa."

"I'll miss you, too, but I won't be gone long."

He released Johnny and stood. "You be good, and go to bed when your ma tells you to. And do your chores without fussing. All right?"

"I will."

With Johnny walking beside him, Jake led his horse

out of the musky barn and mounted with fluid ease. "Bye, Johnny."

Johnny lifted his hand in farewell. "Bye, Pa."

Jake urged the mare into motion, and called back, "I'm counting on you, son."

With one last wistful glance at the house, Jake rode toward the training corrals on the other side of the grove of aspens. Both Charlie and Ethan were with the horses, and Jake stopped near the pen where Charlie worked.

The dark man led the yearling he'd been training toward Jake. "Goin' somewheres?"

Jake nodded. "Red Cliff. I'll be home day after tomorrow."

Charlie narrowed his eyes. "Lawyer work?"

Annoyed by his unspoken accusation, Jake clenched his teeth to bite back a sarcastic reply. "Yes." Jake dragged in a deep, calming breath. "I'd appreciate it if you'd keep an eye out for strangers."

Charlie's broad brow notched upward.

Jake shifted his weight in the saddle, the leather creaking beneath him. "If anyone comes looking for me, he might not care who he hurts to get what he wants."

Ethan joined them. "You finally leaving?"

"Before you start celebrating, I'll be back."

The half-breed angled a glare at him. "Seems to me Miz Thornton and Johnny's better off without you."

Jake rested his forearm on the saddlehorn and leaned down, hoping to intimidate the younger man. "That's Mrs. Cordell."

Ethan's posture tensed.

"He's right, Ethan," Charlie said reluctantly. He looked up at Jake. "We'll keep an eye out. Not because you said so, but because we don't want nobody hurtin' Johnny or Kit. Nobody."

Feeling as welcome as an atheist at a church picnic,

Jake straightened. "I understand. No need to tell Kit. She'd only worry."

Charlie studied Jake a moment, and his features eased. "We won't be tellin' her."

Grateful, Jake nodded and wheeled the mare around to ride away. Although he wished he could be angry with Charlie and Ethan, he couldn't blame them for their protectiveness. He was the interloper, the outsider who'd disrupted Kit and Johnny's lives. But he was tired of being alone. He wanted the past put behind him.

He wanted a future with his wife and son.

Kit pitched another forkful of straw into the wagon. With a groan, she straightened to take a break from the mindless task of cleaning out the stalls. She massaged her lower back and tipped her head from one side to the other to ease the muscles in her neck.

Even though she was exhausted from too little sleep the last few nights, she pushed her body to the breaking point. By working so hard, Kit hoped she wouldn't have time to think of Jake. The physical labor, however, left her mind free to do as it pleased. And it wanted to dwell on Jake.

I love you.

His parting words drifted across her thoughts for the thousandth time since Jake had left. With all her heart she wanted to believe he spoke the truth, but the timing seemed contrived. Was it only another lie to get what he wanted?

Johnny entered the barn, Toby at his heels. "I think Jasper is all healed," the boy announced.

Kit gazed at her son, seeing Jake's chiseled features etched in the boy's face. Her heart lurched. In spite of her bitter disappointment over Jake's betrayal, she couldn't stop loving him, no matter how hard she tried.

She forced a smile for Johnny's sake. "I guess that

means we'd better go let him join his cousins.''

Leaving a disgruntled Toby locked in the barn, they went to the other building where the injured animals were kept.

"Can you lift one end of the cage?'' Kit asked.

"I'm almost six years old,'' came his indignant reply.

A genuine grin claimed her lips. "That's right. Three more weeks and you'll be all grown up.''

"Almost,'' Johnny amended solemnly.

She and Johnny carried Jasper's cage to the edge of the woods.

"Would you like to let him go?'' she asked.

Johnny kicked at the damp soil, and shook his head. "Naw.''

Concern brought a frown to her face. Normally, he'd have been eager to do a grown-up job. "Are you sure?''

"You can do it.''

She pressed her lips together. Something was bothering him. He was always resistant to releasing one of his "pets,'' but his reluctance seemed rooted in something more this time.

She stepped behind the cage, then bent over the top of it to undo the latch. She swung the door open and stepped back beside Johnny.

Sliding her hands in her pockets, she watched the raccoon take its first step toward freedom. Sniffing the ground, then the air, Jasper glanced back at her and Johnny. With a blink of his masked eyes, Jasper ambled off into the brush.

"Do you think he'll come back?'' Johnny asked with a husky voice.

"I don't think so, sweetheart. He has a life out there in the wilds.''

Kit noticed her son had turned his attention to the road leading to the ranch. Abruptly realizing what worried him, she clenched her jaw. She'd been so absorbed in self-pity, she'd failed to see how Jake's departure had affected Johnny. "Don't worry, your father will come back."

"He's been gone two whole days."

Her heart tightened at the anguish in his words. As hurt as she was by Jake's underhanded possession of the ranch, she, too, wanted him back safe and sound. She knelt down in front of Johnny. "This is his home, sweetheart. Besides, he loves you. He would never leave you."

"I miss him." Her son's plaintive tone shafted an arrow of pain through Kit's chest.

"So do I." The truth slipped past her defenses. It didn't matter what he'd done, she loved him. When he returned, she'd listen to his explanation and give him a chance to prove his parting words.

"Let's go back to the house. It's time to get supper on," Kit said, pushing to her feet.

Vertigo assailed her for a moment, and she placed a hand to her temple. She needed a good night's sleep.

After they put away the empty cage, Johnny let Toby out, and she left the two of them romping around the yard. Kit retrieved a basket of potatoes from the root cellar and sat on the porch to clean them for supper.

While her hands were busy, her mind strayed to Jake. This time she didn't fight the image of his endearing smile or twinkling eyes. She wouldn't have been so stubborn, but her pride had been wounded. In the space of less than an hour, she'd professed her love and learned of his deception. Although at first she'd felt angry at his betrayal, now guilt had set in. She'd been a hypocrite. She'd railed at Jake for his silent lie, yet she still carried the secret of T. K. Thorne.

Kit looked around at the leafing trees and the greening grass as if a cloud had lifted. For the first time since

Jake had left, she admitted to herself that she missed him with a soul-yearning intensity.

A horse and rider came into view on the road, and Kit's heart did a somersault.

The sorrel animal the person rode dashed her hopes that it was Jake returning home. Shading her eyes against the setting sun, she watched the visitor approach. As he came into the yard, she recognized the pinstriped suit and black bowler perched on his head. David Preston.

He was the last person she wanted to see. Kit stood and positioned herself at the top of the porch stairs. Preston slid from the saddle and wrapped the leather reins around the hitching post. Fastidiously brushing the dust from his expensive jacket, he walked toward her.

"Good afternoon, my dear Kit," he greeted in a snake oil salesman's voice.

She nodded, keeping her revulsion hidden. "What brings you out here, David?"

"I heard Cordell was out of town."

A shiver shimmied down her spine, and she fought the urge to wrap her arms around her waist. "So?"

Impatience flickered across his aquiline face. "So I thought I'd come out and check on you."

"No need to worry about me. I've got Charlie and Ethan."

He scowled. "Someone needs to be protecting you from them."

Kit's temper simmered. "I trust them with my life. And Johnny's."

"I heard that the brat is Cordell's. Is that true?"

She boiled at his description of Johnny. "Yes."

He grimaced with distaste. "So you and Cordell were more than old friends. And here I thought the nasty rumors about you were nothing more than jealous prattle."

Not bothering to correct his assumption, she laughed.

"The thing that you can't believe is that I chose him over you."

He mounted the stairs, his menacing steps forcing her to retreat a few feet. "I would've given you respectability, a life where you didn't have to work like a common ranch hand."

She shook her head, the first shiver of fear crawling down her spine. "You've never understood me, David. I chose this ranch, and I chose Charlie and Ethan to work for me. I never cared about respectability."

His blue eyes seemed lit from within by a dangerous gleam. His searing gaze slid across her chest and down her legs, then back to her face.

"I've been more than patient with you, Kit. You owe me for that."

Kit reminded herself that he had been her friend. He wouldn't hurt her. "I don't owe you anything, David. We were friends. Anything more was your imagination."

He advanced with the stealth of a predatory beast. She struggled to remain in place and not give in to the urge to withdraw from his intimidation.

"You would've been mine if Cordell's horse hadn't stumbled when I pulled the trigger." He ground out the words between clenched teeth.

The impact of his statement staggered her. She stared at him, mouth agape. "*You* shot Jake?"

"I did it for you, Kit. I knew you would fall for his shallow charms if I didn't save you. For five years I've waited for you." His face twisted into an ugly bitter mask. "Then Cordell shows up, and you can't wait to crawl under him again and spread your legs."

Preston grabbed her unexpectedly, his fetid breath washing across her, and Kit fought a wave of nausea. Stumbling back, she struggled to free herself from his iron grasp. His fingertips bit into her arms as he shoved her across the porch, pinning her against the door.

"What do you think you're doing?" Kit demanded, her knees quaking.

"Taking what should've been mine." He crushed her lips beneath his. A scream crawled up Kit's throat, but was blocked by Preston's cruel ravishment. She tried to wriggle out of his clutches but was defeated by the unexpected hard muscle camouflaged beneath his fashionable clothing.

She kicked at his shins and was rewarded with a grunt of pain. He ended the violent kiss, and Kit gasped for air. The heavy odors of printers ink and damp wool threatened to suffocate her.

"We're going to go in to the house and you're going to give me what you gave Cordell."

"Go to hell," she spat.

"If you don't, that boy of yours and Cordell's will have an untimely accident. If I can get the drop on the great Jake Cordell, can you imagine how easy it would be for me to kill your bastard?"

Cold terror iced her heart and she ceased struggling, although her muscles remained taut. "No! You wouldn't!"

"That'll be up to you, my sweet." Preston chained her wrists in one hand. "Let's go inside where we can be more comfortable."

Kit's frantic gaze searched the corrals for any sign of her hired men. She didn't see them, and hysteria threatened to undo her fragile thread of control.

"They won't be coming to your rescue. You see, I stopped by to let them know I was going to visit my good friend Kit," Preston said, guessing her thoughts.

Her eyes flashed to his smug smile. Below the finespun veneer of civilization lay a perverted sense of propriety. She had to remain calm, and pray she'd be able to escape before he could . . .

Preston shoved her into the house, wrenching her right arm behind her painfully. Her gaze darted about in search of a weapon. Helpless, she watched him remove his black bowler and hang it on a wall peg as if he were a welcome visitor. The stench of his imported hair oil struck her nostrils, and she gagged.

He propelled her toward the stairs. She stumbled, her hip slamming against the baluster. Preston bent her arm behind her back again. Tears sprang to her eyes, and she staggered up the steps.

At the top, he paused. "Which one's yours?"

How dare he violate the sanctuary of her home! She smiled in defiance. "Guess."

A muscle twitched in his jaw. "Your bastard feeds his caged animals between three and four every day except Sunday."

Her skin blossomed with goosebumps. "You've been watching us?"

"I watch over what's mine."

His warped possessiveness pierced her resistance. "The end of the hall."

Preston's upper lip curled in disgust. "As much as I abhor the thought of you and *him* together, I find taking you in the same bed fitting."

Kit pressed a fist to her mouth. He shoved her, and she stumbled down the hall. Inside the bedroom, she closed her eyes against the memories of her and Jake making love.

Preston chuckled, a low, spine-chilling sound. "I'm going to enjoy this."

His laughter brought a resurgence of desperate anger. Jerking out of his grasp, Kit dashed around him, stretching her fingers toward the doorknob. He caught her by the wrist, sending a jolt of agony up her arm, and she cried out in pain. Seeing her hand mirror on the dresser, she grabbed it and swung blindly, striking him and shattering the glass. Preston's hissed curse told her she'd hurt him, but not enough to break his hold.

He flung her to the bed, and her head cracked against the headboard. Her eyes brimmed with involuntary tears.

Preston rubbed his ear. Blood coated his fingers. "That will cost you, Kit."

She scrambled to a sitting position, her skull throbbing. "Not as much as it'll cost you," she threw back. "What do you think Jake will do to you when he finds out what you've done?"

Preston's arrogance faltered a moment, then reasserted itself in his haughty expression. "I'll tell him you were the one who instigated our meeting."

"He won't believe you."

"I think he will." He leaned close to her, and she turned her face away from the sickening odor of his breath. "The town gossip will only support my claim." He dragged his forefinger down her cheek. "Make this easy for both of us. Believe me, you'll enjoy it."

She scooted frantically off the mattress, keeping the bed between herself and Preston.

"You're only making this harder on yourself," he snarled.

He charged around the end of the bed, and Kit jumped across the mattress to the other side in a maniacal game of tag. She dashed to the door and yanked it open, but Preston shoved his palm against it, slamming it with a thunderous crack.

His arm snaked around her neck, and he flung her across the room as if she were a rag doll. Kit's shin struck the solid maple dresser, and she sank to her knees.

Suddenly the door creaked open, freezing the action like a tintype.

Johnny entered, concerned curiosity in his expression. "Are you okay, Ma?" She nodded, and he straightened his shoulders, like a miniature Jake readying for a battle.

"What're you doing up here, Mr. Preston?"

She had to get him away. "Go downstairs, Johnny."

Her son held his ground, his attention on Preston. He frowned with unconcealed dislike. "My pa won't like it that you were here."

"Get out of here, kid."

Johnny shook his head. "You hurt her."

Preston grabbed the boy and shook him.

Fury surged through Kit, and she hurled her battered body against Preston. "Let him be!" She pounded his back with her fists and kicked him.

Preston swiveled his attention to Kit, releasing Johnny. He buried his fingers in her hair and yanked her head back, and she yelped in pain.

Johnny grabbed Preston's leg and bit him above the knee.

Preston howled, trying to shake him off. He backhanded the boy, knocking him to the hall floor. Forgetting Kit, he stalked toward Johnny.

"*Run!*" Kit screamed.

The terror in his ma's voice spurred Johnny into action. He scrambled to his feet as Preston's figure loomed, and raced down the stairs, his hand skimming the railing. He hurried out to the porch, then paused, looking back. Mr. Preston hadn't chased him.

His stomach spun with fear. He had to take care of his ma. His pa was counting on him.

Johnny sneaked back into the house, his heart pounding, tears running down his face. Entering the library, he opened a desk drawer, and his fingers closed around a wooden box. With trembling hands, Johnny withdrew it, lifted the lid, and took out the revolver. Sobbing, he loaded the weapon the way Ethan had taught him.

He hefted the Colt in both hands. He'd never fired it before, but he'd watched Ethan practice shooting. All he had to do was aim and squeeze the trigger.

Tiptoeing up the steps, he paused in front of the bed-room door. His hands shook from the weight of the gun. Sweat mixed with tears rolled down his cheeks. Then his mother's muffled scream shattered his hesitation. He threw open the door and lifted the revolver, using every ounce of his strength and resolve.

He spied his mother lying on the bed, Mr. Preston sitting on top of her. Her shirt was torn, and she was crying.

"Stop it!" Johnny screamed.

Preston glanced at him over his shoulder and laughed. "Put the gun away, kid. You won't shoot me."

His ma tried to get away from Preston, and the man lifted a hand to her.

Gritting his teeth, Johnny aimed the gun at Mr. Preston's back and squeezed the trigger.

Chapter 19

⁓◦◦◦⁓

The explosion registered in Kit's mind a split second before Preston fell forward on her chest. Reacting without thought, she shoved him off her and scrambled from the bed. She stared at his still body, trying to comprehend what had happened. Blood oozed from a wound high on his right shoulder.

She shifted her gaze to the doorway and spotted Johnny on the floor, a revolver beside him. Realization struck like a physical blow. Johnny had shot Preston.

"Dear God," she whispered.

Charlie and Ethan appeared behind her son, and Kit closed her eyes in relief. Ethan knelt down beside Johnny, and his bewildered gaze found Kit. "What the hell happened?"

She hurried to Johnny's side and wrapped her arms around her son. Hugging his shuddering body close, Kit replied in a shaky voice, "P-Preston attacked m-me."

Ethan spewed a string of curses, and Charlie's fingers rolled into ham-sized fists. Charlie strode to the motionless figure on the bed, then he gazed at Kit in alarm. "He was shot in the back."

Kit stared at the dark man, and comprehension

seemed to stagger him. He looked at Johnny, empathy brimming in his eyes.

Charlie turned back to Preston. "The son-of-a-bitch is still alive."

"I can fix that," Ethan growled.

"No," Kit said. Clinging to her sobbing son, she said in a low voice, "We can't let him die. Get the wagon, Ethan. I'll take him to the doctor's office."

The half-breed stared at her for a moment as if he were going to argue, then he glanced at Johnny and nodded.

After Ethan had gone, Kit looked over at Charlie, bent over Preston's still figure. "How bad is it?"

"Looks like the slug's still in him."

"We need to stop the bleeding."

Charlie nodded. "I'll take care of it. You get Johnny out of here."

Grateful for her friend's help, she led Johnny away from the bloody sight and steered him to his room. She lifted him onto his bed and knelt on the floor facing him.

"You did a very brave thing," she began softly.

Johnny scrubbed his damp eyes with his fists. "Pa told me to take care of you."

Kit's heart leaped into her throat, and she had to wait a moment to answer. "Your pa would be very proud of you, but you can't tell him that you shot Mr. Preston."

His dark brows drew together. "Why not?"

Kit took hold of his tiny hands, hands that had just held a gun and shot a man. Moisture burned her eyes. "We'll tell everyone I did it."

Fear skittered across his tearstained face. "You'll go to jail, and I won't ever see you again."

She forced a reassuring smile. "They won't put me in jail for shooting someone who was trying to hurt me."

She shivered with remembered terror, then choked the

fear back. She had to remain strong for Johnny. She had to protect her son. "This'll be our secret. Yours, mine, Charlie's, and Ethan's, okay?"

Worry shadowed Johnny's features. "Won't Pa be mad?"

He'd be furious, Kit thought. Regret stabbed her. No, if Jake found out, there was no telling what he might do. And she couldn't risk the whole town turning against her son for protecting his mother. "Not if he doesn't find out."

Johnny nibbled his lower lip and nodded.

Kit embraced him, drawing him close. "I love you, sweetheart, and I'm very, very proud of you."

He looped his thin arms around her neck and hugged her tightly. "I love you, too, Ma."

Reluctantly, she released him and studied the swelling around his right eye. A week ago, she wouldn't have believed Preston capable of such violence.

"Let's go downstairs and put a damp cloth on that eye for you. Looks like you're going to have a shiner, young man." She kept her voice light to counter the anger churning within her.

Johnny hopped down from the bed and took her hand. She kept herself between him and the doorway to her bedroom and led him down to the kitchen.

As she wet a cloth with cold well water, she heard footsteps on the stairs. In another minute, she heard more coming down. Knowing Charlie and Ethan were carrying Preston out, she kept a light hearted conversation going with Johnny. She talked about Salty and Pepper, and Jasper. And Jake.

If only Jake had been home, none of this would have happened. Kit knew it was unfair to blame him for Preston's actions, but she couldn't help herself. If Jake truly loved her as he claimed, he wouldn't have left them.

Charlie entered the kitchen, followed closely by

Ethan. The brawny man glanced at Kit, then Johnny. "Quite a shiner you got there, Johnny."

"Mr. Preston done it," the boy replied, then glanced guiltily at Kit.

"It's all right, sweetheart. You can tell them the truth."

"Ethan, why don't you take Johnny to the front room and play a game of checkers?" Charlie suggested.

Johnny clung to Kit. "No, I want to stay with Ma."

Gently, Kit loosened his frantic grip from her. "It's all right, sweetheart. Mr. Preston can't hurt us anymore. Besides, Ethan and Charlie are here now. They won't let anything bad happen."

Fresh tears filled Johnny's eyes, and Kit's throat constricted.

Ethan led him out of the kitchen, and Johnny kept his frightened gaze on Kit until he was gone.

"You'd best get yourself cleaned up before you go into town," Charlie said.

She glanced down at her ruined shirt and noticed for the first time that her chemise had been torn, too, exposing a patch of pale skin between her breasts. Kit pulled the sides of her shirt together, and the shakes caught her off-guard. Her whole body quaked. Ragged sobs escaped her throat, and tears ran unheeded down her cheeks.

Charlie wrapped his arms around her and she stepped into his comforting embrace.

"He was going to rape me," she managed to get out.

His muscles tensed, but he only smoothed Kit's hair in a comforting motion. "If I'da known what kind of man Preston was, I wouldn't have let him out of my sight."

"He had everyone fooled with his city manners." She hiccuped. "Especially me. I can't believe I thought he was my friend." She drew out of his arms. "Nobody can know that it was Johnny who shot Preston in the back.'' Her stomach fisted. ''I'm going to say I did it.''

Charlie stared at her in shock, then shook his head vehemently. ''I ain't gonna let you do that. I'll tell them I did it.''

''Once it's out that he was backshot, you'd be strung up without a trial. Same as Ethan.''

''But—''

Kit squeezed his hand. ''No, I won't take that chance.''

''You figure on hidin' it from Jake, too?'' he asked, his tone disapproving.

Kit swallowed her remorse. ''I have to. Jake's a lawyer. He'd feel obligated to tell the truth. He'll get the same story as everyone else. Preston attacked me, and hit Johnny, then I shot the snake.''

He shook his head. ''Tell him the truth. He's your husband.''

''No. I can't risk having him labeled a backshooter for the rest of his life.'' She searched for understanding in Charlie's eyes. ''Johnny wouldn't be punished by the court, but folks would call him a coward and worse as he grows older. I have to protect my son.''

''He's Jake's son, too.''

She hesitated, and said quietly, ''That's another reason I have to do this.'' She turned toward the door. ''I have to go change and get Preston to the doctor.''

''I packed the wound to stop the bleedin'.'' He reached behind him, withdrew the revolver from his waistband, and handed it to Kit. ''Here.''

She took it with trembling hands, recognizing it as the one she kept in her desk drawer: Judge Cordell's Colt revolver. ''Thanks.''

''I'll ride with you into town,'' Charlie said.

''No. I don't want you or Ethan anywhere near Chaney for a little while.''

Kit went to the library, and placed the unloaded gun back in its box. She noticed a packet of envelopes lying on the desk beside the box and tossed them in the drawer with the weapon.

Half an hour later, Kit drove the team of horses down the dusk-lit road. Preston had lost a lot of blood, but his unconscious groans told her he was still alive. Torn between wanting him to die and wanting him to live, Kit struggled with her conscience. She'd never wished for a man's death before, and the savagery of her thoughts frightened her.

She thought of the novels she'd written glorifying Jake's gunfights. Despite the men being outlaws, she had cheapened the lives and deaths of human beings. And made Jake a hero without remorse. Her vision blurred, and Kit removed her spectacles to rub her eyes. Replacing them, she thought of the final dime novel she'd been trying to write. She now knew how to conclude the legend.

Chaney came into sight, and she guided the horses to the doctor's building. She glanced up at Jake's office, blanketed in darkness, and once again wished he'd been home. Dashing aside the useless musings, she hopped to the hard-packed earth and rushed into Dr. Lewis's office.

"The fire station's down the street," Dr. Lewis growled from his desk.

Kit blinked, at first bewildered. "I've got a badly wounded man in the back of my wagon."

He came to his feet with a scowl. "Why didn't you say so in the first place?"

"I—" Kit shook her head. There was no use arguing with him; she'd never win. "He's been shot."

Dr. Lewis rushed past her, surprising Kit with his agility. He looked into the wagon bed. "Looks like the newspaperman."

"It is," she affirmed. "I did it."

"Didn't agree with one of his editorials?"

Despite the gravity of the situation, Kit smiled. "Not exactly."

The doctor shanghaied a couple men out of the crowd who'd gathered around the wagon and had them carry Preston into the examination room.

"You get queasy with blood?" Lewis demanded.

Kit shook her head. "No."

"Good. I need a nurse."

"But—"

"I got no time for shilly-shallying. Get in here."

Kit accepted the inevitable with a sigh and rolled up her sleeves.

For the next hour, she helped Lewis remove the bullet from Preston's shoulder. Tying off the bandage, she glanced at the doctor. "Will he live?"

"I look like God to you?"

Flustered, Kit shook her head. "Well, no." She attempted another approach. "In your medical opinion, will he be all right?"

"Bullet didn't do any real damage. He'll be fit as a fiddle in a few weeks."

Kit nearly collapsed with relief.

Dr. Lewis wiped his hands dry. "Preston do that to you?"

She noticed his attention on her neck, and she covered the painful bruise self-consciously. "Yes."

His eyes gleamed with anger. "Preston got what he deserved. In my day, a man who attacked a woman would've been strung up without a trial." His shrewd gaze remained on her. "Want to tell me who really shot him?"

Startled, she glanced down, and picked up the bloody cloths littering the floor. "I told you, I did."

"How do you shoot a man in the back when he's attacking you?"

"I got away from him and grabbed a gun and shot him. Simple as that," Kit stated, her voice unnaturally loud. "Am I done here?"

He nodded.

Kit watched the doctor gather his tools, then went into the front office. She stopped short at the sight of Mayor Walters, Bertie Wellensiek, and Patrick. The Irishman's usually pleasant expression was absent, and Kit's palms grew moist.

"Is that David Preston back there?" Patrick asked without preamble.

Kit nodded, but didn't offer more.

"Arrest her," Bertie said in a shrewish voice.

Patrick leveled a quelling gaze at the reverend's wife. "I want to hear Kit's side."

Kit recognized the Irishman's struggle to control his temper. Quaking inside, she prayed for courage to keep to her story. "David came out to the ranch. He said he knew Jake was out of town and wanted to make sure I was all right."

Bertie narrowed her darting little pig eyes. "Mr. Preston is a gentleman."

"I hate to shatter your image of the wonderful Mr. Preston, but he's no gentleman," Kit stated shakily. "He attacked me. Fortunately, I was able to get away from him and grab a gun. Then I shot him." She paused. "Dr. Lewis said he'll be fine in a few weeks."

"You shot him in the back, Miss Thornton," the mayor commented.

She pinned him with a glare. "I had reason enough. And it's Mrs. Cordell."

Walters stuck two fingers between his stiff collar and thick neck as if he were suffocating. "Were there any witnesses to the shooting?"

Kit lifted her chin. "No."

Bertie sniffed and dabbed at her beaked nose with a

delicate white lace hanky. "I think Mrs. Cordell enticed Mr. Preston out to her place since her husband was gone. And when Mr. Preston refused her, Mrs. Cordell shot him in a fit of anger."

Kit closed her eyes, wondering if she should laugh or cry. Bertie Wellensiek's storytelling abilities rivaled those of T. K. Thorne.

"Arrest her, Sergeant," the mayor ordered.

Patrick glanced at the pompous little man, then turned to Kit, an apologetic look on his florid face. "I'll have to put you in jail until the judge comes to town."

Panic danced on the fringes of her precarious control. "It was self-defense!"

Misery lined the Irishman's face. "I'm believin' you, lass, but Preston was shot in the back."

Kit's hands trembled, and she curled her fingers into fists. "So I'm going to be thrown in jail as if this was all my fault?"

"I'm sorry, lass."

What would Johnny think when she didn't come home? She couldn't have him blame himself, but she wouldn't be able to reassure him.

Allowing the sergeant to guide her out of the doctor's office, she passed the townspeople lining the boardwalk. Kit heard their murmurings in her wake, and although she couldn't understand the words, she could tell by their tones what was being said. Stiffening her spine, she stared straight ahead and ignored them as she'd learned to do years before.

But deep down she was a ten-year-old girl again, vainly looking for her hero to rescue her.

Jake mopped the sweat from his forehead with his neckerchief, cursing the vagaries of a Wyoming spring. Soon after he'd arrived in Chaney, there'd been a snow-storm. Less than six weeks later, the sun beat down upon him like he was in an Arizona desert. He tied the bandanna around his neck in a loose knot.

Passing the cemetery where his father and Maggie were buried, he sent them a reverent nod but continued on home, anxious to see Johnny and Kit. He hoped Kit had thought about what he'd said and was ready to listen to him. He ached to see her smile again, to hold her in his arms, and to spend the night making love.

Jake chided himself for his eagerness. He'd always made fun of those men who'd been lassoed and heeled. Now he found himself in the same position, and he felt anything but tied down; there was only an urgency to see his family again and make amends with Kit. He was no longer obsessed with the ranch, and he'd prove it to her. Patting his saddlebags, he imagined her expression when he gave her his present.

Darkness had fallen when he arrived at the ranch. He dismounted in front of the house, looping the leather reins around the hitching post. Toby greeted him with his usual enthusiasm, and Jake rewarded him with a pat.

Light blazed from the windows, warming Jake with the welcoming sight. His stomach twisted with nervousness. What if Kit still refused to listen to him?

He struck the fear from his mind. He had never run from a fight, and he wasn't about to begin now. Especially when the stakes were this high. He strode to the house and thundered up the stairs to the porch. He reached for the door, but it swung open and Johnny launched himself into Jake's arms. He lifted the boy up and Johnny hugged him, burying his face in the curve of his neck.

A love more powerful than he'd ever known overwhelmed Jake, and he couldn't speak. He held his son close, savoring his clean fresh scent.

"I'm glad you're home, Pa."

His muffled words held something more than happiness at seeing him again.

"I'm glad, too, son." Easing Johnny's head up, he spied the boy's swollen eye. "What happened?"

"Mr. Preston did it," Johnny replied, tears welling in his eyes. "He was hurting Ma and I tried to stop him."

Bewildered, Jake looked past his son into the house, and found Charlie and Ethan gazing at him. Alarm wrenched Jake's gut. "Where's Kit?"

"Ma's—" Johnny began.

"She's in town," Charlie interrupted. "She took the son-of-a-bitch to the doctor."

Totally confused, Jake glanced at Ethan, whose hostility seemed to have waned since the last time he'd seen him. "What happened, Ethan?"

The young man jerked his head up, and his bronze complexion darkened. "Preston tried to force Kit . . ."

Black rage filled Jake, and he barely controlled his fury.

"I tried to stop him, Pa," Johnny said, his slight body shaking in Jake's arms. "But he was so big, and I thought he was going to chase me." A sob escaped him. "I had to do it."

"Do what, Johnny?" Jake tried to keep his voice calm so he wouldn't further frighten his son.

"Preston was shot," Charlie interjected. "Kit took him into town. That was a couple of hours ago."

A tear rolled down Johnny's face. "It's my fault."

Jake thumbed away the moisture. "It wasn't your fault, Johnny." He looked at Ethan and Charlie; they were holding something back from him. "Did Kit shoot Preston?"

Charlie glanced at Ethan, who stared down at his feet. Charlie hooked his thumbs in his suspenders, and raised his chin. "Nope."

Frustration tensed Jake's muscles. "So you or Ethan did?"

"I shot him," Johnny blurted out. "Don't tell Ma I told you. She told me not to tell."

Jake's breath caught in his throat. He tightened his arms around Johnny. "How bad was Preston hurt?"

"Couldn't tell," Charlie replied.

He pierced Charlie and Ethan with a taloned glare. "Why didn't one of you take him in, instead of Kit?"

"She was afraid them folks in town would string us up," Charlie stated. "He was backshot."

The pieces of the puzzle fell into place. Kit would protect those she cared for, no matter the price she had to pay. "Was she hurt?"

"A few bruises," Ethan replied.

Fury pulsed through Jake's skull. He looked at Johnny. "I'm going into town to get your mother."

The boy dragged his forearm across his eyes. "I want to go with you."

"No. You stay here with Charlie and Ethan."

Jake deposited a reluctant Johnny into Charlie's arms. "I'll be back in a little while."

His fury thrumming a tattoo in his mind, he stalked to his horse. Jake ran a hand down the animal's damp neck, then jumped into the saddle.

Jake tried to keep his mind blank, his thoughts focused on the road and nothing more. If he allowed himself to think about Kit, about what Preston had attempted, Jake was afraid he'd not be able to control his rage.

My son shot a man in the back. Anguish washed through Jake. Johnny'd only been protecting his mother, but the stigma of a backshooter was something Jake never wanted anyone he loved to have to face. Even if his son had done the right thing.

Twenty minutes later, he reached Chaney and hurried inside the doctor's office.

"Dr. Lewis!" Jake hollered.

The cantankerous doctor came out of the back room, scowling at Jake. "What in tarnation is your problem, Cordell?"

"I'm looking for my wife."

"You got married and didn't invite me to the wedding?" Dr. Lewis sounded hurt.

Jake blinked. "Kit and I were married over a month ago. You must've been out of town."

"Well, someone could've told me. I never know what's going on."

"That's for sure," Jake mumbled. "Have you seen Kit?"

"Pretty gal with blond hair?"

Jake choked back his frustration. "That's her."

"Brought that newspaperman here with a bullet in him. Said she shot him."

Why wasn't Jake surprised? She was like a she-wolf protecting her young. A band seemed to squeeze his chest. "You believe her?"

Dr. Lewis shook his head. "Kinda hard for a body to shoot someone in the back if they're being attacked."

So Lewis wasn't nearly as offtrack as he appeared. "Is Kit in the back room?"

"What in tarnation would she be doing back there? Preston is the only patient I got right now."

Relief and disappointment warred in Jake. "Then he's alive?"

"Well, I don't take dead patients."

Jake raked his hand through his hair. "Where's Kit?"

"Down at the jail."

Jake's heart hammered against his ribs. "Was she arrested?"

"Do I look like a judge?" Lewis studied Jake through

his glasses. "You look a bit like a judge I used to know. Judge Cordell. Any relation?"

Jake spun around and hurried out before he lost all patience.

Briskly walking down the boardwalk, he almost bowled over the mayor.

"Jake, good to see you," Walters greeted. "Do you know your wife's in jail?"

"Now I do," Jake stated through clenched teeth.

He strode past the puffed-out pigeon.

Walters retreated, but called out in righteous indignation, "I warned you about her before you got married."

"I think you'd better find out where Fanny spends her evenings before you cast any stones," Jake snarled back.

The mayor's eyes bulged out like a fish's, and Jake took satisfaction in the man's shock. He continued on to the police station and barreled into the office.

Jameson scrambled to his feet, and moved to block the entrance to the cells. "Hold on now, Mr. Cordell. You can't go barging in like you own the place."

Jake stopped toe-to-toe with Jameson. "I'm going to see Kit, and you're not going to stop me."

Jameson crossed his arms, and shook his head. "Forget it, Cordell. She shot a man in the back."

Jake drew back his fist and struck the younger man in the jaw. Jameson crumpled to the floor, unconscious.

Jake shook his stinging hand. "Nobody calls my wife a backshooter." He stepped over the prone officer. "Besides, you've had that coming for fifteen years."

Chapter 20

Kit sensed Jake's presence, and looked past Freda and Patrick to see his approaching figure. Her heart skipped a beat at the wide breadth of his shoulders, and his easy, confident gait. Everything would be all right now. Her tardy hero had arrived.

Jake tipped his hat to Freda. "Evening." He turned to Patrick. "You might want to clean the trash off your floor."

The Irishman narrowed his eyes. "And what trouble have you been gettin' into?"

"Jameson thought he could keep me from seeing my wife."

Kit's grip tightened on the metal bars. *My wife.* The possessiveness in his tone brought a shiver of delight. Did she dare hope he really loved her, as he'd claimed?

He turned his gaze on her, and his expression softened. "Kit."

A lump filled her throat, and she gazed at him with undisguised love.

Jake turned to the police sergeant, his features cast in granite. "Why's she in jail?"

Patrick appeared miserable. "Preston was shot in the back."

343

"The son-of-a-bitch deserved it."

Kit studied Jake, wondering how much he knew.

"I'm agreein' with you, lad, but you know the law better 'n me." The Irishman put his arm around Freda. "Come on, Freda. We'd best be leavin' these two alone."

He guided Freda out, and Kit heard Patrick trying to wake Jameson. Alone with Jake, Kit didn't know how to breach the awkward silence. She could only gaze at him: his dusty clothes, which told her he hadn't taken time to change before he came to Chaney, and the whiskers that shadowed his strong jaw.

Jake moved to stand directly in front of her, then wrapped his fingers around hers. "I'm sorry, Kit."

She blinked. "For what?"

"For not being here."

Unable to meet his sorrowful gaze, she stared at a point behind him. "It wasn't your fault."

"The hell it wasn't!" His forceful exclamation startled her. "If I hadn't gone out of town, he wouldn't have hurt you or Johnny. And you wouldn't be in jail."

She reached through the bars and put her palm against his chest. His heart thumped against her hand as his warmth invaded her skin. "Everything will be all right, Jake."

"These 'good folks' of Chaney are going to be sorry they tangled with Mr. and Mrs. Jake Cordell."

He hadn't asked her what happened, yet he believed without a doubt she was innocent. When had his trust become unconditional?

When he realized he loved you, a little voice in her mind answered.

Kit took hold of his shirt front and pulled him toward her. "Shut up and kiss me, Jake."

He stared at her a moment, then, as a slow smile slid across his sensuous lips, he tipped his hat back off his forehead and leaned forward. Between the cold metal bars, his tender mouth slanted across hers. Sultry heat poured through her limbs, dispersing the cold emptiness of the jail.

Jake broke the kiss a few moments later, his breath coming in a ragged gasp. "I've missed you, Kit."

She swallowed. "I missed you, too, Jake. Have you seen Johnny yet?"

He nodded and grimaced. "I saw him. I shouldn't have told him to take care of you while I was gone. It was too much responsibility for a kid."

"I'm sorry, Jake. I had no idea David would try something like that." She paused. "He's the one who ambushed you and killed Zeus."

Surprise lit his expression. "Are you sure?"

She nodded. "He told me right before he . . ."

"I need to know exactly what happened," he said softly.

She gazed into his empathy-filled eyes. Taking a deep breath, she related how David had shown up at the ranch.

"He threatened Johnny's life if I didn't cooperate with him. I couldn't risk Johnny being hurt or killed, so I did as Preston said. We went up to the bedroom and he—" she faltered. "He kissed me and touched me." Kit shuddered with remembered revulsion. "Johnny must've heard something, because he came into the bedroom and tried to get Preston to stop hurting me. Preston hit him—I thought he was going to kill him. I told Johnny to run."

"Did he?" Jake prompted.

Kit nodded. "Thankfully, Preston didn't chase him. Next thing I knew, Preston was on top of me on the bed." Tears ran unheeded down her cheeks.

"I have to know the rest. How did Preston get shot in the back?"

She looked up at him, and his searching gaze didn't waver from her. Kit had thought she could withhold the truth from him, but she found she couldn't. She had to learn to trust. There had been enough deceit between them.

Swiping aside her tears, she continued. "Johnny got your father's gun, which I kept in my desk." Kit tightened her grip on Jake's hands. "Johnny shot Preston. If he hadn't, Preston would've raped me."

Jake scrutinized her with unfathomable intensity. He eased from her grasp and framed her face in his palms. "I'm glad you told me the truth."

She blinked. "You already knew?"

He nodded. "Johnny let it slip. Our marriage was started on the wrong side of trust, and I didn't help matters when I didn't tell you about the loan papers." He reached into his back pocket, pulling out an official-looking piece of paper. "I know this isn't a very good time, but I want you to have this."

He handed her the document. Kit stared at him a moment, wondering at the almost childlike eagerness in his expression. She scanned the deed, and her vision blurred. He'd signed the ranch over to her. She lifted her teary gaze to him. "You didn't have to do this."

He shook his head. "Yes, I did. The ranch means nothing to me. It's you and Johnny that matter."

She believed him now, as well as the words of love he'd spoken three days ago. Kit slid her hand between the bars and threaded her fingers through his. "Thank you, Jake," she said, her throat raw with love.

Uncharacteristic bleakness darkened his expression. "If we don't have Johnny testify, we're going to have a hard time proving self-defense. And knowing some of our fine citizens, there'll be some pretty ugly gossip, too."

"Like the current one that says I invited Preston over,

then tried to seduce him?'' Bitterness tightened her mouth.

Jake's stomach clenched at her pain, and he wished he could spare her the next few days. Instead, he nodded.

"Words have never hurt me before, Jake. I won't let them start now, especially since the alternative is having Johnny up on the stand," Kit stated, determination ringing in her tone. "You have to protect him."

"No court would convict a five-year-old boy for protecting his mother. Let me talk to Patrick, tell him what really happened," Jake argued.

"No! I'll take my chances."

"What if it looks like Preston will get away with it?"

Her eyes became haunted, but no less resolute. "Do you want Johnny to be called a backshooter? A reputation like that will never disappear. He'd be branded a coward the rest of his life."

He gazed at the stubborn tilt of Kit's chin, the iron will in her somber expression. He'd never known a woman as uncompromising in her beliefs. He'd never known a woman who would die to protect those she loved.

He'd never known a woman like Kit.

He wanted to groan in frustration. Defending her against an attempted murder charge would be easier than defending her against town sentiment. And he'd have to do both, without Johnny's testimony.

The trial ahead frightened him more than any gun duel he'd been involved in, because the stakes were the highest he'd ever encountered. If he lost, Kit would go to prison. Johnny would lose his mother, and Jake wouldn't be able to live with himself, knowing he hadn't done everything he could to defend her.

He hadn't expected his first trial case to be a personal battle for his wife's life.

*　　*　　*

"Damn it, there's got to be somebody around here who's had some bad dealings with Preston." Jake rubbed his grizzled jaw and paced back and forth across the straw-covered floor.

Charlie curried Satan's mane in a hypnotic motion. "I ain't heard anything bad about him the whole time he's been here. What about before he come to Chaney? He get in any trouble back where he come from?"

Jake halted in front of Satan's stall and leaned against the top rail. "I've got someone checking on him back in Chicago. That's where Preston grew up. The problem is, we're running out of time. The trial starts tomorrow, and I have nothing."

"And Preston has everyone eatin' out of his hand," Charlie growled. "Pretendin' he's the hurt one. How's Kit doin'?"

"As well as can be expected. I took some more clothes in for her yesterday morning. Freda got Patrick to let her out long enough to take a bath at her place." Jake held his hand out to the midnight-colored stallion, who nuzzled it with his velvety nose. "She's not sleeping, though, and she's been sick."

"She tell you that?"

Jake laughed without humor. "She keeps telling me she's fine, and not to worry." He spun around, startling the stud horse. "How can I not worry about her? Johnny keeps asking me when his mother's coming home, then he wants to go see her. It damn near kills me to see him cry for her at night."

"What about you?" Charlie asked in a low, rumbly voice. "How're you holding up?"

Flattening his palm against a post, Jake leaned forward and hung his head. "I want her back home where she belongs."

"You love her, don't you?"

Jake straightened and gazed at Charlie. "Helluva lot good it does now."

Pete Two Ponies stepped out of the shadows. "And a lot of good feelin' sorry for yourself is doin' for her, too."

Startled, Jake tossed Pete a glare. "I wish you wouldn't pop in and out like that." He narrowed his eyes. "How do you do that, anyhow?"

Two Ponies shrugged. "Old Indian trick." He approached Jake, aiming a gnarled forefinger at him. "There's only one way to fight fire."

Jake nodded impatiently. "Yeah, with fire. What does that have to do with defending Kit?"

"You say that newspaperman has everyone believing he's one of your god's saints. Maybe you ought to be creatin' your own saint."

A smile grew across Charlie's broad face. "That's a mighty fine idea for a broken-down Indian."

Puzzled, Jake looked from Pete to Charlie and back. "I don't get it."

Two Ponies frowned. "I thought heroes were supposed to be smart."

Charlie snickered and came out of Satan's stall. "At least smarter 'n the bad guys." He clapped Jake on the back. "Let me explain it to you."

Two hours later, Jake sipped coffee in Freda's kitchen.

"What is a 'character witness'?" she asked.

"People who will testify that someone is basically a good person," Jake explained. "I was hoping you would be a character witness for Kit."

Freda nodded vehemently. "I will, if it will help her."

Jake smiled. "I thought you might. I know a lot of folks in this town don't think much of her, but could you come up with a few others who might testify on her behalf?"

She thought a minute, then nodded, a sly grin sneaking across her face. "Many people I know who stay quiet, but Kit has helped them. Maybe if you talk to them, shame them into speaking up, they will do so."

Jake pulled a paper and pencil from his pocket. "Give me their names and what Kit did for them. I'll take it from there."

Kit heard the inner door open, and she laid her pencil and paper on the thin cot. Patrick came to her cell and unlocked the door.

"Time to face the judge," he announced in a gentle voice.

Kit swallowed back the trepidation blocking her throat, and pressed her spectacles up on her nose. Smoothing her dress over her thighs, she stood up. A wave of dizziness threatened to upset her stomach, and she folded her arms, pressing them against her abdomen.

"Are you all right, lass?" Patrick asked in concern.

"I haven't been sleeping very well." She hoped she wouldn't get sick in the courtroom. "I'll be all right."

She could tell she hadn't quelled his worry, but her own fears consumed her. Patrick guided her out of the police station to one of the saloons that doubled as a courtroom. The smell of flat beer, stale smoke, and unwashed bodies nauseated her. She cupped her hand over her nose, blocking out only a portion of the vile odors. She gagged, and only sheer force of will kept her from vomiting.

Keeping her gaze fixed straight ahead, Kit didn't allow herself to look at the people who filled the chairs. Her chest tightened, and she couldn't seem to get enough air into her lungs. Jake's tall, impressive figure came into view and he took hold of her hands, helping her into one of the two chairs at the front. He sat beside her.

"Are you all right? Your face is as white as a sheet,"

he said, keeping his warm fingers wrapped around her ice-cold ones.

Her lungs expanded, replenishing her oxygen, and the nausea abated slightly. She gazed at the familiar angles and contours of Jake's beloved face, the face that had kept her sane during the long, lonely nights in her cell. The loving concern in his expression brought tears to her eyes. All she wanted was to go home and fall asleep in the circle of his arms.

"I'm fine," she managed to say in reassurance.

"Don't worry. Everything will work out."

Kit nodded. "I know. My hero's never let me down before."

A smile twitched Jake's lips. "Not even when he had to be dragged out of the saloon?"

"Only make-believe heroes are perfect," she said gently. "I prefer mine to be slightly flawed."

Jake kissed her, and for a moment they were all alone, oblivious to the roomful of spectators.

The judge entered, and Jake helped Kit to her feet. Once the black-robed man was seated, she lowered herself back into her chair.

Judge Blair banged his gavel once on the scarred poker table, and silence ensued. Glancing at the paper in front of him, the judge scowled. He looked at Jake. "You must be Jonathan Cordell's son."

Jake nodded. "That's right, Your Honor."

"Played poker with your father a few times. A helluva bluffer."

"I didn't know that."

The judge studied Jake. "Couldn't stop talking about his son, either. He was mighty proud of you going to law school."

Kit looked up at Jake, who appeared startled. Sensing his overwhelming emotion, she laid her hand on his forearm.

"Thank you for sharing that with me, Your Honor," he said, his voice husky.

Judge Blair nodded. "I see you're defending your wife. I'd be remiss if I didn't suggest she get another lawyer." He turned his shrewd gaze to Kit. "Would you prefer other counsel?"

She shook her head. "I trust my husband implicitly."

"All right, then let's get on with it," the judge said.

The prosecutor and Jake gave their opening statements, then David Preston was called to the stand.

Kit stared at his expression, full of thinly veiled hostility, and she wondered why no one else could see the evil in him. His face was pale, his steps short and deliberate as he held his slinged arm close to his side. He milked his injury for all the sympathy he could get.

Kit locked her fingers together and laid her hands in her lap. Her insides churned with the remembered terror Preston had caused her. Jake's jaw muscle clenched, but he gave her a reassuring smile before returning his attention to the proceedings.

After Preston was sworn in, the prosecutor began his questioning. "Would you tell us what happened three days ago?"

David Preston grimaced with theatrical flourish. "I rode out to the Cordell ranch to visit Mrs. Cordell. Kit and I were old friends, and I wanted to be sure she was all right with her husband out of town. After I got there, she invited me into the house for a cup of coffee. I accepted her invitation and followed her into the kitchen. There I found out she had more than coffee on her mind. She told me she was unhappy in her marriage to Jake Cordell. She asked me to hold her."

Kit closed her eyes against his vicious lies.

"Did you?" the prosecutor pressed.

Preston sighed. "Yes. I know it wasn't proper, but I

thought she only wanted comfort, and we had been friends.''

"She wanted more?''

"I had never believed the rumors about her.''

"What rumors were those?''

"That she gave her favors freely. I believed she was a decent woman despite her choice of clothing.'' Preston paused melodramatically. "She wears trousers.''

Jake jumped to his feet. "Objection. What Kit prefers to wear has no bearing on the charge.''

"Sustained,'' the judge said.

"So you comforted Mrs. Cordell?'' the prosecutor prompted.

"Yes. Then she began to kiss me. I tried to tell her it was wrong, that she was a married woman, but she wouldn't listen.''

Kit stared at her white knuckles, and her fingernails cut into her palms. She couldn't look at Jake. Did he think there might be some truth to Preston's testimony?

"So you tried to dissuade her?''

Preston nodded. "Then she got angry because I wouldn't do what she wanted me to. At that point I decided I should leave, so I turned around and that's when she shot me.''

Kit couldn't hold back her indignant rage any longer. She jumped to her feet. "You're lying! You were the one who tried to—''

Judge Blair banged his gavel on the table. "Sit down, Mrs. Cordell.''

Jake grabbed her shoulders and leaned close to her. "Kit, do as he says.''

Jake's voice brought some control back to her outrage. Bile inched up her throat, and she clasped her palm to her mouth. "I'm going to be sick.''

He turned to Freda, who sat directly behind them. "Take her outside to get some air.''

The petite woman put her arm around Kit's waist and helped her out of the saloon. Kit made it to the alley before she lost what little was in her stomach. Freda rubbed her back with circular soothing motions, and after a few minutes, Kit wiped her damp brow with her forearm. With some embarrassment, she saw that Patrick had joined them.

She mustered a reassuring smile. "I'm sorry. I thought I could handle Preston's lies."

"It's all right, lass," Patrick said. "I'll take you back to your cell so you can lie down. Jake'll be along in a bit. He's goin' to cross-examine Preston, then the judge will probably be adjournin' for lunch."

With Patrick and Freda flanking her, Kit returned to the jail. She lay on her lumpy cot and closed her eyes.

A little later, Jake joined her in the cell, concern in his rugged face. "How're you feeling?"

She nodded and sat up. Jake lowered himself to the thin mattress beside her.

"How does it look, Jake?" she asked, unable to hide a tremor in her voice. "And don't lie to me."

"Judge Blair has a reputation for being fair." Jake sighed. "But Preston did a damn good job of making himself look like the injured party."

"And the bullet wound helped," Kit added. "What's going to happen this afternoon?"

"The prosecutor will call in character witnesses for Preston."

Kit worried her lower lip between her teeth. "The things Preston said about me—I couldn't bear it if you thought any of it might be true."

"You know I believe you, Kit." Jake's face turned stormy. "Preston's a lying son-of-a-bitch who's going to get his due when I get my turn to call witnesses for the defense."

She looked up, alarmed. "You aren't going to put Johnny on the stand, are you?"

Jake glanced down at their twined hands. "I don't know."

"You said you wouldn't."

He captured her with an intense gaze. "Were you telling the judge the truth when you said you trusted me implicitly?"

Kit searched his eyes, finding nothing but concern. With jerky motions, she nodded. "Yes."

"Then trust me."

He wrapped his arms around her, and Kit leaned into his embrace, resting her cheek against his suit jacket. His heart pounded with a steady comforting rhythm.

"I want to go home, Jake," she whispered hoarsely. "I want this nightmare to end."

"It will, honey, it will," he said softly.

An hour later, Kit sat in the same chair at the front of the courtroom. For the entire afternoon, she listened to Mayor Walters, Bertie Wellensiek, and others extol the virtues of David Preston until she thought she'd be sick again. When the judge adjourned for the day, she was actually relieved to return to her cell.

She urged Jake to go home, tuck Johnny into bed, and make sure the boy said his prayers.

"He asks God to bring you home every night," Jake said as he left.

Kit kept her tears at bay until she was certain Jake was gone. Then she buried her face in her hands and allowed the wave of homesickness to overcome her. She missed Johnny so much that she physically ached to hold him. She had promised she'd teach him how to work with the yearlings, and now she might not be able to keep that promise.

Her only consolation was that his father was with him. Two months ago, Kit wouldn't have believed Jake would be able to handle fatherhood, but he'd proved her wrong. A powerful bond existed between him and Johnny, a bond that would never be broken.

In the solitude of her cell, she offered a prayer of thanks to God for bringing Jake home and for giving her the courage to reveal the truth. If she was convicted, she'd be comforted by the fact that her son would be loved and protected.

After Johnny had cried himself to sleep, Jake restlessly wandered downstairs. The house seemed lifeless without Kit's presence, and desolation filled his chest. He wanted her home, lying beside him at night. If it weren't for those sanctimonious hypocrites Bertie Wellensiek and Mayor Walters, Kit wouldn't be sitting in a jail cell. For the first time, Jake wished he was more like the fictional hero. *That* Jake Cordell wouldn't be fretting his defense.

Wandering into the library, Jake sank into the chair behind the desk. Kit's floral scent drifted around him, deepening his loneliness for her. Hoping to divert his thoughts, he opened the desk drawer to find the box that held his father's Colt—the gun Johnny had used to shoot Preston.

He reached for the weapon, but his gaze settled on a stack of envelopes tied together by a frayed piece of cloth. Picking up those instead, he held them up to the moonlight streaming in the window behind him. They were addressed to him.

Puzzled, Jake lit a lamp and settled back in his seat. The neat handwriting was obviously a woman's. It wasn't Maggie or Kit's penmanship. What other woman would've written him? He glanced at the date on the first envelope: 1870, nearly twenty-five years ago. Unease prickled through him.

His fingers trembling, he plucked the tie from the letters. He opened the top one and carefully unfolded the brittle yellow parchment. Silently he began to read.

> *My dearest Jake,*
>
> *I hope you are doing well. I think of you often and pray for your safety. I know you're too young to understand, but I couldn't live out there. I wanted to take you with me to live in the city, but your father wouldn't allow it. In his own way, he loves you more than even he realizes. Be good, and please don't blame yourself for my leaving. It was nothing you did, my dear son. I will always love you, and I will always be with you even though you cannot see me.*
>
> *Love, Mother*

Jake's throat closed, and moisture filled his eyes. He picked up the next letter and read that. Two hours later, he set the last one down on the desk. He scrubbed his wet face with his palms.

His mother hadn't abandoned him; she'd loved him all these years, and he hadn't even known. The last letter was dated six years ago, right before his father had been killed. She had probably continued to write, but the letters had been undeliverable.

He seethed with anger and pain. Why had his father hidden them from him? Perhaps it the same reason Kit hadn't told him about Johnny. Maybe Jake's father been afraid he'd lose his son, just as Kit had been fearful he would take Johnny from her.

Judge Blair's words drifted through his thoughts: *he was mighty proud of you.*

His eyes burned anew. He had believed neither one of his parents had loved him. Now he knew he'd never been without love. He couldn't blame his father; he was only doing what he thought best. But could he put twenty-five years of bitterness behind him?

He resolved to write his mother tonight and hoped it wasn't too late.

But first, he had to give Johnny the choice Jake hadn't been given: the choice to keep his mother.

Chapter 21

Kit had slept little the night before, and the stench of the courtroom triggered her nausea again. She had eaten little supper and no breakfast, so she was able to hold the sickness at bay. Jake, looking as exhausted as she felt, greeted her with a smile and kiss.

"It's our turn today," he said.

Kit tried to muster a measure of confidence, but all emotion seemed to have been drained from her. How could Jake prove her innocence? The only witness was Johnny, and Kit didn't want the young boy subjected to the probing questions and accusations that might lead to the truth.

As if living someplace between reality and dreams, Kit rose when the judge entered. After four nights in jail and being under the constant scrutiny of narrow-minded townsfolk, she wanted it over.

Jake took hold of her arm and urged her to sit. "Trust me, Kit."

She blinked, and the fog cleared. Taking a deep steadying breath, she nodded.

After one last concerned look at Kit, Jake called his first witness. "Defense calls Henrietta Jacobs."

Kit frowned, wondering what Mrs. Jacobs had to do

with Preston's attack. The mousy, brown-haired woman took the stand. She kept her gaze lowered as if afraid to look anyone in the eye.

"State your name," Jake said.

"Henrietta Lolita Jacobs."

"Mrs. Jacobs, do you know the defendant Kit Cordell?" Jake asked in a gentle voice.

She nodded, and smiled shyly at Kit. "I've known her since she was a little girl."

"Has she ever exhibited the type of behavior Mr. Preston accuses her of?"

The woman's eyes saucered. "Heavens, no. She was such a quiet girl, always fixing up hurt animals and helping folks."

"Has she ever helped you?"

"Yes." Mrs. Jacobs finally raised her head and met Jake's gaze. "When my youngest was sick, Kit came over every day to tend her." She glanced at the judge. "My husband had died a few months earlier, and I had six other children to care for."

Jake smiled at the woman. "Thank you, Mrs. Jacobs."

"Cross examination?" Judge Blair asked the prosecutor.

He shook his head.

"You may step down," the judge said.

The woman returned to her seat.

"Next witness."

"Defense calls Abraham Zoller," Jake said.

Kit frowned. What was Jake doing?

After the preliminaries, Jake asked. "How do you know the defendant, Mr. Zoller?"

"She come and helped me with my young'uns after my wife died," the big overalled man said. "If she hadn't, I woulda lost my farm."

"How's that?"

"I wouldn't have been able to get my crops in."

"Do you believe Mr. Preston's claim that Kit Cordell is not a decent woman?"

The prosecutor jumped to his feet. "Objection."

"Your Honor, he opened this line of questioning by denigrating Mrs. Cordell's reputation," Jake argued.

Judge Blair thought for a moment, then nodded. "Overruled. You may continue, Cordell."

After Zoller's statement of support, he left the stand. Jake continued to called a parade of witnesses to defend Kit's character. There was Mr. Brown, whose doctor bill she'd paid; Jenny Darling, whom she'd taken to a nearby town to visit her dying sister; and Joseph Landowers, to whom she'd given food and clothing when his cabin had burned down. Astonished by the number of people who'd come forward to testify on her behalf, Kit wondered how Jake had learned of all of them.

Jake called his next witness. "Defense calls Freda Finster."

Holding her head up, Freda took the stand and was sworn in.

Jake stuck his thumbs in his vest pockets. "When did you meet Kit Cordell, Mrs. Finster?"

Freda smiled at her. "After my husband died. I was alone and not knowing a soul. Helped me she did, when I had no money or place to go."

"How did she help you?"

"She helped me buy my house and start a bakery."

"What did she demand in return?"

Freda shook her head. "Nothing. Out of the kindness of her heart she did it."

"Would you say that Kit has ever behaved indecently?"

"No." The single word echoed in the expectant silence. "She is a good woman."

"Thank you, Mrs. Finster."

Freda returned to her chair, giving Kit a quick pat on the shoulder as she passed.

Embarrassed and touched by the testimonies, Kit kept her teary gaze on Jake. He winked at her and announced the next person.

"Defense calls the Reverend Wellensiek."

"You can't do that," Bertie said indignantly.

Judge Blair pinned her with a sharp gaze. "And why not?"

Bertie sputtered in protest.

"That's enough, Englebertina," the reverend said firmly to his wife.

She stared at him as if he'd never spoken to her in that tone before, and Kit doubted the mild-mannered man ever had.

"How long have you known the defendant, Reverend?" Jake questioned.

"Twenty-three years. Ever since I came to Chaney."

"Does she attend Sunday services regularly?"

The minister nodded. "More often than most."

"Do you think she's capable of the type of behavior Mr. Preston accuses her of?"

"Objection," the prosecutor spoke up. "The question is subjective."

Jake arched his dark brow. "On the contrary, the Reverend Wellensiek deals with sinners all the time. I would think he would be an expert at picking one out."

A few chuckles greeted his words, and Kit found herself admiring Jake's quick wit.

"Overruled," the judge decided. "Answer the question, Reverend."

"Based on my experience, I would have to say Kit Thornton Cordell could not have done what Mr. Preston described."

Kit wondered if Bertie had fainted yet.

"Thank you, Reverend." Jake glanced at the opposing counsellor. "Would you like to cross-examine?"

The prosecutor stood. "Reverend Wellensiek, have you ever been wrong?"

The minister blinked owlishly. "Only God is perfect, but Mrs. Cordell—"

"Thank you, Reverend," the prosecutor interrupted.

"You may step down, Reverend," Judge Blair said. He glanced at his pocketwatch. "How many witnesses do you have left, Mr. Cordell?"

Jake grinned. "How many do I need?"

Blair harrumphed. "I believe you've made your point."

"Then I have only one more."

"In that case, we'll adjourn for an hour, then come back for the last witness and closing arguments." Judge Blair pounded his gavel on the table, ending the morning session.

After he left the room, Kit faced Jake. "How did you find out about all of them?"

He shrugged, although a boyish pride lit his handsome face. "Freda told me about most of them, and Patrick and Charlie gave me a few more names. A couple of them had to be persuaded to be witnesses, but most of them wanted to help you." Jake gazed at her, his eyes quizzical. "Why didn't you tell me?"

She turned away. "Tell you what?"

"That you'd put Bertie Wellensiek to shame with all the good deeds you've done," he replied. Gently, Jake captured her chin between his thumb and forefinger and raised her head. "I knew you were kind-hearted, but I had no idea how loving and generous. What did I ever do to deserve you, Kit?"

Tears, which lately seemed ready to flow at the drop of a kind word, rolled down her cheeks. "You were just you, Jake. That was more than enough."

Holding Kit's hand, Jake walked her back to the police station. Patrick followed at a discreet distance until Kit and Jake were in the cell. Leaving them alone, the Irishman returned to the office.

"Pretty soon it'll all be over," Jake said.

She nodded. "For better or for worse. Even with all the testimonies this morning, it still doesn't look good, does it?"

"I'd feel a whole lot better if I could poke some real holes into Preston's story." He paused. "Johnny is my last witness."

She didn't want Johnny on the stand, but a part of her had expected Jake would need his eyewitness testimony. "You can't let him admit to shooting Preston."

"It wasn't my decision."

"Yes, it is. Johnny's too young to make that choice."

Jake grasped her shoulders. "I want our son to grow up with a mother. I gave him the choice I never had." Time-weary pain shimmered in his eyes. "I found a stack of letters in your desk."

Kit frowned. "What letters?"

"They were in the same drawer as my father's gun."

She nodded, remembering tossing them in there the night of the shooting. "They must've been in the gun case. I'd never seen them before."

Jake swallowed. "They were letters from my mother addressed to me. My father must've gotten them and hid them."

Sympathy tugged at her heart, and she asked softly, "What did they say?"

"You were right, Kit. She never stopped loving me."

"I'd wondered how she could've abandoned her own child."

"I wrote her a long letter last night. I hope she's still alive to get it."

"I wonder why your father didn't just throw the letters away?"

He shrugged. "Maybe deep down he wanted me to have them someday. I know now that he loved me—he just didn't know how to tell me."

Kit hugged him. "No matter what happens, I'll always love you and Johnny," she whispered, in a voice filled with unshed tears.

He smiled. "I've been waiting for you to say those words again. I love you, Kit."

In spite of her uncertain future, she savored a peaceful contentment. Even if she had no more time with Jake, she would always remember this moment.

Kit barely picked at her lunch, both fearful and anxious to see her son for the first time in four days. It was longer than they'd ever been apart. Returning to the courtroom, she couldn't sit still in her chair. She swiveled around, looking for Johnny.

"Freda will bring him in when I call his name," Jake whispered.

Disappointment welled in Kit. She'd wanted to hug him and talk to him before he got up on the stand. Forcing herself to relax, she eased back in her seat. Judge Blair entered, and Kit stood, then resumed her place.

Jake remained standing, and he unbuttoned his suit coat. "Defense calls Johnny Cordell."

Her heart hammering in her throat, Kit saw the door at the back open and Johnny entered, holding Freda's hand. He looked neither right nor left as he walked down the aisle. Kit spied his black-and-blue eye and nearly cried aloud. She looked over at Preston, her hatred so strong she could taste it.

Johnny finally looked around, and his face beamed when he spotted her. He made a move toward her, then he glanced at Jake, who seemed to send him a silent message. Licking his lips, Johnny continued up to the front. He appeared small and vulnerable in the large chair, and Kit ached to reassure him.

"Do you know what we're here for?" Jake asked his son.

He swung his feet back and forth a few inches above the floor. "Ma's trial."

"Do you understand that you have to answer truthfully, no matter how much it might hurt?"

He bobbed his head up and down.

"Can you tell everyone here your name?"

"Jonathan Jacob Cordell the third," he replied proudly.

A few gasps and murmurings sounded from the audience. One glare from the judge and the exclamations ceased.

Jake stood close to Johnny. "Can you tell us what happened the day Mr. Preston came to visit?"

"Me and Ma let Jasper go." He looked at the judge. "Jasper's a raccoon. He got hurt and we fixed him."

Blair smiled.

"Go on, Johnny," Jake urged gently.

"Well, after that, I played with Toby, my dog."

"Where was your mother?"

"She was on the porch cleaning potatoes and watching us."

"Is that when Mr. Preston showed up?"

Johnny nodded, squirming on the wide seat. "He and Ma talked for a few minutes and then I guess they went in the house, because when I looked again, they were gone. I stayed outside for a little while, but I got hungry so I went in to find Ma."

"Was she in the kitchen?"

"No. I yelled, but she didn't answer, so I went looking for her." He paused, and swallowed, his Adam's apple sliding up and down.

"Where did you find her?" Jake asked, in a voice so quiet Kit could barely hear it.

"She was in her bedroom, with Mr. Preston." Johnny

lifted his accusing gaze to the reporter who stared back at him without a hint of emotion. "He was hurting her."

"How do you know he was hurting her?"

Kit leaned forward, planting her elbows on the table, and pressing her fisted hands against her mouth. She didn't want him to have to relive the horrible scene. How could Jake make him do this?

Johnny licked his lips nervously. "I opened the door and saw Ma on the floor crying. She told me to go downstairs."

"Did you?" Jake prompted gently.

"No. Then Mr. Preston grabbed me, and Ma hit him, trying to make him let me go. He got mad at her and pulled her hair." His eyes filled with tears. "I jumped on him and bit his leg, but he hit me."

The saloon had grown hushed with expectancy.

"Is that how you got your black eye?"

Johnny nodded, and a tear spilled down his pale cheek. "He was too big. I couldn't stop him."

Kit closed her eyes, fighting her own tears.

"So what did you do then?" Jake asked.

Kit's eyelids flew open, and she leapt to her feet. "Stop it! Leave him alone. He's only a child."

Jake laid a hand on Johnny's shoulder and gazed at Kit. "I let him make the decision. He wants his mother to come home."

The raw pain in Jake's eyes staggered Kit. She stumbled back and sank into her chair. How could she blame him? How could she deny Johnny his decision to protect her, when she'd done the same for him?

"Tell us what happened then, Johnny."

The boy drew his forearm across his damp face. "Ma told me to run. I went and got my grandpa's gun from Ma's desk."

"Had you ever shot a gun before?"

Johnny shook his head. "Ma didn't want me to until

I was older. She said guns weren't toys. That they hurt people.''

"Your mother's a smart woman," the judge approved.

"I put some bullets into it and went back to Ma's room." He looked at Jake. "I was scared, but you told me to take care of her. I heard her scream and went inside." Johnny pointed a finger at Preston. "He was on top of her on the bed. She was crying and trying to get away. He had his hands around her neck and her shirt was ripped. I told him to stop, but he just laughed at me."

Silence stretched out in the courtroom. A man coughed and another person shifted their feet. A fly buzzed, resounding in the eerie quiet.

"And what did you do?" Jake asked, his voice barely a whisper.

"I pulled the trigger." A tortured sob racked his small body. "I didn't want to, but he was hurting my ma. He's a bad man!" He stumbled out of the witness chair and ran over to Kit.

She enfolded him in her arms, tears running down her face as he cried on her shoulder.

A movement beside her made Kit glance up, and she saw Jake standing by them.

"You raised Johnny to tell the truth, Kit, and that's what he wanted to do. You can't blame him for doing the right thing. He takes after you."

Her throat closed, and she could only nod in return. As Johnny clung to her, Kit settled him on her lap, wrapping her arms tightly around him.

Jake moved to the center of the room. "Defense would like to call David Preston to the stand for further cross examination."

The newspaperman's pale face matched his white

sling, and hatred glittered in his eyes. With shuffling footsteps he walked to the witness chair.

"Did you attack Kit Cordell?"

He flushed. "As I stated before, no, I did not."

Jake leaned close to him. "I want to remind you that you are still under oath."

"I am aware of that." His brittle tone echoed in the hushed courtroom.

"Are you saying Johnny Cordell's testimony is a lie?"

"Yes."

"Did Johnny bite you?"

Preston's bloodless lips thinned. "No."

"May we see your legs, Mr. Preston?"

"Objection," the prosecutor called out.

"Johnny says he bit Mr. Preston's leg. Mr. Preston said he did not. If we're to determine who's lying and who's telling the truth, we need to see the proof," Jake argued.

"Objection overruled," Judge Blair said. He looked at Johnny. "Show us which leg you bit, son."

Kit lifted him off her lap. "Go ahead, Johnny. Your father won't let him hurt you."

Reluctantly, he shuffled over to Jake. Holding her breath, Kit watched her son point to Preston's left leg.

"Raise that pants leg, Mr. Preston," the judge ordered.

"There's ladies in the room," Preston argued.

Blair sighed. "Ladies, if the sight of a man's leg will shock you, please close your eyes."

Kit kept hers wide open as Preston lifted the hem of his trousers a few inches.

"I bit his knee," Johnny said.

"Higher, Mr. Preston," Blair commanded.

As the material was raised, a bruise came into view,

a black and blue ring with obvious teeth marks. Voices buzzed, and Preston glared at the boy.

Jake kept his arm around Johnny. "In light of this new evidence and the fact that Preston has obviously lied, I move that the charges against Kit Cordell be dropped."

Judge Blair nodded without hesitation. "I agree. Sergeant O'Hara, place Mr. Preston under arrest for assault."

"And attempted murder," Jake added. Blair sent him a questioning look. "Of me, Your Honor."

A smile flitted on the judge's stern lips. "You heard Counsellor Cordell—assault and attempted murder."

"He also killed my horse," Jake added grimly.

"Add destruction of personal property, Sergeant," Judge Blair said.

"Yes, sir, Your Honor," Patrick replied with a grin. "With pleasure."

Kit collapsed in her chair. Jake had done it—her hero had saved her again!

Patrick came forward and escorted Preston out of the noisy courtroom. As the newspaperman passed Kit, he sent her a look brimming with virulence. No longer afraid, she held his gaze until he looked away.

Judge Blair banged the gavel on the table. "Case dismissed. Court is adjourned."

Jake and Johnny rushed over to Kit, who stood and opened her arms wide to receive their embraces. Jake wrapped his arms around her, hugging her with Johnny caught between them. Tears flowed down Kit's face, making everything a blur.

The judge approached them, and Jake withdrew but kept his arm around her. He shook Blair's outstretched hand.

"Your father would be proud of you. You handled

yourself very well.'' Blair patted Johnny's head. ''I'll bet your papa is proud of you, too.''

Jake rested a protective hand on his son's shoulder. ''Yes, sir, I am.''

With a smile, Judge Blair left the room.

The townsfolk swarmed around them, slapping Jake on the back congenially and offering Kit their congratulations. Many even apologized for believing the worst of her. She had strived for acceptance most of her life, and now that she had it, she found all she wanted to do was go home and be with her family.

Jake captured her lips with his as they stood in the circle of well-wishers. He drew back and gazed at her with loving adoration. ''You've always taken care of everyone else. Now let us take care of you.''

''You always have, Jake.'' She smiled through tears of happiness. ''Didn't you know? You're *my* dime novel hero.''

Jake glanced at her quizzically.

Kit's joy changed to eager anticipation. ''I have a feeling that T. K. Thorne can finally write Jake Cordell's final chapter.''

Epilogue

⌁⌁

Looking out the kitchen window, Kit saw the two buckboards enter the snow-covered yard. She pressed her hands to her lower back and tried to alleviate the perpetual ache eight months of pregnancy had produced. It didn't help, but Johnny barreling into the house made her forget her discomfort for a few moments. Wintry air eddied around her ankles.

"Here's the mail, Ma," Johnny announced, handing her a stack of papers. "We saw Pa, too, and he took me and Charlie and Ethan to lunch."

Before Kit could comment, the boy dashed outside, a bundle of energy packed in his wiry body.

She smiled. Only Jake could have gotten a town to leave behind its prejudices and allow a Negro and a half-breed to eat in a restaurant. There were still a few folks who held onto their biases, but on the whole, Charlie and Ethan were treated like everyone else.

Charlie carried in a box of supplies. "Jake gave me strict orders to put this stuff away and not let you anywhere near it." His white teeth shone brilliantly against his dark skin. "So don't you be gettin' me in trouble with him."

Kit shook her head ruefully. Women had babies all

the time, but Jake was bound and determined to treat her like she might break at any moment. It was only another one of his exasperatingly endearing qualities she loved. "Will he be working late again?"

Charlie shook his head. "Said to tell you he'd be home in time for supper."

"I'm glad. He's been working too hard lately."

"If Judge Blair had his way, Jake would be runnin' for governor."

Pride surged through her. Jake had already gained a reputation as a good lawyer and, more important, a man with integrity. She had no doubt that if he wanted to, Jake could someday be governor of Wyoming. Jonathan would have been very proud of his son.

She glanced in the box Charlie had set on the table. "Was the material I ordered for the baby clothes in?"

He grinned. "Why do you think I needed two wagons?"

"I didn't order that much, did I?"

"Nope, but Jake did."

He ducked out of the kitchen before Kit could question him further. Knowing her soft-hearted husband, he'd gone overboard with presents, intending to make up for all the Christmases he'd missed.

Shaking her head, she glanced down at the mail Johnny had given her. She sighed. A couple of bills, a note from one of her regular horse buyers, and a letter for Jake from his mother. The seventh one in as many months.

The last and largest envelope sent Kit's heart into a stampede, and she eased down into a chair. The day of reckoning had arrived. How often had she practiced her confession?

"I have some news for you, Jake," she said calmly.

She was always cool and collected as she faced her image in the mirror.

"About those dime novels, the ones written by T. K. Thorne? Well, I'm T. K. Thorne."

Then Jake would look suitably impressed, and tell her he was proud of her.

Kit buried her face in her hands. In reality, Jake would be madder than a stepped-on snake. He'd wonder why she'd waited so long to tell him. She'd asked herself the same question numerous times. And the answer was fear. Life had been near-perfect since the trial, and she'd been scared to upset the buggy.

Taking a deep breath, she pushed her bulky body upright. She'd tell him tonight. She couldn't put if off any longer.

At supper that evening, Jake read the letter from his mother. "She'll be here in less than a week."

"My grandma's gonna be here for Christmas?" Johnny asked excitedly, forgetting he had just forked a mound of potatoes into his mouth.

"That's right," Jake affirmed. "And what have we said about talking with your mouth full?"

Johnny swallowed his food. "Sorry. What's she like, Pa? Is she like Ma? Is she as old as Pete? Does she talk like Mrs. Finster?"

"That's Mrs. O'Hara now," Kit reminded him. Freda had finally taken the chance, accepting Patrick's assurance that he wasn't like her dead husband and wouldn't break her heart with his drinking.

"I have a feeling she's something like your mother, Johnny," Jake replied, a sad smile playing across his rugged face. "And I don't think she's as old as Pete." He winked at Kit. "Nobody's as old as Pete."

"How long will she be here?" Kit asked.

"Long enough to see her second grandchild come into the world. She says she's missed too much already."

Kit reached across the table and laid her hand on Jake's. He squeezed it gently. "You told her she's welcome for as long as she wants to stay, didn't you?''

Jake nodded. He took a deep breath and pushed his empty plate back. "Come on, Johnny, time for bed." He waggled a finger at Kit. "And you sit there until I come down. I'll do the dishes."

She arched her brow and waited until he and Johnny were upstairs before she stood and began clearing the table. By the time Jake returned to the kitchen, she had the dishes washed and wiped but not put away.

Jake wrapped an arm around her shoulders and steered her toward a chair in the kitchen. "Sit."

Kit giggled, but sank into the seat. "I think you've been spending too much time training Toby."

"And I think my wife is too mule-headed and stubborn," Jake retorted.

Watching him place the dishes in their proper places, she should have been content. However, the last dime novel lay heavily on her mind. Would he still treat her with such loving concern after he heard her confession? Her stomach roiled and the baby kicked, startling her.

Jake was at her side in a moment. "What's wrong?"

Seeing his beloved face creased in worry sent her heart spiraling. "The baby moved." She took Jake's hand in hers and laid his palm on her stomach's ample curve. Another kick. "Did you feel that?"

Wonder lit Jake's face, reminding her of Johnny's when the boy found an interesting worm. She laughed softly at the analogy.

"I wonder if Johnny moved this much," Jake said reverently.

Kit nodded. "More. Maggie would let me feel him kicking. It was such a strange feeling." She smiled. "Now it's not strange at all. Just wonderful and comforting at the same time."

He was silent a moment, although he kept his hand on Kit's belly. "I didn't love Maggie."

Kit met his poignant gaze. "She knew that, but you cared for her. And for Maggie that was enough." She began to stand, and Jake helped her the rest of the way up. "Let's go to bed."

He arched a brow. "Is that an invitation?"

Kit glanced down at her ungainly body. "I'm fat, Jake."

Stepping behind her, he slipped his arms around her, below her breasts, which had grown fuller during her pregnancy. "You're not fat. You're carrying our child."

He kissed the sensitive nape of her neck, and she shivered. It would be so easy to postpone her confession. Another day. Then another day, and another . . .

No, she had to tell him tonight. No matter the consequences, she had to tell him the truth. It was the only barrier left between them.

"I have an early Christmas present for you," she said, her voice fluttery.

Although he appeared puzzled, he followed her up the stairs, a steadying hand at the small of her back. Once inside the bedroom, Jake seated himself on the edge of their bed.

Her insides trembling, Kit reached into a dresser drawer and withdrew the book. With her back to Jake, she clutched the dime novel to her chest and breathed a silent prayer, asking for courage.

Turning slowly, she handed it to Jake. "Merry Christmas."

He glanced at the cover, frowned, and looked back at Kit. "*The Final Adventure of Jake Cordell*?"

She nodded. Her heart pounding like she'd run a mile, she said, "It's autographed."

He opened the cover and read the words Kit knew by heart. *This is my dime novel hero's last adventure, but you and I have the rest of our lives to write our own happily ever after. All my love, Kit.*

He turned his bewildered gaze to her. "I thought you meant the author autographed it."

"She did."

"I don't get it."

She sank onto the mattress beside him before her quaking knees buckled. "T. K. Thorne is the pseudonym for Theodora Katherine Thornton." She took a deep breath. "*I* wrote the dime novels."

He stared at her like he'd never seen her before, and Kit's fears intensified.

"Why?"

Her hands balled into fists to keep them from trembling. "You've been my hero for years, Jake. The stories were my way of thanking the knight in shining armor for rescuing the ten-year-old damsel in distress; my way of staying close to you." Anguish filled her. "I never thought they'd put your life in danger, or get Zeus killed. That was the last thing in the world I wanted."

His silence unnerved her. He shook his head. "Preston didn't shoot Zeus or me because of your books. You can't blame yourself for those things." He twined his fingers with hers. "We've been lucky no one's come gunning for me, but if someone does, that won't be your fault, either."

Kit frowned, puzzled.

"What a person does after he reads the stories isn't your responsibility," he said softly.

"But you hated the dime novels. You said they'd made your life miserable."

A sad smile tugged at Jake's lips. "*I* made my life miserable. T. K. Thorne was only the scapegoat."

"Then you're not mad at me?"

Jake set the book on the nightstand and embraced Kit. "How can I be, knowing why you wrote them?"

She wound her arms around his neck, savoring his heartachingly familiar scent.

"And if someone had told me I'd be married to T. K. Thorne, I would've said they were crazy." He kissed her forehead tenderly. "The only craziness is you loving someone like me."

She threaded her fingers through his thick silky hair and flashed him a saucy smile. "Must've been a moment of insanity."

He grinned. "Feel like doing something a little crazy right now?"

An hour later, as Kit dozed, snuggling close to him in the aftermath of their abandoned lovemaking, Jake gazed down at her tenderly. He brushed a golden curl from her forehead, then feathered a kiss across her smooth brow. A slight smile touched her passion-swollen lips, as if she recognized his touch even in slumber.

Carefully, so he wouldn't disturb her, Jake reached for the book sitting on the stand. Below the title, *The Final Adventure of Jake Cordell*, he spotted the subtitle in smaller letters: *Shut Up and Kiss Me, Jake*. He laughed quietly.

With T. K. Thorne nestled close to his side, he began to read her last tribute to her dime novel hero:

Jake Cordell's search had finally come to an end . . .